Phil Robinson

The poet's beasts

Phil Robinson

The poet's beasts

ISBN/EAN: 9783337304478

Printed in Europe, USA, Canada, Australia, Japan

Cover: Foto ©Andreas Hilbeck / pixelio.de

More available books at **www.hansebooks.com**

THE POETS' BEASTS

A SEQUEL TO "THE POETS' BIRDS"

BY

PHIL ROBINSON

AUTHOR OF

"IN MY INDIAN GARDEN," "NOAH'S ARK," "UNDER THE PUNKAH,"
"SINNERS AND SAINTS," "THE POETS' BIRDS," ETC.

London
CHATTO AND WINDUS, PICCADILLY
1885

This Volume

IS MOST GRATEFULLY DEDICATED TO

TWO POETS,

JEAN INGELOW AND *EDWIN ARNOLD*,

IN RESPECTFUL ADMIRATION

OF

THEIR RARE SYMPATHY WITH NATURE,

AND THEIR TENDER INTERPRETATIONS OF

"THE SPEECHLESS WORLD."

EXCULPATORY NOTE.

By way of partial explanation of the errata and repetitions which the Reader will find flourishing in the later and unrevised pages of this volume, I would venture to draw his generous attention to my present address. Leaving England for the front at very short notice, I had not the necessary time for finishing my proof-correcting; and though this fact is no sort of justification for the original mistakes, it appears to me to be somewhere on the road to an excuse for their being left unmolested.

PHIL ROBINSON.

HEADQUARTERS CAMP,
SUAKIM FIELD FORCE, *April* 1885.

CONTENTS.

THE POETS' BEASTS.

I.

THE KING OF THE BEASTS.

THERE are many who deprecate the lion's coronation as the King of Beasts. But, after all, it should not be forgotten by this noble animal's critics that it is only contended on its behalf that it is the King of *Beasts;* and, remembering this, it is very difficult, I think, to dispute its claim to monarchy. It may have vassals actually as strong as itself, powerful Warwicks or Burgundies, but it is still, I think, their liege lord. Its gait, eye, voice, and uplift of head all make it royal in presence—and as for its character, taking one thing with another, it is as good as that of any other beast. Its personal advantages, therefore, are all so much "to the good," as it were, while in its natural life, and in its traditional glories, the lion is indisputably majestic.

There are two lions, the real and the imaginary. The former exists in nature only; the latter in heraldry, myths, and poetry. But both are royal; the former from attributes of person, the latter from attributes of mind.

A writer,[1] for whom I have a great respect, calls the King of Beasts "a great carnivorous impostor," challenges

---

[1] Frances Power Cobbe.

its claim to majesty, and asks proof of its "supposed mag-nanimity and generosity beyond the blandness of its Harold Skimpole countenance, and the disdainful manner in which it throws back its mane as if it were quite incapable of the pettiness (of which it is, nevertheless, frequently guilty) of picking up and eating a humble black-beetle." But though it is quite true that it is sometimes excelled in size and generally in ferocity by the tiger, in elegance of form by the leopard and jaguar, and in beauty of colouring by most of the great cats, "yet it would" (as Professor Kitchen Parker says) "be useless, even if it were advisable, to try to depose the lion from the throne it has, by the universal consent of mankind, so long occupied." It would be use-less, because the magnificent presence and kingly voice of the lion would always suffice to rethrone it as often as it was deposed. And it wou'd be unadvisable, as no other beast could be crowned in its stead. The ermine would hardly become the unwieldy elephant with its petty anti-pathies to pigs and porcupines and mosquitoes, its secluded herbivorous habits; and there is too much blood on the tiger's claws for a sceptre. The violent rhinoceros, with its vicious little eyes, might force its way to temporary dictator-ship during a popular revolution, or the tusky wild boar by pertinacity of courage enforce a general respect. But neither of them could be presented with sufficient dignity to the people as the Anointed and Elect. So, failing a suc-cessor worthy to fill its place, the lion must remain king.

Its glorious head and full intelligent eye, the terrible composure of its bearing, the impressive ease of its step, the awe-compelling voice—"the rocks tremble while he seeks his prey"—are all kingly. But in many of its habits it declines from this high standard. It is not really coura-geous. Thus, the ancients gave their statues of Fear the heads of lions. It avoids conflict with formidable antago-nists, and dreads man and all his works. It haunts well-wooded and, if possible, rocky places, where it can lie hidden and pounce upon passing prey. If it misses its aim it sulks, but does not pursue.

Of course, the imaginary lion, the lion of the poets, is a very different animal. It is a king of "sandy deserts," reigning in a majestic solitude. It courts danger by provoking men to combat, and never knows when it is beaten.[1] It scorns a weak foe, and generously overlooks everything not its equal—for which perhaps the poets might quote that episode near Bethel when the lion killed the prophet, but refused to harm his ass. There is only one rebel against its authority, Spenser's "prowd, rebellious unicorn."

But much of the poets' mistaken eulogy is condoned by their fidelity to tradition, and the result is that, while the lion is credited with noble qualities that he does not possess, he is also debited with many very culpable human weaknesses. So, though the poets must be held largely responsible for the perpetuation of the ideas of the royalty, magnanimity, and general infallibility of the lion, there can be no doubt that, taken as a whole, their presentation of the "King of the Beasts" is a tolerably fair one. It is not, perhaps, quite so impartial as the American poets' exposition of their country's "Eagle"—but then that, as I have said elsewhere, is what might be called in vulgar English "altogether phenomenal"—but it will stand, nevertheless, like Landseer's bronzes, as being a thoroughly gratifying and sufficiently accurate statement of the lion's pretensions. For the poets assume the attitude of historians rather than of courtiers towards "the forest king," and—following the old fabulists faithfully—compound a sovereign that has both the virtues of royalty and the weaknesses. Thus, though the lion is regal, it is at times tyran-

---

[1] Solomon himself says that it is "the strongest among beasts, and turneth not away from any." But Solomon probably did not know of the tiger.

nical, and, though usually magnanimous, it is also on occasion "inhuman." It is "the awful lion's royal shape" in one place; in another we meet only "the shaggy terror of the wood." While Cowper portrays the beast sparing a victim "on the terms of royal mercy, and through generous scorn to rend a victim trembling at his foot," Armstrong writes of "the ruthless king of beasts, that on blood and slaughter only lives."

In spite too of its prodigious strength, it is well worth noting that no incident of man's triumph over the lion is neglected, and—as Pausanias tells us that Polydamas, the athlete, killed a lion, "although he was unarmed"—it is particularly recorded (whenever such was the case) that the man was without weapons during the encounter. In the same spirit the Assyrian king has left the proud chronicle on stone how "I, Assar-Banipul, king of multitudes, by my might, on my two legs, a fierce lion, which I seized behind the ears, in the service of Istar, goddess of war, with my two hands killed."[1] In the same spirit of pride at such a conquest, the son of Jesse makes his boast before the king, and afterwards, being himself king, he places among his "mighty men," and before "the Thirty," that man of calm courage Benaiah, who "went down and slew a lion in the midst of a pit in time of snow," and who also slew, terrible as himself, two "lion-like" men of Moab. Our own Richard—"he who robbed the lion of his heart" —after three days' fasting, so the legend goes, in the dungeons of "Almayne," was especially glorified by the ballad-singers of his day, because he had torn a lion to pieces, and this, too, "without his weapons in his hands." So, too, "irresistible Samson," who "tore the lion as the lion tears the kid" ("and he had nothing in his hand").

---

[1] "Who drew the lion vanquished? 'twas a man."—*Pope.* "Avec plus de raison nous aurions le dessus si mes confrères savaient peindre," says the lion in La Fontaine.

> " Withouten wepen save his handes twey
> He slew and all to-rente the leon
> Toward his wedding walking by the way."

And David (in Cowley)—

> " Saw a lion and leapt down to it ;
> As eas'ly there the royal beast he tore,
> As that itself did kids or lambs before."

And Hercules (in Darwin)—

> " Drives the lion to his dusky cave,
> Seized by the throat the growling fiend disarms,
> And tears his gaping jaws with sinewy arms."

So in Glover's "Leonidas," "This unconquered hand hath from the lion rent his shaggy mane." So Drayton in the "Polyolbion" has a hero smashing two lions' heads together "against the hardened earth" till "their jaws and shoulders burst," reminding us of St. George's feats with a diversity of dragonish things ; and Montgomery peoples the world before the Flood with beings who pulled lions about as if they had been rabbits, and who were themselves ruled over by giant kings whose robes were "spoils of lions."

> " Throned on a rock the Giant-King appears
> In the full manhood of five hundred years ;
> His robe the spoil of lions, by his might
> Dragged from their dens and slain in fight."

Cervantes speaks of Don Quixote's adventure with the lions as "the last and highest point at which the unheard-of courage of the Knight ever did, or could, arrive," and Don Quixote was himself so much of the same opinion, that he gave the world to know that thenceforward he called himself the Knight of the Lions.

"Are the lions large?" asked Don Quixote. "Very large," replied the man in the fore-part of the waggon ; "bigger never came from Africa." But the Knight insists upon them being led forth. They will not come. One of them, "of a monstrous size and frightful aspect," approaches the open door, stretches itself, gapes, yawns, "then thrusts out half a yard of tongue, with which it licks the dust off its face," puts its head out of the cage, and after looking about it "awhile," turned its back upon the Don, without paying any attention whatever to his "vapourings and bravado," and "very contentedly lay down again in its apartment." So perhaps "the lion is not so fierce as painted," as Fuller—plagiarising from Herbert's "Jacula prudentum," itself a plagiarism—allows.

In most cases the poets represent the lions calling, like the Earl of Chatham, or Mr. Winkle, for their antagonists to "come on;" but occasionally, as in straight-thrusting Quarles—

> " They faint, and show
> Their fearful heels if Chaunticleer do crow ; "

and I find in Sir Thomas Browne the following note : " In our time in the court of the Prince of Bavaria one of the lions leaped down into a neighbour's yard, where, nothing regarding the crowing or noise of the cocks, he did eat them up, with many hens." Our own lions of the Tower used, I find, to be regaled occasionally on " cocks and hens."

Though usually so chivalrous as to refuse to take advantage of " equal foes," Byron tells us how—

> " 'Mid the sad flock at dead of night he prowls
> With murder glutted, and in carnage rolls ;
> Insatiate still through teeming herds he roams,
> In seas of gore the lordly tyrant foams." [1]

---

[1] Phineas Fletcher has the following, identical in spirit :—

> " As when a greedy lion, long unfed,
> Breaks in at length into the harmlesse fold—
> So hungry rage commands—with fearful dread
> He drags the silly beasts ; nothing controlls
> The victor proud ; he spoils, devours, and tears.
> In vain the shepherd calls his peers."

As a rule "courteous" to their subjects, we read in
Butler that

> " Lions are kings of beasts, and yet their power
> Is not to rule and govern but devour.
> Such savage kings all tyrants are."

Again, though the sovereignty is one that "makes all
nature glad," and the beasts unanimous in loyal submission (the fox says " Thee all the animals with fear adore "),
yet we find the lion's subjects abused for submitting to his
supremacy. "No better than mere beasts that do obey,"
says Butler, and Pope—

> "If a king's a lion, at the least
> The people are a many-headed beast."

So that, even from this scanty sample of quotations, it is
evident that the poets had not arrived at any such unanimous opinion as to the lion idea as they have about many
other animals. As the King of Beasts it is merely the corre-
late of the eagle. But as the fabulists' lion, done into verse,
it remains the same mock-heroic animal that the folk-lore
of the world has bequeathed to us.

Above all, of course, the lion is royal ; not so super-
lative, perhaps, in sovereignty as the eagle, but still very
emphatically the King of Beasts. "The sovereign lion "—
"the forest king "—"the lion king "—"dread king "—"im-
perious lion " (Cowper), and so forth, are to be collected for
the gathering by bushels. Morris' "yellow lords of fear "
is exceptionally fine. Nor, seeing how unanimously the
past has conspired to crown the lion, is it easy to quarrel
with the poets for perpetuating the monarchical idea. But
it is essentially a poetical form of procedure to accept a
fiction on the statement of professed fables and myths, and
then to build upon it according to individual imagination.
Thus, nothing is so popular with poets as the image of a

lion, like some chivalrous knight of the Crusades, challenging attack from overwhelming numbers, and defying superior strength.

No lion in the flesh behaves as Dryden's "kingly beast" that guides his pursuers to where he stands, " with roar of seas directs his chasers' way," that "provokes the hunters from afar, and dares them to the fray," and that " roars out with loud disdain, and slowly moves, unknowing to give place ; " or, as Thomson's—

> " Despising flight,
> The roused-up lion, resolute and slow
> Advancing full on the protended spear,"

or as many other lions of poetry do, that scorn to turn from a foe.

As a matter of fact. the lion, of all beasts of prey, is one of the readiest to avoid a scrimmage. King James used to try to divert his friends with lion-fights in the Tower, but, according to Howes' Chronicle, his Majesty always failed, owing to the captives' objections to fighting. "Then were divers other lions put into that place one after another, but they showed no more sport nor valour than the first ; and every one of them, so soon as they espied the trap-doors open, ran hastily into their dens. Lastly, there were put forth together the two young lusty lions which were bred in that yard, and were now grown great. These at first began to march proudly towards the bear, which the bear perceiving came hastily out of a corner to meet them, but both lion and lioness skipped up and down and fearfully fled from the bear ; and so these, like the former lions, not willing to endure any fight, sought the next way into their den." But perhaps this forbearance is like that of the late Mr. T. Sayers, who, it is said, " never liked to hit a man who didn't know who he was." He was afraid of killing him in all his ignorance. So before he hit him he always told the victim that he was Sayers. In the same way the poets' lion always "roars" before attacking.

"Something almost like a lion" came "a great padding pace" after the Pilgrim. It had "a hollow voice of roaring."

This passage reminds me somehow of the poetical Beast of Beasts. It is almost like a lion, and has a hollow voice.

> *Snug.* Have you the lion's part written? Pray you, if it be, give it me, for I am slow of study.
> *Quince.* You may do it extempore, for it is nothing but roaring.

Now, to complete the poetical lion it is necessary that in all its moods it should be classic; not only in those that are heroic but those that are pathetic also. For are not strong passions merely strong feelings? So the lion in grief is the most grievous beast imaginable. No parents created (except eagles) feel the loss of their young so keenly as lions and lionesses; none are so quickly apprehensive of danger to their hearths and cradles; none are so frantic in revenge. Therefore, from Spenser, with his "felle" lion that "grudging in his great disdaine, mournes inwardly, and makes to himselfe mone," to Burns, who, anxious to give expression to an overwhelming melancholy, cries out for the voice of a lioness "that mourns her darling cubs' undoing," we find the poets punctually magnifying the tenderness of the species. It was necessary, of course, that this should be done—just as one hears it said, describing some utter ruffian, that, "after all, his heart is in the right place." Thus, some of Ouida's tawny heroes are very leonine. They crunch up bronze candlesticks between their fingers in agonies of suppressed passion. But their violet eyes overflow with liquidity at the first appeal of pathos.

The "stately lion," that "stalks with fiery glare" and "dauntless strides along," offers in its majestic gait an obvious simile that is abundantly and handsomely availed of. Omitting the interminable series of individuals that have been leonine in deportment, the surpassing dignity and sense of power that ennobles the lion's pace have been admirably transferred to, among other objects, an army (Mrs. Hemans):

> "With a silent step went the cuirassed bands,
> Like a lion's tread on the burning sands"—

lines which might be happily applied to the march of the brigade of Guards across the sands to Tel-el-Kebir. Wordsworth employs the simile for primeval man—

> "His native dignity no forms debase,
> The eye sublime, and surly lion-grace:
> The slave of none, of beasts alone the lord."

When tranquil in mind, there is a simplicity and ease in the lion's movements, though full of a tremendous consciousness of strength, that is eminently beautiful. When slightly out of temper this stateliness increases by the addition of a splendid sullenness—"with sullen majesty he stalks away" (Broome)—but the simplicity is lost. When it flies into a passion both stateliness and simplicity are gone, for the lion reverts at once to a furious rough-and-tumble wild beast.

But the poets measure its kingliness by its fury, and the more "woode" it becomes the more royal. This is an error, not only of fact, but of grace. When Jove gets angry he grows undignified. Gods and kings should always keep their tempers, for sceptres do not become furious hands. Mortals begin to question divinity when they see such passions *cælestibus animis*.

Sometimes, but very seldom, he is merely "the shaggy lion" (Prior), "the forest prowler" (Byron), "bristly savage" (Young), "terror of the wood" (Broome), that "grins dreadfully"—the lion of nature pure and simple, "lapping at the palm-edged pool" (Jean Ingelow); the husband of the "tawny" lioness that, robbed of whelps, "forgets to fear;" the father of the brindled cubs "blood-nurtured in their grisly den." And it is worth noting that, just as the cock comes off, both in poetry and proverb, with such honours, while the hen is left behind to cackle and be generally ridiculous, so the lioness fails to receive from her spouse any adequate reflection of his dignities. She is desperately cruel, and, in defence of her young, exceptionally fierce. Because one, being robbed of her whelps, is said to have killed the Ambracian king, they all seem athirst for homicide. But the poets know little else of her. Pope calls her "stubborn," Spenser, King, and several others "fell," Montgomery, in the sense of mad with rage, "wild," and all the rest speak of her as the incarnation of maternal fury. But the poets should not call the lioness or her cubs "brindled," nor speak of "lionets," or as heraldry calls little lions, "lioncels,"[1] as "shrieking." For lion-kittens are spotted, and mew—"slumbering in milk and sighing" like any other cat's kittens.

But their home, "Gurden the lion's palace," the grisly den, all strewn with victim-remnants, cannot be too dreadfully rendered, and the poets' grimness[2] rises to the subject.

> ' The air as in a lion's den
> Is close and hot."

> " Terrific as the lair
> Where the young lions couch."

> " Giant rocks at distance p'led
> Cast their deep shadows o'er the wild.
> Darkly they rise.
> Away ! within those awful cells
> The savage lion of Afric dwells."

---

[1] " The Lyoncel from sweltrie countries braughte,
    He locketh with an eie of flames of fyre."
    —*Chatterton's " Tournament."*

[2] *Inter alios* Wordsworth, Thomson, Hemans, Montgomery, Young.

> " In weary length
> The enormous lion rests his strength.
> For blood in dreams of hunting burns ;
> Or, chased himself, to fight returns,
> Growls in his sleep, a dreary sound,
> Grinds his wedged teeth and spurns the ground."

> " There, bent on death, lie hid his tawny brood,
> And couched in dreadful ambush, pant for blood ;
> Or stretched on broken limbs, consume the day
> In darkness wrapt, and slumber o'er their prey."

That lion-cubs eat tiger-cubs (Southey), but avoid bears and bulls till they are grown up (Cowley), are two details of poetical natural history which seem to rest on an insufficient foundation of fact. The following also seems to be a sketch from Southey's imagination :—

> " A lion vainly struggled in the toils,
> Whilst by his side the cub, in furious rage,
> His young mane floating to the desert air,
> Rends the fallen huntsman."

Of the beast in nature poetry is full, from the half-created lion of the morning of the sixth day " pawing to get free his hinder parts " (Melton)—

> " The roaring lion shakes his tawny mane,
> His struggling limbs still rooted in the plain " (*Darwin*)—

to the final lion of the Apocalypse that shall have six wings, and eyes before and behind ; from the cub, whelped upon a litter of mumbled bones, to the old toothless brute blundering into the Kafir's pitfall, and—

> " By the wily African betrayed,
> Heedless of fate, within its gaping jaws
> Expiring indignant."

But, as a rule, the lion is not merely the natural beast, it is the " dread king," autocrat of the forest and desert, the "blood-nurtured monarch of the wood" (Southey), with terrific attributes of eye and voice and stride—

> "The lordly lion stalks
> Grimly majestic in his lonely walks.
> When round he glares, all living creatures fly;
> He clears the desert with his rolling eye."

Each special feature in turn engages the poets' deference, and each in turn is cited—like the birth-marks on the Christian Champions, on the Fatal Children, or Eastern Messiahs of all kinds and heroes generally—as an indisputable proof of natural dominion and a birthright of sovereignty. Thus of the lion's eye—

> "A lion o'er his wild domains
> Rules with the terror of his eye."—*Montgomery.*

And the undoubted majesty of the lion's gaze when startled into apprehension or anger is a frequent metaphor—

> "Like a lion turns the warrior,
> Back he sends an angry glare."—*Percy's Reliques.*

> "As a leon he his loking caste."—*Chaucer.*

> "A lion's noble rage sits in their face.
> Terribly comely! arm'd with dreadful grace."—*Cowley.*

Its voice, "the prowling lion's Here I am" (Wordsworth); that "doubles the horrors of the midnight hours" (Broome); "how fearful to the desert wide!"—is one of the poets' finest resources whenever terror is needed in a stanza or panic-striking catastrophe requires a simile from Nature.

> "Not with more dismay
> When o'er Caffraria's wooded hills
> Echoes the lion's roar, the timid herd
> Fly the death-boding sound" (*Southey*),

than puny enemies before the battle-cry of heroes of the lion ramp, conspirators before the discovering lantern-flash, or evil-doers at the voice of God ; and, in short, everything in Nature that at one time or another may be suddenly startled into the propriety of precipitate self-preservation.

As a rule it is heard roaring at night—"midnight listens to the lion's roar" (Byron) ; but sometimes in broad daylight "the lion's sullen roar at noon resounds along the lonely banks of ancient Tigris" (Akenside). As a rule, too, the lion roars only when alone ; when, that is, it is calling to its mate or seeking one—"the solitary lion's roar" (Montgomery) ; but occasionally travellers have heard them roaring in company, and justifying therefore Montgomery's fine simile of—

> "Mad as a Lybian wilderness by night
> With all its lions up."

So that the poets have no room for error. But it is not a fact, as Prior supposes,[1] that lions go about roaring seeking for hunters to rend.

Yet, reverent as the majority are, there are poets who (in spite of Eliza Cook's warning[2]) have been found audacious enough to "talk as familiarly of roaring lions as maids of thirteen do of puppy-dogs," and even to make fun of the tremendous voice.

> "*Bombastes :* So have I heard on Afric's burning shore
> A hungry lion give a grievous roar ;
> The grievous roar echoed along the shore.

---

[1] "So the fell lion in the lonely glade,
His side still smarting with the hunter's spear,
Tho' deeply wounded, no way yet dismay'd,
Roars terrible, and meditates new war.
In sullen fury traverses the plain
To find the vent'rous foe, and battle him again."
—*Ode to the Queen.*

[2] "Let the lion be stirred by too daring a word,
And beware of his echoing growl."

Artax. :   So have I heard on Afric's burning shore
Another lion give a grievous roar,
And the first lion thought the last a bore.

Or, as in Swift's delightful " Hyperbole on a Lion : "

" He roar'd so loud and looked so wondrous grim,
His very shadow durst not follow him."

The prodigious fervour of the lion's attack—or rather the exaggerated ideas once entertained of the general fierceness of the animal—has stereotyped Chaucer's comparison "as feres as a lion"—"as lions fierce."

" Ne in Belmarie there n'is so fell leon
That hunted is, or for his hunger wood.
Ne of his prey desireth so the blood
As Palamon."

And again—

" This Palamon
In his fighting were as a wood leon."

So Thomson and Parnell—

" On just reason, once his fury roused,
No lion springs more eager to his prey.
Blood is a pastime."

" So proud, inhuman, numberless and strong,
Like desert lions on their prey they go."

Hence numerous metaphors taken from the same aspect of the animal have become almost proverbs with poets of the Eliza Cook calibre—" She'll take a blow and face a foe, like a lion turned to bay "—" Go face the hungry lion in his path," &c.   But the ferocity idea is certainly elongated to absurdity when we read that—

" The lion may yield, let him sink, let him bleed,
But seek not to tame him, to bind and to lead ; "

for as a matter of fact the lion has been very frequently

tamed. Among the ancients it was considered a regular appendage of the hunting *cortège*, being trained for the chase, in Abyssinia notably, just as the lynx and cheetah are trained still in the East. Nor were the Assyrians singular in keeping this beast as a pet, for several heroes and kings both to east and west of Nineveh are reported to have kept tame lions; while in art the docile species is by no means infrequent—

> "About that king ran many a tame leon and leopart."

And so we find, among others, St. Mark, St. John, and St. Jerome, Sir Gwain de Galles, De Latour, Saladin, Hildebrand, Una, and the Fairie Queene, all maintaining lions as pets or servants, while in the various classics, Cybele—

> "Four maned lions hale
> The sluggish wheels; solemn their toothed maws,
> Their surly eyes brow-hidden, heavy paws
> Uplifted drowsily, and nervy tails
> Cowering their tawny brushes—

and Bacchus, and Love, Indras, Prakrit, and Bala share with other divinities and personages the dignity of a lion-steed.

Again, in popular works of fiction, from the "Arabian Nights" to the "Pilgrim's Progress," the lion appears as a janitor or guardian, faithfully ferocious to the suspicious-looking stranger and the evil-doer, but as tame to its own household and friends as Una's companion or Androcles' acquaintance.

Nor in this "ferocious" connection is it impertinent to note how carefully the poets credited the fiction of the lion finding it necessary to exasperate itself up to the necessary point of fury by lashing its own body with its tail,[1] just as

---

[1] This fiction, it is just possible, arose from the curious claw-like prickle or "thorn" found sometimes at the tip of the animal's tail, and for which naturalists are still puzzled to provide an explanation.

Picrochole had to goad himself into courage against Grand-gousier by self-reproaches. "Roused by the lash of his own stubborn tail," says Dryden, happily hitting off the British characteristic of abusing ourselves into action ; while Waller is more precise—

> "A lion so with self-provoking smart
> (His rebel tail scourging his noble part)
> Calls up his courage ; then begins to roar
> And charge his foes."

That the lion wags its tail when angry has passed into a proverb, and those who have hunted the splendid animal, either in Asia or Africa, always record the preliminary "lashing of the tail" of a lion that has made up its mind to charge. So Darwin's "indignant lions rear their bristling mail, and lash their sides with undulating tail." Cowley's "bold lion, that, ere he seeks his prey, lashes his sides and roars and then away," and others are not only within "the literal verity," but the extension of so common a feline gesture into a leonine singularity—above all, for so absurd a purpose as stinging itself into courage—is a prolongation of the idea that is decidedly poetical, but certainly little else.

Indeed, the poets seem to recognise the dilemma in which undue insistence on the unmitigated ferocity of the lion would place them—

> "Fie
> Upon a lord that wol have no mercie,
> But be a leon both in word and deed !"

ejaculates Chaucer, after having exhausted the lion-idea to magnify the heroic fury of Palamon. For if the lion is not magnanimous it is evidently unworthy of the royal title. So the poets "hedge," so to speak, on all their ferocity by explaining that under certain particular circumstances the lion is quite lamb-like, and with very special classes of persons, "roars you as gently as any sucking dove."

You are never, of course, to be in any doubt as to the capacity of the lion for being terrible on occasion—"Mind you, Todgers's can do it when it likes." But, on the other hand, Hercules can calm down to the distaff, and Mars play with pet sparrows. Did not Cœur-de-Lion himself withdraw his hand on one or two occasions from committing unnecessary murders? So just as the partial historian tempers the crimson story of the first Richard with dabs and specks of white clemency, so the poet, afraid of finding his monarch-beast a complete Nero, qualifies its blood-thirstiness with legendary and mythical suggestions of an occasional magnanimity. Thus Moore diverges from his usual importraiture to call it, in one of his Fables, "generous lion," and Dryden (using generous in the best sense, as Prior has "the hungry lion's gen'rous rage") goes on to say—

> " So when the gen'rous lion has in sight
> His equal match, he rouses for the fight.
> But when his foe lies prostrate on the plain
> He sheaths his paws, uncurls his angry mane,
> And, pleas'd with the bloodless honours of the day,
> Walks over, and disdains th' inglorious prey : "

which is industriously untrue to fact—while sheathing his *paws* is an extraordinary performance even for a poet's lion. The *bear* really does act in the whimsically magnanimous way described in the above lines. But not the lion.

"The royal disposition of that beast to prey on nothing that doth seem as dead " is a fiction.

> " And I no less her anger dread
> Than the poor wretch that feigns him dead
> While some fierce lion doth embrace
> His lifeless corpse and licks his face.
> Wrapt up in silent fear he lies,
> Torn all to pieces if he cries."

This reads well enough in Waller's song, but it is deplorably beyond doubt that the lion will even prey on things that are obviously and outrageously defunct. Its opportunity really comes when "the foe lies prostrate on the plain." Above all, it prefers to surprise its "equal match" when he is asleep by the camp fire. The same agreeable fiction is very frequently repeated. In one of the oldest of our ballads we find—

> " As the lyonne which is of bestes kynge,
> Unto thy subjects be kurteis and benyngne ; "

whereas in nature the lion will even condescend to pick up off its royal path 'such inconsiderable "subjects" as mice, lizards, frogs, and even cockroaches. The larger ones keep out of sight, knowing his majesty's omnivorous propensities, and disregard Wyatt's assurance that "the lion in his raging hour forbears that sueth," or Broome's, that "the fierce lion will hurt no yielden things." Dr. Livingstone once saw a very fine lion in Africa that had just captured a fawn only a few hours old. Yet Quarles tells the fawns that "hungry lions, woo'd with tears, will spare," and Spenser the lady—

> " The lyon lord of everie beast in field
> His princely puissance will abate,
> And mightie proud to humble weak does yield,
> Forgetful of the hunger which of late
> Him prickt, in pittie of such sad estate."

Thus, in St. George's adventures, two lions, after killing the eunuch, lay their heads in Sabra's lap. But the Knight comes up and slays them, for which I can never sufficiently forgive him. He goes on, however, to say : " Now, Sabra, I have by this proved thy fidelity : for it is the nature of the lion, be he never so furious, not to harm but humbly lay his bristled head upon a maiden's lap. Therefore, divine paragon, thou art the world's chief wonder for love and chastity." Later on, in the adventures, I think, of St. David, where the King of Babylon's daughter is in great trouble, her father wishing to kill her, Fidelia hangs about the king's neck "like a lioness," and says : "Thou monstrous murderer, more cruel than the mad dogs of Egypt, why dost thou determine to slaughter the most chaste and loyal lady in the world, even she within whose lap untamed lions will come and sleep ? "

But women were the special objects of leonine forbearance, particularly if they were chaste—

> " 'Tis said that a lion will turn and flee
>   From a maid in the pride of her purity ; "

and again—

> " Harpers have sung and poets told
>   That he, in fury uncontrolled,
>   The shaggy monarch of the wood,
>   Before a virgin, fair and good,
>   Hath pacified his savage mood ; "

so that if Byron, Scott, and the rest be correct, "a lion among ladies " need not after all be so " dreadful " a thing as Snug supposed.   Nor if they are of royal blood will the royal beast do them hurt, as in Beaumont and Fletcher's play—

> " Fetch the Numidian lion I brought over.
>   If she be sprung from royal blood, the lion
>   Will do her reverence ; else, he'll tear her."

Una, it will be remembered, was at first attacked by the beast, but, recognising her virtue, it fawned upon her, kissed her feet, licked her hands, and followed her to the death.

As a matter of (poetical) fact, lions will not hurt princes under any consideration.   Nor are many individual instances of leonine generosity wanting.   To say nothing of the frequent allusions to Androcles his lion, Shakespeare, Waller, Blake, Fairfax, Cowper, and others cite examples of the lion's unexpected clemency to such as were in misfortune, or those who had befriended it.

Thoroughly consonant with this theory of the occasional gentleness of "the terror of the wood," is the poet's cheerfulness in endorsing its amiable familiarity with the lamb. Everybody, probably, remembers the astonishment of the Seven Champions of Christendom, even though they were accustomed to "untamed lions" laying their heads in the laps of Angelicas, when they saw lions and lambs together. But the poets are not to be surprised by such trifles. The Orpheus and Amphion myths redound to the credit of the muse,[1] and it is not therefore altogether unnatural that lions "by tuneful magic tamed," "by verses charmed," and "led by the ear," should now and then be found "dandling the kid," or "gambolling with the bounding roe." They write, however, on a point of a high prescription. We read in Howe's "Chronicles" how King James had a lamb lowered into the Tower lions' den, the company expecting to behold a thrilling murder. On the contrary, "Being come to the ground, the lamb lay upon his knees, and both the lions stood in their former places and only beheld the lamb. Presently the lamb rose up and went unto the lions, who very gently looked upon and smelled on him, without any hurt. Then the lamb was softly drawn up again, in as good plight as he was let down." In the earliest past, as we know from Holy Writ, "the lion gambolled with the kid" in Spenser's Paradise—

> " The lyon there did with the lambe consort,
>   And eke the dove sate by the faulcon's side;
>   Ne each of other feared fraud or tort,
>   But did in safe securitie abide,
>   Withouten perill of the stronger pride."

We can also surmise, from sacred promises of a future of universal peace and idyllic amiability, what Shelley, dreaming of the hereafter, foresees—

---

[1] Poets claim both as of their craft : also Arion.

> " The lion now forgets to thirst for blood :
>   There might you see him sporting in the sun
>   Beside the dreadless kid ; his claws are sheathed,
>   His teeth are harmless ; custom's force has made
>   His nature as the nature of a lamb ; "

and that then, blessed as in Montgomery's " Pelican Island," [1] where " nor lion nor tiger shed innocent blood,"

> " The steer and lion at one crib shall meet,
>   And harmless serpents lick the Pilgrim's feet."

The weary Progress will then be over : the chained lions and the loose ones will have no further terrors for Faithful, and the beasts that came along after the pilgrims "at a great padding pace " will have been forgotten by Christian.

In heraldry it is a more conspicuous beast than even the ordinary familiarity with the armorial lion would lead the uninitiated to suppose, for (as Planché tells us [2]) it was once upon a time the *only* beast thought worthy to be worn on shields and helmets. Thus, kings of England, Scotland, Norway, and Denmark, Princes of Wales and Dukes of Normandy, Counts of Flanders, Earls of Arundel, Lincoln, Leicester, Shrewsbury, Pembroke, Salisbury, and Hereford, all bore lions—indeed, up to the twelfth century, heraldic zoology begins and ends with the King of Beasts. Later on, the leopard came upon the heraldic field, not only to divide honours with the lion, but to usurp its place. For leopard and lion—notably in the arms of England—are the one and same animal, the difference of attitude alone deciding the nominal species. In other words, "leopard" is used in heraldry, not to represent a specific beast, but only a particular attitude of the lion. Thus lion-leopard means a lion passing and seen in profile, while a leoparded-lion means a lion full-faced. For the lion, pure and simple, heraldry

---

[1] " Lion nor tiger here shed innocent blood."—*Pelican Island.*

[2] Planché, " The Pursuivant of Arms : " Chatto & Windus.

insists that it shall be "rampant." That attitude belongs to it, as a matter of course. According to further details of position, couching, standing, stalking, &c., the lion symbolises sovereignty, circumspection, sagacity, magnanimity, valour, counsel. But heraldry has played strange pranks with the animal, for it has degenerated into many unworthy varieties, double-headed and double-tailed, fork-tonged and winged, blue and red, silver and gold, black and white—and even spotted.

As our national emblem the lion cannot fail of course to meet with abundant and flattering recognition. But there has been, on the whole, a generous forbearance from the topic that deserves our gratitude. Nevertheless, whenever treaties are signed, "the British lion kisses the feet of peace," and whenever they are broken "our lion roars." In subsequent battle "the lion-glance appals the foe," and after the victory it "learns to spare the fallen foe." But many other countries claim the lion for their cognisance, or have at one time or other earned the leonine epithet, for, besides "the Anglian lion, the terror of France,"[1] there is "the ruddy lion that ramped in gold" in "proud Scotland's royal shield;" "the winged lion of St. Mark,"[2] where "Venice sate in state, throned on her hundred isles," but now

> "St. Mark sees his lion where he stood,
>   Stand, but in mockery of his wither'd power."

There is "Belgia," with her lions "roaring by her side,"—"the Belgic lion in full fury roars" (Phillips), and "the Assyrian lyonesse," and "the lion of Neustria," and (whatever that was) the Tartar lion, and "victorious Salem's

---

[1] That "oft prowling, ensanguined the Tweed's silver flood, but, taught by the bright Caledonian lance, learned to fear in his own native wood."—*Burns.*

[2] "Sullen old lion of grand St. Mark
    Lordeth and lifteth his front from the dark."—*Joachim Miller.*

lion-banner," " Judah's lion," and others of more or less celebrity.

Yet, with all their homage, the poets can hardly exceed the measure of this animal's dignity in prose. Even to dream of lions was a splendid prognostication. It is the ensign of Hercules, Hector, and Achilles; the Egyptian hieroglyph of divine strength; the " vehicle " of many gods both of the East and West, and of the heroic all the world over, from Scandinavian Rollo to Ethiopian Candace. The Persian Xerxes also is a lion, though it was those beasts that, by attacking his camel-train, put his campaign in peril. The gods of Greece borrowed its form, and the chiefest of Olympus and of the earth accepted its spoils as the insignia of imperial strength. To describe or paint Jove himself, men have had to take the lion as their model, and in the imaginative Orient the figure is repeated in the forces of Nature and the pageantry of the Pantheon. Its effigies supported the throne of Solomon and dignified the decorations of the Temple. It stands, the mere name alone—" Sinha," lion—as the honourable affix of every member of one of the noblest nations of Hindostan, whose king all the world knew as Runjeet Singh, " the lion of the Punjab." But what a roll of heroes that title summons up to the fancy— " the lion of Persia,"[1] Ali, " the lion of God," " the lions of Judah," " the lion-kings of Assyria," " the lion of the north," " the lion of the Prophet," " the lion of Bavaria "—and so forth in endless list, till we have enough Cœur-de-Lions and Leos to re-establish a Lemberg or a Leontopolis, and to justify the redemption of " that sweet land of Lyonnesse " now lying forty fathom under Cornish water. To take its name was the crowning affectation of the chivalrous, just as to have killed a lion was so often—from Hercules to Don Quixote—considered the climax of their courage.

[1] That splendid prince who met his death, unhappily, while chasing an ass.

> " A man huge of limb,
> Grey-eyed, with crisp-curled hair 'twixt black and brown,
> Who had a lion's skin cast over him,
> So wrought with gold that the fell showed but dim
> Betwixt the shreds, and in his hand he bore
> A mighty club."

It adds a dignity to the light offence of the fleet maiden and her lover that for their disregard of her groves they joined Cybele's chariot-team ; and even the firmament borrows a splendour from its terrific lion-constellation. Homer himself is the grander for his lions, and what notable blanks there would have been on the gates and walls of fortress and palace and city had there been no lion for the sculptor, and what beauties been missing on canvas and in literature.

Egypt was so indiscriminate in her zoological reverences that it adds little to the dignity of the lion, that the Pharaoh who bowed before beetles should have paid it sacred honours, though there is something originally fine in the fact that the priests of the " Lion-town " chanted during its meal-times to the beasts as they crunched their bones. Our church-gargoyles are said to be a relic of this worship by the Nile, a vestige of the old-world homage paid to Leo, in the ascendant at the rising of the Great River; and whether this be true or not—and we owe a great deal more to the pagans than unfortunately, " Pagan being dead this many a day," we can ever repay them—the Florentines supply a half-way link in the coronation of the lions on St. John's Day, the Solleone, when the sun enters that sign.

Individuals dignified with lion compliments are "too numerous for specification." But they include British sailors ("the lion-spirits that tread the deck ") and British soldiers (" the lion-heart of British fortitude "); most British kings, from Richard I., "monarch of the lion-heart," to George III., and a very large number of heroes from St.

George to Nelson, as also most European celebrities—
Henri IV., Napoleon, Tell, Charles XII., Luther, and
others; "classical" notables, varying in degrees of merit,
from Ulysses to Tarquin, and all the heroes of poets' fancy,
the Douglases, Alberts, and Tracy de Veres, besides a prodigious series of miscellaneous personages of very diversified
character, ranging from Cain to Jonathan, and from the
Messiah to Satan.

The singular elasticity of the lion idea is thus abundantly
illustrated.   But when we remember that in Holy Writ the
animal stands as the symbol of such very different things as
dignity and falsehood, courage and craft, the enemies of
truth and of wickedness: that in one part of Holy Writ it
typifies the devil, in another is a type of the Saviour; also,
that in all fables the lion is presented to us in every possible
variety of character, from supreme grandeur to ridiculous
meanness, we perceive that the poets have been faithful to
their sources of information.

But it is in the metaphors and morals which the King of
Beasts affords that his many-sided nature is perhaps best
illustrated.   Independence is (in Smollett) "Lord of the
lion-heart;" Ambition is (in Cowley) "the lion-star;"
Truth, "lion-bold;" Danger (in Akenside) has a "lion-
walk;" Wrath (in Spenser)—

> "And him beside rides fierce avenging Wrath
> Upon a lion, loth for to be led."

Passion and War (in Churchill), "fierce as the lion roaring
for his prey, or lioness of royal whelps foredone," are on
one side, while Peace, Cruelty, and Self-interest (in Young)
may be cited on the other.   Tennyson has a noble simile—

> "Slowly comes a hungry people as a lion creeping nigher,
> Glares at one who nods and winks behind a slowly dying fire."

an ass: The sea is often a lion, and sometimes with admirable force. Thus, in Hood, " Three monstrous seas came roaring on like lions leagued together ;" or, in Hemans, " Like angry lions wasting all their might." So Montgomery, " the ocean roaring in his wrath, mad as a Lybian wilderness by night, with all its lions up, in chase or fight." In Jean Ingelow, Time, " A. grim old lion gnawing lay, and mumbled with his teeth a regal tomb." Into innumerable other facets is the lion-stone cut. It does homage (in Grahame) to the announcing angels of Bethlehem—

> " The prowling lion stops,
> Awe-struck, with mane upreared, and flattened head,
> And, without turning, backward on his steps
> Recoils, aghast, into the desert gloom ; "

it spares the prophet, thus characteristically " Emblem "-ed by Quarles,—

> " Fierce Lyons roaring for their prey ! and then
> Daniel throwne in ! and Daniel yet remaine
> Alive ! There was a Lion in the Den
> Was Daniel's friend, or Daniel had been slaine.
> Among ten thousand Lions, I'd not feare
> Had I but only Daniel's Lion there ; "

it is soothed, in Darwin for instance, by music—

> " So playful Love on Ida's flowery sides
> With ribbon rein the indignant lion guides ;
> Pleased on his brindled back the lyre he rings
> And shakes delirious rapture from the strings.
> Slow as the pausing monarch stalks along
> Sheaths his retractile claws and drinks the song ; "

and is a pattern of connubial constancy—

> " The lion's constant to his only miss
> And never leaves his faithful lioness,
> And she's as chaste and true to him again."—*But'er.*

This may be true of the lion—for Nature has enforced monogamy upon nearly all dangerous or noxious (male) beasts—but it is far from the truth with regard to the lioness.   She is a very Messalina, at once faithless and cruel.

"In consequence of the great mortality of female cubs during the process of dentition, she possesses over European ladies the advantage of not being 'redundant,' as Mr. Greg calls it—nay, of being, on the contrary, at a high premium. Every third lion prowls about the desert sands, roaring vainly for a mate ; and the consequence is, of course, an immense exaltation of value, and perhaps, also, some additional cruelty on the side of the lioness."   Miss Cobbe then goes on to give a terrible illustration of this cruelty— but the facts are, perhaps, too familiar to need repetition. Suffice it to say that the lioness manages by her coquetry to bring rival suitors into each other's presence, and, having excited them to combat, leaves them to bleed to death for her sake while she strolls away in search of fresh conquests.

"The lion," says Professor Kitchen Parker, "enjoys the honourable distinction of being strictly faithful to his spouse, although report says she is by no means so virtuous, but only cleaves to her mate until a stronger and handsomer one turns up."

II.

THE HEPTARCHY OF THE CATS.

Nothing can be more unsatisfying than the poets' treatment of the splendid family of the Cats. Excepting the lion, to which, as I have shown, they do conspicuous justice, the poets have apparently no appreciation whatever of the grand Parable of the Carnivora. They say the tiger is very fierce, and the leopard and the panther very beautiful; but there they end. Their powerful compeers, the jaguar, puma, ounce, and cheetah, which complete the Heptarchy—the Lion-state enjoying the "hegemony" of the confederacy— are not utilised, so that virtually the noble Beasts of Prey afford the poets no more than two similes—one of excessive cruelty, and one of personal elegance. Here and there, of course, tradition, heraldic association, or Biblical mistranslation, betrays the poet into some oblique injustice to the proud vassals of the beast paramount—"the lonely lords of empty wilds and woods"—but these aberrations do not materially affect their treatment. They do not recognise apparently the nobility of this family of courageous and beautiful beasts in Nature's wild-life scheme, nor appreciate the purpose they serve as her chief ministers of state.

Individually the tiger, leopard, and panther are each of them largely utilised, but, as will be seen, with very meagre aims and results, considering the possibilities of such subjects.

With regard, however, to this class of beautiful and dangerous beasts, it is due to the poets to point out that antiquity used "pard" for the cheetah; that tradition made the "leopard" a hybrid between pards and lions; that the "mythical panthera," of European fancy, was first imagined somewhere about the Reynard-the-Fox Age, and has survived as the panther of modern times; that when heraldry commenced in earnest, the leopard was merely the lion in certain attitudes; that early writers mixed up tigers with leopards and panthers as part of the emblematic retinue of the Greek gods; that modern zoologists are still divided as to the identity or variety of the leopard and panther; that America calls the puma both "panther" and "mountain lion;" that in Ceylon the panther is called the "tiger;" that in the South African Colonies the leopard is called "tiger" also; and that all over India the same native names are hopelessly bewildered among not only panthers, leopards, and cheetahs, but also extended to hyænas.

TIGER.

The Tiger—"the deep-mouthed tiger, dread of the brown man," as Morris calls it—is a very frequent image with the poets, whether "holding its solitude in desert dark and rude,"—"crouching to await its helpless prey,"—"darting fierce, impetuous, on the prey his glance has doomed,"— or "returning to its den before the sun may see it." But it has nevertheless only one aspect, namely, of ruthless voracity. To this every other feature is made to contribute. The "tiger's plunge," from its impetuosity, is used as if denoting a malignity of purpose greater than when the royal lion does the same thing; and when it lies in ambush—a particularly leonine trick—the stratagem is condemned as savouring of treachery, though lions may do it by right divine.

The tiger—"cruel and unkind, that with greediness thirsts after blood,"—"formed to cruel meals," stands, in fact, in the poets for the symbol of pure bloodthirstiness—"with fell clawes full of fierce gourmandise, and greedy mouth wide-gaping like hell-gate "—

> "As when some tiger, to his haunt from day
> Returns, bloodfoaming, with his slaughtered prey,
> Grim-pleased that there with undisturbed roar
> He'll glut and revel o'er the reeking gore ;
> Glares in wild fury o'er the gloomy waste,
> And growls terrific o'er the mangled beast ;
> Now drags relentless down the rugged vale,
> And stains the forest with a bloody trail."

This episode from Wilson is characteristic of a hundred other passages equally untrue to nature, for the tiger is not by many fathoms such a fool as to drag his prey to his haunt, "and stain the forest with a bloody trail" which would inevitably lead to his destruction. Nor does he roar at his meals. Another popular poets' error is preserved in Montgomery, where, in an otherwise excellent passage, he speaks of the tiger dragging the buffalo to his lair and "crashing through the ribs at once unto the heart," for this animal never commences its meal either at the heart, or, as other poets say, at the throat, but at the buttocks of the prey.

"The tigress in her whelpless ire," "the cubless tigress in her jungle raving" (Byron), "the tiger-dam with red fangs" (Cook)—is a very favourite simile for supreme ferocity, carried in Marvell even to the point of suicide—

> " So from Euphrates' bank, a tigress fell
> After her robbers for her whelps doth yell,
> But sees enraged the river flow between.
> Frustrate revenge, and love by loss more keen,
> At her own breast her useless claws does arm—
> She tears herself."

Arcité in the " Knight's Tale " is a " felle tigre."

> " There was no tigre in the Vale of Galaphey
>   When that hire whelpe is stole
>   So cruel."

But, after all, where shall we give the palm of maternal fondness?   As Byron says—

> " The love of offspring's nature's general law,
>   From tigresses and cubs to ducks and ducklings ;
>   There's nothing whets the beak, or arms the claw,
>   Like an invasion of their babes and sucklings,
>   And all who have seen a human nursery, saw
>   How mothers love their children's squalls and chucklings.'

Connubial affection is not the tigress's forte, for, with all wild animals of her sex, she shares the deplorable tendency to transfer her charms from her spouse to any other male that overcomes him in battle, and is indeed much maligned if it be not true that she actually incites her lord and master to fight, as if not altogether indifferent to a change of husbands.   The lines " Oh, e'en the tiger slain hath one who ne'er doth flee, who soothes his dying pain," are not therefore in invariable or even frequent harmony with the facts of the tiger's wedded life.   For the tigress licks the wounds of the conqueror, irrespective of previous domestic relations.

Nor, as a matter of fact, is the tiger a specially ferocious criminal.   As the greatest authority on Indian natural history says, it is " a harmless, timid animal."   It feeds on animals that are prodigiously injurious to crops, and there are on record in India the complaints of villagers about the increase of deer and wild pigs in consequence of the destruction of the tigers in their neighbourhood.   When it gets too feeble to catch wild animals it begins to eat tame ones, or easier victims still, the men or women who are in charge of the cattle. It then becomes, as a " man-eater," a criminal against humanity—and death cannot overtake it too soon.

But it is only those who know the Hindoos thoroughly who can credit their amazing apathy, even when in imminent danger. So long as it is not actually visible they refuse to take precaution against peril, and I remember during the Afghan War having to thrash some lazy camp-followers in order to arouse them to a proper sense of the necessity of saving their own lives. They had squatted down to smoke by the roadside in the Khyber Pass, though they knew the enemy was lurking both in the rocks above them, and in the grass-jungle behind them, and though they had with their own eyes seen the corpses of camp-followers lying where they had been murdered—when, like themselves, they had sate down contrary to orders to smoke. In the very same way, the herdsman comes loafing home in the twilight, shouting out a song at the top of his voice as he goes (to let the beast know that he is coming probably), and suddenly the tiger flashes out of the sugar-canes, and there is an end of that herdsman. But the next man will probably do the very same thing. He will take another road of course on his way home, but he will lag behind his cattle and sing to himself in the same ridiculous way, and out from under the bair-tree springs the same old tiger.

Indeed, it is one of the problems of Indian administration how to keep the natives from suicide. They prefer to have half the village down with small-pox and then to carry a dead chicken round the stricken hamlet on the end of a pole, than to be vaccinated. They prefer to lose a prodigious number of their acquaintances by drowning rather than protect their open wells. They prefer to have tens of thousands of men and women bitten by snakes in the toes and thumbs, and die therefrom, than to let enough light into a hut to see the difference between a faggot and cobra.

Not that I wish to extenuate the immorality of the tiger in eating human beings, even when it finds them lying about, so to speak, as if they were worth nothing. It is a practice that should be discouraged even more forcibly than it is, and be made an imperial matter. But, on the other hand, it is unfair, even to tigers, to speak of them as if they were for ever going about mangling. They are ferocious enough—indeed, they set the lion a very splendid example —when they are attacked and have to fight. But such ferocity is not to be spoken ill of. It is heroism. The historian can give our handful of soldiers in the Indian Mutiny no further praise when he has once said that "they fought *like tigers.*" The poet, therefore, who calls Bertram a tiger, because he has not enough courage to show fight against odds, does the noble beast a gratuitous injustice. Scott, moreover, stretches his metaphor beyond its capacity when he makes Bertram, couching in the brake and fern, hide his face "lest foemen spy the sparkle of his swarthy eye!"

Nor, in the poets, does any majesty appertain to the tiger, "that doth live by slaughter." It is "tameless"— which of course tigers are not, seeing that they have very frequently been tamed—and affords frequent similes for irresistible ferocity. But there is no dignity attaching to the beast apart from his pre-eminence in criminal fury. It is, in fact, described as rather a mean animal, toying, as in Hurdis, with the kids when caught, " whetting his appetite by long restraint," and, in Spenser—

> "When he by chance doth find
> A feeble beast, doth felly him oppress."

It worries sheepfolds, stalks "gentle fawns at play "—

> " As a tiger, who by chance hath spy'd
> In some purlieu two gentle fawns at play,
> Straight couches close, then rising changes oft

> His couchant watch, as one who chose his ground
> Whence rushing he might surest seize them both
> Gripped in each paw " (*Dryden*),

kills for killing's sake, " roams all abroad and grimly slays," and continues to slaughter even when dying itself.

> " As a grim tiger whom the torrent's might
> Surprises in some parched ravine at night
> Turns, even in drowning, on the wretched flocks
> Swept with him in that snow-flood from the rocks,
> And to the last, devouring on his way,
> Bloodies the stream he has no power to stay."

Moore's zoology, however, is, as a rule, of the wildest kind ; but it is strange that the notorious fact—notorious at any rate from the days of the Ramayana and before Homer—that in presence of a common danger tigers and sheep lay aside their mutual antipathies, should not have made his metaphor move more cautiously. I have myself known of a tiger and a herd of cattle on the same half-acre of ground during a flood, and the tiger seemed the most ill at ease of all the company. Thus accurate Tennyson, "Gareth and Lynette," has, the "lion and stoat isled together in time of flood ;" and Leyden, in the "Scenes of Infancy"—

> " When the storm through Indian forests runs,
>
> .   .   .   .   .   .
>
> Floats far and loud the hoarse, discordant yell
> Of ravening pards, which harmless crowd the dell.
>
> .   .   .   .   .   .
>
> The barbarous tiger whets his fang no more
> To lap, with torturing pause, his victim's gore.
> Curb'd of their rage, hyænas gaunt are tame,
> And shrink, begirt with all-devouring flame."

Its appearance, the poets say, commands no such respect from other beasts as the lion's is said to do—though Livingstone says those who meet a lion will be much disappointed if they expect to see anything but a very large dog-like animal. Its eyes are "glowing flames" (Chatterton), and "fire-ball" eyes "that make horrid twilight in the sunless jungle"[1] (Montgomery); they "flash" and "glare." But there is nothing of awe in the aspect of the tiger, according to the poets, except to such poor things as lambs and kids and fawns. Blake is a notable exception, in the poem commencing—

> " Tiger ! tiger ! burning bright
> In the forests of the night :
> What immortal hand or eye
> Could form thy fearful symmetry ? "

Its voice is "dreadful," it "growls terrific," but it has no effect upon the surrounding forests and its inhabitants, such as the roar of lions is supposed to have when they burst

> " From dreams of blood, awaked by maddening thirst,
> When the lone caves, in which they shrunk from light,
> Ring with wild echoes through the hideous night,
> When darkness seems alive, and all the air
> Is one tremendous uproar of despair."—*Montgomery.*

The "thirsting tiger's yell," "hideous howl," "voice more horrid than the roar of famished tiger leaping on his prey," and other expressions of objection to the sound are very frequent, but none of them give any notion at all of the supreme awfulness of the real voice in nature, that literally hushes the jungle and fills the twilight with horror. Not that tigers roar much. When, as in Darwin, "with kindling flame, he hears the love-lorn night-call of his brinded dame," the tiger has a very solemn and dreadful utterance, but Mont-

---

[1] So Jean Ingelow :—

> " In tangles of the jungle reed
> Whose heats are lit with tiger eyes."

gomery comes nearer to the actual sound when he calls it a "groan." As a matter of fact, it is something between a cough and a groan.

Is the lion or the tiger the superior in courage and strength? There is little evidence on record to help us to a decision, but all that there is is completely in favour of the tiger. The two animals have often been put together to fight, but the lion has invariably declined the combat. They have accidentally got into each other's cages, and the tiger has killed the lion. Feats of strength are authenticated of the tiger to which the lion can, on evidence, lay no claim; and as regards their comparative courage in the presence of man, the evidence goes to prove the superiority of the tiger. Says Livingstone, for instance, "Lions would seem to be inferior in power to the Indian tiger." For myself, then, I give the preference without hesitation to the tiger.

Yet in the poets the tiger forms, of course, part of the courtier-retinue of the lion—"Gaunt wolves and sullen tigers in his train" (Collins)—for the lion, as Spenser, Allan Ramsay, and others state, defeated the tiger in single combat, when the prize was the sovereignty of the animal world. Cowley speaks of the lion as thirsting for tigers' blood, and again of the "dreadful" (that is, full of dread) tiger trembling at even the slumbering lion—

> "When he lies down the woods a dreadful silence keep,
> And dreadful tigers tremble at his sleep."

Southey, imitating this fancy, does the same, and speaks of tigers "trembling" while the lion sleeps; while several others describe the two as meeting, and the tiger giving way. Thus Wilson—

> "The shaggy lion rushes to the place,
> With roar tremendous seizes on his prey.
> Exasp'rate see! the tiger springs away,

> Stops short, and maddens at the monarch's growl;
> And through his eyes darts all his furious soul.
> Half willed, yet half afraid to dare a bound,
> He eyes his loss, and roars, and tears the ground."

Yet in spite of the poets I am of opinion that a very considerable dignity attaches to the Raja of the Jungles. Sportsmen know well what a solitude the tiger creates for itself by its simple presence, and what an overwhelming awe possesses all wild life when its voice is heard. The wild boar, it is true, will turn upon it, but then the wild boar is the type among the beasts of a chivalry that is Quixotic in its rashness; and the tiger by this presumptuous conduct often arrives at pork that he could not otherwise have captured. Sometimes, however, he is killed by the boar. But what supremacy in the world is not challenged at some time or another by foolhardy subjects or overweening rivals? Does the lion " walk his kingly path " unchallenged? On the contrary, he has to yield the path very often.

In the tiger's manner of life, lording it over the unrivalled jungles of India, there is an undoubted majesty, while its amazing physical powers bespeak the monarch of a kingdom where might is right, and befit it as the steed of Hari and the emblem of Shiva.

In metaphor, therefore, though frequently recurring, the tiger has but a very narrow range. Spenser's Spumnador rides on one—

> " Upon a tygre swift and fierce he rode,
> That as the winde ran underneath his load,
> While his long legs nigh raught unto the ground."

All very bloodthirsty personages, like royal enemies of Great Britain, " daring the lion," or their soldiers—" Gallia's tigers," for instance, who " fight with tiger zeal;" or disreputable heroes of the Byronic Corsair or Moore's Ghebir type; or wicked sycophants of the powerful, or oppressors of the weak, are all "tigers." So Wrong itself and Evil Passions are symbolised by the tiger, Wrath is "tiger-passioned" (Keats), and—the climax of insidious and abominable cruelty—the gout is "half tiger, half a snake" (Armstrong). Once only is the beast amiable, and that is in a general revolution of animal character which Darwin delightfully imagines in his "Loves of the Plants:"—

> "Charmed on the brink, relenting tigers gaze,
> And pausing buffaloes forget to graze ;
> Admiring elephants forsake their wood,
> Stretch their wide ears, and wade into the flood.
> In silent herds the wondering sea-calves lave,
> Or nod their slimy foreheads o'er the wave ;
> Poised on still wing attentive vultures sweep,
> And winking crocodiles are lulled to sleep ;"

and once again, when Chatterton sees them "wanton with their shadows in their stream."

But in Chatterton all things were permissible;[1] and Moore, perhaps, need create no surprise when he assures us that even the hungriest tiger will not eat a "Ghebir" man, knowing him to be "a thing untamed and fearless as themselves." But why does Shelley make tigers fight with sea-snakes out in mid-ocean? or Campbell sing of tigers stealing along the bank of a North American river? or Somerville describe them in Mexico? or why do Cowley and Byron speak of *spotted* tigers?

> "The tiger's litter ; but whoe'er
> Would seek to save the spotted sire or dam
> Unless to perish by their fangs?"

---

[1] For instance, this impossible convention of animals—

> "The rampynge lyon, felle tygere,
> The bocke that skyppes from place to place,
> The olyphaunte and rhynocere
> Before me throughe the greene-woode I did chase."
> —*Parlyamente of Sprytes.*

> " He swells with angry pride,
>   And calls forth all his spots on every side."

For once the poets have nearly managed to make a wild beast a real wild beast, and these variations from nature are as deplorable as they were unnecessary.

As I have said before, "there is no nonsense about the tiger, as there is about the lion." He does not go about imposing on people. Wolves may, if they like, pretend that they are only dogs gone wrong from want of a better bringing-up, and the lion swagger as if he were something more than a very large cat; but the tiger never descends to such prevarication, setting himself up for better than he is, or claiming respect for qualities which he knows he does not possess. There is no ambiguity about anything he does. All his character is on the surface. "I am," he says, "a thoroughgoing downright wild beast, and if you don't like me you must lump me; but in the meanwhile you had better get out of my way." There is no pompous affectation of superior "intelligence" about tigers. If they are met with in jungles, they do not make-believe for the purpose of impressing the traveller with their uncommon magnanimity, or waste time like the lion in superfluous roarings, shaking of heads, or "looking kingly." On the contrary, they behave honestly and candidly, like the wild beasts they are. They either retire precipitately with every confession of alarm, or in their own fine outspoken way "go for the stranger." Nor when they make off do they do it as if they liked it or had any half mind about it—as the lion, that Livingstone tells us trots away slowly till it thinks itself out of sight and then bounds off like a greyhound—wasting time in pretentious attitudes or in trying to save appearances. They have no idea of showing off. If they mean to go, they go like lightning, and don't for a moment think of the figure they may be cutting. But if, on the other hand, they mean fighting, they give the stranger very little leisure for misunderstanding their intentions.

The tiger, therefore, deserves to be held in respect, as a model wild beast, for he knows his station, and keeps it, doing the work that Nature has given him to do with all his might. Life has only one end for him, the enjoyment of it, and to this he gives the whole of his magnificent energies. Endowed with superb capabilities for taking lives and preserving his own, he exercises them to the utmost in this one direction, without ever forgetting for an instant that he is only a huge cat, or flying in the face of Providence by wishing to be thought anything else. One result of this is that the tiger finds no place in folk-lore outside of India and (in a demoniacal form) Cathay. There was, it is true, a stream somewhere in Fairyland that turned donkeys into " tigers," but the name is used here only as the extreme antithesis of the inoffensive ass.

LEOPARD.

Owing to the mystery in heraldry about the identity of the Leopard, and the confusion in myths and folk-lore, not only between this animal and the panther—which is allowable, seeing that science is still unable to decide the question of their variety—but even between the leopard, lion,[1] and tiger, the poets have found in it (whether we call it libbard, pard, pardel) a thoroughly suitable subject for poetical treatment. Having no definite individuality, it can be treated very liberally as to manners, appearance, and attributes, and there is little margin for criticism of the liberties which poets may take.

They have, therefore, this justification for their " leopards," that the sources from which they usually draw their zoolo-

---

[1] Thus Broome makes Achilles terrific in "a leopard's spotted spoils."

gical information are exceptionally muddy on the question of *felis pardus.*

Thomson calls "the lively shining leopard, speckled o'er with many a spot," "the beauty of the waste;" Wordsworth has "the lively beauty of the leopard;" Dryden, "the lady of the spotted muff;" Morris has "spotted leopards fair, that through the cane-brakes move, unseen as air;" Moore, "such beauties might the lion warm;" Jean Ingelow has "the fair leopard, with her sleek paws laid across her little drowsy cubs," and so on : while the other touches of Nature —"elegant," "light," " of easy grace "—all connote a thing of beauty. "Freckled like a pard," says Keats, wishing to enhance the loveliness of the Lamia snake; and Tennyson has, "eyed like the evening star."

In Darwin it is the lover—

> " And now a spotted Pard the lover stalks,
> Plays round her steps and guards her favoured walks.
> As with white teeth he prints her hand, caressed,
> And lays his velvet paws upon her breast,
> O'er his round face her snowy fingers strain
> The silken knots."

In Leyden, the "brinded panther fierce" does not matter, but why should Heber, with his Indian experience, say "the brindled pard?" Truly may Herbert, though in another significance, say, "in a leopard the spots are not observed." Campbell, with his characteristic independence in matters of fact, places "panthers" in New South Wales.

Otherwise they have no place in poets' Nature. Keats has "pard with prying head," a delightful phrase; Hood speaks very happily indeed of a sound "distantly heard, as of some grumbling pard," and Morris, always in sympathy with Nature, has "the stealthy leopard whining" as it creeps from out the thicket. But except Moore's absurd conceit of leopards mistaking loosened stones for prey, and

> " Long heard from steep to steep,
> Chasing them down their thundering way,"

and one or two incidental " pards " that happen to fit into rhymes, the animal does not appear.

Yet when we remember the importance of the leopard in heraldry, and its frequent appearance both in art and the fancies of antiquity, it seems somewhat curious that it should have found such scanty favour. As part of " panthered Bacchus' jolly retinue " we meet with it in Keats and one or two other poets, while in Shakespeare, Scott, and elsewhere, allusion is made to our national " leopard." As referred to in Holy Writ in connection with the indelible Ethiopian, it receives due notice from the worthy Hurdis and from Cowper as being a beast of prey, and therefore, in the coming days of a universal peace, predestined to lie down with the lamb.

Sacred to Pan, Chief President of the Hills, and the favourite of Dionysus, its skin was once the honourable badge of priesthood ; the Greek gods and Greek heroes wore it on state occasions, and it is still one of the supreme insignia of royalty in Africa.

PANTHER.

When the Panther—" the viceroy panther " of Dryden's parable—is mentioned by name, it generally adds something of solitude to the leopard idea. The poets' leopard is a graceful, pretty beast, fit to be a lady's pet. The panther is of a somewhat gloomier sort. It " ravens " occasionally, and is often found in the dreadful company of tigers, hyænas, and other beasts of reproach. A savour of covert malignity attaches to the animal.

But it is still beautiful. Says Dryden, " fairest creature of the spotted kind ;" Shelley, " a pard-like spirit, beautiful and swift," and again, "sleeping in beauty on the mangled prey, as panthers sleep;" Wordsworth—

> " He was a lovely youth !   I guess
> The panther in the wilderness
> Was not so fair as he,"

and so with others. In the East a "panther waist," "panther elegance," is a stereotyped phrase in the description of Oriental beauty. But even in these (Dryden's having a covert significance), the touch of the beast of prey is not wanting—it is fleet of foot, a thing of the wilderness, sleeping on its mangled prey—while in the majority of references it is a downright wild beast—"skulking," the guilty accomplice of wolves, "the bloody panther" by which A. Wilson must mean the cougar or puma, or else mean nothing, for there is no large *spotted* carnivore in North America, "ruthless panther," "furious pard," and so forth. At sunset it rushes out after prey "from the roots of Lebanon," ravages the red man's "fold" (in E. Cook—whom the Saints preserve !); "in his desperate fierceness, defying and bold;" is found (in Glover) on Hydaspes' side or Eastern Indus cooling his "reeking jaws" after "feasting on the blood of some torn deer,"

> " Which nigh his cruel grasp
> Had roamed unheeding in the secret shade ; "

and very often besides is spoken of as a fierce carnivorous brute—which, in spite of its beauty and fragrance, the panther or leopard undoubtedly is. To kill this animal, therefore, was, the poets tell us, "the highest glory and the greatest joy" of North American foresters, and its spoils "the prime trophy" of Ethiopian spears. Somerville, therefore, includes the panther in the beasts of chase, and gives the following singular receipt for the successful hunting of the beast, though it might be objected that the carrying about of large mirrors, when out after panthers, in such scenes as they inhabit would be a cumbrous matter—

> " Fierce from his lair springs forth the speckled pard,
> Thirsting for blood and eager to destroy ;
> The huntsman flies, but to his flight alone
> Confides not : at convenient distance fix'd,
> A polish'd mirror stops in full career
> The furious brute ; he there his image views :
> Spots against spots with rage improving glow.
> Another pard his bristly whiskers curls,
> Grins as he grins, fierce menacing, and wide
> Distends his op'ning jaws ; himself against
> Himself oppos'd, and with dread vengeance arm'd,
> The huntsman, now secure, with fatal aim
> Directs his pointed spear, by which transfix'd
> He dies, and with him dies the rival shade."

The poets, in fact, divide their leopard into two (as many sportsmen do for the sake of augmenting their trophies) so as to seem to be talking of more than one animal, reserving the leopard to convey ideas of grace without undue ferocity, and the panther for ferocity that even personal beauty does not condone. It is a "bearded" beast of "panther-peopled solitudes" (Shelley), that "howls" in the wilderness (Campbell), and dies of the sirocco in African deserts (Darwin). And, indeed, in Nature, it is by no means a mere plaything. For the "panther"—by which name Oriental sportsmen call the larger specimens or, as some zoologists affirm, the larger *species* of leopard—is very often a man-eater. And this not from the necessities of decrepitude, as with the tiger, but from choice. For the panther frequently enters huts to carry off an inmate, though the village cattle, past which it had come, offered a less perilous capture. Its strength is surprising, for it can break the neck of full-grown cattle, and carry sheep over a wall seven feet in height. When attacked, it is, in the opinion of many sportsmen, quite as formidable as the royal wearer of the stripes. It feeds only on the largest game, the sambhur stag, nilghai, cattle, horses, and man—one panther in the Gwalior state having been known to kill fifty human beings in one district. If wounded from a tree it will climb up to its assailant and attack him there, and will charge an elephant as cheerfully as the tiger does.

The leopard (I am here accepting the theory that there really *are* two species of the animal), though not so formidable, is still a dangerous antagonist, but, as a rule, it does not aspire to larger victims than sheep and goats, the smaller varieties of deer and antelope, calves, and, above all, dogs. Now the poets, as Broome and Somerville, seem to think the leopard looks upon the dog as its natural master and conqueror, whereas the fact is that the leopard looks upon the dog as its natural food. The leopard's taste for dogs is certainly one of the most extraordinary phenomena in natural history. We say that cats like fish and that monkeys are fond of nuts, but these are mere passing whims, caprices of the moment, compared to the constant passion of leopards for dogs. It is a very Chinaman for its delight in puppy, for it will follow a man for miles like his shadow if a dog be at his heels,—and it will be a very extraordinary dog indeed if it does not at last give the leopard its chance. The best of them sometimes commits the indiscretion of loitering behind its master or running out of sight round a corner in front of him, and if it does this with a leopard on the track nothing more is ever seen of the dog, and nothing more heard of it but a last squeal as it is swiftly snatched up off the path and carried, with a sudden rustle of foliage, down the hill-side. At night, leopards will prowl round the tent, sniffing under the canvas for the dog that they can smell within, or in the hill stations will boldly come down among the houses and carry off the pet of the establishment, though servants may be moving about. It is on record that in the station of Gumsoor not a single dog escaped, and nearly every resident of India who has ever camped out in the jungle where leopards are, or has lived in "the hills," has had some tragic experience of this mania of the leopard for dogs.

In about the same degree, but obviously for very different reasons, the monkey takes the most profound interest in the leopard, and when one is afoot the four-handed folk follow him as closely as they dare, shaking the branches in their absurd rage, chattering furiously at their enemy, and making faces at him. Sometimes, however, the leopard stops abruptly and glares at them, and the wretched monkeys, gathering overhead, get so excited in their demonstrations that one of their number is pretty sure to lose its balance and tumble into the leopard's mouth.

A tradition was once widely current that the panther was sweetly-scented—says Dryden, "the panther's breath was ever famed for sweet"—and that this fragrance was so fascinating to some small animals that it enticed them to their death in the jaws of the aromatic beast.[1] It is a fact, however, that the panther itself is peculiarly sensible to perfumes, and among other instances is one of undeniable authenticity of a panther being tamed with lavender water.

A part of this tradition is no doubt the existence of a mythic animal called the "panthera," of which the bones were of great lustre and exquisite odour. One of the three "rarities" which Reynard the Fox pretended he had got for the Queen was a comb. "This comb was made of the bone of a noble beast called Panthera, which lives between the greater India and earthly Paradise. He is so beautiful that he partakes of all the loveliest hues

---

[1] Spenser thus alludes to another tradition—the power of the panther to fascinate, like the snake, by sight—

> "The panther, knowing that his spotted hyde
> Doth please all beasts, but that his looks them fray,
> Within a bush his dreadful head doth hide,
> To let them gaze whylst he on them may prey."

under heaven; and the smell of him is so sweet and wholesome that the very savour cures all infirmities. He is the physician of all animals that follow him, and has one fair bone, broad and thin, in which, when slain, are contained the whole virtues of the animal. It can never be broken nor consumed by any of the elements : yet it is so light that a feather will poise it, and it can receive a fine polish."

In metaphor these twin animals are very unfruitful in the poets' hands. As being beautiful but of faulty character, they supply the fabulist with a satire—in Dryden on the English Church, in Gay on a vain beauty, in Spenser a cruel one, in Moore a dissolute one. And as being fierce, a simile for impetuous soldiery, as "the sword of the Moslem," and the British attack.

JAGUAR, PUMA, CHEETAH, OUNCE.

Two or three poets mention the " Jaguar " and the "fell Puma that feeds on the colt and the steer," and once by inference (in Somerville) the cheetah is indicated. Nor in the case of the last-named is obscurity altogether unjustifiable, for, except as part of the hunting equipage of princes, Asiatic and African, or—in the case, for instance, of Semendmanik, the favourite of Akhbar—as royal pets, the cheetah is an inconspicuous animal in its own countries.

At the same time it should not be forgotten that the cheetah is the real "pard" of the ancients, and therefore the animal that the poets really mean, though they do not know it, when they refer to "leopards" of antiquity.

But, in the case of the other two furred princes, the truly royal jaguar, and the very picturesque and sometimes very ferocious puma—or cougar,[1] mountain lion, or panther of Western America—such neglect is perhaps more noteworthy.

---

[1] " Cougar's deadly spring."—*Mrs Hemans.*

The lives of these creatures are in themselves poems, when we think of the territories they rule over, and the romances of the country—Mexican, Red Indian, Peruvian—in which they lord it, among the ruins of a desolated civilisation in the midst of dwindled nations. Around these animals numerous legends have of course gathered. Thus, the jaguar and boa are supposed to have an hereditary blood-feud—a fact Shelley would have delighted to know—and the jaguar, again, will not harm children, while the pretty story of Maldonata and her puma revives with graceful additions the old Androcles tradition.

Shelley and Keats both mention the Ounce by name, the former in error for the cheetah, in the line—

> " As hooded ounces cling to the driven deer,"

the latter to get a rhyme for " pounce "—" pard or ounce." This animal, however, is simply the leopard adapted by / nature for existence in a bitterly cold climate, and is probably the most beautiful wild-beast on our earth—and one of the most powerful. It is the " snow-leopard " of Eastern sportsmen, and its fleecy skin, silvery white or primrose yellow, with black rings and rosettes and rather larger than an average leopard's, is one of the choicest trophies of the Himalayan shikarry. The Zoological Gardens have never possessed a specimen of this rare and lovely carnivore.

To conclude this chapter with a quotation from my *Essay in Unnatural History* [1]—

"The lesser carnivora," as they are called, play a very important part in the political system of the beasts. They are the great feudatory princes or viceroys of the wild world. Claiming kinship with royalty, they possess within their respective earldoms all the privileges of independent

---

[1] " Noah's Ark, an Essay in Unnatural History." Sampson, Low, & Co.

sovereigns, and the powers of life and death.   At the head of fierce clans, they often defy the central authority, and, retiring within their own demesnes, maintain there almost royal state.   Such are the puma, jaguar, leopard, and panther.   The two latter are to the East what the others are to the West, and their lives, whether we consider the kindliness of Nature to them in their beauty and strength, or their strange immunity from harm, are equally to be admired and envied.   They live, it is true, within the empire of the lion, but only as, in the days of the Heptarchy, the Mercian or the Northumbrian prince would have called himself "within the realm" of the Bretwalda; as in the early days of France the Dukes of Soissons or Burgundy acknowledged their vassalage to Paris; or, earlier still, only as Acarnacia or Locris confessed the supremacy of Sparta. There is respect on both sides, and therefore a large measure of peace within the satrapies of the Cats."

Though it cannot claim an equal dignity with any of the seven animals I have grouped under the Heptarchy, the Lynx is distinctly of the aristocracy.   Moreover, it is a delightful wild beast, savage, carnivorous, and something of an assassin, as wild beasts should be—and all the more delightful for being European.   We have so few picturesque ferine touches in the domesticated Nature of our civilised Continent that the lynx could hardly be spared.   There is the wolf, of course—but the wolf is, perhaps, too serious an animal.   Failing sheep, it will content itself with children. There is the bear too, but the bear is seldom in the way. Its habits are retiring; its diet, by preference, innocent. So that it cannot be considered a disagreeable addition to European Fauna.   The lynx comes midway between the two. It has a taste for mutton, but would prefer the lambs coming into its private retreats to having to go and fetch them out of the public meadow. Now, when we speak of the ravages that wild animals commit, we forget that they are usually of our own prompting or creating. We set to work and cultivate a district, and populate it, driving out or exterminating the natural food of the beasts, and then fill large spaces with our own helpless "domestic" animals. After this, if the wild beasts eat these we exclaim against them, quite overlooking the fact that in most cases we have made such consumption a necessity of ferine existence, and in all have put temptation in the wild beasts' way in a most immoral manner.

And lynxes do not hesitate to avail themselves of their opportunities, and this with such wastefulness that they will kill far more sheep than they eat. But then beasts do not know any better. When they get amongst lambs they are like children among daisies, who murder the poor innocent flowers by thousands, leave them lying in heaps close by where they picked them, and go dripping daisies along the road all the way home.

For some reason or another these animals have acquired the reputation of an extraordinarily piercing eyesight, and from thee arliest times have been credited with the power of seeing through opaque bodies. This fiction would appear to constitute its chief claim to poetical regard. "Watchful," Crabbe, Byron, Drayton, and others call it.

> " Thus parents also are at times short-sighted,
>   Though watchful as the lynx."

Nor is the epithet misapplied, for, like every other species of cat, it is very watchful, and indeed in the patience of its ambuscades exhibits a somewhat special vigilance. So "calculation" is, poetically, lynx-eyed. It is the antithesis of the mole and bat. The prophet borrows its vision—

> " Now with a lynx-eye
> I see, looking into future time,"

says Cowper's Adam.   From this reputed keenness of sight,
"lynx" comes to signify a cruel eagerness in detection, as
of officers of the Inquisition ; and Keats, by a curious form
of what may be called metastasis, make the eyes which
can see far be themselves seen from a distance—

> " As deep into the wood as we
> Might mark a lynx's eye."

He does not, of course, mean a long distance, but the
transference is worth nothing.

Mrs. Hemans, referring to the Piedmontese variety, has
the armed Jäger pursuing it

> " Above the clouds of morn ; "

and there is probably no length to which the hunter, if he
saw any chance of bagging it, would not follow such a
quarry, for the lynx wears a very valuable and beautiful fur
—said to be worth three times as much as the sable's—and
is moreover a beast well worth the hunting if only for its
endurance and courage.   It is still to be found in Scandinavia, the greater part of Central Europe, and, of course, in
Russia, and as one of the three beasts of prey worth calling
such—the other two being the bear and the wolf—deserves
to be considered really notable.

But it is not, as is supposed, "untamable."   The Gaek-
war of Baroda has a regular pack of trained lynxes, for
stalking and hunting pea-fowl and other kinds of birds.   I
have myself seen a tame lynx that had been taught to catch
crows—no simple feat—and its strategy was as diverting as
its agility amazing.   It would lie down with the end of a
string in its mouth, the other end being fast to a stake, and
pretend to be asleep, dead asleep, drunk, chloroformed,

anything you like that means profound and gross slumber. A foot or so off it would be lying a piece of meat or a bone. The crows would very soon discover the bone, and collecting round in a circle, would discuss the probabilities of the lynx only shamming, and the chances of stealing his dinner. The animal would take no notice whatever, but lie there looking so limp and dead that at last one crow would make so bold as to come forward. The others let it do so alone, knowing that afterwards there would be a free fight for the plunder, and the thief probably not enjoy it after all. So the delegate would advance with all the caution of a crow —and nothing exceeds it—until within seizing distance. Then it would stop, flirt its wings nervously, stoop, take a last long look at the lynx to make sure that it really *was* asleep, and then dart like lightning at the bone. But if the crow was as quick as lightning, the lynx was as swift as thought, and lo ! the next instant there was the beast sitting up with the bird in its mouth !

Now its procedure was very singular. It knew that it was no use jumping straight at the crow ; it would be sure to miss it, and go under it. So at the moment that the bird darted at the bone, the lynx flashed up into the air, and caught the crow at the instant it had left the ground.

Next time it had to practise a completely different manœuvre. The same crows are not to be " humbugged " a second time by a repetition of the being-dead trick. So the lynx, when a sufficient number of the birds had assembled, would take the string in its mouth and run round and round the stake at the extreme limit of its tether as if it were tied. The crows, after their impudent fashion, would close in. They thought they knew the exact circumference of the animal's circle, and getting as close to the dangerous line as possible without actually transgressing it, would mock at and abuse the supposed-to-be-tethered brute.

But all of a sudden the circling lynx would fly out at a tangent right into the thick of its black tormentors, and, as a rule, bag a brace, right and left.

Cowley has a very singular passage in one of his Juvenile Pieces, which is this—

> " Let Cygnus pluck from the Arabian waves
> The ruby of the rock, the pearl that paves
> Great Neptune's court ; let every sparrow bear
> From the three sisters' weeping bark a tear ;
> Let spotted lynxes their sharp talons fill
> With crystal, fetch'd from the Promethean hill ;
> Let Cytherea's birds fresh wreaths compose,
> Knitting the pale-fac'd lily with the rose."

The reference here—the lynx bringing crystals—is to the old-world fable of the "lyncurium," a misnomer of the lapidaries of the time for "the Ligurian stone" (a repetition of the "g" in the Greek making the error of sound a very easy one) or "jacinth."   This gem was supposed to be produced naturally by the lynx, that of the male being held in higher estimation than that of the female, as of purer colour and finer lustre.   The jacinth is a lovely crystal, "much more agreeable and superior in tint to the best Brazilian topaz" (King's *Nat. Hist. of Gems*), but modern jewellers would appear to have confounded it with one of the garnets or cinnamon stones.   The ancients, however, prized the "lynx-stone" highly, and attributed to it strange potencies against jaundice and other ailments.

In European fables the lynx is rarely mentioned, its place being filled for minor affairs by the cat, for greater by the leopard.   But it has its traditions.   Its eyesight was considered so piercing that it could see through solid matter and long paces of time, so that Lynceus, who could see three weeks ahead, and Apollonius' lynx, that looked through the earth and observed the proceedings of the devils in hell, are quite within its legendary potentialities.   Another

Lynceus was one of the Argonauts, and discovered obstacles long before they were in sight, to the great advantage of the Heroes—as every schoolboy knows. The Lynx Academy of Rome took the name as significant of the depth and keenness of the insight into Nature to which, in their studies, they hoped to attain.

III.

BEARS AND WOLVES.

" *Slender.* Why do your dogs bark so? be there bears i' the town ?

" *Anne.* I think there are, sir ; I heard them talked of.

" *Slender.* I love the sport well ; but I shall as soon quarrel at it, as any man in England.—You are afraid, if you see the bear loose, are you not ?

" *Anne.* Ay, indeed, sir.

" *Slender.* That's meat and drink to me now : I have seen Sackerson loose twenty times, and have taken him by the chain : but, I warrant you, the women have so cried and shrieked at it, that it passed : but women, indeed, cannot abide 'em ; they are very ill-favoured rough things."

IN Nature, bears and wolves have very little indeed in common.   They are opposed in appearance, habits of life, and character ; yet it would be difficult in all Poetry to find two wild animals more intimately associated.   The shambling, fruit-eating, retiring, straightforward, and mild-mannered bear [1] differs most conspicuously from the agile, flesh-preferring, aggressive, crafty, and ferocious wolf. Never-theless in poetry they are as punctually bracketed together
    In ... and linnets.
being fil...
leopard. ...

BEARS.

sidered so pic...
and long paces ...ast, has lost caste in public estimation, first
three weeks ahead, ...nominious familiarity which its dancing
the earth and obser...eak of the grizzly bear, and I do not therefore
hell, are quite within i...

and being baited have induced; and, secondly, from its apparently awkward personal appearance.

Yet in freedom it is by no means a clumsy or ridiculous animal. When it sets itself going after any one it wishes to catch, the bear displays an agility and address which those who have been hunted by it declare to be amazing. And when it wants to extract beetle-grubs from the ground, or ants out of their nest, honey from a bee-tree, fruit off a slender bough, or birds' eggs out of a nest, it shows itself to be as ingenious and skilful as any other animal that has to live by its wits. To get, for instance, at the beetle-grubs, it scratches off the upper earth and then sucks them up out of the ground—an application of a scientific process which no animal without a prodigious reserve of air-force could hope to accomplish. When it wishes to empty an ant-hive, it knocks the top off with its paws, and then, applying its mouth to the central gallery of the nest, inhales its breath forcibly, thereby setting up such a current of air that all the ants and their eggs come whirling up into his mouth like packets through a pneumatic tube. When robbing a hive it keeps one paw over its nose, its only vulnerable point, and when in quest of wild apricots or acorns it not only balances itself with all the judgment of a rope-walker, but uses its weight very cleverly so as to bring other boughs within reach of its curved claws. Nor, while doing this, does it guiltily conceal what it is about. On the contrary, when sucking at an ant-heap or grub-hole it makes such a noise that on a still evening it can be heard a quarter of a mile off, and when up a tree, and not alarmed, it goes smashing about among the boughs as if bears were not only the rightful lords of the manor, but as if there were no such things as enemies in the world.

This secluded, simple-minded, unsuspecting animal contrasts very strikingly with the guilty-seeming, stealthy, blood-preferring wolf. The poets, however, bring the two beasts into company as if they were constant associates in real life and habitual accomplices in crime.

In poetry there are two kinds of bears—the "wild-wood bear" and the bear at the end of a chain. The former is divided into the polar animal and the bear general—which also, it should be noted, is something polarish also; Southey speaking of the common bear as seeking its food "o'er track-less snows," Thomson of it as icicled and so forth. The latter, that is to say, the captive bear, is also subdivided into the purely saltatory and the baited bear.

Neither of them is popular with the bards. For the former, "the wild-wood bears," an unjust suspicion that it eats human beings,—a suspicion as old as our ballads—

> " With bears he lives, with bears he feeds,
> And drinks the blood of men "—

appears to prejudice the minds of some of our poets. Many others look upon them as animals that resemble tigers in their habits and tastes. As Butler,

> " Bears naturally are beasts of prey
> That live by rapine."

They are "cruelly fanged," as in Keats; and gloat over victims before devouring them, as in Spenser. "The bloody bear, an independent beast," says Dryden. In this aspect they are "rugged," "shapeless," and "shagged," "felon bears," and (in Heber) "heathen bears." They "howl" and "snort" in concert with wolves.

Much more true to Nature is Hiawatha's apostrophe— remembering only that "coward" is the regular phrase of Red Indian challenge—

> " Hark you, Bear, you are a coward,
> And no brave as you pretended ;
> Else you would not cry and whimper
> Like a miserable woman !

> Bear ! you know our tribes are hostile,
> Long have been at war together.
> Now you find that we are strongest,
> You go sneaking in the forest,
> You go hiding in the mountains !
> Had you conquered me in battle
> Not a groan would I have uttered :
> But you, Bear ! sit here and whimper,
> And disgrace your tribe by crying,
> Like a wretched Shangodaya,
> Like a cowardly old woman."

Bret Harte's address to the "Grizzly" is perfection.

But it is to the maternal triumph of licking her cubs into shape that the poetical attention is chiefly drawn;[1] the poet's supercilious satisfaction being very much increased by the discovery that after all her labours the mother produces nothing better than a bear.   Thus Shenstone—

> " What village but has sometimes seen
> The clumsy shape, the frightful mien,
> Tremendous claws and shagged hair,
> Of that grim brute yclep'd a bear.
> He from his dam, the learn'd agree,
> Receiv'd the curious form you see,
> Who with her plastic tongue alone
> Produced a visage—like her own."

And Pitt—

> " Thus when old Bruin teems, her children fail
> Of limbs, form, figure, features, head or tail ;
> Nay, though she licks her cubs, her tender cares
> At best can bring the Bruins but to bears."

---

[1] It is too late in years to refute this fiction seriously.   But Sir Thomas Browne's argument against its verity (after having otherwise shown its complete fallacy) is worth quoting.   "Besides," says he " (what few take notice of), men hereby do in a high measure vilify the works of God, imputing that unto the tongue of a beast which is the strangest artifice in all the acts of Nature."

And Pope—

> "So watchful Bruin forms with plastic care
> Each growing lump, and brings it to—a bear!"

Not, for myself, that I see anything derogatory to a she-bear in being the mother of bear-cubs, and nothing more.

Nevertheless, the bear-cub she has *not* licked affords a delightful point. Thus Churchill, "a bear whom, from the moment he was born, his dam despised and left unlicked in scorn;" and Byron, "the she-bear licks her cub into a sort of shape; my dam beheld my shape was hopeless."

It is evident, though, that the poets are conscious of their want of familiarity with the wild animal. For, whether we meet it in a hot country as "the shaggy monster of the wooded wild," or see, with Darwin,

> "Slow o'er the printed snows with silent walk
> Huge shaggy forms across the twilight stalk;"

or with Savage, "the crackling vales, embrown'd with melting snows, where bears stalk, tenants of the barren space," it is an undefined, mysterious, and, so to speak, still unlicked monster. Not, however, without a weird majesty; in strict sympathy with the natural facts in Jean Ingelow—

> "The white bears all in a dim blue world,
> Mumbling their meals by twilight."

Spenser's "white bears" are creatures of fancy—

> "I saw two Bears, as white as any milk,
> Lying together in a mighty cave,
> Of mild aspect, and hair as soft as silk,
> That savage nature seemed not to have,
> Nor after greedy spoil of blood to crave;
> Two fairer beasts might not elsewhere be found,
> Although the compassed world were sought around.
> But what can long abide above this ground
> In state of bliss, and stedfast happiness?

> The cave, in which these Bears lay sleeping sound,
> Was but of earth, and with her weightiness
> Upon them fell, and did unawares oppress,
> That, for great sorrow of their sudden fate,
> Henceforth all worlds felicity I hate."

As a performer on the village green, or as a retainer of the household, "creeping close amongst the hives, to rend an honeycombe," it has a distinct individuality, but as a wild beast none. Perpetually in use as an adjunct of savage scenes, it never seems to be described from the life. It always looms out from a distance, or from gloom, and seldom comes close enough to us to be tangible or seen in detail. It is a convenient beast, but a shadowy one, and Butler (in his portrait of Potemkin) seems to me to sum up with tolerable fairness the whole of the poets' bear-lore—

> " The gallant Bruin march'd next him,
> With visage formidably grim,
> And rugged as a Saracen,
> Or Turk of Mahomet's own kin,
> Clad in a mantle delle guerre
> Of rough impenetrable fur ;
> And in his nose, like Indian king,
> He wore, for ornament, a ring ;
> About his neck a threefold gorget,
> As rough as trebled leathern target ;
> Armed, as heralds cant, and langued,
> Or, as the vulgar say, sharp-fanged ;
> For as the teeth in beasts of prey
> Are swords, with which they fight in fray,
> So swords, in men of war, are teeth
> Which they do eat their vittles with.
> He was by birth, some authors write,
> A Russian, some a Muscovite,
> And 'mong the Cossacks had been bred,
> Of whom we in Diurnals read,
> That serve to fill up pages here,
> As with their bodies ditches there.
> Scrimansky was his cousin-german,
> With whom he serv'd and fed on vermine ;

> And when these fail'd he'd suck his claws,
> And quarter himself upon his paws."

Unlike the Puritans, who hated bear-baiting—not because it gave pain to the bear, but because it gave pleasure to the spectators—the poets condemn the pastime as being cruel to Bruin.

> " How barbarously man abuses power !
>   Talk of the baiting, it will be replied
>   Thy welfare is thy owner's interest,
>   But wert thou baited it would injure thee,
>   Therefore thou art not baited.   For seven years—
>   Hear it, O heaven ! and give ear, O earth !—
>   For seven long years this precious syllogism
>   Hath baffled justice and humanity."—*Southey.*

Their sympathy is always with the bear that has "off-shakt" the "curres," and when the "cruell dogs" get the better of him the poets punctually note that the bear was chained or muzzled.   They use the simile of "ragged roaring bears rearing up against the baiters"[1] for nobles attacked by those of lower degree, or for men of might beset by numbers.   They knew well the spectacle—

> " When through the town, with
>   Slow and solemn air, led by the nostril,
>   Walked the muzzled bear."

The Bankside bear-garden and Hockley Hole were familiar names, and the dancing Bruin has given at least three poets the subject for a poem, Leyden drawing the "moral" from the exhibition that men learnt to dance from the bear, and might still improve their own saltations by imitating it—

> " From bears the dancer's art at first began,
>   To monkey next it past and then to man ;

---

[1] Hood borrows the expression for the waves during a storm.   " Black, jagged billows rearing up in war, like ragged roaring bears against the baiter."

> And still from bears, by Fate's unerring law,
> Their dance, their manners, men and monkeys draw " —

and Southey, with excellent humour, using the old slave-trade arguments to persuade the bear that dancing is good for it—

> " We are told all things were made for man,
> And I'll be sworn there's not a fellow here
> Who would not swear 'twere hanging blasphemy
> To doubt that truth.   Therefore as thou wert born,
> Bruin, for man, and man makes nothing of thee
> In any other way, most logically
> It follows, that thou must be born to dance,
> That that great snout of thine was formed on purpose
> To hold a ring, and that thy fat was given thee
> Only to make pomatum.
>
>   To demur
> Were heresy.   And politicians say
> (Wise men who in the scale of reason give
> No foolish feelings weight) that thou art here
> Far happier than thy brother bears who roam
> O'er trackless snows for food ; that being born
> Inferior to thy leader, unto him
> Rightly belongs dominion ; that the compact
> Was made between ye when the clumsy feet
> First fell into the snare, and he gave up
> His right to kill, conditioning thy life
> Should thenceforth be his property.   Besides,
> 'Tis wholesome for thy morals to be brought
> From savage climes into a civilised state,
> Into the decencies of Christendom."

Nor were they ignorant of that other elegant Elizabethan pastime of "whipping blind bears."

But of the "awkward," "uncouth," "shuffling" beas which they are so ready to put into their verse—

> " Rough tenant of the shades, the shapeless bear,
> With dangling ice all horrid "—

they had only the most delightful ignorance.

Yet what a large place the bear has filled in the past. And how multitudinous and honourable are its associations. As the God of Thunder, the Bear-king of Storms, Bruin is perfectly majestic in cloud-myths. The tempest demons, black-bearded, are his children, and the thunder-clouds, ragged and gloomy, go rolling and roaring and foaming overboard, bears every one of them, and close on the heels of their prey. Turn it round to the sun-myth, and lo! "the shining ones," the luminous sky, the bear—"Woful Calisto, when that Dian grieved was." In the one aspect horrific, as the bear-fiends of Dardistan or the shaggy terrors, every hair of iron, that awe the Russian peasant ; in the other, benign, "the honey-finder," or in Lapland, "the dog of God," or in Russia, "the old man with the fur cloak." On the one hand, the cruel instrument of the prophet at Bethel, a synonym for lurking mischief in the classics and in Holy Writ ; on the other, the nurse of Paris and of Atalanta—

> " Folk say that her, so delicate and white
> As now she is, a rough root-grubbing bear
> Amidst her shapeless cubs at first did rear.
> In course of time the woodfolk slew her nurse,
> And to their rude abode the youngling brought,
> And reared her up to be a kingdom's curse " (*Morris*)—

the docile disciple of Saints, the gentle animal that played at soldiers with the children and so prettily befriended Snow-White and Rose-Red.

Poetry, however, so diligent sometimes in availing itself of legend, takes no cognisance of the unusual prominence of the bear in history, heraldry, art, and folk-lore. The story of Valentine and Orson affords the subject of a ballad.

> " ' But who's this hairy youth ? ' she said,
> ' He much resembles thee.'
> ' The bear devoured my younger son,
> Or sure that son were he.'

> ' Madam, this youth with bears was bred,
> And reared within their den,
> But recollect ye any mark
> To know your son again ? ' "

And the Russian and "the Persian beares," the badges of Warwick and Leicester, are referred to. But not a word for the legends of St. Ursus and St. Ursula, St. Maximin, St. Anthony, and St. Medard ; for Oursine or the Orsinis ; for the Cities of the Bears or the Bear Hills ; for the virgins of Artemis or the unhappy rival of Juno, mother of constellations, the terror of the Tyrrhenian mariners, who had unawares given Bacchus a free passage ; nor the bears of story, Gundramnus the church-builder, Restaurco the musician, and Tony Lampkins' bear that only danced to " the genteelest of tunes ;" Sackerson and Martin, Rollo and Marco, " the good bear of Lorraine," the ursine monsters of the Ramayana—the bear-kings, friends-in-arms of the Solar Hero—or all the hundred bear-myths of the world. How is it that not a hint of these distinctions in literature, and of ten times as many more that I have omitted, do not find even a passing reference in the poets ? Is it possible that, having formulated a bear of their own, which is " obscene " in Nature and ridiculous in captivity, they purposely avoided all appearance of countenancing the condoning dignities of Bruin's past ?

Once more, then, whence arose this strange antipathy to the bear ? It could not have come from previous information, for all precedent honoured the animal. Nor was it from any knowledge of the bear in Nature. For the bear in Nature—I am speaking of the species which the poets supposed themselves to be speaking of—is really almost a lovable animal. It is a vegetable and fruit feeder, when it can get such food, and, failing its favourite viands, eats by preference insects. It is a delightful touch where Wilson makes the bear gaze ferociously on—beech-nuts. But, above

everything, it doats on honey. Do you remember the
shabby trick of Sir Reynard when he takes poor Bruin from
Malepardus to the carpenter's house on the pretence of
giving him honeycombs? The bear arrives at the castle
of the defaulting fox, and finds Reynard pretending to be
sick. He had eaten, he said, something that had disagreed
with him. "What was it?" asks the bear with a friendly
solicitude.

"'Uncle,' replied the other, 'what will it avail you to know? The
food was simple and mean ; we poor gentry are no lords, you know,
but are glad to eat from necessity what others taste for mere wanton-
ness. Yet not to delay you, that which I ate was honeycombs, large,
full, and very pleasant. But, impelled by hunger, I ate so very immoderately that I was afterwards infinitely distempered.' 'Ay !'
quoth Bruin, 'honeycombs, do you say? Hold you them in such
slight respect, nephew? Why, sir, it is food for the greatest emperors
in the world : help me, fair nephew, to some of these honeycombs, and
command me while I live ; for only a small share I will be your servant
everlastingly.' 'You are jesting with me, surely, uncle,' replied the
fox. 'Jest with you !' cried Bruin, 'beshrew my heart, then ; for I
am in such serious good earnest, that for a single lick of the same you
shall count me among the most faithful of your kindred.' 'Nay, if
you be,' returned Reynard, 'I will bring you where ten of you would
not be able to eat the whole at a meal. This I do out of friendship,
for I wish to have yours in return, which above all things I desire.'
'Not ten of us !' cried the bear, 'not ten of us ! it is impossible ; for
had I all the honey between Hybla and Portugal, I could eat the whole
of it very shortly myself.'"

So Bruin goes, gets his head caught in a cleft log, and
is very nearly killed.

Its life is particularly innocent, and its manners, as a rule,
are the reverse of ferocious. Having satisfied itself with
berries and buds, the bear returns to its cave, and there, putting its paws into its mouth, lies humming to itself like some
great baby, sucking its thumbs and crooning. It takes few
precautions against surprise, will stay out eating wild strawberries or acorns till the sun is fairly up, and will then
go into a cleft in the rock or hollow tree, and murmur

contentedly to itself, and so loudly that sportsmen are frequently guided from a distance to the purring spinning-wheel sound[1] which betrays it.

There is something very touching, so I think, in the story of the men who, following up a wounded bear, found the beast behind an ice-boulder trying to staunch the flowing blood with snow. I like too to think of the other which discovered an empty whaling boat and got in, and—the moorings giving way under its somewhat violent boarding—went off on a cruise on its own account, and was seen by the unfortunate owners of the boat sitting up in the stern with every appearance of the most complete satisfaction.

Folk-lore, as a rule, is just, and folk-lore is always kind to the bear. There are no fairy-tales or legends in which the bear is a villain. He is a blundering fool in several fables, but he is never unamiable.

Writing many years ago on the " Fairies of Dardistan," I put into a hunter's mouth the following fragment of local folk-lore :—

" I myself have never seen either Fairies or Demons, but I am a familiar of the Bears. It is not generally known, perhaps, but bears are the offspring of a man who, unable to pay his debts, went off to the woods and never came back again, for he married some wild forest thing and lived amongst the fir-trees to the end of his days. And his descendants understand our language, fall in love with human beings,

---

[1] Cuvier's bear " was particularly fond of sucking its paws, during which operation it always sent forth a uniform and constant murmur, something like the sound of a spinning-wheel."

" The sucking of the paw, accompanied by a drumming noise when at rest, and especially after meals, is common to all bears, and during the heat of the day they may often be heard puffing and humming far down in caverns and fissures of rocks." The cause of this has often been speculated on, but Tickell imagines that it is merely a habit peculiar to it, and he states " that they are just as fond of sucking their neighbours' paws or the hands of any person as their own paws" (*Jerdon*).

and marry their children to each other much as we do.   I have seen a bear's wedding.   It was just after the Feast of Firs, and I was coming back tired along the Ghilgit road from Astor across the hills when I suddenly chanced upon a great convention of bears.   There were a hundred at least—brown and black, big and little—and they were all dancing round the wood-fires which they had lighted.   Some of them had wreathed their heads with wisps of straw and flowers, and were dancing solemnly, each by himself.   Others had in their arms tussocks of long grass and faggots of fir-wood which they used as partners, while others danced two and three together, holding hands and going slowly round and round.   At each corner sate a bear crooning harmoniously for the others to dance in time to.   And while I was watching them an old fellow, the largest bear of the company, got up from where he had been eating honey, with a long fir-branch in his hand, and made all the others fall into two long lines, and then the bride and the bride-groom (who had been up a tree all the time) were called down and placed at the end of the row.   And they took each other's hands and danced, turning slowly round and round, down between the long rows of bears, and when they reached the other end all the company gave a howl together, and scattering themselves among the woods began collecting viands for the feast.   As some of them came in my direction I ran off as fast as I could, and saw no more."

Sir Bruin of the Reineke Fuchs is of the common type. He has great physical strength and fidelity of character, but he is so simple that adversaries always outwit him.   He is. no match for foxes, any more than the bear-heroes Sir Bors, or Jubal or Earl Arthgal of the Table Round, or any of those heavy slumberous giants, upon whose persons small, agile, and invincibly-armed heroes performed such prodigies of valour.

The bear is the sleepy summer thunder of Scandinavian myth.   It is of a mumbling grumbling kind, happy enough in an old-country-gentleman sort of way when unmolested, but testy in the matter of strange neighbours and trespassers. It is a stubborn Conservative, a Legitimist, a protest of Routine against Reform.   Daniel makes it a symbol of faithlessness ; but he evidently did not know as much about bears as he did, or ought to have known, about lions, or he would have been aware that bears are very generous, never returning to harm a helpless or fallen adversary. "Women," says Slender, "cannot abide them, they are very ill-favoured rough things;" but there is an abundant dignity about them nevertheless. They are among the seniors of the quadrupeds in Nature, and in Art they brought no declension from eminence to such as bore them on their shields —the greatest of monarchs, of earls, and of painters.

WOLVES.

> "' Well is knowne that,' sith the Saxon king,
> ' Never was wolf seene, many nor some,
> Nor in all Kent, nor in Christendom.'"

But there was a time, as Keats says, "while yet our England was a wolfish den," when our ancestors called January "the wolf month," and prayed in their litanies for defence against them when estates were held on wolf-head tenure; and many poets, Dryden, Somerville, Drayton, Addison amongst them, gratefully allude to the purging of our isles of these destructive pests.

> "Cambria's proud kings (tho' with reluctance) paid
> Their tributary wolves, head after head,
> The full account, till the wood yields no more,
> And all the rav'nous race extinct is lost."

To the poets, therefore, with their allowable extensions of horizon and chronology, the wolf is a British animal: not in the way that the lion has become one, but on the more practical basis of previous existence in the country.

> " Full many a year his hateful head had been
> In tribute paid, nor since in Cambria seen."

So it comes, perhaps, more familiarly off their pens than other animals. Its name, moreover, has become, almost universally, a synonym for twilight ferocity, so that the poets are to some extent justified in their attitude of detestation. In the cloud myth, the rough dark wolf is of course the night, and the white morning sheep-clouds escape from its clutches. But more especially it is the twilight, "the grey one"—in Holy Writ it is always "the evening wolf," or the "wolf of the evenings,"—that wolf-gloom wherein malign influences are abroad, *entre chien et loup.*

Sir Isegrim in Reynard the Fox is the type of the rapacious baron. The king, more distant from the people, may pass for a lion, but the baron in his castle on the rock yonder, domineering over the servile plain, is the wolf, a present power for evil. So folk-lore and fables represent under this symbol the sentiments of European serfs or "villeins" towards their feudal oppressors. The hectoring style of argument with lambs; the use of forced labour from asses; evasion of contracts with cranes; double-dealing affabilities to old she-goats with kids; insidious counselling of dogs for disastrous combinations against their shepherds; treachery towards neighbouring wolves—in these and a score of other features the resemblance between wolf and baron is traced in popular literature.

Worked in with these symbolical sketches are touches straight from the real wolf-life. Its surpassing cunning, its more than ferine intelligence, "effrayant de sagacité et de calcul," distinguish it as the Bandit of the Beasts, and like all other communities of outlaws and criminals, the wolves are singularly superstitious. Elsewhere I note how easily they may be frightened, but I cannot help thinking that there is in this trait a striking analogy to the suspicious, superstitious timidity which characterises every gang of human wolves; and which, sooner or later, brings them to the gallows or their deserts. But it is very interesting to remark the poetical method of bringing the wolf within the sweep of poetical opprobrium.

By daylight they make it the accomplice of vultures, and by night of owls, so that there is nothing too bad to say of the wolf. The fact is true enough of the animal in Nature, for it really is the Thug among the beasts. In other languages besides our own Saxon, the criminal outlaw, the bandit, was said in legal phrase to be "wolf-headed"—there was a price on his life, and his destruction as a beast of prey was authorised and rewarded. But the synthetical process by which the poets arrive at the full compass of the wolf's iniquity is very pleasing. Tyranny and darkness are their special aversions, so the poets construct a wretch that preys by preference on the very weak, the most innocent, and the youngest, and then make it commit its violences *by night*. By this means the wolf not only alienates all the sympathies of the chivalrous and generous, but is branded as the nocturnal companion of such obscene, night-prowling things as owls and bats, night-ravens and hyenas. A dash of man-eating is then thrown in to exasperate the general sentiment of the sanctity of human life; and, finally, to enlist against it human reverence for the dead and the beautiful maternal instinct, the beast is touched up with such details as the desecration of graves, corpse-eating, and baby-snatching.

It is the "night-prowling," "savage," "fierce-descending," "insatiate," "surly," "stern," "grim," "gaunt," "guilty," "wild," "shaggy," "black-jawed," "robber" wolf. Its voice is a "long" and "deep" howl, or "shrill" or "a low whine," "lugubrious dreary yell," and "death-boding."

A dreadful adjunct of all scenes of dismal horror—"Near him the she-wolf stirred in the brake, and the copper-snake breathed in his ear" (Moore). Whenever a tragedy is on hand, the neighbouring thicket holds a wolf, or the rocky pine-glen yonder knows their lurking tread. There are few circumstances of more than ordinary wretchedness that are not accompanied by one of these animals, or a pack of them, and at night the wolf's "howls" rise almost as punctually as the moon.   It may be in Wilson's wild country—

> "Shrill, wildly issuing from a neighbouring height,
> The wolf's deep howlings pierce the ear of night;
> From the dark swamp he calls his skulking crew,
> Their nightly scenes of slaughter to renew;
> Their mingling yells sad savage woes express,
> And echo dreary through the dark recess."

Or in (Faber's) civilisation—

> "From time to time a restless watch-dog bayed,
> And a cock crew, or from the echoing hill
> The wolf's low whine, prolonged and multiplied,
> Possessed the ear of night and over-ruled
> All other sounds."

Being thus a thing of night, it becomes in poets' phrase "obscene," as in Leyden—

> "Beasts obscene frequent the lonely halls,
> Howling through windows waste the wolf appear'd."

Or in egregious Thomson—

> "Wolves and bears and monstrous things obscene,
> That vex the swain and waste the country round;"

and it is punctually associated with that delightful fiction of the poets, the poetical owl.   They are as thick as thieves, these two creatures, and always "on the patter" together. If you see Charley Bates coming up the street you may be sure the Dodger is in the immediate neighbourhood. The rascals converse in highwayman's slang.   "The owlet whoops to the wolf below."   The chances are they are decoys for each other, and divide the spoils of the victims whom they assassinate in company.   Was there ever such an abominably comic partnership in crime—owls and wolves!

And just as owls, after taking all the lower degrees of criminality, become in poetry "shrikkes" (which are of a specially venomous sort), so wolves graduate into "were-wolves" or "war-wolves"—that fearful fancy of the *loup-garou* that has kept its hold upon popular terror in every country ever since the day when "wild Lycaon, changed by angry gods, and frighted at himself, ran howling through the woods." Their hairs are then used like owls' feathers by witches to mix with "madd dogges foames and adders eares." They haunt Coleridge's woods with "vampyres" and other monstrosities, and their voices are alike "death-boding."

This were-wolf superstition is a more ancient and persistent one. The horrid "Hyrcanians" were said to "become wolves" in the heat of battle, a more allowable metaphor, since historians talk commonly of British soldiers being "lions" and "tigers." So also the Newri and Hirpini: and much later the same simile was frequently used in the Sages for the Berserkers; and later still, in our own time, for the men of Norway and of Iceland, who "become wolves" in conflict. In Ireland I suspect the phrase would be found still extant, for the Irish, according to their own legends, are specially liable to being "people not of one skin," which is a euphemism for lycanthropes. Many individual instances are on record, notably that of the family whom St. Nathalie turned into were-wolves for seven years. But these could retaliate on occasion, as, for example, when St. Patrick turned Vereticos, king of Wales, into a wolf. Ireland, indeed, would in this matter appear to be our Arcadia— the land of superstition; for that province was conspicuous for its wolf traditions. Lycaon himself was a king of Arcadia, and the *loup-garou* was a household word in that "emerald-state." The hyæna and the vampyre are in some countries curiously mixed up with the wolf-myth, but by itself it possesses a very dreadful individuality.

> " Therewith stalked forth into the way
> From out the thicket a huge wolf and gray,
> And stood with yellow eyes that glared on me.
>
> . . . .
>
> My folly made me see
> No wolf, but some dread divinity in him."
>
>   (*Hopponons loq.*)

To this day the supernatural wolf is an article of popular belief in Europe, and, if I am not mistaken, the men-wolves are far more dreaded than the beast-wolves in, say, Litherania. At the feast of the Nativity they used to assemble in the churchyards, so it was said, and proceed at midnight to search for the dead or the belated living. They were, in fact, ghouls. Indeed the literature of this amazing superstition passes belief. What are we to say of a whole multitude turning were-wolves in the canton in Jura, hunting for human flesh in pack, and being executed six hundred at one time !

Beware of men with meeting eyebrows ; it is from these that legend says the were-wolves recruit their packs.

That wolves—"assiduous in the shepherds' harms" (King) —prey on flocks, is in itself quite sufficient to set poets against them. Does not the vulture suffer miserably in poetry from being accused of "pouncing" doves? And are not doves and lambs equally engaging; and is not, therefore, the wolf as detestable as the vulture, with which, indeed (when it is seen abroad in daylight), it is nearly always to be found in partnership. So the poets have little sympathy for "the grim wolf that with privy paw daily devours apace," even when it is most hungry. Hunger, indeed, would hardly seem to be allowable at all in wolves : " wolf's-nagen " is a term of reproach. It is an aggravation of the offence instead of a palliation. If they would consent to eat strawberries they might fare no worse than the bears, but, as it is, that they should deliberately go forth and satisfy their detestable cravings with mutton—and now

and then with the mutton-herd himself—enrages the ordinary
poet.   Nor, when this infamous appetite for butchers' meat
is indulged by a meal of lamb, are even the better poets able
to control their generous indignation—

> " The gaunt wolf crouches to spring out on the lamb,
>   And if hunger be on him, he spares not the dam."

Worse than this is Colin's complaint—

> " They often devoured their owne sheepe,
>   And often the shepheards that did hem keepe ;
>   *This was the first source of shephcard's sorrow.*"

The last line is a delightful one.

Savage, Akenside, Rogers, and others extend their tenderness from the lamb to its cousin the kid, but there is always,
curiously enough, a reservation of sympathy from the fact
that the kid was "straying."   The lamb, on the other hand,
is generally where it should be, " bleating near its fleecy
dam ;"   and the unprincipled conduct of the wolf takes
therefore a deeper dye from the outrage on the ewe's feelings which accompanies that on the lamb's, while if the
victim be carried out of a sheepfold there is the crime
of housebreaking superadded.   Supreme, however, in this
particular class of offence was that wolf who married a lamb,
and then ate her up after they had been only wedded
a week.

But sometimes it arrives that the shepherds get the better
of the wolf, as in Chatterton's " Battle of Hastings "—

> " As when the shipster in his shadie bower
>   Hears doublying echoe wind the wolfin's rore,
>   That neare hys flocke is watchynge for a praie,
>   With trustie talbots to the battel flies,
>   And yell of men and dogs and wolfins tear the skies."

Or in " The Wanderer "—

> " When lo ! an ambush'd wolf, with hunger bold,
>   Springs at the prey and fierce invades the fold,
>   But by the pastor not in vain defy'd,
>   Like our arch-foe by some celestial guide."

Or in Cowley—

> " Such rage inflames the wolf's wild heart and eyes
>   (Robbed, as he thinks, unjustly of his prize),
>   Whom unawares the shepherd spies, and draws
>   The bleating lamb from out his ravenous jaws."

In metaphor this salvation of the lamb (and its attendant parents) is a very frequent figure, showing very pleasantly the general tendency of the poets to rejoice with the virtuous and innocent over their escape from consumption, and with the loyal custodian of another's property over his triumph against the wicked-minded vagabond.

Yet it is wonderful to note how often the legendary wolf appears in a benign aspect. For instance, we are told by Baronius that a number of wolves attacked a monastery and slew all the monks therein who held heretical opinions. Another pack tore to pieces the sacrilegious soldiers of the Duke of Urbino who had plundered the Loretto shrine. It was a wolf that guarded the head of St. Edmund the Martyr from the other beasts, and a wolf that stepped in to defend St. Oddo, when on pilgrimage, from the attacks of wild boars. Just as it showed the Abbot of Cluny his way home, so the legend says it guided Adam, and the priests of Ceres, and Deucalion. It dragged the cart of St. Eustorgius, and tended the sheep of Norbert. In Italy and Sicily its hide and head are supposed to endow the wearer with courage : they are charms against many perils, and a more than Stygian panacea for pain of all kinds. As a foster-nurse the she-wolf is perpetually recurrent in an amiable light, and legends in which the animals are benign are very numerous indeed. In Red Indian stories the amiable and pathetic sides of the wolf-idea are well brought out.

Thus Manobozho the mischief-maker meets a magician and his family, who are wolf-wizards, and is changed into the same form. They are very good to him, and keep him alive during a very severe winter. At times they play practical jokes upon him, but each has its moral for his advantage, and eventually Manobozho leaves them with much regret. In another story also the magician takes the wolf-shape in order to befriend the hero. In the legend of " Sheem the Forsaken " the benevolent trait is even more conspicuously illustrated. The child has been deserted by his elder brother and sister—the family being orphans—and is on the point of starvation, but seeing some wolves at their meal he goes up to them and, waiting till they have finished, picks up the morsels they have left. This he continues to do, until at last the animals take notice of their small dependent, and hearing his story are lost in amazement at the cruel heartlessness of human beings, and adopt Sheem on the spot. Now it happens that one day Owasso, the elder brother, comes in his canoe to the place, and hearing a sorrowful voice of wailing on the bank, thinks he recognises the deserted child, and landing goes to seek him. All of a sudden there leaps out from the bushes a creature half-wolf, half-boy, which flies from him along the shore. Owasso calls out to him, " Stay, brother ! " But the wolf-boy goes leaping on his way, and crying as he goes, " Neesia, Neesia—a-wee ! You left me, going away in a canoe, and I am half-changed into a wolf—E-wee. Half-changed into a wolf—E-wee ! " and he howled between his words. And Owasso, stricken with brotherly love, cried after him, "Sheem ! Sheem ! Sheem ! " But the child fled on, alternately complaining and howling, and all the while kept changing more and more into a wolf. Then all of a sudden he reached a bank, and leaping on to it turned, and, looking back at his brother, cried in tones of most pathetic reproach, " I am a wolf "—and vanished. On the other hand, it is beyond doubt that the image was one used, as a rule, to represent a fraudulent, double-dealing, heartless, and pitiless monster. Night, and Winter, and Cold put on the wolf's skin. It is then gloomy, sinister, malignant, diabolical. How terrible, for example, are those wolves of Odin, "Gari and Freki," who hunt down his enemies—the "Odin's hounds" of more modern folk-lore—the truly awful Feuris-wolf whom the gods tried to bind with chains but could not, but at last was fettered by most delicate links to the rock Amsvartner to await Ragnarok—those dread Finland jinns who live in the Wolf-Valley by the Lake of the Wolves—the red wolf that waylays the souls of bad men going to the nether world.

But the wolf's name would not have been terrible in legends had it merely plundered the sheepfold. It is its crimes against mankind that have made it so gruesome a beast in folk-lore and so perilous in Nature ; and the poets do not fail to take note of the solitary pilgrims, mountaineers, goat-herds, and travellers that the wolves make their prey, nor of the horrid duties they share with birds of carrion on deserted fields of battle ; nor yet of greater crimes than all these —the murder of infants in their mothers' arms, and their violation of graves. In the following truly Thomsonian nonsense the poet catalogues the animal's iniquities :—

> " Cruel as death, and hungry as the grave !
> 　Burning for blood ! bony, and gaunt, and grim,
> 　Assembling wolves in raging troops descend ;
> 　And, pouring o'er the country, bear along,
> 　Keen as the north wind sweeps the glossy snow.
> 　All is their prize. They fasten on the steed,
> 　Press him to the earth, and pierce his mighty heart.
> 　Nor can the bull his awful front defend,
> 　Or shake the murdering savages away.
> 　Rapacious at the mother's throat they fly,
> 　And tear the screaming infant from her breast.
> 　The godlike face of man avails him nought.
> 　Even beauty, force divine ! at whose bright glance

> The generous lion stands in softened gaze,
> Here bleeds, a hapless undistinguish'd prey.
> But if, appris'd of the severe attack,
> The country be shut up, lured by the scent,
> On churchyards drear (inhuman to relate !)
> The disappointed prowlers fall, and dig
> The shrouded body from the grave ; o'er which,
> Mix'd with foul shades and frightened ghosts, they howl."

Each enormity in Thomson's catalogue finds abundant individual condemnation in the poets. Thus Leyden—

> " The prowling wolves that round the hamlet swarm
> Tear the young babe from the frail mother's arm ;
> Full gorged, the monster, in the desert bred,
> Howls, long and dreary, o'er the unburied dead."

Chaucer's wolf, "with eyen red and of a man he ete ; " Dodd's gaunt wolf, that, " blood-happy, growling feeds on the quivering heart" of the belated Switzer ;[1] Mackay's score of wolves "rushing like ghouls on a corse new-dead ;" Montgomery's "gorged wolves, howling in convulsive slumber o'er their corses ;" and Webster's

> " But keep the wolf far hence, that's foe to men,
> For with his nails he'll dig them up again."

How this ghoul attribute of the wolf gained currency it is not easy to guess, for no work of natural history charges the wolf with doing that for which it is by nature unfitted to accomplish. A wolf might of course scratch up a corpse that was only lightly covered with soil, but it has not got the claws necessary for rifling any decent grave.

The climax of horror is of course reached when, like Wordsworth's, the wolf is a baby-eater—

> " Vexed by the darkness, from the piny gulf,
> Ascending nearer, howls the famished wolf,

---

[1] The mountaineer, naturally, is more often the prey of poets' wolves than other classes of solitary-lived men, shepherds alone excepted.

> While through the stillness scatters wild dismay,
> Her babe's small cry that leads him to his prey."

But surely Thomson unjustly aggravates the wolf's obliquities when he makes it loitering on sea-shores "there awaiting wrecks;"[1] as Shelley when he says—

> " They knew his cause their own, and swore
> Like wolves and serpents to their mutual wars
> Strange truce, with many a rite which earth and heaven abhors."

But inasmuch as the poets sometimes need to use the wolf, their symbol of ruthless cruelty, as comparing favourably with men whom they consider worse than wolves, they have to absolve the animal from its supreme crime of cannibalism in order to have this one extra point in infamy to reproach human beings with. So men are wolves and "cannibals" in addition, though it is a fact that of all animals in the world the wolf is itself the most egregious cannibal. Most wild beasts will eat their own species on occasion, but the wolf habitually does so. No other explanation of this, of course, is needed than the hunger of the hour aggravating a natural bloodthirstiness; but if it were, it would doubtless be found in the instinct that tells these brutes that they, of all wild beasts, cannot afford to have lagging comrades, and that it is better therefore for the commonwealth to eat them up as soon as they are crippled. In the same way savages on the war-path massacre their sick (and sometimes eat them), for they cannot afford to drag about with them in time of war a burden of invalids.

While, on the one hand, therefore, the wolf escapes a reproach that he is fairly liable to, man, on the other, is libelled by the unjust comparison—

---

[1] Phillips has "the starving wolves along the main sea prowl." Neither poet is referring to the Arctic wolf.

> " Whoever saw the wolves that he can say,
> Like more inhuman us, so bent on prey,
> To rob their fellow wolves upon the way.
>
> .   .   .   .   .   .
>
> The fiercest creatures we in nature find
> Respect their figure still in the same kind ;
> To others rough, to these they gentle be,
> And live from noise, from feuds, from factions free."

And again—

> " But man, the wildest beast of prey,
> Wears friendship's semblance to betray ;
> His strength against the weak employs,
> And where he should protect, destroys."

Not that I would be thought to defend our kind from these charges, for they may be well founded. I only complain of the wolf not being fished with the same net.

But the chief feature of the wolf-symbol appears to me neglected—namely, the altogether disproportionate accession of horror that surrounds wolves when in a pack, as compared with the solitary animal. Individually the animal is almost despicable, collectively it is terrific. Alone, the wolf is a highwayman, an individual bandit ; in company they are furies. A small dog, a little child, a burning stick, Campbell's " wolf-scaring faggot," a fluttering rag, a " bogy-trap " of any kind, will suffice to keep off a single wolf; but a squadron of cavalry will hardly stop the rush of a pack. The hunter hears a solitary howl and looks to his rifle; but the wind brings down to him a chorus of voices, and he thinks only of escape. Men ride down single wolves in the snow and kill them with whips; but the hunters become the hunted when a dozen wolves sweep down from the rocks—

> " The death-doomed man
> Felt such a chill run through his shivering frame,
> As the night-traveller on the Pyrenees,
> Lone and bewildered on his wintry way,

> When from the mountains round reverberates
> The hungry wolves' deep yell; on every side
> Their fierce eyes gleaming as with meteor fires,
> The famished troops come round."—*Southey.*

To its craftiness—the stealthy "evening wolf" of the Bible—the poets bear ready witness, but not probably since Hobbinole discoursed with Diggon Davie on the Kentish Downs has wolfish cunning received more amazing and delicious testimony. Diggon tells his companion how "a wicked wolfe, that with many a lambe had gutted his gulfe," taught itself how to bark ("learned a curre's call"), and then, dressing up in the fleece of one of its victims. ("his counterfeit cote"), allowed itself to be penned up with the flock in the fold at night; and how at midnight it would begin to howl, at which Roffin the shepherd would send out his big dog Lowder to scour the country, and how, while Lowder was away scouring the country, the wolf would "catchen his prey, a lambe, or a kid, or a weanall wast,[1] and with that to the wood would speede him fast." But this was not the worst—

> "For it was a perilous beast above all,
> And eke had he cond the shepheard's call,
> And oft in the night came to the sheep-cote
> *And called Lowder, with a hollow throte,*
> As it the olde man selfe had beene;
> The dogge his maister's voice did it weene,
> Yet half in doubt he opened the dore
> And ranne out as he was wont of yore.
> No sooner was out, but swifter than thought,
> Fast by the hyde the wolfe Lowder caught,
> And had not Roffy renne to the steven,[2]
> Lowder had been slaine thilke same even."

In metaphor the wolf does not fail to meet with its deserts, or what are supposed to be such. Rapine, Lust, Cruelty, Treachery are all wolves. Spenser sees Envy "riding on a

---

[1] Youngling. [2] Noise.

ravenous wolf." Crime (in Mackay) has a "wolfish grin;"
Plague (in Shelley) is "a winged wolf;" Pride and Avarice
(in Cowper) "make man a wolf to man;" Bigotry (in
Watts) is "half a murdering wolf;" and again, in Shelley—

> " Wolfish Change, like winter, howls to strip
> The foliage in which Fame, the eagle, built
> Her aerie, while Dominion whelped below."

Dryden calls the Presbyterians, and Milton the Papists,
"hireling wolves," and mischievous teachers "grievous
wolves "—

> " Help us to save free conscience from the paw
> Of hireling wolves whose gospel is their maw."

Pomfret bewolfs the soldiers of Kirke, Southey those who
fought against Joan of Arc, Byron the enemies of Greece
and Scotch Reviewers, and Gay the Irish. Holy Writ,
no doubt, gives the poets their inspiration for many of
their expressions—" ravening," "in sheep's clothing," and so
forth ; and the animal is used throughout the Scriptures as
the symbol of a cunning blood-thirstiness, from princes
of Moab to a false prophet. As an emblem of ferocity
it was given to Benjamin, whose standard bore the wolf
couched in a field of green corn.

Poetical proverbs about the wolf are numberless : as a
specimen the following—" The wolf knows what the ill
beast thinks "—" As wolves love a flock, these love the weak "
—" A bad dog never sees the wolf "—" The death of a young
wolf doth never come too soon "—" The wolf must die in his
own skin "—" Who hates a wolf for his master needs a dog
for his man "—" Wolves give a good account of sheep, left
to their vigilance to keep "—" The wolf unseen and trembling lies, when the hoarse roar proclaims the lion near "—
" Hungry wolves, though greedy of their prey, stop when
they find a lion in their way."

The Assyrian was not more fierce in his attack upon

doomed Jerusalem; Orcas "his wolfish mountains rounding" not more fearful; Satan "lighting on his feet" in Eden not more bold-stealthy, than the wolf that "leaps with ease into the fold." Even Rome's founder—so bitter is the poets' hostility to "the howling nurse of plundering Romulus"— is followed into after-life by reflections upon his wet-nurse.

Byron, however, makes, in a single stanza, a large measure of amends—

> "And thou, the thunder-stricken nurse of Rome!
>   She-wolf! whose brazen-imaged dugs impart
>   The milk of conquest yet within the dome
>   Where, as a monument of antique art,
>   Thou standest :—Mother of the mighty heart,
>   Which the great founder suck'd from thy wild teat,
>   Scorch'd by the Roman Jove's ethereal dart,
>   And thy limbs black'd with lightning—dost thou yet
> Guard thine immortal cubs, nor thy fond charge forget?"

IV.

SOME BEASTS OF REPROACH.

POETS use wild beasts chiefly as terms of reproach. They seem to see no moral beauty, and recognise little good, in them. Being wild beasts, they are bestial, and being bestial, they are types of corresponding deformities in human nature. For poets do not, as a class, seem to have the generosity that belongs to the true lover of Nature, to admire the wild-beastiness of wild beasts, and to contemplate them in the orderly scheme of creation, outside the hackneyed phases of popular ignorance, or beyond the sphere of man's own common needs.

Servile animals they overload with flattery. The independent wild beast they traduce. Sheep are virtuous Christians : tigers are the infamous heathen.

A certain number of animals contemplated by the poets as being harmless—the camel, giraffe, elephant, hippopotamus, kangaroo, opossum, beaver, and bison—are used, of course, as similes of patience, stateliness, sagacity, bulk, agility, timidity, vigilance, and strength respectively—and among the British fauna the deer, hare, rabbit, squirrel, and dormouse are symbols of admirable docility, amiable weakness, cheerfulness, and dozy contentment. Yet even each of these receives, in turn, more or less cynical treatment at times, while all of them are mentioned so casually, or contemplated from a standpoint of such lofty condescension, that the poets' sentiment towards them is hardly more than one of acidulated toleration.

Sheep, cattle, deer, and dogs, the domesticated animals in fact, are favourites of the poets. For very few poets view Nature except in its relations with man. It is the chief charge against the wolf that it eats the mutton intended for human beings; and if an owl frightens Chaw-bacon, it is, therefore, an obscene and death-boding fowl. But sheep and cows, horses and dogs and deer, being servile animals, are flattered with the same exaggerated attentions as "the meek birds of the dove-cot" that fill pigeon-pies, and the bees that "yield their honey'd stores" for the poet's breakfast. Yet even with these, their inordinate favourites, the poets sometimes fall out. They are never tired of reminding sheep that they are silly, abusing the bull for using his horns against men, libelling dogs when of low degree, and horses that are "jades." So that neither the "harmless" animals nor the "domesticated" meet with complete urbanity.

But outside these two classes stand nearly all the Wild-Beast world, and to them, the bravest and most beautiful of Nature's ministers, the poets are all uncharitableness. The lion is the one exception, but then the lion of poetry is a magnificent creation of the poets, and not the creature of Nature at all. For the rest, the lords of the forest and plain, the peerage of jungle-duchies and desert-earldoms, the marquisates of river-side and cañon—the tiger and leopard, panther, puma and jaguar, ounce, ocelot and lynx, cheetah, bear, wolf, rhinoceros—there is nothing but reproach. And for what reason? Only the most egotistical and whimsical. Those that are not afraid of man are, on that account, monsters of ferocity, and when they despoil man's property, they are called utterly abominable; while the rhinoceros, grand old recluse of reedy hermitages, is abused for having a horn on the tip of his nose, just as the

hedgehog and porcupine are calumniated for having quills
on their backs.

The monkeys, again, another large and admirable feature
of wild nature, are pelted with unmitigated scorn because
they seem to resemble man, and can be taught to burlesque
him, as if the poets really believed that all the monkeys of
the world live in cages or on barrel-organs. Or take
another class, the foxes and jackals, delightful parables
both of them, or the hyæna, one of the gloomiest touches
in Nature, and we find it is the same, and that the poets
are similarly deficient in sympathy and tenderness. Now,
for myself, keeping no poultry-yard, I like young foxes just
as much as I do chickens or ducklings; and having no
friends buried in Syria or Abyssinia, I can view the hyæna
apart from corpses. For the poets, of course, it will be
argued that they project themselves into the affections of
others, and feel for the chickens of neighbours and the
graves of Ethiopians as keenly as if they were their own.

I had once in India a favourite dog carried off by a
leopard; yet I do not hate leopards on that account. I
also kept a pet leopard once, and I liked it just as much as
I did the terrier which its relatives previously consumed.
The leopard did quite right to eat my dog, even though it
might have known it would provoke me to ill-nature by
doing so; and though I should have been glad at the time
to see that particular one murdered, I certainly bore no
grudge against all the leopards of the world, much less
against all their glorious congeners as well. So that the
poets, even after they have presumably projected their sympathies into everybody's hen-roost and thus absorbed the
concentrated sentiments of all the poultry-fanciers of the
world, are still, I take it, not justified in abusive generalities
about foxes. That these pretty beasts eat chickens is solely
our own fault, for we have deprived them of every other
source of food. But the great majority of foxes in the world

never even saw a chicken or heard of one, while every fox, chickenivorous or not, is a beautiful and useful animal.

It is ferocious.   But of this the poets take no heed. For the ferocity of the fox is not directed against the person of man, just as the weasel, quite as ferocious as the tiger, escapes reproach on this score, because it never turns man-eater.

The poets, then, judge the great beast-world from a some-what narrow and selfish point of view, and seem to award their praise or blame in proportion to the direct utility to man of the animal under notice.   To make a wild-world, therefore, that should be to the poets' taste, every beast in it ought to contribute either wool or butchers' meat to the needs of human beings, and there ought not to be a four-legged thing afoot with more ferocity in it than a bolster. They would like tigers to wear boxing-gloves, and rhino-ceroses, before going abroad, to unscrew their horns. Wolves should be fleecy and say "baa," and everything be toothless.

Among the special Beasts of Reproach may be enume-rated swine, bats, hyænas, foxes, the jackal, and rat.   Others, of course, are largely used for the same purpose.   Thus, the ape is the symbol of brainless mimicry, of loveless passion, of silly conceited buffoons, of despicable men generally—

> " She to the window runs where she had spied
>   Her much-esteemed dear friend, the monkey, ty'd,
>   With forty smiles as many antic bows
>   As if 't had been the lady of the house :
>   The dirty chattering monster she embraced,
>   And made it this fine tender speech at last :
>   Kiss me, thou curious miniature of man,
>   How odd thou art, how pretty, how Japan !
>   Oh ! I could live and die with thee." [1]

And the ass, "whose very name all satire does comprise,"

[1] Rochester.

is the emblem of all that is solemnly stupid, perverse,
ignobly meek—

> " Half witty and half mad, and scarce half brave,
> Half honest (which is very much a knave) ;
> Made up of all these halves, thou canst not pass
> For anything whatever but an ass."

The heavy mule—"a thing of jadish tricks "—"who, if
they've not their will to keep their own pace, stand stock-
still "—provides the poets with as easy a nickname as its
relative the ass—

> " Some neither can for wits nor critics pass,
> As heavy mules are neither horse nor ass " (*Pope*) ;

and the worst kind of all is "that reasoning mule "—a man.
But I have myself only a very qualified sympathy with the
mule, which is, after all, not a natural animal, but an
artificial.   Man made mules, and may abuse his own productions if he chooses.   I have the utmost admiration for
the mule's intelligence—

> "Shunning the loose stone on the precipice,
> Snorting suspicious—while with sight, smell, touch,
> Trying, detecting, where the surface smiled ;
> And with deliberate courage, sliding down,
> Where, in his sledge, the Laplander had turned
> With looks aghast "—

and for the intrepid self-reliance (to which I have myself
been indebted for personal safety) which Rogers celebrates
in verse ; and consider its capacity for finding water one
of the most conspicuous marvels of all marvellous Nature.
But I do not, all the same, count the mule as a regular
animal.

Bears are types of either monstrous imbecility or rugged
brutality.   In freedom, they are the terror of the wood ; in
captivity, the jest of every clown ; in death, pomatum.   Un-

couth men with unkempt manners are, therefore, bears. Misshapen and abortive plans are Bruin's cubs.

The cruel fair are panthers. Tigers are standards of cruelty by which to measure the greater enormities of man. As in Pomfret—

> "A tiger! worse, for 'tis beyond dispute,
>   No fiends so cruel as a reasoning brute."

> "What tygre or what other salvage wight
>   Is so exceeding furious and fell,
>   As wrong when it hath armed itselfe with might?
>   Nor fit 'mongst men that doe with reason mell."—*Spenser.*

And so, too, the wolf. "Rapacious, rough, and bold" is Moore's description, and all the poets use it as the beast-symbol of pitiless ferocity among men, distributing the epithet impartially among all classes—"For man to man is fiercer than the wolf, more cruel than the tiger"—Churches of different creeds, politicians of different parties, cruel wickedness of all kinds.

The hyæna "that feeds on women's flesh" is a pet abhorrence—

> "Eftsoones out of her hidden cave she cald
>   An hideous beast of horrible aspect,
>   That could the stoutest corage have appald:
>   Monstrous, mishapt, and all his backe was spect
>   With thousand spots of colours queint elect;
>   Thereto so swifte that it all beasts did pas;
>   Like never yet did living eie detect;
>   But likest it to an hyæna was
>   That feeds on women's flesh, as others feede on gras."

Among this animal's epithets are—"dire," "fell," "fellest of the fell" (Thomson), and they are not from a poetical standpoint altogether misapplied, for the hyæna may veritably be called the ghoul among the beasts. Its alternating cowardice and fierceness, its shadowy mist-of-evening colour, its laughter, broken by sobs and groans, are all horribly ghostly. And as if to keep up this imposture of being phantom-beasts, they move more stealthily and silently than even the wolf itself, and are, in fact, perpetually mistaken by those who see them (especially on nights when clouds are driving across the moon) for shadows on the ground. They can be *heard breathing* before they can be seen, and have been observed sniffing at a sleeping watchdog.

It is not, therefore, surprising that the poets should consider hyænas fair subjects for imaginative writing. So we find it meeting " the vulture and the snake, in horrid truce to eat the dead "—revelling in scenes of carnage from which " the very vultures turn away,"—" smiling " over a " rank corse " (Leyden)—" over his loathed meal, laughing in agony, raving " (Shelley)—" shedding tears and biting the while she's howling " (Barry Cornwall) — " tearing and grinning, howling, screeching, swearing, and with hyæna-laughter died despairing " (Byron). But, inasmuch as it is essential for complete horror that the hyæna shall be the direct foe of man, it is described as " bursting " upon man, and man as " flying the hyæna's famished howl."

> " And oh ! to see the unburied heaps
> On which the lonely moonlight sleeps ;
> The very vultures turn away,
> And sicken at so foul a prey !
> Only the fiercer hyæna stalks
> Throughout the city's desolate walks
> At midnight, and his carnage plies.
> Woe to the half-dead wretch who meets
> The glaring of those large blue eyes
> Amid the darkness of the streets."—*Moore.*

In metaphor the hyæna is unexpectedly infrequent. But women in general are called hyænas. In Otway—

> " 'Tis thus the false hyæna makes her moan
> To draw the pitying traveller to her den.
> Your sex are so !"

So, in particular, are the Delilas.   Samson cries—

> "Out, out, hyæna ; these are thy wonted arts,
> And arts of every woman false like thee."

Cruel foemen, the priests of the Inquisition, and unnatural mothers are hyænas, and so are bigotry, tyranny, and lust—

> "And tyranny, hyæna big with young,
> Dreading the sound, shall farrow in affright,
> And drop, still-born, her sanguinary cubs."—*Mackay.*

That the jackal is "the lion's provider" is one of those antique articles of belief which, in the light of modern observation and knowledge, it is very difficult to discredit—

> "Be you the lion to devour the prey ;
> I am your jackal to provide for you :
> There will be a bone for me to pick."—*Dryden.*

That the jackal for some mysterious reason very frequently accompanies the tiger is beyond all doubt ; and the lion is (in India) a neighbour of the tiger.   Is there any reason, then, for supposing that the jackal will not do as much for the one as for the other?   The poets certainly do not think so ; among others, Byron—

> "Ye jackals ! gnaw the bones the lion leaves,
> But not even these till he permits."

And again—

> "So lions o'er the jackal sway,
> The jackal points, he fells the prey.
> Then on the vulgar yelling press
> To gorge the relics of success."

Shelley has—

> "The jackal of Ambition's lion-rage."

And Dryden—

> "Meantime the Belgians tack upon our rear,
> And raking chase-guns thro' our sterns they send ;
> Close by, their fire-ships like jackals appear,
> Who on their lions for the prey attend."

As befits such a mean sycophant as they suppose it to be, "the thin jackal's" turn comes last at the feast. In Byron—

> " So when the lion quits his fell repast,
>   Next prowls the wolf, the filthy jackal last :
>   Flesh, limbs, and blood, the former make their own,
>   The last, poor brute, securely gnaws the bone."

Its voice chiefly attracts the poets. Crime has a "jackal-cry." Leyden calls it a "dismal shriek;" but Heber (writing in Bengal) says—

> "The jackal's cry
>   Resounds like sylvan revelry ;"

and of the two Heber is certainly more correct. Faber's "like plaining infants wearied the still air" is pure fancy; while Byron again (writing from Greece, a jackal country) describes it as

> " A mixed and mournful sound,
>   Like crying babe and beaten hound ; "

A stubborn, ugly, dirty, gluttonous, discontented, quarrelsome swine is the poet's pig. Says Burns—

> " In seventeen hundred forty-nine,
>   Satan took stuff to make a swine
>   And cuist it in a corner ;
>   But wilily he changed his plan,
>   And shaped it something like a man,
>   And ca'd it Andrew Turner."

So we may guess what Andrew Turner was like. And all men that are either stubborn, ugly, dirty, gluttonous, discontented, or quarrelsome, are called swine. It is the "filthy," "guzzling," "whining," "wallowing," "grumbling" hog; it lives in an "impure" and "stinking" "sty;" it eats "greasy draff." Thomson gives an unlovely sketch of the porker on its way to market—

> " Even so through Brentford town, a town of mud,
>   An herd of bristly swine is prick'd along ;

> The filthy beasts, that never chew the cud,
>   Still grunt, and squeak, and sing their troublous song.
> And oft they plunge themselves the mire among ;
>   But aye the ruthless driver goads them on,
> And aye of barking dogs the bitter throng
>   Makes them renew their unmelodious moan ;
>   Nor ever find they rest from their unresting fone."

Their voice, appearance, gait, food, habit of wallowing, and sleeping, all suggest comparisons with other "vile noises," other "hog-snouted features," or "pigs' small eyes ;" other "bestial indolences," other "miry ways."

Fat men are compared with "the fattest hogs in Epicurus' sty," and crowds with "rampant raging herds of swine;" gormandisers are fit only to "grunt with glutton swine," and indolent folk, as in Parnell—

> "Very silent and sedate,
>   Ever long and ever late,
>   Full of meats and full of wine,
>   Take their temper from the swine."

Yet as a feature of rural woodland life, where it is a cleanly, cheerful, active animal (as it always is in a natural state), the porker could not be overlooked.   So we meet in Clare with—

> " The grunting noise of rambling hogs
>   Where pattering acorns oddly drop,
> And noisy bark of shepherd dogs
>   The restless routs of sheep to stop."

In Gay we see them revelling "'mid a feast of acorns ;" in Montgomery grubbing "for dainty earth-nuts and nutritious roots ;" in Johnson "returning home fat with mast."

A common object of the country is Joanna Baillie's "grumbling sow that in the furrow feeds," nor far off her is Drayton's hog—

> "And in the furrow bye where Ceres is much spilled,
>   Th' unwieldy larding hog his maw there having filled,
>   Lies wallowing in the mire, thence able scarce to rise."

Nor unfamiliar is the mud-mashed corner, by the farm-yard gate, where Gay's "batt'ning hogs roll in the sinking mire,"—for your "pig is a philosopher, who knows no pre-judice."

But Blomfield is emphatically the poet of the pig, and some of his vignettes are delightful. Thus the indolent pig being tickled by geese—

> "As when by turns the strolling swine engage
> The utmost efforts of the gander's rage,
> Whose nibbling warfare on the grunter's side
> Is welcome pleasure to his bristly hide ;
> Gently he sleeps, or stretched at ease along,
> Enjoys the insults of the gabbling throng
> That march exulting round his fallen head."

Or this other of the frequently occurring panic among piglings—

> "No more the swains with scatter'd grain supply
> The restless wandering inmates of the sty ;
> From oak to oak they run with eager haste ;
> And wrangling share the first delicious taste
> Of fallen acorns ;
> The trudging sow leads forth her numerous young,
> Playful, white and clean, the briars among ;
> Till briars and thorns increasing fence them around.
>
> With bristles raised the sudden noise they hear,
> And ludicrously wild, and wing'd with fear,
> The herd decamp with more than swinish speed,
> And snorting dash thro' sedge, and rush, and reed ;
> Through tangling thickets headlong on they go,
> Then stop and listen for the fancied foe,
> The hindmost still the grunting panic spreads."

Clare, too, was a pig-observer, and here is an excellent touch of the evening farmyard—

> "Hogs with grumbling deafening noise
> Bother round the server boys,
> And far and near the motley group
> Anxious claim them suppering up :

> From the rest, a blest release,
> Gabbling home, the quarrelling geese
> Seek their warm straw-littered shed,
> And waddling, prate themselves to bed."

This frequent connection of pigs and geese is characteristic of the best observers of country life. I have noticed it already in Drayton, Leyden, and Blomfield, and Clare again has—

> " In autumn time he often stood to mark
> What tumults 'tween the hogs and geese arose,
> Down the corn-littered street."

So that Miss Frances Power Cobbe's exquisite story of the geese that used to make the pigs run the gauntlet of the flock every evening, and grab their fat skins and tweak them as they passed, is a real incident of this funny feud.

But I have read Charles Lamb too well to be unamiable to the pig, for whom a far better defence can be made than Southey's humorous odes. For in its natural state it is cleanly both in food and person, of remarkable intelligence, activity, and courage. They are perpetually bathing, they eat only fresh vegetable food, are as difficult of approach as wild geese, and as nimble in escape as goats; while for downright pluck, there is not a single animal in all the round world—the wolverine, perhaps, excepted—that can compare with it. At any rate, it is the only living beast that will wilfully challenge the tiger to combat. Nor is the tiger always the victor.

In a domesticated state, except on the best managed farms, appearances are very much against hogs. But the young pig, the porkerling, is a very queer and engaging little person. Its inquisitiveness, resulting, as a rule, in tumultuous panic, its utterances, so full of interrogations and astonishments, its manner of sidelong frisking and unexpected cavorts, are all immensely diverting. Nor are adult swine without their humour and sentiments. Farm hands sometimes grow curiously attached to their grunting charges—

> " But now, alas ! these ears shall hear no more
> The whining swine surround the dairy door ;
> No more her care shall fill the hollow tray,
> To fat the guzzling hogs with floods of whey.
> Lament, ye swine ! in grumbling spend your grief,
> For you, like me, have lost your sole relief."—*Gay*.

And need I refer to the national affection that exists between the Irish peasantry and their pigs ? Among the poets who refer to this Hiberian taste is Wilson—

> " Here streams of smoke the entering stranger greet ;
> Here man and beast with equal honours meet ;
> The cow loud bawling fills the spattered door,
> The sow and pigs grunt social round the floor ;
> Dogs, cats, and ducks, in mingling groups appear,
> And all that filth can boast of, riots here."

In the matter of those bedevilled hogs of Gadara, and the prodigal son, with other references to them in Holy Writ, the pig arrives at some adventitious consequence. Further dignity, too, attaches to him from the ceremonious consumption at Yule-tide of his head, "crested with bays and rosemary," and of the "brawne of the tusked swine" that Chaucer respected so sincerely. Indeed, its complete edibility (for which it has been called "a perfect gentle-man, eatable from the tip of his nose to the tip of his tail ") set Islam a problem which, to this day, the Moulvies have not solved. But it must be confessed that the poets are very chary of compliments to swine, the sagacious truffle-hunting animals "that grubbed the turf and taught man where to look for dainty earth-nuts and nutritious roots," and that, next to their "dirtiness," they seem to recognise most keenly their absurdity. That they are credited with seeing the wind gives them a joke against the pig, and the ring in its nose, the curl in its tail, and the absence of wool on its back, are all considered as fair subjects for ridicule as the soaped pig hunted at the fair—

> " Painful regale
> To hunt the pig with slippery tail,"

says Green ; and Clare—

> " And monstrous fun it makes to hunt the pig,
>   As soaped and larded through the crowd he flies ;
> Thus turn'd adrift he plays them many a rig,
> A pig for catching is a wondrous prize,
> And every lout to do his utmost tries ;
> Some snap the ear, and some the curly tail,
> But still his slippery hide all hold denies."

Now the hog, if regarded aright, is by no means a contemptible creature. It is a purely modern fancy (and one that the poets are, to a very great extent, responsible for) that swine are things to laugh ill-naturedly at. For, as a matter of fact, the vast majority of contemporary mankind, and all antiquity, invest the hog with a very strongly marked intelligence and strength of character. Whatever else it may be, they never call it ridiculous.

In one aspect, the pig is positively *terrific.* The Vedic pig is a thunderbolt, red,[1] bristling, terrible. In the solar myth the deities and powers of the elements frequently assume the swine form when in troublous, threatening moods, and the sun himself when malignant is a hog. It is then, in fact, a demoniacal symbol. At other times it is simply potent without malignity, as when Freya's chariot, in Scandinavian myth, is drawn by a hog with a luminous head, or when the Hindoo Indra appears to the earth in his boar avatar, or Vishnu is " the tusked one."

---

[1] Chaucer's pigs, by the way, are red, " rede as the bristles of a sowe's eres ;" and again, " his beard as any sowes or fox was rede." So too in all ballads the " rede " swine.

At other times, again, it is the placid emblem of fatness, an honourable obesity. For it is only in modern civilisation that fatness has been laughed at. In more than half the world it commands respect, for beyond the energetic limits of Europe, physical exercise after manhood is considered one of the disagreeable accidents of poverty, the fate of the necessitous, just as leanness of limb is the livery of the underfed. And the Oriental, therefore, receiving as he does the deference of his neighbours on account of the portliness of his person, prefers to move about in the adipose discomfort of a well-to-do appearance rather than to be seen in the pauper's uniform of bones.

I do not go so far as to say that I would join the superstitious in their vigils in pig-styes on Christmas eve—at least not with becoming alacrity—or would join in the train of suitors for the wealthy pig-faced lady, or " hog-faced gentlewoman," as the chap-book of the period styles her. But, on the other hand, I have no propensity to faint, as that stout marshal of France used to do at the sight of one, nor to object to being taxed, as the country folk thereabouts do, with being born at Hogg's Norton. I do not share Isaiah's prodigious objections to pork.

Indeed, between an excessive enthusiasm and a bigoted detestation there is the more becoming medium of sobriety, and I am content, therefore, to commit myself no further than to say I had rather hear the cheery horn of the swineherd calling his charges to their banquet under the Campanian oaks, than the last squeals of the hog on the altars of Bacchus.

The poets, therefore, are not romping on such safe grounds as they think when they frolic over the fatness of swine. Nor should they have forgotten to allow pig-legends to temper their severity. It is only by giving all evidence its due weight that judges arrive at the cold neutrality of impartiality. Now, was not the hog sacred to Thor, and is it not under the very special protection of St. Anthony,[1] the friend of all animals and protector of weddings? Did they never hear that pork gives the eater acuteness of ear and intelligence? That a pig's bristles have strange occult influences when the proper arrangements are made for working a charm? That Rome, "the nameless city," once had the hog, "the nameless beast," for its badge and cognisance? That "please the pigs," now a contemptuous phrase, really means "please the Holy Virgin," or may mean "please the girls"?[2] To laugh at "a hog in armour" is a poor jest enough even for those who think "hog" means a pig, and wherein lay the joke of a Chinaman's queue—a lank dependent plait of hair four feet in length—being called a "pig-tail" I never could understand. The pig's tail, by the way, provides the poets with as much fun as it does, when soaped, the clowns who try to catch hold of it, and there is a proverb to the effect that it is beyond the capacity of human ingenuity to convert the caudal appendage of a swine into an instrument of sibilation. But this is not the case, as in the city of Chicago I myself saw a whistle made out of a pig's tail, and an excellent one, not one that would merely on occasion emit an exiguous squeak, but a rousing whistle that would fetch every hansom, within a radius of half a mile, to your door.

That the tail should curl amuses the poets; but I am not sure that such flippancy is not blameworthy. They do not even care whether it curls to the right or the left. Yet it depended once upon the direction of the twist whether the hog was acceptable in sacrifice or not. All deities of taste abhorred the twist-sinister.

In short, I cannot help thinking that there has been

---

[1] "St. Anthony is universally known for the patron of hogs, having a pig for his page in all pictures."—*Fuller's Worthies.*

[2] Pigeon maiden (Danish), hog youth of both sexes (Gaelic). *Sic aiunt cognoscentes.*

much mutual misunderstanding between the poets and their pigs. Indeed, if only on the ground of the pig's eatableness throughout, I should have expected some occasional scintillations of gratitude from men and women with such far-reaching and subtle sympathies as poets claim.

For there is no finicking reservation of himself about the pig ; he keeps back. nothing, excepts no part of his person from the general consumption. He puts himself up to be eaten " without reserve," generously closing the door against possibilities of subsequent misunderstanding. He goes the whole hog with himself. The inventory of his effects is complete, and without any fraudulent withholding of items ; he puts himself into your hands bag and baggage. When you have finished eating him, there is no gleaning after you—

> " It would be well, my friend, if you and I
> Had, like that pig, attained the perfectness
> Made reachable by nature."—*Southey.*

The hog, then, is unanimous, and from this fact have risen two singular phenomena so opposed in character that it is a wonder they should have sprung from the same source. The first is the Moslems' consumption of the entire animal ; the second, the Jews' entire abstinence from it.

Mahomet, as is well known, enjoined upon all the Faithful that they should not eat pork ; for, said he—

> " There is a part in every swine,
> No friend or follower of mine
> May taste, whate'er his inclination,
> On pain of excommunication."—*Cowper.*

But the prophet did not actually specify the sinful part, but left the point at large, to the great perplexity of Islam, and no little discontent, inasmuch as

> " For one piece they thought it hard
> From the whole hog to be debarred."

The Moulvies, therefore, met in consultation to settle what joint Mahomet had in mind. And Cowper goes on—

> " Much controversy straight arose :
> These chose the back, the belly those,
> By some 'tis confidently said
> He meant not to forbid the head ;
> While others at that doctrine rail,
> And piously prefer the tail.
> Thus, conscience freed from every clog,
> Mahomedans eat up the hog."

There was no intermediate position tenable, for so numerous and bigoted were the admirers of the several good points of a cooked animal that it was impossible to find any one bit of the animal that somebody did not swear was the very best morsel in him. Yet see to what contrary ends the same symmetry of perfection worked with regard to the Jews. Not only did they not eat swine, but, recognising the solidarity and homogeneity of the animal, the very strictest Jews refused even to admit that such an animal existed !

They would not rest even at the half-way toleration of Accadian nomenclature, and fetch a compass about it by calling it "the one that wears a ring in his nose," or "it with a tail like a ringlet," or "the bristly thing that grunts." They decreed at once its complete banishment into the limbo of nameless nothings.

So they spoke of it as "the other thing," the "you know what I mean," the "what do you call 'ems," the "abomination." They were afraid even to utter the insidious word "pork." To talk of "crackling" was, they knew well, the first step to eating it. So they cut the name out of their language. But what a pitiful illustration of moral weakness ! Not to be able to look a pig in the face without incontinently debauching on brawn !

But this weakness is in my opinion aggravated by the

suspicion that these same strict Jews, who would not for the world think of mentioning the name of the pig, used, as a matter of fact, to have it served surreptitiously. Or how is it that we find pigs so numerous in the Judæa of Holy Writ? Were they *all* Gentiles' pigs?

Not that my suspicion is altogether pure assumption. For —apart from the fact that we never find preachers denouncing practices that do not exist—history tells us that the Egyptians tried very hard indeed to keep from pork, but could not do it. They formally anathematised it as "impure;" but formally also they ate it, affecting, by the vast ceremony with which they consumed their bacon, that they were performing a religious rite. They were never tired of saying that it was abominable and vowing it to Tycho, the spirit of evil, but with all this fuss of terrible abnegation, they solemnly gave themselves up twice a year with a profusion of ceremonial and dumb-crambo to eating pigs. And mark the sagacity of the ancient Egyptians, those " serpents of old Nile." On the two authorised pork-days they "sacrificed" (so they pleasantly termed it) immense numbers of hogs to their equivalent for Bacchus. But did they destroy them by fire before his shrine? waste the precious carcase by useless incineration? Not a bit of it. They gave the bodies to the swineherds. And why? *Why?* To be made into bacon, of course.

The swineherds lived on the preserved flesh of their charges, and understood these little matters of smoking and curing. Nor is it without significance that the Egyptians were very careful as to the age and condition of the pigs they thus "sacrificed," and that they killed their pigs just as farmers do nowadays, twice in the year. If any one, therefore, would try to convince me that the jolly old Egyptians did not have bacon and ham, brawn, tripe and sausages, chine and pettitoes all the year round, I should be as deaf as a wilderness of adders. Nor do I believe that the Jews were ever any stricter than they are now; and I think he would be a foolhardy man who should walk past a Hebrew pickpocket with a rasher of bacon sticking obviously out of his coat-tails.

It is not likely that any one, with eyes to see and ears to hear, could write a paragraph descriptive of a summer evening without mentioning the bat. So the regular occurrence of the bat-feature in Clare, Hurdis, Blomfield, Wilson, Garth, Grahame, Wordsworth, Collins, Gay, Shelley, and all the others who have sung of twilight, was only to be expected. But it is curious that none should have made remark of the flitter-mouse's amazing eyesight, admired its unrivalled dexterity on the wing, or wondered at its voice —those needle-points of sound, which are too keen and quick for many ears to catch.

Recent investigations by railway companies have shown what a dangerous proportion of humanity is wholly or partially colour-blind, and similar inquiries would prove that a very large number of persons are unconscious of their being partially deaf. A test case is the bat's acute voice. So Tennyson, requiring a simile, says " our voices were thinner and fainter than any flitter-mouse shriek." I have myself known four persons out of a company of six unable to catch the sounds uttered by bats when hawking overhead. Coleridge, for instance, says "the bat wheels silent by," as if it was the regular thing for bats to be silent, whereas the fact is, that it is very unusual for bats to be silent when wheeling after insects. So the chances are that Coleridge was bat-deaf. Yet he hears (in the same stanza) " the solitary humble-bee singing in the bean-flower " —one bee in a bean-field and not a score of bats overhead ! But perhaps his humble-bee was really a cockchafer, or ten thousand of them, busy among the beans. Crabbe could hear the bats " feebly shriek," and speaks of the sound as the note of " their melancholy love." Clare also calls the bat " shrieking." But except for these and perhaps half-a-dozen more, I do not know that any of the many poets who have introduced the bat into their evening sketches remark its extraordinary voice.

The flutter of its wings attracts their notice frequently. Thus Collins has—

> " The weak-eyed bat,
> With short shrill shriek flits by on leathern wing."[1]

Grahame—

> " Round the strawy roof
> Is heard the bat's wing in the deep-hushed air."

And again—

> " The whirring wing of the dark bat."

Now here again comes in the fact that the bat's flight is singularly noiseless. When it turns a sudden somersault, there is a supple flutter heard, and when it drops down out of the air close to the watcher's face in pursuit of a dodging moth, the soft crumpling of its wings is audible. But it does not " whir," nor, as Byron says, " flap "—

> " The long dim shadows of surrounding trees,
> The flapping bat, the night-song of the breeze."

But Byron perhaps, writing from Greece, heard the large frugivorous bat.

As regards the flight itself, the descriptive touches are commonplace enough. Clare's " scouting bats begin their giddy round " is good, and so is Grahame's—

> " And even the reremouse when the twilight sleeps
> Unbreathing, spreads her torpid wings and round
> From stack to house or barn and round again,
> With many a sudden turn, flits and eludes
> The eye : "

---

[1] How many poets use the "leathern wing?" Crabbe has "webby," and Garth "sooty," but the rest when they specify the wing say "leathern."

for each specifies a fact of observation—the "scouting" of
the bat, which, like a pigeon thrown up into the air, first
casts about in the sky for a while till it gets its bearings,
and then settles down to its work, and the sudden evanish-
ments of bats on the wing, eluding the eye by marvellous
nimbleness. Shelley has "quick bats in their twilight
dance," and Hurdis, with his usual clumsy fidelity—

> "What time the bat
> Hurries precipitous on leathern wing,
> Brisk evolution in the dusky air
> With sudden wheels performing."

But all the rest of the "fluttering," "wavering," "flitting,"
"mazy" bats are studiously commonplace, and thrown in
as it were by way of a touch of local colour, just as bees
are sprinkled about in a flowery verse by poets who need
a little insect life.

But why should the bat be taunted as being "torpid,"
"drowsy," "lazy-lurking?" It is no lazier than the sky-
lark. The only difference is that it usually (not as a rule)
sleeps all day, instead of sleeping all night. Are the
printers of the London morning papers "torpid," "drowsy,"
and "lazy-lurking?" Yet they have to do the same. One
poet only, A. Wilson, does the little mouse-on-wings justice :

> "The bat, the busiest of the midnight train,
> That wing the air or sulky tread the plain,
> Sees morning open on each field and flower,
> And ends her mazes in yon ruined tower."

So much for the poets' best side of the bat, the bat
natural ; but even to it, imperfect as it is, has to be added
the normal error of the poets of thinking that the bat was
a bird, "an ominous fowl"—

> "Oui, je te reconnais, je t'ai vu dans mes songes,
> Triste oiseau ! sœur du hibou funèbre."

So says Victor Hugo, and the error of the bird-bat is

probably, therefore, a widely spread one. Æsop gave countenance to it in his bat "half bird, half beast;" and many poets give themselves the advantage of the doubt. Spenser commences his list of "fatal birds" with "the leather-wingéd bat." Southey makes fun of the mistake in

> "The midnighte howre when all the fowles
>   Are housed and hushte save battes and owles,
>   Yatte screche they're bodynges shrille;"

and Dryden makes a happy hit in the couplet—

> " Nor birds nor beasts, but just a kind of bat,
>   A twilight animal, true to neither cause."

But why should Montgomery have included the bat among his "*Birds*" or Scott perpetuated the fiction?

On the other, its fanciful side, the bat is a thing of reproach, pure and simple. Because it flies by night, it is "obscene," and everything, therefore, that goes on by night is bat-like. For it is no innocent thing this poets' bat. It is "ghastly" and "blood-loving," the vampyre—

> " In the air a ghastly bat bereft
>   Of sense has flitted with a mad surprise."

In this aspect, however, it does not belong to my present subject, but to the Fauna of Fancy. But there is a modification of it that properly belongs to the Beasts of Reproach—the "ill-omened bat"—and this is by far the most frequent view which the poets take of the grotesque but harmless creature. For then, the bat adds a desolation to desolate places and a horror to the horrible. Shattered thrones, empty harem-bowers, crumbling beds of state (Crabbe), and rifted minster-spires, are the perches of bats; ruins are their pleasure-haunts, deadly nightshade their bower, and wolves their boon companions—

> " Come list and hark, the bell doth toll
>   For some but now departing soul,

> And was not that some ominous fowl—
> The bat, the night-crow, or screech-owl?"

Rogers' bandit greets as old companions, in his hiding-place, "the bat, the toad, the blind-worm, and the newt," and Darwin's naturalist hears

> "Shrill scream, the famished bats and shivering owls,
> And loud and long the dog of midnight howls."

"Through darksome gulfs the bats for ever skim, the haunts of howling wolves and panthers grim" (Wilson); "nocturnal bats and birds obscene" (Pope); "the bat flies transient o'er the dusky green, and night's foul birds along the sullen twilight sail" (Beattie); "the bat takes airy round on leathern wings, and the hoarse owl his woeful dirges sings" (Gay).

It is easy, therefore, to anticipate the place that bats fill in poetical metaphor. As "vampyres" they symbolise the foulest crimes and the worst enemies of humanity. As the bat ominous, they are all sorts and conditions of men that are abroad at night with evil intentions, and are emblematic of hovering disaster. As the bat natural, they represent drowsy, day-shunning indolence, purblind ignorance, and from the weirdness of their form and feature suggest things from another world—

> "Then did whisper low
> Some of the little spirits that bat-like clung,
> And clustered round the opening."—*Jean Ingelow.*

This is permissible. It is quite fair to the bat to say that its gnome-like countenance and self-absorbed, self-enwrapped attitudes should be used as similes for that which is impish and uncanny, just as Swift aptly gives riches the wings of bats, and Parnell calls them the "dire imps of darkness." But it is a crime against poetry to make the bat itself obscene and abominable, a thing of reproach. If

the poets wished to find hard things to say of the creature, why did they not say that its caves stink like a wilderness of polecats, or that its fur is incredibly swarming with
vermin?

To those who have seen the "flying foxes" of tropical
countries—stretching nearly five feet across the wings—
flapping their solemn way across the evening sky, or have
seen them with softly fanning wings wheeling round the wild
fruit trees, the "vampyre" and generally weird idea of the
bat is easily explicable. But that the busy, merry, little
harlequin of our English twilight should have earned for
itself the ill name it possesses, shows a fertility of superstition which is very interesting.

> "Bloody, bloody bat,
>   Come into my hat!"

cries the country urchin, holding his cap over the bridge as
the tiny flickering things tumble about in the air in pursuit
of moths and beetles. He expects this prodigious spell to
fascinate "the night-flier" into the cap which he holds out
for its reception. Nor are his elders more sensible. In
Scotland they call them "bawkie birds," thing of ill-
and over a large part of rural England they ar the fox that
be blood-suckers, and in league with the , namely, its
"the other world." But public opinion has *ntre chien et*
them from the first.   t is the hour

At the Creation, so they say, the bat affect nythical un-
ostrich) to be neither beast nor bird, in the
ing the task which Allah was apportioning se, and for
punished in the end by being told that all th fox-hunting
the night were already distributed, and that i of course,
shift for itself as it could with those hours which
the one nor the other. The Mosaic law pronou
—"the fowl that creeps, going on all fours"—
tion, and the Rabbis carried on the national pre

Egypt, meanwhile, it had attracted attention, been adopted into the menagerie of worship, and solemnly dedicated to Darkness. Rome and Greece took their bat from Egypt, and we find the bat drawing the car of Nox through the sky, and transformation into the bat one of the gloomiest penalties within the imagination of the myth-maker.

Here and there, however, it is redeemed from opprobrium, as by the Moslem legend of Isa making a bat, " Khopash," out of clay and endowing it with life, so that it might come and tell him in his seclusion among the mountains when the sunset-hour for the suspension of the Ramazan fast approached.

So to-day we find this useful little animal, a mouse on wings, regarded by a majority of mankind with apprehension and dislike. Its appearance when seated is certainly against it; but on the wing it is the very incarnation of buoyant happiness. Under the inquiries of science its amazing sensitiveness to touch, amounting indeed almost to the possession of a new sense, has been the admiration of naturalists, while its extraordinary suspension of life for part of the ʼdar (differing altogether in character and degree drowsy, ʼ ʼhiʼ-sr nation of dormice and bears) ranks certainly from the weirʼonders of Nature. But apart from science, is from another ʼgratitude due to a creature that has ventured
iginality in the matter of nose? It is horn-
sed, sometimes it wears a crest on the top of
Som. a fleur-de-lys, sometimes a mimic horse-shoe ;
And
ys fantastic and unexpected. It is the very
This is permiss.
that its gnoʼhe fox " for my subject, I should be over-enwrapped a it, for Reynard covers a whole volume of which is impiʼolk-lore. But, fortunately, it is only the poets' the wings of ʼterns me, and this is a very meagre and single-darkness." . Not that it does not abound in verse—it bat itself obʼut, then, it is always the same old fox. It has

its den in solitudes, and issues stealthily forth to rob the
neighbouring poultry-yard, and by-and-by the huntsmen
meet and the "ruthless," "bloody-minded" fox is done to
death. It is, therefore, a suitable simile for all crafty and
guileful persons, especially those who meet with just punishment for their crimes.

But this is not the animal that was made for the earth,
and of the two foxes I prefer the natural one. I should
like to have found here and there in the poets a reference
to the beautiful ruddy fox that by its simple presence, passing across a scrap of woodland scenery, startles the landscape into unwonted picturesqueness, and marshals all the
surrounding foliage into a back-ground for the little living
spark of colour moving in front; or a word for the small
foxes, the prettiest wild-thing cubs in the world, with the
innocentest faces and most winning ways; or a word of
sympathy for the vixen, that will run before the hounds
with a cub in her mouth for miles and miles, and after
hiding it, will double and turn upon her course, careless
for the time of her own life, in the hope of leading away
the hounds from her treasure—a word, in   or the
pretty little beast of prey that is still a native
and, but for encroaching farmsteads and gar   the fox that
would be abundantly content to live entirely, namely, its
birds and animals. But of this creature,   *ntre chien et*
and brave little English fox, the poets kn   t is the hour
Even its cheery voice is called "an on   mythical un-
(Grahame), and said to "make approaching
dismal fall."   se, and for

It is "ruthless," "gaunt," "noxious," "wicl fox-hunting
"greedy," "stinking," "obscene," "vagrant;" "   of course,
fox;" "felon" and "villain;" "the nightl
the fold;" "abhorred alive, more loathsome
dead."

And why all this pother? Simply because

the property of man.   It runs off with a cock, and lo ! the
chorus of the poets !—

> " They crieden out, harow and wala wa !
> A ha the fox ! and after him they ran
> And eke with staves many another man
> Ran Colle our dogge, and Talbot and Gerlond,
> And Malkin with hire distaf in hire hond,
> Ran cow and calf, and eke the veray hogges
> So fered were for berking of the dogges,
> And shouting of the men and women eke,
> They ronnen so, hem thought hir hertes breke.
> They yelleden as fendes don in helle ;
> The dokes crieden as men wold hem quelle,
> The gees for fere flewen over the trees,
> Out of the hive came the swarme of bees.
> So hideous was the noise, a benedicite !
> Certes he Jakke Straw, and his meinie,
> Ne maden never shoutes half so shrille,
> Whan that they wolden any Fleming kille,
> As thilke day was made upon the fox.
> Of bras they broughten beemes and of box,
> Of horn and bone, in which they blew and pouped,
> And therwithal they shriked and they houped :
> It seem'd as that the heven shulde fall ! "

"green ruins" and "gaping tombs," "looks
windows of the desolate dwelling of Moira,"
or the night in caves where none else but the
ouses.   This gives the fox the necessary degree
ty."   But as the "subtle pilfering fox," "the
tal foe," it has often to be found less remote
bitations of men and chickens.   It is most
therefore, as a farmyard prowler, as a hen-
metimes, as in Somerville, it seizes "the poor
lamb, whose sweet warm blood supplies a rich
in Pope, Dryden, Dyer, Grahame, prowls round
sking in the sun, the frisking lambs on the bank,
"to seize a straggling prey."   And Piers tells
wonderful story of the false fox that comes in

pedlar's guise and tempts little "Kiddie" to its doom, in spite of his mother's warning words before she "yode forth abroad unto the greene wood." Quoth she—

> " Many wilde beastes liggen in waite,
> For to entrap in thy tender state,
> But most the foxe. maister of collusion,
> For he has vowed thy last confusion.
> Forthy, my Kiddie ; be rulde by me
> And never give trust to his trecheree ;
> And if he chaunce come when I am abroade,
> Sperre the yate fast, for fear of fraude ;
> Ne for all his worst, nor for his best
> Open the dore at his request."

But of course Kiddie does, and of course the false fox "ranne away with him in all hast."

But, as a rule, it is the rape of the hen that inflames the poets to most indignant declamation, like Clare's—

> " Housewives discoursing 'bout their hens and cocks,
> Spinning long stories, wearing half the day,
> Sad deeds bewailing of the prowling fox,
> How in the roost the thief had knaved his way,
> And made their market profits all a prey."

Yet it is not often that the poets attribute to the fox that which in all other fabulists is its chief failing, namely, its going about its larcenies by twilight. The *Entre chien et loup* is "the great epical hour of the fox." It is the hour of betrayals and perfidies, of doubts and mythical uncertainties.

Some score of poets sing the glorious chase, and for downright brutality commend me to your fox-hunting poet, Bloomfield emphatically excepted—and, of course, Cowper.

> " The reeking roaring hero of the chase
> I give him over as a desperate case ;
> Physicians write in hopes to work a cure
> Never, if honest ones, when death is sure ;

> And though the fox he follows may be tanned,
> A mere fox-follower never is reclaimed :[1]
> Some farrier should prescribe his proper course
> Whose only fit companion is his horse :
> Or if deserving of a better doom
> The nobler beast judge otherwise, his groom."

The squire, when he goes to the cover-side, never affects a sympathy with chickens, or maudles about "the turkey's callow care." Most of the hunt are there because they enjoy the excitement of the hard ride, a few because they take an extra pleasure in seeing hounds working well, but all of them hunt the fox *because it is brave.* Probably, also, not a man in the field, except the huntsman, cares whether the fox is killed or not. They want to overtake it, to break down the pluck of the "game" little beast by a combination of their hounds' sagacity, their horses' power, and their own straight riding. The huntsman likes to see the fox killed simply from a professional point of view. It encourages the pack, and the brush is "good for a sovereign." But the fox-hunting poet musters his hounds and huntsmen out of sheer revenge, and murderously pursues the fox because it has killed a chicken, and exults over the actual mangling of the little body.

> "Here, huntsman, from this height
> Observe yon birds of prey ; if I can judge
> 'Tis there the villain lurks, they hover round,
> And claim him as their own. Was I not right ?
> See ! there he creeps along, his brush he drags,
> And sweeps the mire impure : from his wide jaws
> His tongue unmoisten'd hangs, symptoms too sure
> Of sudden death.
>
> Ha ! yet he flies, nor yields
> To black despair. But one loose more, and all

---

[1] " The fox's brush still emulous to wear,
    He scours the county in his elbow-chair."
                    —*Rogers : Pleasures of Memory.*

His wiles are vain. Hark ! thro' yon village now
The rattling clamour rings. The barns, the cots,
And leafless elms, return the joyous sounds.
Thro' ev'ry homestall, and thro' ev'ry yard
His midnight walks, panting, forlorn, he flies.

Thro' ev'ry hole he sneaks, thro' every jakes
Plunging he wades besmear'd, and fondly hopes
In a superior stench to lose his own :
But faithful to the track th' unerring hounds
With peals of echoing vengeance close pursue.
And now distress'd, no shelt'ring covert near,
Into the hen-roost he creeps, whose walls with gore
Distain'd, attest his guilt.

                        There, villain ! there
Expect thy fate deserv'd. And soon from thence
The pack, inquisitive, with clamour loud,
Drag out their trembling prize, and on his blood
With greedy transport feast. In bolder notes,
Each sounding horn proclaims the felon dead,
And all th' assembled village shouts for joy.

The farmer, who beholds his mortal foe
Stretch'd at his feet, applauds the glorious deed,
And grateful calls us to a short repast :
In the full glass the liquid amber smiles,
Our native product ; and his good old mate
With choicest viands heaps the lib'ral board,
To crown our triumphs and reward our toils."

Now fox-hunting, I take it, requires no condoning from
anybody. But to go about to condone it, by pretending
that the fox is "the terror of the hamlet," "the farmer's
mortal foe," a "bloody-minded villain," and must be killed
itself in retribution for ducklings eaten, is to condemn the
sport as inhuman, and fox-hunters as monsters of cruelty.

               " Give ye Britons ! then
Your sportive fury, pitiless, to pour,
Loose on the mighty robber of the fold !
Him from his craggy winding haunts unearthed,

> Let all the thunders of the chase pursue.
> Happy he . . .
> Who sees the villain seized and dying hard,
> Without complaint, though by an hundred mouths
> Relentless torn ! "

Cowper is bad enough, but read Leyden. The fox is supposed to have gone to earth, but a terrier turns him out—

> " His guilt glares hideous when, in open day,
> The villain stands revealed, with dumb dismay,
> When guileful rapine's hoarded spoils are viewed,
> And guilty caverns stained with guiltless blood.
> None grieve when low the trembling felon lies,
> Who unlamenting,[1] unlamented dies ;
> His limbs the hungry brood of ravens feed,
> Abhorred alive, more loathsome still when dead."

And all this about a fox ! The innocence of the poet as to the procedure and incidents of "the thunders of the chase" are as delightful as his animus is discreditable above all to a poet. But Somerville is, perhaps, the most brutal of the versifying fox-hunters, for he rejoices alike over the "greedy transport" of a score of big hounds swallowing one small fox, and over the killing of foxes in traps ! So that he not only brutalises the sport which he professes to enjoy, but sins against it in the worst manner a fox-hunter can.

> " Nor hounds alone the noxious brood destroy.
> The plundered warrener full many a wile
> Devises to entrap his greedy foe,
> Fat with nocturnal spoils. At close of day
> With silence drags his trail, then from the ground
> Pares thin the close-grazed turf, and with nice hand

---

[1] On this point of the silence with which the fox handsomely meets death, compare Scott's "he took a hundred mortal wounds as mute as fox 'mongst mangling hounds," and Thomson's "dying hard, without complaint, though by an hundred mouths relentless torn."

> Covers the latent death, with curious springs
> Prepared to fly at once, whene'er the tread
> Of man or beast unwarily shall press
> The yielding surface.   By th' indented steel
> With gripe tenacious held, the felon grins
> And struggles, but in vain ; yet oft 'tis known
> When every art has failed, the captive fox
> Has shared the wounded joint, and with a limb
> Compounded for his life.   But if, perchance,
> In the deep pitfall plunged, there's no escape,
> But unreprieved he dies, and bleached in air,
> The jest of clowns, his reeking carcase hangs."

"We [1] can but raise our feeble voice in mild protest against the cruel misrepresentations to which the fox is exposed in *Reineke Fuchs*, wherein he is credited with every vice under the sun, and wins his final victory over his enemy Sir Isegrim by the basest perfidy on record.   The fox of natural history, we venture to plead, is not so bad as all this.   He is simply a robber—at once a highwayman, burglar, and garotter—but he is not a hypocrite (at least, more than his profession requires); and as to his private morals, he is an excellent husband and *père de famille*, taking unusual pleasure in the sweets of domestic life and the gambols of his infant offspring. . . . The stories about the race are mostly base fabrications. *Reineke Fuchs* is, as we have already said, one long unpardonable libel."

Now "Reynard the Fox" is exactly the fox of poetry, and, indeed, it is very possible, considering the extraordinary popularity of that "pleasant history," that the poets really borrowed their Reynard from that ancient work.

But in the Middle Ages the fox had a literature to itself, and has been ever since one of the most conspicuous features of folk-lore—but always in the same aspect of a practical joker of a sinister kind.   To my mind he resembles the Manobohzo of Red-Indian legends, "the mischief-

---

[1] Francis Power Cobbe, "False Beasts and True."

maker," and the Loki of Scandinavia. Earliest, perhaps, of all myths is the so-called "solar," and in it the fox perpetually figures as the grim humorist that is perpetually keeping chanticleer in alarm. Each is perpetually outwitting the other, and will continue to do so till the sun ceases to rise and set.

The fox-twilight just comes on the scene as the cockdaylight is disappearing from sight, and gets weary again of waiting for the cock's return just as his patience was on the point of being rewarded by the breaking of dawn. Towards sunset the fox comes stealing into sight, but the cock is at that moment making off. Next morning the cock, seeing his adversary ("the fox-shadows") slinking away, pops out his head and crows. And so the old contest goes on.

Following this ancient precedent, therefore, folk-lore makes the fox get into trouble himself as often as into mischief—for though Reynard is one of the most cunning of beasts, his cunning, like that of the wolf, is constantly overreaching itself.

V.

ASSES AND APES.

" Your asses and your apes,
And other brutes in human shapes."—*Beattie.*

ASSES.

"The ass, that heavy, stupid, lumpish beast" (*Oldham*) ; "slouth-full" (*Spenser*) ; "whom Nature reason hath denied " (*Groome*) ; "heavy-headed thing" (*Wordsworth*) ; "slow beast " (*Southey*) ; "obstinate, dull," &c. (*Swift, Gay, &c.*) ; "serious" (*King*) ; "solemn, puir lang-legs" (*Allan Ramsay*).

GLORY has been pernicious to the ass. So saith an ancient of wisdom ; and it may be that the donkey, satisfied with past honours, and conscious of the worth that was once set upon him, has become indifferent to the opinion of a degenerate race of men who knew him not in his prime—his golden prime, in the good old time of Haroun Al-Raschid. So he retires from public favour, like some great actor or author who has pleased the taste of his day, but finds a generation overtaking him that has no congenial sympathies ; and so, loftily withdrawing with his obsolete laurels, he walks the world wrapped as in a cloak with self-conscious merit and voluntarily undistinguished.

For myself, when I watch a donkey at his work, be his master a good or a bad one, there grows upon me somehow a suspicion that the animal "whose talent for burdens is wondrous " is deliberately concealing other talents, and that its meekness arises from condescension rather than submission; that it prefers to subject itself to perennial crucifixion rather than tediously prove its patents to nobility.   Legend says it bears the cross upon its back to keep men in recollection of the exaltation of the humble to offices of honour, and that its meekness is to remind us that even under such honours we should still remain humble.[1]   But legend is often audaciously wrong.   For when our Saviour went into Jerusalem on an ass, He selected the beast upon which it was then considered most honourable to ride.   The donkey was—as it still is—the steed of the rich, the high in place, and the luxurious.   There was no humility intended or expressed in that notable procession; on the contrary, it was our Saviour's one and only assertion of personal consequence, His solitary condescension to the earthly ambitions of the disciples.   Moreover, viewed naturally instead of traditionally, the cross-stripe on the donkey's back gives the "heavy-headed thing" a very interesting significance, for it may be the last lingering vestige of a zebrine ancestry. All the other stripes have been thrashed off its hide.   Bewildered by ill-usage, they have run together and blended into a colour that, like the character of the wearer, is monotonous, dull, serious, solemn.   I prefer then the natural and matter-of-fact explanation of the emblem on the donkey's back to the legendary one, for it directly associates the poor animal with its proud wild-life past, and by a single line of colour suffices to restore "the heavy, stupid, lumpish thing" of the poets to its original Asiatic and African honours and freedom.

> " Didst thou from service the wild ass discharge,
>   And break his bonds, and bid him live at large ;
>   Through the wide waste, his ample mansion, roam,
>   And lose himself in his unbounded home ?

---

[1] In Scotland, they say the stripe is the bruise of Balaam's staff.

> By Nature's hand magnificently fed,
> His meal is on the range of mountains spread ;
> · As in pure air aloft he bounds along,
> He sees in distant smoke the city throng ;
> Conscious of freedom, scorns the smothered train,
> The threat'ning driver, and the servile rein." [1]

The poets, *more poetico*, accept the dull significance of the monkish fancy in preference to the more eloquent parable of the scientific fact, and refer the cross to Calvary rather than Central Africa. So Rogers, seeing "the panniered ass browsing the hedge by fits," did not probably recognise therein the old instinct of asinine vigilance when the wild ass—"the ass of savage kind," as Watts calls it—grazed only two steps at a time, and kept stopping between mouthfuls to raise its head, in order to scan the horizon and sniff the breeze. Nor perhaps did Wordsworth, who saw the ass,

> "With motion dull
> Upon the pivot of his skull
> Turn round his long left ear,"

associate the gesture with days of suspicious freedom, when the long left ear of the sentinel ass caught the first whisper of approaching danger and gave timely warning to the herd of otherwise fatal surprise.

For once upon a time the wild asses, the onagers, were the only representatives of the family, and they were so swift of foot and so courageous that the east and the south wore their hides as robes of honour, and kings and chiefs took the wild ass for their cognisance and badge. It was hunting an ass, then a royal sport, that Bairam, Prince of Persia, lost his life, plumping into the pool in the Vale of Heyris and being never seen again. Oriental children wore shreds of ass-skin round their necks that they might grow up generous and brave. Did Ali, "the Lion of the Lord,"

---

[1] Young's paraphrase of Job.

intend any disparagement of the Prophet's favourite horse when he named his own donkey Duldul after it? Thus prized, the wild ass soon came under domestication, and the under-sized drudge of the London streets is the latest and most degraded variation of the species. But intermediate between the proud vagabond of the desert and the costermonger's "moke" come many animals more worthy, physically, of their lineage. In Egypt, the white ass still claims something of the respect, and fetches the high price, of olden days ; and during the Egyptian war I remember seeing more than one of these animals figuring conspicuously in the British camp. A distinguished general, a baronet, and two M.P.'s, rode to the front, as used to ride the fifty sons of Jair. All over Asia Minor the donkey of superior caste is the recognised "hack" of the well-to-do, and I have seen them not only in the Levant, but in Southern Europe and in Eastern Africa, sumptuously caparisoned as steeds, and of a size and form that dignified their office far better than some of the ponies of the Cossacks of the Don, the tattoos of India, the bronchos of Western America, or the rat-like chargers of Beluchi warriors.

And I have overwhelming authority from the Past for my respect for donkeys. The purely stupid ass was unknown to antiquity. Take Hindoo mythology alone. There we find the donkey in divine, demoniacal, or Ghandarvic aspects—that is, benign, malign, or merely vagabond and loose-moralled—but never ignominious or ridiculous. The ass of Indra is a potent personage, and, as the warrior that conquers at Yama, rises to the dignity of the Solar Hero, the Sun itself. Or, if you will, take the more familiar Greek and Latin. What was the ass Lucius but the Sun ? Sacred to Bacchus, it paced along triumphant in Dionysic feasts ; it was honoured, as it well deserved, in the worship of Vesta, and sacrificed as a worthy offering to the God of War.

A god, it is true, gave Midas donkey's ears, but it was just like the intolerance of a divinity to do so. The perpetrator of the insult was Apollo (who ought to have known better), whose music the Phrygian king had pronounced inferior to that of Pan, and so—in order to gag honest criticism—the god, forsooth, gave Midas donkey's ears! For myself, admiring fearlessness in critics, and admiring also the music of Nature above that of art, I shall always believe that Midas was right and that Apollo was fairly beaten, just as I shall continue to believe that George the Fourth was really fat even though Leigh Hunt had to go to prison for saying so. And mark the mean ingenuity of Apollo's retaliation. Pan, whom Midas preferred, sometimes wore asses' ears himself. They were his emblem of acute hearing, of a perception open to the subtlest harmonies of the woods and fields, and therefore in lengthening the Phrygian's ears the sulky divinity thought to put an affront upon Midas' patron too. It is for posterity to avenge the critic on his petty-minded tormentor.

Again—

> " Silenus on his ass,
> Pelted with flowers as he on did pass
> Tipsily quaffing,"

is not, either in Keats or the classics, made ridiculous by his vehicle; for it should not be forgotten that the jolly old man being placed on an ass points to the importance of the animal in Bacchic worship, and is not intended to derogate from the dignity of the boon companion of the gods. Says a learned commentator upon the pageant, " The ass was in fact the symbol of Silenus' wisdom and his prophetical powers."

But I regret that the esteem in which it was held should so often have marked out the donkey as a proper object for sacrifice. But so it was. The Scythians slew it in honour of the god of battles, and the Egyptians in honour of the god of learning. When it was a red one, the Copts thrust it with much pious ceremonial over the top of a precipice, as a "scape-ass" for the people. Hence, by an oblique prolongation of the vicarious-sinner idea, "wicked as a red ass" became a Coptic proverb. In the same vein, the Nagas to this day select red cocks for augury and sacrifice. Not that red was always an honoured tint. Cain's hair, they say, was red, and Nebuchadnezzar's, for his sins, was turned to the same colour.

As for its voice, "the loud clarion of the braying ass," as Pope calls it, the donkey fares badly at poets' hands. And, indeed, I defy any one to hear a donkey fairly out and not to laugh at the cavernous melancholy of the animal's concluding notes. It commences with an ardour that has something of military enthusiasm in it, but suddenly, as if the memory of secret griefs had supervened, the voice drops from the full-breathed outcry that rings across the Bikaneer wastes, to a dolorous pumping up of hollow groans and husky sobs that had justified the venerable Philemon in his mirthful death far better than the sight of a donkey eating figs. But Philemon, poor dry old soul, was in his ninety-seventh year, and needed no great excuse for dying. Yet if I had to find some excuse myself for dying of laughter, when I was only three years off the century, I think I should have myself transported to some spot on the banks of holy Ganges where Hindoo washermen congregate, and there pleasantly demise while laughing at their donkeys braying.

> " To all the echoes south and north,
>   And east and west, the ass sent forth
>   A loud and piteous bray."

And again—

> " Once more the ass did lengthen out
>   More ruefully an endless shout,
>   The long, dry, see-saw of his horrid bray."

Wordsworth, like the other poets, here recognises the melancholy of the donkey's voice, but (like the others), afraid of making the animal natural, takes no notice of the unrivalled ludicrousness of the sounds it produces. When it frightened John Gilpin's horse, the ass "did sing most loud and clear," but this is the nearest approach to appreciation of this great jest of Nature that I know of in verse.

Not that even its voice is altogether ridiculous. "The braying of Silenus his ass" (*intempestivos edidit ore sonos*) "conduced much to the profligation of the giants."

> "So, when at Bathos earth's big offspring strove
> To scale the skies, and wage a war with Jove,
> Soon as the ass of old Silenus brayed,
> The trembling rebels in confusion fled." [1]

And though the "*auctor clamoris*" may be subsequently sacrificed, it is not from any depreciation of his resonant services, but rather in recognition of them. It finds honourable mention in Holy Writ, and in the Ass-mass of the monks, commemorative of the flight into Egypt—

> "Asinus egregius,
> Asinus dominorum,
> .   .   .   .
> Super dromedarios
> Velox Madianeos,"

there was a hee-haw refrain, the choir on one side taking the *hee*, and on the other the *haw*. Moreover, in the myths of many countries, and the fairy tales of nearly all, the donkey's voice plays sometimes a serious and important part.

> "Ah! those dreadful yells, what soul can hear
> That owns a carcase and not quake for fear?
> Demons produce them doubtless, brazen-clawed
> And fanged with brass, the demons are abroad." [2]

---

[1] Garth, "The Dispensary."   [2] Cowper, "Needless Alarms."

Its character in fable and folk-lore is not always that which the poets attribute to it. It has other traits than stupidity and credulity. For though it is outwitted and betrayed by the fox, it outwits the wolf, and kicks all its teeth down its throat. Though it absurdly proposes to chirp like a grasshopper, and undertakes the *rôle* of lap-dog, it philosophises very sagaciously on the fortunes of the war-horse.

> " The ass, whom Nature reason has denied,
> Content with instinct for his surer guide,
> Still follows that and wiselier does proceed ;
> He ne'er aspires with his harsh braying note
> The songsters of the wood to challenge out ;
> Nor, like this awkward smatterer in arts,
> Sets up himself for a vain ass of parts." [1]

The frogs, it is true, make fun of it, but the ass in turn flouts the mule. Under a mistaken sense of its own powers, it amiably proposes to serenade the beasts—Swift calls it "the nightingale of brutes"—and, with a self-respect that is not unbecoming, falls into the error of supposing that the homage paid to the image which it carries is intended for itself. But, on the other hand, it is always found sensibly selecting creature-comforts over mere vain-glory, and possessed of a considerable sense of humour. Till its glee overcame its discretion, the donkey in the lion's skin had a " high old time of it," as the Americans say, and kept all the beasts of the forest in a ridiculous stampede by its well-acted part ; and I can quite understand the long-eared one laughing prodigiously over the consternation and hubbub he was causing. Indeed, I am half inclined to think, with Bloomfield, that when the donkey played the part of the " Fakenham Ghost " he did so with full sense of the practical joke.

[1] Oldham, " Satires of Boileau Imitated."

Nor while mirthful itself has it failed to conduce to mirth in others, for, besides Philemon's disastrous cachination, we know that Chrisippus also fatally over-laughed himself on seeing an ass eat apples off a silver dish, and that Agelastus (Crassus of that ilk) only laughed once in all his life, and that was on seeing an ass eat thistles.

Butler, I may note, confounds these two catastrophes for the sake of his rhyme—

> " Or he that laughed until he choked his whistle
> To rally on an ass that ate a thistle."

The poets, however, have recognised only one aspect of the animal, namely, the familiar " cuddy," and, of its classical and historical honours, only two or three. " The blameless animal" of Balaam finds due reference ; but, so it seems to me, in order to point a personality or a jest. Thus Crashawe—

> " The ass of old had power to chide its wilful lord,
> And hast not thou the power to speak one word?
> Not less a marvel, sure, this silence is in thee,
> Than that the ass of old to speak had liberty." [1]

---

[1] Crashawe has the same idea again ; applied, however, to the ass that carried the infant Saviour into Egypt. He says to it—

> " Hath only anger an omnipotence
>   In eloquence ?
> Within the lips of love and joy doth dwell
>   No miracle ?
> Why else had Balaam's ass a tongue to chide
>   His master's pride.
> And thou (Heaven-burthened beast) hast ne'er a word
>   To praise thy Lord ?
> That he should find a tongue in vocal thunder
>   Was a great wonder ;
> But oh ! methinks 'tis a far greater one
>   That thou find'st none."

Marvel has—

> " We ought to be wary and bridle our tongue,
> Bold speaking hath done both man and beast wrong.
> When the ass so boldly rebukèd the prophet,
> Thou know'st what danger had like to come of it.
> Though the beast gave his master ne'er an ill word,
> Instead of cudgel Balaam wished for a sword."

As an occupant of the stable on the first Christmas Day, it commands deference. Faber curiously and pleasantly explains its patience thus—

> " For long the ass with silent shadowy head
> Gazed on the infant Saviour.
>
> .   .   .   .
>
> And for the ass
> To gaze on Him who saves both man and beast,
> Lifted his patient nature to a calm
> Transcending far the purposes of sleep."

Allan Ramsay has a donkey that is a very particular fool —" egregiously an ass," as Othello says; but Peter Bell's, on the other hand, is an unnatural monster of drivelling intelligence. Crabbe, however, strikes the just middle in his " Resentment "—

> " Close at the door where he was wont to dwell,
> There his sole friend, the ass, was standing by,
> Half dead himself to see his master die."

But there were many asses (besides those I have already referred to) of which the world has wide cognisance. The " Bricklebrit " donkey that wept sequins ; Ali Baba's drove ; the ass with the silver nose that hunted hares, and the little ass which the Queen bore and that itself married a queen ; the donkey-cabbages and the musician of Bremen —yet nowhere in folk-lore is it odious or even unlovable. But the poets have need of an animal that shall illustrate, as they think, an easy sneer, so when they do not use the owl they use the donkey.

Metaphors and images are therefore abundantly drawn from this animal. Every one, from Moore's Sovereign—

> " A royal ass, by grace divine
> And right of ears, most asinine,"

to Crabbe's Schoolboy, is pelted with the epithet.

" The man's a donkey—let him bray," suffices in Mackay to stand by itself as all-sufficient and not requiring explanation. Mankind in general belong to the species : says Cowper—

> " Man is the genuine offspring of revolt,
> Stubborn and sturdy, a wild ass's colt."

So do nations collectively and separately ; as in Byron—

> " The world is a bundle of hay,
>   Mankind are the asses who pull ;
> Each tugs it a different way,
>   And the greatest of all is John Bull."

Or as Oldham in his Satires, placing a donkey in London, asks—

> " What would he think on a Lord Mayor's Day
> Should he the pomp and pageantry survey,
> Or view the judges and their solemn train
> March with grave decency to kill a man?
> .   .   .   .
> What would he say, were he condemned to stand
> For one long hour in Fleet Street or the Strand ;
> To cast his eyes upon the motley throng,
> The two-legged herd, that daily pass along ?
> .   .   .   .
> If, after prospect of all this, the ass
> Should find the voice he had in Æsop's days,
> Then, doctor, then, casting his eyes around
> On human fools, which everywhere abound,
> Content with thistles, from all envy free,
> And shaking his grave head, no doubt he'd cry,
> Good faith ! man is a beast as much as we !"

Individual classes of persons are specifically asses. Thus, in Falconer, kings—

> " While fools adore and vassal lords obey,
>   Let the great monarch ass thro' Gotham bray ; "

and, in Barry Cornwall (I cross myself saying it), aldermen—

> " Oh ! the tradesman he is rich, sirs,
>   The farmer well to pass,
>   The soldier he's a lion,
>   The alderman's an ass ! "

Lovers—"the grave lover ever was an ass" (Johnson); sailors—"though he plays the ass on shore, he is lion of the sea" (Cook) ; and courtiers (Moore)—

> " Lord Harrowby, hoping that no one imputes
>   To the Court any fancy to persecute brutes,
>   Protests, on the word of himself and his cronies,
>   That had these said creatures been asses and ponies,
>   The Court would have started no sort of objection,
>   As Asses were there always sure of protection."

And, need I say it, *critics ;* as in King—

> " The twilight owl and serious ass
>   Would needs for modern critics pass."

Individual personages addressed by this title are "too numerous to mention," and, from Swift's Duke of Marlborough to Byron's Wordsworth, they are most of them not only ass, but partly also ape.

Summing up, then, the poets' donkeys, I find them a dull pack, for the poets as a rule seem to use the animal merely as the schoolboy does—as affording a ready epithet of abuse that comes within the comprehension of the meanest capacity—and to agree with Burns that the donkey's thick hide[1] was given it by a compassionate Providence as a pro-

---

[1] " Thou gavest the ass his hide, the snail his shell."—*To R. Graham.*

vision against pre-ordained cudgelling. But if any other view of the Ass be worth taking, I venture to think the poets should have been the first to find it out and to utilise it.

A P E S.

"Freakish monkey" (*Oldham*) ; "abhorred baboons" (*Montgomery*) ; "apes with hateful stare" (*Hood*).

The poets' apes—under which name I include (with due apologies to naturalists) the baboons and monkeys—are a deplorable creation. They are not "hateful" in the natural sense that the octopus or man-eating tigers or rattlesnakes might be, but they are unnaturally deformed into a despicable travesty of man at his worst and meanest. "A chattering, idle, airy kind," as Parnell calls them, is just criticism, and so is Shelley's "restless apes;" and so, too, Morris' "quick-chattering apes that yet in mockery of anxious men wrinkle their brows," for these are epithets from Nature ; but it is scarcely generous, I think, first of all to fancy a questionable resemblance between ourselves and monkeys, and then to abuse the monkey for all the vices and meannesses of the worst among us. The ape, they say, is the worst kind of a libel on a man—and an ape besides. Having reduced the human to its lowest, they call the monkey human and add "brute" besides ! The truth is, as the wise of all times have pointed out, man has a grudge against the Simian folk for being so like himself in body. Other animals, less amiable in themselves, are accepted with resignation, condoned with apologies, or treated with deference. But, as Congreve says—

> " Baboons and apes ridiculous we find,
> For what ? for ill-resembling human kind ;"

and poets find them worse than ridiculous : they find them
every whit as bad as men.   Says Goldsmith—

> " Of beasts it is confessed the ape
>   Comes nearest us in human shape ;
>   Like man, he imitates each fashion,
>   And malice is his ruling passion."

And yet, when the monkey itself suggests that it is a man,
parrots and foxes are deputed to laugh down its pretensions.
Says one of the species, in Barry Cornwall—

> " For a monkey is much on a par with man.
>   There's a difference——
> *Parrot.* Ho, ho ! I shall crack my sides.
> *Monkey.* Though few see't till we sit side by side.
>   On the one hand a man has a longer nose,
>   And struts in clean linen wherever he goes ;
>   But what has he like to the monkey's tail ?——
> *Parrot.* Ho ! ho ! ho ! ho !"

And again in Spenser's delightful " Mother Hubberd's
Tale," when the fox and ape rob the sleeping lion of his
sceptre, crown, and robe, and then fall to disputing as to
who should wear the regalia, the ape claims the preference
over its companion on the ground of its resemblance to
man.

> " Then too I am in person, in stature,
>   Most like a man, the lord of every creature."

But the fox flouts it—

> " Where you claim yourself for outward shape
>   Most like a man, man is not like an ape
>   In his chief parts, that is, in wit and spirit."

So in Æsop, when the ape, passing through a graveyard,
falls to deplorable weeping, its comrade, the donkey, asks
the reason for such immoderate melancholy, and at the
ape's reply that it always weeps thus when in the presence

of its "poor dead ancestors," the long-eared one laughs hugely.

This resemblance, however, being postulated, the poets run easily on to debit the ape and its cousins with every human weakness that is especially contemptible. They are "pert" and "vain" and "dapper" in a score of poets ; "coxcombs," "beaux," "lady-killers," in others. Now, every one of these epithets connotes a purely artificial character, and are all of them therefore inapplicable to the animal world.

It is the "monkey-beau," "the buffoon-ape "—

> " Long did the beau claim kindred with the ape,
> And shone a monkey of sublimer shape ;
> Skilful to flirt the hat, the cane, the glove,
> And wear the pert grimace of monkey-love ;
> Of words unmeaning poured a ceaseless flood,
> While ladies looked as if they understood ;
> So chats one monkey to his brother,
> Chatters as if he understood the other."—*Leyden.*

"The mimic apes" "that love to practise what they see."

Yet, except in these very restricted phases, the poets have seldom sought for metaphor or moral from these singularly suggestive animals. Young finds an analogy between the monkey grasping at the reflection in the glass and man striving to find happiness in riches—

> " As monkeys at a mirror stand amazed—
> They fail to find what they so plainly see ;
> Thus men in shining riches see the face
> Of happiness, nor know it is a shade,
> But gaze, and touch, and peep and peep again,
> And wish, and wonder it is absent still."

The ape epithet is applied as liberally and promiscuously as the asinine, and falls therefore on many of the same classes and individuals. Mankind generally are apes as

well as asses, and so are certain nations, notably Frenchmen
—"monkeys in action, parroquets in talk"—and so again
also certain classes of men and women, such as courtiers,
lovers, and (*horresco referens*) critics—

> " The critics hence may think themselves decreed
>   To jerk their wits and rail at all they read,
>   Foes to the tribe from which they trace their clan,
>   As monkeys draw their pedigree from man."
>   —*Fenton's Epistle.*

Nor does the alderman escape this time either, for,
though he is freely written down an ass, Somerville says—

> " A genius can't be forced, nor can
>   You make an ape an alderman."

Asses and apes in fact go together with much of the same
arbitrary association as the bat and the owl among the poets'
"birds."   Anything or anybody that the poet takes a fancy
to dislike for the moment is either ape or ass, or both.   To
such curious extremes is this sometimes carried that Ambition is both monkey and donkey.   Says Herbert, "the
higher the ape goes the more he shows his tail;"[1] and
again Young—

> " What Nature has denied fools will pursue,
>   As apes are ever walking upon two."

---

[1] Herbert forgets apes have no tails at all.   This loss of the caudal
ornament is accounted for by Spenser as follows : The ape and fox
having stolen the sleeping lion's crown and usurped his palace, mis-
govern so infamously that high Jove is incensed, wakes up the slumbering monarch, and tells him what has happened.   The lion returns
roaring to his palace, bursts in and captures the usurpers :—

> " The ape's long taile (which then he had) he quight
>   Cut off, and both eares pared of their height ;
>   Since which all apes but half their eares have left,
>   And of their tailes are utterly bereft."

While in Shenstone, ambition "pricks up asses' ears!' Again Rochester, in his attack upon Sir Car Scrope, makes the knight both ape and ass—

> " When in thy person we more clearly see
> That satire's of divine authority,
> For God made one on man when he made thee,
> To show there were some men, as there are apes,
> Framed for mere sport, who differ but in shapes :
> In thee are all these contradictions joined,
> That make an ass prodigious and refined."

Yet the monkey is not a fool—certainly not "a fool of the greatest size," as Christiana would say. In fables it is often the butt of other creatures, but it is its inquisitiveness as a rule that gets it into trouble, not its folly. The poets describe it as half an idiot, and with very bad intentions— "just skilled to know the right and choose the wrong"— but I have so often myself taken advantage in their wild forest state of their generous credulity and otherwise laudable thirst for knowledge, that I speak as an expert when I say that though I have harmlessly astonished them with trains of gunpowder and frightened a whole community out of all gravity by striping one of their number an agreeable vermilion, I never saw anything in their behaviour, sober or drunk, composed or alarmed, that led me to think them particularly foolish, as compared with men. Indeed, when undisturbed in mind the monkey has a philosophical gravity which attracts my admiration, although I confess the alternating fits of monkey frivolity and indecorum exasperate me.

> " Since Father Noah squeezed the grape
> And took to such behaving
> As would have shamed our grandsire ape
> Before the days of shaving." [1]

---

[1] Wendell Holmes.

If they would only sit still a little longer and look me fairly in the eyes, I should like to ask the monkey, baboon, or ape some questions of which the solutions interest me greatly.   Why are they always so sad-faced, when evidently the most content?   And where is "the missing link?"   Is it true that they speak among themselves in a *lingua franco* of their own, and that under the impulse of hidden panic they can articulate?

I remember once, in India, hearing at the Allahabad Club of a monkey which in a frenzy of terror had called out to its native attendant *by name*.   It had seen a cobra coming towards it, and distinctly articulated its master's servant's name—so, at any rate, more than one person vouched for.   Is then the tradition correct that monkeys refuse to talk lest they should be made to work?

> " Play at dummy like the monkeys
>   For fear mankind should make them flunkeys."

I should like, too, to ask them about the ape-faced men of Tartary and the Soko and the Pongo, Susumete and Engeena, and to get at the truth about Du Chaillu's gorillas. But as they are, the monkeys are impossible in conversation. They are too sudden, too unforeseen in their transformations from sense to ribaldry to be rational, too furtive in expression to be straightforward in reply, too fond of scratching neighbours to keep to the point.   What a curious community of fur this is, by the way!   I know nothing like it, except the unanimous scratching of Hindoo fakirs.

They seem to me sometimes to be the " fatal children " of the animal world, predestined to go wrong.   They do not, it is true, rise to the achievements of King Arthur, Sir Tristram of Bevis, or Olga the Dane, Telephos, Perseus or Œdipus, or any other of the famous "sons of sorrow," but they often arrive innocently like them at great catastrophes, their Kismet apparently leading them by the nose right up to, and over the precipice. At other times they seem deliberately affecting humanity, just as Bunyan had a craze to be thought a Jew; at others they convene in solemn assembly on purpose, so it seems, to burlesque us, for the whole Sanhedrim when assembled will gravely fall to, and search the fur of the smallest of the congregation; very much as Domitian would ceremoniously convene the Senate, and then ask them the best stuffing for a mullet.

As they exist in Nature—the sunny, merry, monkey-world of tree tops—the four-handed folk meet with hardly a reference. In his " Reign of Summer," Montgomery brings them into the dread presence of the jaguar—

> " The monkeys in grotesque amaze
> Down from their bending perches gaze ;
> But when he lifts his eye of fire,
> Quick to the topmost boughs retire."

And again in the "Pelican Island" we have a glimpse of wild life—

> " A monkey pilfering a parrot's nest,
> But ere he bore the precious spoil away
> Surprised behind by beaks and wings and claws
> That made him scamper gibbering."

And once more—

> " The small monkeys capering on the boughs
> And rioting on nectar and ambrosia,
> The produce of that paradise run wild ;
> No—these were merry if they were not wise."

But even Montgomery, with an unusual deviation from his characteristic sympathy with the animal world, breaks off suddenly into abuse of the monkey cousins, the baboons—

> " Man's untutored hordes were sour and sullen
> Like those abhorred baboons, whose gluttonous taste
> They followed safely in their choice of food,
> And whose brute semblance of humanity

> Made them more hideous than their prototypes
> That bore the genuine image and inscription,
> Defaced, indeed, but yet indelible."

This poetical reversion of the more orthodox theory of evolution is curious.

Rogers gives a passing line to "the marmoset," that

> " Dreams on his bough and plays the mimic still."

And Gay out of his fancy draws an excellent picture of the "bhunder-logue" on the Ganges—

> " Ah ! sir, you never saw the Ganges—
> There dwell the nations called Quidnunkies
> (So Monomotapa calls monkeys) ;
> On either bank, from bough to bough
> They meet and chat (as we may now) ;
> Whispers go round, they grin, they shrug,
> They bow, they snarl, they scratch, they hug,
> And just as chance or whim provokes them,
> They either bite their friends or stroke them."

But, as usual, this is only the introduction of spiteful analogy—

> " Thus have I seen some active prig
> To show his parts, bestride a twig ;
> L—d ! how the chattering tribe admire !
> Not that he's wiser, but he's higher ;
> All long to try the vent'rous thing
> (For pow'r is but to have one's swing) ;
>
> From side to side he springs, he spurns,
> And bangs his foes and friends by turns."

The tremendous honours of the tribe in the Egypt of the past, the India of to-day, receive no fuller recognition than in such lines as Oldham's—

> " In Egypt oft has seen the sot bow down
> And reverence some deified baboon."

Nothing more than this!—for these decayed divinities of an old-world worship, for the green monkey of Ethiopia that had a shrine in every temple in Memphis; for Thoth, the god of letters; the moon, the Bacchus of the Nile; for Pthah, the all-wise pigmy baboon that Hermopolis revered; for "the wise ones," the sacred monkeys and baboons of Hindostan; the ourangs, "the wise old men" of Malaya; for the creatures that the Sanskrit renders as the sun, the insignia of Arjuna, the dread son of Indra; for Sugrivas, prince of the baboons and Balin the snow-white ape; for the great "pluvial monkey"—delicious beast—that Gubernatis is so wise about; for the " Lords " of the Benares temples; for the lineal posterity of Hanuman himself! Was ever a more tremendous monkey, ape, or man, than the long-tailed friend of Rama? How magnificent his flight across Asia! The rivers in their courses turned, the trees on the hills tore themselves up by their roots, the mountains themselves swayed over, to follow in the fierce rush of the current made by his passage! And then, was ever tail greased, before or since, to such momentous purpose as when Hanuman let the Philistines of Ceylon grease his, thinking, poor dupes, that the strength would go out of him thereby: and then, rising Samson-like, he sets his own tail ablaze, and, rushing through the royal city of Lanka, fires it in every quarter, and from a neighbouring peak surveys, in the tranquil complacency of accomplished revenge, the prodigious conflagration!

VI.

SOME HARMLESS BEASTS.

IN proportion as beasts are harmless, and less useful therefore for comparison with the wickednesses and failings of men, the poets appear to find them uninteresting. Amiability among wild animals, unaccompanied by utility to man, would seem to be considered a deviation from poetical requirements which ought not to be encouraged. At any rate, to the lover of wild nature, the poets' treatment of the beasts appears to be a perpetual cynicism. But, inasmuch as many of the "harmless" animals—the elephant, beaver, deer, camel, bison, and so forth—contribute to the welfare of human beings, the poets' survey of them, though of a distant, half-hearted kind, is not unfriendly.

Thus, they compliment the elephant, "the huge earth-shaking beast" that hath "a serpent twixt his eyes," on its unusual sagacity and on employing it in the service of man, remember the beaver's fur in its favour, credit the camel with conveying merchandise across deserts with great patience, and do not overlook the claims of the bison upon the hunter who eats him. Others, again, like the rhinoceros and hippopotamus, do not, so far as the poets know, contribute directly to the comfort of humanity, nor do they attack man. They are addressed therefore not only without acrimony, but without sentiment of any kind. Each is a name for a very large beast which man by his superior intelligence and strength can always overcome when he chooses.

> " His arm can pluck the lion from his prey,
>   And hold the horned rhinoceros at bay."

A conspicuous exception to all the rest, however, is the poets' treatment of the deer. It is the dove among the beasts. And the hind and the fawn are the turtle-doves.

But it is evident to me, studying the poets among their animals, that very few indeed cared for any one of the beasts any further than it assisted them to a simile for something human. That this can be justified I easily allow; but at the same time it is a matter for fair surprise that *poets*, when the name of a wild beast suggested to them a mental picture of the actual thing in Nature, did not enrich their bald references with one or other of the many beautiful and picturesque images which are at once conjured up.

Had I been born a poet, I should never have tired, for instance, so it seems to me, of the elephant symbol—

> " The huge elephant, wisest of brutes !
>   O truly wise, with gentle might endowed,
>   Though powerful not destructive."

It is so comprehensive, so intelligent, so versatile. Elephants do most things that men do, and a great many besides that men cannot. Every one of them is a whole Cleopatra's-needle-full of hieroglyphics and significances. They knock down the walls of houses with their foreheads and pick up pins with their trunks. One elephant bumping against another knocks it over, yet elephants have been taught to dance on the tight-rope. It seems to have most of the virtues in ordinary times of an honest man ; at others it develops a depth of cunning malignity that all the Newgate calendar cannot match. However, this is not the poets' elephant.

> " Behold the castle-bearing elephant
>   That wants no bulk, nor doth his greatness want
>   An equal strength.   Behold his massy bones
>   Like bars of iron ; like congealed stones
>   His knotty sinews are ; him have I made,
>   And given him natural weapons for his aid.
>   High mountains bear his food, the shady boughs
>   His cover are, great rivers are his troughs,
>   Whose deep carouses would to standers-by
>   Seem at a watering to drain Jordan dry.
>   What skilful huntsman can with strength outdare him ?
>   Or with what engines can a man ensnare him ? "

So speaks Job Militant ; and after Quarles many poets refer to the "elephant endorsed with towers," the "castled elephant," the "towered elephant," and so forth, omitting to remember how those same swine which they so much reproach and ridicule once wrought havoc in the "embattled front of elephants proud-turreted."   The story is a simple one, and better perhaps in the original English.   Alexander, invading India, was told that elephants were terrified at pigs, and finding opposed to him a formidable array of "olyphauntes berynge castelles of trees on theyr bakkes and knyghtes in ye castelles for ye batayle," the great Emathian ordered up a drove of swine to the front of his army, and the "jarrynge of ye pygges" upset the olyphauntes altogether, for we read that they began "to fle eche one and keste down ye castelles and slewe ye knyghtes.   By this meane Alysaundre had ye vyctorie."

It is a creature of colossal bulk, yet it is the most gently docile of man's servants ; indeed, almost of creatures.

> " Calm amidst scenes of havoc, in his own
>   Huge strength impregnable, the elephant
>   Offended none ; but led his quiet life
>   Among his old contemporary trees."

Though of vast strength, it is curiously sensitive to small annoyances.   It detests the squeaking of mice.   Mosquitoes infuriate it. In the fable, the frog and the ant compel it to commit suicide out of sheer misery. Spenser's elephant, assailed by an ant, is one of the poet's types of the " World's Vanity "—

> " Soone after this I saw an elephant,
>   Adorned with bells and bosses gorgeouslie,
>   That on his backe did beare (as batteilant)
>   A gilden towre, which shone exceedinglie ;
>   That he himselfe, through foolish vanitie,
>   Both for his rich attire, and goodly forme,
>   Was puffed up with passing surquedrie,
>   And shortly gan all other beasts to scorne.
>   Till that a little ant, a silly worme,
>   Into his nostrils creeping, so him pained,
>   That, casting down his towres, he did deforme
>   Both borrowed pride, and native beautie stained.
>   Let, therefore, nought that great is therein glory,
>   Sith so small a thing his happines may varie."

But infinitely more admirable than its mammoth bulk (in itself no credit to it), or its strength, so often perverted to bad ends, is the character of the elephant's intelligence. It is almost human, not because it imitates, but because it draws rational deductions and acts upon them.

To give one illustration only, an original one. An elephant, when driven every day from the stables at Agra, found his passage inconvenienced by a post standing up in the path. To this post a monkey was chained, and the elephant and the monkey were good friends. But one day, on coming out as usual, Behemoth found Pug gone, and, concluding that the tiresome post was of no further use, wrenched it up and passed on comfortably. Now, so long as the monkey was chained to the post the elephant recognised its utility, and accepted without complaint the inconvenience it caused him. But as soon as the reason for the post ceased to be obvious he removed the obstruction.

This intelligence makes the giant a very valuable ally of man ; for once it recognises that its driver is a careful and trustworthy person, it abandons its natural timidity and develops an extraordinary sense of discipline. But if the driver is changed, the next man has to satisfy the elephant as to his moral character and personal reliability *ab initio.* Elephants take nothing on trust—except the pitfalls with which Thomson's Asiatics and Somerville's Africans "mine with cruel avarice his steps."

> " And now the treach'rous turf
> Trembling gives way, and the unwieldy beast,
> Self-sinking, drops into the gulf profound."

This splendid beast is one of the few indisputable relics of the epoch of giants, the last survivor of the mastodons and mammoths that the sons of Noah hunted. In Jean Ingelow's poem, the wife of " the world's great shipwright " has allowed the lads, our progenitors, to go out mammoth-hunting, and is anxious about them—

> " For they are young. Their slaves are few,
> The giant elephants be cunning folk ;
> They lie in ambush, and will draw men on
> To follow—then will turn and tread them down."

And I think, too, there is something very striking in the fact of the elephant being gregarious in death. They lay their bones in the vaults of their ancestors, and socially defer to the solemnity of the rites of sepulture.

In eastern warfare it is still to this day as conspicuous as when (in Somerville)—

> " High upon his throne,
> Borne on the back of his proud elephant,
> Sate the great chief of Timur's glorious race ;
> Sublime he sate amid the radiant blaze
> Of gems and gold ;"

for the elephant can carry loads over places impracticable

for wheels, but it is no longer the " castelle " whence warriors fight, though it carries the standards of princes in
front of their hosts, and is the rallying-point and centre for
the fiercest conflicts.

> " From the dread front of ancient war
> Less terror frowned ; her scythed car,
> Her castled elephant and batt'ring beam,
> Stoop to those engines which deny
> Superior terrors to the sky,
> And boast their clouds, their thunder, and their flame."

But of itself it takes no part in war, no longer

> " rages 'mid the mortal fray,
> Astonished at the madness of mankind."

In man's warfare against wild beasts it still, however,
retains all the importance of the olden time when the
Moguls went out against the striped terror of the jungles,
and

> " high upon his throne,'
> Borne on the back of his proud elephant,
> Sate the great chief of Timur's glorious race."

Of all animals it is the most majestic figure in Oriental
mythology. The gods loved the colossal brute, but by-
and-by, when Vishnu had warred with Indra, it became
an object of fear to the Celestials. Then came forth the
vulture-god to fight with the elephant. It is the Atlas of
Hindostan, an elephant standing at each corner of the earth
—what a noble image ! As the symbol of strength it was
among the honorific titles of the greatest emperors, and the
supreme significance in their architecture. As the emblem
of intelligence the gods of India wear its head. The stateliness of its walk gives the invariable simile of grace with
dignity to the poets of the East. In its gloomy bulk
mythology sees the steed of the pluvial god, the Rain-cloud.
So Keats nobly beheld it—

K

> " Up-piled
> The cloudy rack slow journeying in the west
> Like herded elephants."

The white elephant—curiously enough a " demoniacal " form of the animal in Vedic myth—meets with only humorous reference as a monstrous monstrosity, though the immense dignities of this beast from time immemorial should perhaps have invested it with a somewhat mysterious dignity. Morris, however, has " huge elephants, snow-white, with gilded tusks." " The elephant," or " the lord of elephants," is a distinction proudly assumed by many rajahs ; but " the white elephant," or " the lord of the white elephant," only by the premier prince of Hindostan or a sovereign. Then, too, that white elephant of Vedic myth who malignantly hunts the hermits up and down the hills of India, allowing them no leisure for meditation on their travels, who is the mortal enemy of Jatayus the bird-god, the adversary in eternal conflict of the tortoise and afterwards of Garuda, the eagle-deity, but whose ultimate ruin, as already foretold in legend, will be wrought by a sparrow—what a delightful personage he is !

Elephant sagacity is of course notorious—

> " The huge elephant, wisest of brutes !
> O truly wise, with gentle might endowed
> Though powerful."

"Take from the elephant instruction wise," says Cunningham ; "the wise and fearless elephant " (Shelley), and so on with many others. Its great age is hardly less widely accepted—

> " As though he drank from Indian floods
> Life in a renovating stream ;
> Ages o'er him have come and fled,
> 'Midst generations of the dead
> His bulk survives."

Thomson, Montgomery, and Drayton, all, curiously enough, like to think of it as coeval with the trees among which it lives—"its old contemporary trees." Equally familiar is the fiction of the elephant sleeping standing, in consequence of its having no joints in its legs—as thus, in Swift and Herbert—

> " For elephants ne'er bend the knee."

> " Most things sleep lying ; the elephant leans or stands."

Montgomery also has—

> " The palm which he was wont to make
> His prop in slumber."

Another agreeable fiction is the hereditary feud which the elephant maintains against its neighbour the rhinoceros. Says Adam (in Cowper)—

> " Behold that dusky beast
> That with white tusks of an enormous size extends its weighty jaw ;
> That now forgetting to revere the moon,
> Intractable, ferocious, beyond its native temper,
> Rushes in anger with its fibrous trunk that serves it for a nose,
> Against the horn which the rhinoceros sharpens of hardest stone."

Was ever greater nonsense given to the world before as poetry ? Cowper knew something about hares' rumps, but nothing about rhinoceros' horns or elephants' noses. And imagine Adam, who was a thorough naturalist not only by inspiration but personal observation, talking in such slipshod manner about a beast he knew so well—presuming it to have existed. And the suspicion of plagiarism is added to the absurdity by reading in Glover how—

> " In the wastes of India, while the earth
> Beneath him groans, the elephant is seen
> His huge proboscis writhing, to defy
> The strong rhinoceros, whose pond'rous horn
> Is newly whetted on a rock." [1]

---

[1] Pliny says, on an agate, hence this frequent error.

It was evidently a moot point with the poets whether the elephant or the rhinoceros were the better in open lists. As a rule, they are merely seen (as in Glover's poem) at the opening of the duel—

> " Anon each hideous bulk encounters.
> *   *   *   Earth her groan
> Redoubles.   Trembling from their coverts fly
> The savage inmates of surrounding woods,
> In distant terror."

Dryden, however, decides against the rhinoceros (the female), calling the elephant "her unequal foe ;" and so does Lovelace, who makes it die "under his castle-enemy." Cowper, on the other hand, and Darwin, make the rhinoceros the better of the two.

> " Go, stately lion, go ! and thou with scales impenetrable armed,
> Rhinoceros, whose pride can strike to earth the unconquered elephant."

Their tone is generally very respectful to the rhinoceros— "the horned rhinoceros," "the armed rhinoceros," "the mailed rhinoceros that of nothing recks ;"—but what does Johnson mean by saying, " He speaks to men with a rhinoceros nose " ("which he thinks great"); or Moore by "rhinoceros' ivory ? "

Yet the rhinoceros in its simple, secluded, harmless life might have afforded an occasional illustration of strength not abused, of a dignified retirement, of magnificent solitude.   The ponderous hermit slowly crashing its way through the cane-brakes is a striking figure, and I like to think of it—the solitary rhinoceros, tranquilly wading along the river's edge, with no companions larger than the otter that watches it from mid-stream, the little reed-birds swinging on the flags, and the small white egrets catching the frogs which the giant's progress startles out from the ooze.

Hippopotamus is not an accommodating word for a verse,

and when it is referred to it is as "Behemoth," or "river-horse." It then becomes "Job's beast," "scaled," and "spouting," and, therefore, more or less fabulous or more or less mixed up with crocodiles and whales. Montgomery, however, gallantly takes the whole name into a line, and for his isolated courage, in spite of his absurd misrepresentation of the comfortably-browsing pachyderm, deserves quotation—

> " The hippopotamus amidst the flood,
> Flexile and active as the smallest swimmer,
> But on the bank ill-balanced and infirm ;
> He grazed the herbage with huge head declined,
> Or leaned to rest against some ancient tree."

But I confess that the river-horse has less significance than many animals. There is much, of course, that is pleasant enough in the manner of its life—its lazy lounging existence in warm streams, its circumstances of perpetual plenty, its innocent pastimes when undisturbed, its helpless ferocity when attacked. But, except as living a slothful and apparently useless life under conditions of unalloyed hippopotamus-happiness, as a symbol for pure, feral enjoyment in its utmost expression, this monstrous grotesqueness—as if from some "great chronicle of Pantagruel"—this familiar of old Nile in his cradle, has little significance.

As Behemoth it is a delightful fiction, but in its actual carnal bulk it is only a hippopotamus. The Rabbins said that there were never more than two Behemoths at a time in the world. They inferred this from the compassionate goodness of the Almighty. For if there were to be more than two at a time, they doubted if the whole earth could provide them sufficient sustenance. It is a pity in one way that the day of beliefs in unique existences is past; for what zest it would have lent to travel and sport if there had been a possibility of meeting with *the* pair of hippopotami, *the* phœnix, or the one and only unicorn !

Nor does Montgomery hesitate at the giraffe (though he has to make the second syllable short[1]). But the very few others who refer to the animal prefer to call it "the camelopard." Hood has a sportive ode to the "great anticlimax" as he calls the animal, "so very lofty in its front, but so dwindling at the tail;" but he does not exhaust, or even tap, the potentialities of fun which the giraffe suggests : "For this sky-raking animal, that passes all its life, so to speak, looking out of a fourth-storey window, that looks down into the birds' nests as it browses, and seldom sees the ground except when it lies down on it, is about the best instalment of the impossible that has been vouchsafed to us."[2]

With the camel, one of the most provoking, discontented animals in the world, the poets express a very pleasing sympathy; and Byron in his phrase, "the patient swiftness of the desert ship," sums up compendiously three of the reasons for the poets' tenderness; while, if we add Thomson's "patient of thirst and toil, son of the desert," we have them all four. Its extreme patience and extraordinary swiftness are two proverbial, and erroneous, attributes of "the bunchback camel"—as Quarles (adopting Isaiah's epithet) calls it —while the voyaging of the "helmless dromedary" (Byron) over the sandy oceans of the desert and its supposed independence of wells naturally commend it to poetical fancy.

But here is the camel to the life, in Jean Ingelow—

> " The Red Sahara in an angry glow
>   With amber fogs, across its hollows trailed
> Long strings of camels, gloomy eyed and slow,
>   And women on their necks, from gazers veiled,
> And sun-swart guides who toil across the sand
> To groves of date-trees on the watered land."

---

[1] " From rude Caffraria where the giraffes browse
With stately heads among the forest boughs."—*West Indies.*

[2] " Noah's Ark."—*Phil Robinson.*

Here and there besides are pleasant touches of camel life —and what a poem the beast really is !—"the tinkling throng of laden camels," "the browsing camels' tinkling bells "—

> " 'Neath palm trees' shade
> Amid their camels laid
> The pastoral tribes with all their flocks at rest."

But, as a rule, the poets' attention is unfortunately turned to those aspects of the camel which are now known to be fictions. Leyden matches it against "the swiftest courser," and Heber and Sir William Jones, both of whom should have known better, compare the camel with the ostrich for speed—"the camels bounded o'er the flowery lawn like the swift ostrich "—and make it even excel it—"not the ostrich speed of fire my camel can excel." As a matter of fact, and in spite of its having carried Mahomet in four jumps from Jerusalem to Mecca, seven miles an hour is the camel's best pace, nor can it maintain this rate over three hours. Its usual speed is about five miles an hour—a slow, lounging pace beyond which it is dangerous, with nine camels out of ten, to urge them, or else, as Asiatics say, they "break their hearts" and die on the spot. For, once a camel has been pressed beyond this speed and is spent, it kneels down, and not all the wolves of Asia will make it budge again. The camel remains where it kneels, and where it kneels it dies.

And this stubbornness is really what the poets call "patience." An Oriental proverb says that "the camel curses its parents when it has to go up hill, and its Maker, when it has to go down," and "camelishness" is a term of abuse for one who is obstinate past all reasoning. As a matter of fact the camel is one of the most impatient brutes in existence ; it will remain motionless as long as you permit it to do so, or till hunger arouses it. But remaining

motionless is just what camels like. Once begin to load
them, and the camel grumbles and roars as if its vitals were
being wrenched out. "So habitual is this conduct that if
a kneeling camel be only approached, and a stone as large
as a walnut laid on its back, it begins to remonstrate, groan-
ing as if it were being crushed to the earth with its load." [1]
"We have all been to Egypt or Syria, and many of us have
been bitten by his long front teeth, trampled over by his
noiseless feet, deafened by his angry roar, and insulted by
the affected, not to say sanctimonious, *tournure* of his head
and neck and the protrusion of his contemptuous upper
lip. No one who thus knows him at home retains a spark
of belief in the beast's patience, amiability, fidelity, or any
other virtue. The camel must be reckoned among the
lost illusions of youth !" [2]

Urge it to get up on to its legs, and it remonstrates voci-
ferously ; but once get it going, with the string through its
nose tied to the tail of the camel in front of it, and it will
keep on going just as long as the one in front of it keeps
on pulling its nose. But the moment one camel in a line
stops, they all stop. There is " patience " of course in this
perpetual plodding, but, so far from being admirable, it
used to exasperate the British soldier, both in Afghanistan
and Egypt, into the most ludicrous paroxysms of indignation. The brutes moved like machines, at a regulated rate
of motion, and not one step would they take faster than
another. To the bewilderment of Tommy Atkins, they
paid no attention whatever to sticks ; but suddenly, as if it
had made up its mind that life was not worth more trouble,
a camel would come down on its knees with a thump—
and there remain. The gap would be made good, the file
pass on, and the sulking camel be left where it had knelt,
with its head upheld superciliously in the air and gazing

<hr>

[1] " Bible Animals," Rev. J. G. Wood.
[2] " False Beasts and True."

vacantly into distant space. And there it would patiently starve to death. It was no use taking off its load ; the camel had refused to "hold the fort" any longer, and, persisting in thinking life impossible, insisted on dying.

Nor, unfortunately for poetry, does the camel's abstinence from water hold quite good in fact. It is one of the thirstiest of animals, and ought not to be allowed to go without water for any length of time, if it is expected to be of any use. In this respect a horse has more endurance. But Nature has provided the camel with an arrangement of cells in the stomach which it can fill with water if it pleases.

> " Unwearied as the camel, day by day,
>   Tracks through unwatered wilds his doleful way,
>   Yet in his breast the cherished draught retains,
>   To cool the fervid current in his veins."

But if Montgomery had often ridden camels, he would have wondered why the brute did not drink some of the cherished draught sometimes, instead of wanting to replenish itself at every possible opportunity.

> " The all-enduring camel, driven
>   Far from the diamond fountain by the palms,
>   Who toils across the middle moonlit nights,
>   Or when the white heats of the blinding noons
>   Beat from the concave sand, yet in him keeps
>   A draught of that sweet fountain that he loves,
>   To stay his feet from failing, and his spirit
>   From bitterness of death."

Keats carries the idea one stage further, and has "slake my greedy thirst with nectarous camel-draughts "—an admissible prolongation of the original, inasmuch as it conveys to the mind an immediate consciousness of the extreme aridity of deserts—"long. long deserts scorch the camel's foot "—and the terrible drought from which the camel has so often, poor beast, to suffer.

> " Even the camel feels,
> Shot through his withered heart, the fiery blast."

But it will hardly be believed that the " ship of the desert " takes an immoral advantage of this kindly arrangement to enjoy the deplorable pleasures of illicit tippling.   Yet such is said to be the sad fact, for the date juice (so it is stated) sometimes finds its way into these water cavities, lies there, and ferments ; so that while every one is admiring the camel as such a prodigious teetotaller, the Bedouin quadruped has really got a spirit-cask inside it instead of a water-butt.

In spite, however, of this grievous falling away from Islam, the camel receives extraordinary honour from the Faithful. Are not the names of Al Kaswa and Al Adha, the camels of Mahomet, as sacred to the Arab as those of any of the nine wives of the Prophet?   And has not Mahomet promised the camel all the enjoyments of Paradise—which no other animals share with it except Al Borak, the Prophet's horse, and Ketura, the Dog of the Seven Sleepers, Tobit's dog, Balaam's ass, and the cuckoo?   When it carries the sacred cloth to Mecca in the annual pageant-pilgrimage of Al Sherif, what man in all the caravan has such honour of Islam as the camel that bears the musnud?   Had it not been for a camel would Zem-Zem ever have been found, and without Zem-Zem would man have ever attained to Paradise?

One poet speaks of its " ear attentive," though the camel's ear is certainly not a " feature " of the animal.   Its hearing is dull—though it is not so deaf but that it stops when it hears no voices—and the ears themselves are so small that the Arabs have a legend to account for it.   Once, they say, it had long ears and asked Allah for horns to match them, but Allah in reply cropped its ears.

Spenser has Avarice riding on a camel, and elsewhere speaks of it as "simple" and the victim of carnivorous ferocity, the tiger and—the boar !

This idea is of course borrowed from fable, in which the camel often falls a victim to the superior astuteness of the boar, wolf, fox, and other animals.

As a remote kind of beast that does not concern the poets, the bison, or buffalo, finds little recognition. Jean Ingelow is a very notable exception, and uses the headlong herd very finely on two occasions—

> " Raging up like doom
> The dangerous dust-cloud that was full of eyes—
> The bisons ; "

and again—

> " The mad
> Masterful tramping of the bison herds
> Tearing down headlong, with their bloodshot eyes
> In savage rifts of hair."

Byron pays it the compliment of "stately," and describes it tossing about, as it were a mere pastime, the pack of wolves that have attacked it. And here and there we meet with the casual bison careering ; while Leyden has a Scotch bison not known to these degenerate days, "whose bounding course outstripped the red deer's speed," who shook a "yellow lion-mane" and "tossed his moony horns around." This beast appears to have been slain in mad charge by "the chief from whom their line the Turnbulls drew," and it left, unfortunately, no posterity.

> " Bold was the chief from whom their line they drew,
> Whose nervous arm the furious bison slew.
> The bison, fiercest race of Scotia's breed,
> Whose bounding course outstripped the red deer's speed.
> By hunters chafed, encircled on the plain,
> He, fuming, shook his yellow lion-mane,
> Spurned, with black hoof, in bursting rage, the ground,
> And fiercely tossed his moony horns around.
> On Scotia's lord he rushed, with lightning speed
> Bent his strong neck, to toss the startled steed.

> His arms robust the hardy hunter flung,
> And rolled the panting monster on the ground.
> Crushed, with enormous strength, his bony skull;
> And courtiers hailed the man who turned the bull."

But, as a rule, it is the American bison of which the poets treat—not the reem,[1] the extinct Urus, of which the Bible speaks, and which (according to legend) had to be towed behind the Ark, as its horns would not allow it to get in by the door.   Asks Young in his paraphrase—

> " Will the tall reem which knows no lord but me
> Low at the crib and ask an alms of thee?
> Submit his unworn shoulder to the yoke,
> Break the stiff clod, and o'er thy furrow smoke?"

Not the magnificent gaur of Asia, that the natives say takes up stones with its nostrils and discharges them at its assailants with the force of a musket-ball !—nor the great Arna of the wondrous horns that ramps at large in the swampy jheels of Bhutan, charges the elephant whenever it meets it, and lords it over the dense marshy thickets bristling with canes and wild rose, nor its African congener of equally terrible armament, but the animal that the Red Indian knows so well, and with which his whole life was at one time bound up: the bison that has been called the true pioneer of Western America, and, once "spread o'er the vast savannah, ranged masterless" is now being fast exterminated by the amazing progress of the New World—

> " In these plains
> The bison feeds no more.   Twice twenty leagues
> Beyond remotest smoke of hunters' camp,
> Roams the majestic brute in herds that shake
> The earth."

But the bison is an animal of extraordinary picturesque-

[1] Mentioned by Drayton and Young.

ness, and round it gather centuries of the history of the nations of the red men.

Kangaroos are not poetical beasts in the poets' sense, and except, therefore, when they are made fun of, as in Hood's verses, receive no attention—

> " A pair of married kangaroos
>   (The case is oft a human one too)
> Were greatly puzzled once to choose
>   A trade to put their eldest son to.
> It came—no thought was ever brighter—
>   In weighing every why and whether
> They jumped upon it both together,
>   Let's make the imp a shorthand writer."

Lovelace refers to them vaguely as "cubs of India," and, addressing the snail, says that, like them—

> " Thou from thyself a while dost play,
>   But, frighted by a dog or gun,
>   In thine own belly thou dost run ; "

which is a delightful confusion of epitaphs.

Some score of allusions to the beaver are to be found in the poets, but they present nothing of interest. As a " furry nation " and " fur-bearing," also as supposed to furnish a perfume, they are benignly treated, for conducing to the best of their small abilities to the welfare of lordly humanity. But, so far as the poets are concerned, they are things of prodigious solitude " where earth's unliving silence all would seem, save where on rocks the beaver built his dome "—a passage characteristic of blundering Campbell —and the comrade in Mackay's " Arctic Regions " of " the white wolf that howls to the moon." Dyer, too, has some delightful nonsense about it.

In Darwin, however, it is the " half-reasoning " beaver, and Drayton preserves the following very interesting fact of British natural history in his quaint rhyme—

> " More famous long agone, than for the salmons leape,
>   For bevers Tivy was,[1] in her strong banks that bred
>   What else no other brooke of Britaine nourished ;
>   Where nature, in the shape of this now-perisht beast,
>   His propertie did seeme t' have woundrouslie exprest ;
>   Being bodied like a boat, with such a mightie taile,
>   As serv'd him for a bridge, a helme, or for a saile."

Several poets give the ermine a place.

> " I will disdain, and from your proffers fly,
>   As from vile dirt the snowy ermine."

Cowper here refers to a pretty fiction, still current, I find, about this little creature, to the effect that it detests contact with any impurity.

There are some ants, which Sir John Lubbock knows all about, that hate untidiness and "messes" so much, that if you throw rubbish over their nests they all decamp precipitately.   They absolutely refuse to live in a parish where sanitation is not properly attended to.   But the ermine carries its aversion even further than this, for it prefers death to dirt.

> " Better to die than be sullied."

This was the motto on the ermine-device borne by kings of Naples and of Castille.   There was also a Breton "Order of the Ermine," with the same legend, and the device was adopted by "La Reine Duchesse," Anne of Brittany, wife of Charles VIII., and afterwards of Louis XII.   These words, "*Plutôt mourir que souiller*," or "*Malo mori quam fœdari*," in the original, allude to the fancy that if an ermine be encircled with mud it will fastidiously prefer capture to crossing the dirty barrier.   "It is of so pure a nature that it will choose rather to be taken than defile its skin."   Trappers, therefore, were supposed to take advantage of this suicidal cleanliness, and build walls of dirt round the ermines, and so catch them ; but, it might well be added,

---

[1] " Inter fluvios Cambriæ . . . solus hic [Teivi] castores habet."

"the wiser and older hunters preferred putting salt on the ermines' tails."

However, the superstition greatly enhanced this dainty little animal's unsullied reputation. Thus Marvel makes the small exquisite one of the creatures of Paradise—

> " In fair Elysium to endure,
>   With milk-white lambs and ermines pure ; "

while in the present world it has been selected as the most befitting emblem of sovereignty—

> " Whose honour, ermine-like, can never suffer
>   Spot or black soil."

So the robes of royal and noble personages are lined with this fur, "to signify," says the author of " Historic Devices," "the internal purity that should regulate their conduct."

At one time it was the only fur represented on coats of-arms, and was the natural white, with black tail-points—

> " Tipped with jet,
> Fair ermines, spotless as the snows they press. '

But afterwards, like every other object in Nature, it wandered into varieties—"counter-ermine," which was black, with white tail-tips ; "erminois," gold, with black points ; and "erminite," white, with black points edged with red.

A special interest attaches to the whimsical exaltation of this elegant creature, as the ermine is really—under a climatic variation of fur—only the *stoat*, which is as guileful, stealthy, and wicked a little assassin as ever ran on four legs.

Yet, we ask, "What's in a name?"

Just as the hedgehog is reproached for having " thorns " on its back, so the porcupine for wearing quills. Its mythical power of shooting its quills at assailants is accepted. Thus " like porcupine she sends a piercing dart " (Jenyns), and " more dangerous than porcupine his quill " (Somerville).

" Fretful " is an excellent epithet for the porcupine.   Yet
I cannot help thinking that in the Ghost's speech "fretted"
would perhaps have been better.   For though it is perfectly
true that the former characterises the animal's disposition to
take offence quickly, the latter would have assisted out the
spectre's meaning.   " Each particular hair on your head,"
he would then have said, "would stand on end with horror,
like the quills upon the porcupine when he is out of temper."
As it is, he seems to imply that the animal's quills are always
standing on end—which is not strictly true.   Now Milton
has the line, " Chafed wild boar or ruffled porcupine;"
and "ruffled" is admirable, inasmuch as it conveys two
facts in one word—the agitation both of body and mind.

The occurrence of this beast in another poet, also con-
joined with the boar, is perhaps noteworthy, as in myth
the porcupine is a vague sort of animal, occupying a place
somewhere between the boar and the hedgehog.   In the
" Dragon of Wantley " we have the other association presented to us—its hedgehog side—

> " Had you but seen him in this dress,
> How fierce he looked and how big,
> You would have thought him for to be
> Some Egyptian porcupig.
> He frighted all, cats, dogs, and all,
> Each cow, each horse, and each hog ;
> For fear they did flee, for they took him to be
> Some strange outlandish hedgehog."

Yet the poets—three at any rate—employ the metaphor in
regard to woman.   Thus Cowley, singing of Beauty, says—

> " They are all weapons, and they dart
> Like porcupines from every part."

And Byron has—

> " Those cursèd pins,
> Which surely were invented for our sins,
> Making a woman like a porcupine,
> Not to be rashly touched."

Qui s'y frotte s'y pique was the legend on Charles the Bold's device of a porcupine. Another heraldic whim about this animal, and one that might have attracted the poets, is the Colonna's motto of *Decus et tutamen in armis*, wherein is contained a wholesome moral both for individuals and nations, and a practical fact, of which the porcupine is most thoroughly well aware.

The reference in Cowley's lines, quoted above, to the "darting," is an allusion, of course, to the fiction—a very ancient one—that the porcupine can shoot its quills like arrows. When the animal charges an enemy—which it does *backwards*, by the way—it often, no doubt, leaves a quill or two sticking. Also, when the skin is contracted for the erection of the quills, a loose one may, no doubt, sometimes fall out; and seeing how sudden and violent the muscular action is, it is not inconceivable that such a loosened quill might seem to be "shot" off. But there is no capacity for deliberate archery in the beast. It is not so deficient in sagacity as to fire its weapons away.

I find in Mrs. Bury Palliser's fascinating volume the following passage :—

"In 1397, Louis, Duke of Orleans, instituted the Order of the Porcupine, and on the occasion of the baptism of his son Charles he took this animal as his emblem, with the motto ' Near and Afar,' alluding to the vulgar error that the porcupine is able not only to defend itself from close attack, but can throw its quills against more distant assailants, Duke Louis meaning thereby to convey that he would defend himself with his own weapons, and that he would attack his enemy, John, Duke of Burgundy, as well at a distance as near. Louis XII. abolished the Order after his ascension to the throne, but retained the hereditary badge of his family, and took two porcupines for the supporters of his arms. His cannons were marked with the porcupine, and his golden ' écus au porc-epic ' were much sought after by the curious." To this is added a note: "On the submission of Paris, in 1436, the Constable, Richemont, goes to dine at the Duke of Orleans' Hotel du Porc-epic, and in 1438 the Order was conferred on a lady, Mdlle. de Murat."

From the French name, of course, comes our own word, porcupig.

There are few passages in Nature more beautiful throughout than the deer poem. Whether we see them as the "playmate fawns," the "gentle hinds," or the "noble stag," they are equally poetical and lovable. No wonder, then, that so exquisite a theme attracts poets.

Every period of life, indeed almost every action, of these dainty creatures affords a beauty to their verse, and the appreciation of the surpassing charm of deer as they really are in nature seems to have so completely contented the poets, that they pay little attention to the legendary animal, do not care to seek for metaphors or similes from them, and do not venture to let improving imagination meddle with a picture already so complete.

No epithet or phrase that conveys a compliment seems misapplied to creatures that can never be ungraceful or unpicturesque. The light-stepping deer, the rustling deer in the thickets, the tread of the fawn, the hind's soft eyes of love—even the most commonplace phrases, if the word "deer" occur in them—receive a gentle grace from the association.

The dainty and delicate fawn, confiding and yet so timid, is indeed one of the sweetest touches of Nature, and the poets take a delight in leading it out to play upon lawns begemmed with dewdrops, to drink at babbling brooks, and fall asleep in beds of fern and moss. Nor less the hind with its large soft eyes, the gentle, careful mother of "the dappled fawn." It is perpetually recurring as an image of tranquil innocence.

Very often, of course, it is hunted, or its fawn killed, and

the grief of the hind then ranks with the poets only second
to that of the "turtle-dove" when similarly afflicted. But
no amount of sympathy seems excessive for the loss of
such offspring by such a parent.

In all circumstances of life, therefore, the deer is picturesque, whether "crushing the heath-bells as they tread"
the mountain side, or in the hollows, "belling from ferny
bed" (Faber). The poet—

> "Sunk deep in fern marks the stealthy roe,
> Silent as sleep or shadow, cross the glade,
> Or dart athwart his view as August stars
> Shoot and are out."

At rest, when "the summer sun shines on the trees, and
the deer lie in the shade" (Mary Howitt) ; or when, " in
summer's moonlight, the gentle deer lie sleeping ; "

> "The gentle deer lie sleeping in the moon,
> With their own fairy shadows at their side" (Faber) ;

or (Grahame) "in ruminating peace, the fallow deer, a
grove of antlers."

In the daytime, under the elms, " in herds, the troubled
deer shake the still-twinkling tail and glancing ear" (Wordsworth), or "couched on the close sward, while ears and
antlers in the grass with restless movement twinkle"
(Faber). So Bloomfield has "with rattling horns and
twinkling ears."

The solitary stag quenching his thirst at noon ; the hind
leading her fawn in the evening to the stream ; the whole
herd pacing out from the tree-shadows to drink ; the stag,
starting to run, " proudly tossing his antlered head."

Cowper's quiet park, "haunt of deer, and sheep-walks
populous with bleating lambs ; " Mackay's "nooks where
the shy deer browse the bent;" Thomson's forest glade
where the wild deer trip and, often turning, gaze ; Campbell's birchen glades, with the deer "glancing in the sun-

shine." Its grace when first aroused, its haughty flight, its courage when it stands "with hornie bayonnettes at bay"—

> "The chase is up—but they shall know
> The stag at bay's a desperate foe"—

are all insisted upon again and again, and the wood-nymphs and the fairies are for ever being called in to help the hunted favourite.

Its horns—"the stag's large front," as Thomson curiously calls it, or as Denham, with more enthusiasm—

> "On whose sublime and shady front is reared
> Nature's great masterpiece"—

give the stag that unusual stateliness of gait which is familiar to all, and which the poets are never tired of admiring. "Stately as a deer with antlers" is Longfellow's simile for surpassing dignity of bearing. They note its growth and renewal, always introduce the antlers in the foremost passage of the description; and on this point the deer's supposed regret at having so "heavy a head" when hunted, they give fancy play.

Shedding its horns, or, as Surrey says, "hanging his old head on the pale"—unantlered; "flying to the wood to hide his armless head" (Marvell)—rehorned, "gracefully pacing, the wild-eyed harts, to their traditional tree, to clear the velvet from their budded horns" (Jean Ingelow) —we meet it in every stage.

Nor do the poets fail to do full justice to that striking episode of the deer's closing life, its retirement into solitude to die—"as the stricken deer withdraws himself alone"—"so the struck deer in some sequestered part lies down to die" —"I was a stricken deer that left the herd, long since" (Cowper).

> "So wings the wounded deer her flight,
> Pierced by some ambushed archer of the night,

> Shoots to the woodlands with her bounding fawn,
> And drops of blood bedew the conscious lawn ;
> There hid in shades she shuns the cheerful day,
> Hangs o'er her young and weeps her life away." [1]—*Darwin.*

Nor are the poets unaware of the real reason for this retirement—namely, the instinct of the herd to drive away from their company any individual that is crippled or infirm, as being a source of common danger. The limping comrade might bring the huntsman on its heels, upon the whole herd at rest, and the forester coming upon a sick deer would know that the rest of the antlers were not far off.

This selfishness is carried to a cruel extreme when deer, seeing one of their number in distress, refuse him asylum ; and the habit of the herd to repulse a member when in danger is noted by Leyden and by Thomson—"the watchful herd alarmed, with selfish care avoid a brother's woe." Scott, too, refers to it in—

> "The Douglas like a stricken deer
> Disowned by every noble peer."

Somerville also has of the hunted stag—

> "He mingles with the herd where once he reigned
> Proud monarch of the groves, whose clashing beam
> His rivals awed, and whose exalted power
> Was still rewarded with successful love.
> But the base herd have learned the ways of men—
> Averse they fly, or with rebellious aim
> Chase him from thence."

---

[1] Pope has—

> "So the struck deer, in some sequestered part,
> Lies down to die (the arrow in his heart) :
> There, hid in shades and wasting day by day,
> Inly he bleeds and pants his soul away."

Another peculiarity of the deer kind, their often fatal curiosity, finds very frequent notice; as Spenser's "amazed deere;" Greene's "deer that doat the gaze, mazed dismayfully;" Shakespeare's "poor, frightened deer that stand at gaze;" Broome's "tim'rous deer, swift starting as they graze, bound off in crowds, then turn again to gaze;" Rogers' "with fearful gaze;" Quarles' "with strange amaze, and senseless half, through feare they stand at gaze," and a score of others.

One result of this tenderness for the deer is that deer-hunting seldom meets with admiration from the poets. With the fox it is very different. Having condemned Reynard beforehand, they see no cruelty in the pack of hounds that murder the brave little beast, but applaud the hunters as if they had overtaken and slain some desperate bandit. The crimes of the fox are supposed to have earned its death, so it dies unpitied.

> "Not so the stately stag, of harmless force,
> In motion graceful, rapid in his course;
> Nature in vain his lofty head adorns
> With formidable groves of pointed thorns.
> Soon as the hounds' fierce clamour strikes his ear,
> He throws his arms behind, and owns his fear;
> Sweeps o'er the imprinted grass, the wind outflies—
> Hounds, horses, hunters, horns, still sound along the skies.
> He, trembling, safety seeks in every place,
> Drives through the thicket, scales the lofty steep;
> Bounds o'er the hills, or darts through valleys deep;
> Plunges amid the river's cooling tides,
> While strong and quick he heaves his panting sides.
> He from afar his loved companions sees,
> Whom the loud whoop that hurtles on the breeze
> Into a crowded phalanx firm had cast,
> Their armèd heads all outward round them placed.
> To these he flies, and begs to be allowed
> To share the danger with his kindred crowd;
> But must, by general voice excluded, know
> How loathed the sad society of woe.

> The cruel hounds pour round on every hand;
> Desperate, he turns to make a feeble stand,
> Big tears on tears roll down his harmless face;
> He falls, and sues in vain, alas! for grace."

Thomson's imitation of this poem is well worth noting. It differs from Leyden's admirable lines chiefly by its errors and its lack of force. But he repeats all Leyden's sympathy for the stag.

Drayton, after a passing word of wonder that no poets before himself should have sung the chase,[1] invokes Diana, and commences to tell in rhyme of the hunting in Arden Forest.

But Drayton, though fired by the sport of the chase, keeps his sympathy with the stag. The hunters are "bloody hunters," and the hounds are "cruel and ravenous." Quarles tells us how the stag's "weeping eyes beg silent mercy from the following hounds," and from the chase draws this vigorous metaphor—"Before a pack of deep-mouthed lusts I flee."

Grahame, in his "October," has—

> " The clamorous pack rush rapid down the vale,
>   Whilst o'er yon brushwood tops at times are seen
> The moving branches of the victim stag.
> Soon far beyond he stretches o'er the plain;
> Oh! may he safe elude the savage rout,
> And may the woods be left to peace again!"

Nor can Scott be charged with want of sympathy for the "bold red deer." How he triumphs with the "antlered monarch of the waste," that, sleeping in lone Glenartney's hazel shade, suddenly awakes to the deep-mouthed blood-hounds' heavy bay—

> " Then, as the headmost foes appeared,
>   With one brave bound the copse he cleared,

---

[1] Drayton's memory was at fault.

> And, stretching forward free and far,
> Sought the wild heaths of Uam-var!"

Leyden, as has been seen, is also full of sympathy, but confesses to a regret that the stag does not make better use of his "formidable grove of pointed thorns;" as Waller also—

> " So the tall stag upon the brink
> Of some smooth stream about to drink,
> Surveying there his armèd head,
> With shame remembers that he fled
> The scornèd dogs, resolves to try
> The combat next. But if their cry
> Invades again his trembling ear,
> He straight resumes his wonted care,
> Leaves the untasted spring behind,
> And, winged with fear, outflies the wind."

Several poets even go so far as to make the stag regret its armament as cumbering it in its flight. For instance, Davenant—

> " As deer that mourn their growth of head with tears
> Where the defenceless weight does hinder flight."

But this is probably only a reminiscence of the familiar story of the stag proud of its antlers that met with Absalom's fate.

In other poets besides those who sing specifically of the chase, all the details of the deer-hunt " where we did chase the fearful hart of force," and all redounding to the honour of the quarry—" the frighted roebuck and his flying roe " —will be found abundantly scattered.

Somerville alone is cruel, after his wont. He has a wretchedly cruel account of a stag-hunt, in which he follows, with a detail that seems like gloating over suffering, the wretched stag's agonised flight. He compares its terror to that of " the poor, fury-hunted wretch (his hands in guiltless blood bestained) that still seems to hear the dying shrieks,

and the pale threat'ning ghost moves as he moves, and, as
he flies, pursues." In a burst of sycophant solicitude he
implores royalty not to go too near the stag even though a
score of hounds are worrying it ; and when at last the stag
is at the point of death, and—

> " Beneath the weight of woe he grows distressed,
>   The tears run trickling down his hairy cheeks,"

the King " beholds his wretched plight, and tenderness
innate moves his great soul," and he orders off the pack.
Upon which the poet—

> " Great Prince ! from thee what may thy subjects hope,
>   So kind and so beneficent to brutes,
>   O mercy, heav'nly born ! "

&c. &c. But from reading Somerville it might be imagined
that he knew nothing of humaneness.

In legendary allusions both the milk-white doe of fairy-
tale and the black roe of Oriental myth, as also Æsop's
stag, "a creature blameless, yet something vain," are to be
found, with here and there an enchanted hind that was
"hunted to his hurt" by some mythical knight or prince.
But, as I have said above, the poets seem too well satisfied
with the deer as it is in Nature to try to assist it to sympathy
and honour by the adventitious graces of tradition or the
exercise of a fanciful license.

Yet deer enjoy remarkable prominence in myth and folk-
lore. In " elemental " symbolism, they appear as luminous,
variegated, or dark, according as the sky is ruddy, dappled,
or lowering, and they drag the chariots of the wind-fiends,
the spirits of the storm, and are the heralds of the elephant,
"the hurricane." And in folk-lore, how many a hero both
of East and West has the magic fawn, the milk-white doe,
that beautiful but dangerous quarry, or the enchanted hart
—"a creature that was current then, the hart with golden

horns "—beguiled into the forest depths to the hunter's woe. In our own ballads, momentous disasters sprang from "the hunting of the deer." And in semi-sacred legends what an important place it holds, the cross-bearing stag, the celestial hind. And how European history would have been altered if kings had never chased the deer. In the East it is even more fateful. Many princes'have come by their adventures following the deceptive quarry. The whole "Ramayana" turns upon the hero being beguiled from his leafy hermitage in pursuit of the silver-spotted stag. In fact, the deer of myth, whether "stag," "hind," "gazelle," or "antelope," is a thing universally desired, but almost invariably the cause of perplexity and trouble to its pursuer.

Superstitions about them are very frequent. They are captivated by music, as several poets tell us, and when wounded—

> " For his secure an herb can find
> The arrow to withdraw."

Some say this is the " Lancashire asphodel," but others that " the hart, wounded with an arrow, runs to the herb dittany to bite it, that the shaft may fall out."[1] Every one knows, too, that a hart's horn burnt drives all the snakes away from the neighbourhood, and that the deer is the most dreaded foe of the serpent, for it sucks up the air out of the snake-holes, and the snakes cannot help but follow ; and then, when the snake appears, the deer eats it like a stalk of celery. So if you wear deerskin no snake will ever touch you. But deer folk-lore, if it were collected, would be found to be prodigious in quantity and traversing half our philosophies. Dig deep into the earth under the roots of the dread ash Ygdrasil, and you will find four stags on the guard there. Look up above you into the sky, and

---

[1] This healing herb has many pretty legends.

you will see the deer's head, Orion, glittering in sleepless vigil.

Several other species of horned animals share in the popularity of the British deer. Thus the "antelope"—a vague creature enough in Campbell, Thomson, Moore, and Shelley, who make it "snow-white with silver feet" and "feeding on lilies"—is used as a type of timid innocence, is called "sweet antelope," and affords similes of feminine elegance and beauty—

> " Sister-antelopes
> By one fair dam, snow-white, and swift as wind,
> Nursed among lilies near a brimming stream."—*Shelley.*

The grace of its neck makes a goddess envious; the lightness of its step is the despair of nymphs; its eyes—

> " The lady rising up with such an air
> As Venus rose with from the wave, on them
> Bent, like an antelope, a Paphian pair
> Of eyes,"

and carries off Don Juan into delightful captivity. And no wonder that antelopes should attract the poets, for they are even swifter and more graceful than the deer. The peculiar charm of their movements, their elegant impatience, so airy and impulsive, are happily rendered, as in Moore's " fleet and eager down the slope, like antelopes the bright nymphs bound ; " and " down the slope, the silvery-footed antelope, as gracefully and gaily springs," "with light sound ;" or Shelley's "antelope in the suspended impulse of its lightness ;" and "the wild antelope, that starts whene'er the dry leaf rustles in the brake, suspends her timid steps to gaze." The antelope is one of the constellations of the Indian zodiac, sacred to Chandra, and the recognised symbol of feminine grace.

" Gazelle" is nearly synonymous with antelope. "Its airy step and glorious eye" find equal favour with Byron, and Moore, and Shelley. "Its soft black eye," "large and languishingly dark," "glorious," "now brightly bold or beautifully shy," is almost a poetical proverb, and "gazelle-eyed" one of their supreme compliments—

> "Her eye's dark charm 'twere vain to tell;
> But gaze on that of the gazelle,
> It will assist thy fancy well."

But the poets were wrong to speak of them as going in vast herds, or to make them "of many a colour, size, and shape," and still more to place their wild gazelles among lilies and on "flowery champaigns." In Nature it is beautifully placed in sandy wastes and amongst the barrenness of the wilderness.[1]

Among the later poets the chamois meets with occasional reference, as the companion of the eagle in mountain heights that "mock the hunters' might," and "baffle the hunters' ken." It is the "flying chamois," leaping across "the dark-blue crevasse," skipping over "the glaciers bright," an emblem of Swiss independence and liberty generally: "shy as the jealous chamois, Freedom flies."

The elk, "in his speed and might," though a vague entity, is no doubt that favourite figure of red man's myth and tradition, the mighty animal that in the epoch of the bison was one of the noblest trophies of the northern Indians and the feast-dish of the braves. Thomson happily depicts the elk in one of its picturesque situations—

> "Scarce his head
> Raised o'er the snowy wreath, the branching elk
> Lies slumbering sullen in the white abyss;"

and Moore refers to a curious tradition—

------

[1] Says a great naturalist, "It prefers the bare plain, rocky hill, or sandy waste, and a barren country to a rich one."

> " In the woods of the North there are insects that prey
> On the brain of the elk till his very last sigh ; "

his application thereof being—

> " O genius ! thy patrons, more cruel than they,
> First feed on thy brains and then leave thee to die."

But I am unable to find any grounds for the poets' facts, at any rate in special relation to the elk.

Another northern "deer" that is occasionally met with in verse is the reindeer. Montgomery is specially fond of it. Campbell makes it the steed of Winter—

> " Howling Winter fled afar
> To hills that prop the polar star :
> And loves on deer-borne car to ride
> With barren darkness by his side."

The gemsbok gives Jean Ingelow the subject of a powerful vignette—

> " Or far into the heat among the sands
>   The gemsbok nations, snuffing up the wind,
>   Drawn by the scent of water, and the bands
>   Of tawny-bearded lions pacing, blind
>   With the sun-dazzle in their midst, opprest
>   With prey, and spiritless for lack of rest ! "

And "the brindled gnu" finds also a single reference.

VII.

BRITISH WILD BEASTS.

I REMEMBER once, when lying dozing under a tree in a very quiet scrap of English woodland, seeing a badger. The very suddenness of such an apparition is in itself a delightful touch of wild nature—for Nature is always sudden in these glimpses of her inner life.

Thus I remember, when in India, waiting for bear or leopard to be driven past my post, the spectral visions of boar and pea-fowl or fox that would rise up as it were from the ground. One instant absolute solitude, and the next, and lo! a great sambhur stag, with all its pride of antlers, standing out in the open. It takes two steps and is gone again—for ever. Was it ever there at all? You feel inclined to rub your eyes. A twig snaps. You look up : there is nothing. You begin to think of phantoms and Shelley's "panther-peopled solitudes." And look! from opposite you steps out a peacock. For half a second you see it with all its pomp of trailing brilliance. How it lights up the undergrowth ! But on a sudden it turns, and the glittering undulating plumes vanish behind a bush, noiseless and splendid like a coil of some great burnished snake, and once more gloom settles deep on the glade. And so it goes on all the time you wait. Sudden and silent things come and go, and in each flash you catch a glimpse of Nature's self, a peep into her private diary.

So it was with my English badger. And of all animals the "brock" is one of the most suitable for an apparition ; for the colouring and the shape of the beast make its whole body, when it is facing you, look like only the head of some much huger creature. It seemed to me for a second, therefore, that some subterranean monster had thrust its head up above the ground. But the badger lifted one of its hind-paws and scratched its nose, and then I recognised my visitor. It did not see me, and began to root its way along among the bracken. My botanising tin was lying in its path, and the badger came upon it. "A trap!" said the beast, as plainly as ever a grunt said anything, and turning round, my visitor pattered back into the hazels whence it had emerged.

But there was something very picturesque and very engaging in this unexpected verse of poetry. We have very few wild animals, and the sight of one, whether otter or weasel, badger or fox, at its ease and unsuspecting, makes a day's walk memorable to me for ever. "That is where I saw so-and-so," I say to myself whenever I pass near the spot or hear it mentioned. A rare flower—"Sole sitting by the shores of the old romance," makes something of the same impression on me. It carries the place back into the far past. Antiquity comes up with us again.

But poets are averse to badgers.[1] They notice "the tod" as being hunted with terriers and "vexed" in barrels. And they are quite content that it should be. Popular errors have no doubt given poets their bias, for the brock is a beast of ill-omen in parts of rural Britain, and the poets' phrase, "uneven as a badger," comes from the mistaken idea that the legs of the animal were shorter on one side than on the other. Another tradition is to the effect

---

[1] Has the phrase to "badger" a person come from the practice of badgering badgers? It should properly therefore mean "to make a badger of a person."

that the badger is a very cleanly person, and that the fox takes advantage of this amiable weakness to drive it out of its burrows, which it then occupies. Thus Phineas Fletcher—

> " So where the neatest badger most abides,
>   Deep in the earth she frames her prettie cell,
>   And into halls and closulets divides ;
>   But when the stinking fox with loathsome smell
>   Infects her pleasant cave, the cleanly beast
>   So hates her inmate and rank-smelling guest,
>   That far she flies and leaves her loathèd nest."

But there is no foundation for this pleasant fiction of the fastidiousness of the badger. On the contrary, it is rather an ill-savoured animal—to " stink like a badger " is a proverb—and is no enemy of the fox, the two being sometimes unearthed together. So in " Reynard the Fox," the badger, Grimbard, husband of the garrulous Lady Slopard, is the nephew of the hero, and the only one of all the beasts that has any influence for good over him.

Another relative of the fox in the same fable is the striking and picturesque animal, the otter, which is similarly wasted by the poets. " The otter to his cavern drew," and " forth from his den the otter drew," are the usual references, and even these are singularly few, to the otter. Rogers has the otter " rustling in the sedgy mere," and two or three others introduce it as an adjunct of the rural scene.

> " This subtle spoiler of the beaver kind,
>   Far off, perhaps, where ancient alders shade,
>   In deep still pool, within some hollow trunk
>   Contrives his wicker couch, whence he surveys
>   His long purlieu, lord of the stream, and all
>   The finny shoals his own."

Thus, one of the most picturesque and poetical of our native wild beasts is as neglected as most of our more picturesque and beautiful birds, the kingfisher, bittern,

woodpecker, and heron.   Its analogy in poetry to the heron
is very close, for like that bird, it is referred to occasionally as a fish-destroyer, but chiefly as a quarry for
trained hawks; so it fares with the poor " water-dog." Scott
devotes to it one good passage, but he, the poet of the
Scottish stream and loch, ought to have devoted at least
a dozen.

> " Grayling and trout their tyrant know,
>   As between reed and sedge he peers,
>   With fierce round snout and sharpened ears ;
>   Or, prowling by the moonbeam cool,
>   Watches the stream or swims the pool."

Though sometimes mentioned as a fish consumer, it is more
frequent as a beast of chase.   Thus Somerville in his cruel
" poem "—

> " Yon hollow trunk,
> That with its hoary head incurved salutes
> The passing wave, must be the tyrant's fort
> And dread abode.   How these impatient climb,
> While others at the root incessant bay !
> They pull him down.   See there he dives along !
> Th' ascending bubbles mark his gloomy way.
> Quick fix the nets, and cut off his retreat
> Into the shelt'ring depths.

> Ah ! there he vents !
> The pack plunge headlong, and protended spears
> Menace destruction, while the troubled surge
> Indignant foams, and all the scaly kind,
> Affrighted hide their heads.   Wild tumult reigns,
> And loud uproar.   Ah ! there once more he vents ;
> See ! that bold hound has seized him, down they sink
> Together lost ; but soon shall he repent
> His rash assault.

> Again he vents ;
> Again the crowd attack.   That spear has pierced
> His neck, the crimson waves confess the wound.

> Fixed is the bearded lance, unwelcome guest,
> Where'er he flies ; with him it sinks beneath,
> With him it mounts, sure guide to ev'ry foe.
> Inly he groans, nor can his tender wound
> Bear the cold stream.
>
> 　　　　　　　　　See ! there escaped he flies
> Half-drowned, and clambers up the slipp'ry bank
> With ooze and blood distained.　Of all the brutes
> Whether by Nature formed or by long use,
> This artful diver best can bear the want
> Of crystal air.　Unequal is the fight
> Beneath the whelming element, yet there
> He lives not long, but respiration needs
> At proper intervals.
>
> 　　　　　　　　Lo ! to yon sedgy bank
> He creeps disconsolate : his num'rous foes
> Surround him, hounds and men.　Pierced thro' and thro'
> On pointed spears they lift him high in air ;
> Wriggling he hangs, and grins, and bites in vain.
> Bid the loud horns, in gaily warbling strains,
> Proclaim the felon's fate.　He dies, he dies !"

Gay also is an enthusiast in his hatred of the otter, and in other poets "this subtle spoiler of the beaver kind," "the sly goose-footed prowler," is marked out as a proper object of the chase.

> " Would you preserve a num'rous finny race,
> 　Let your fierce dogs the rav'nous otter chase,
> 　Th' amphibious monster ranges all the shores,
> 　Darts thro' the waves and ev'ry haunt explores.
> 　Or let the gin his roving steps betray,
> 　And save from hostile jaws the scaly prey."

In myth the otter is a creature of formidable character— "like a swift otter, fell through greedinesse" is Spenser's simile for the invader from over-sea, and there was nearly as much trouble in Asgard over the killing of the great otter, brother of Fafnir, as in the Troad over the rape of

Helen. The otter, Enudris of the Edda, is a fearsome beast, and so too is the other which, in Muscovite legend, carries off the Czar's son under the winter sea, and with its snoring makes the sea ebb and flow, nine miles at each breath.

As might have been expected, the hedgehog, being prickly, has no friends among the poets. They do not forgive it its spines.

> " Who whilst in hand it gryping hard behent,
> Into a hedgehogge all unwares it went,
> And prickt him so that he away it threw."

" Ugly urchins, thick and short," is Spenser's description. " The thorn-back hedgehog dull," says Quarles. If poets were fairies and given to tumbling about in hedgerows and copses by moonlight, the prickly animal might be objected to—as indeed Titania does object to the " thorny " thing ;— but that any rational man with boots on should bear a grudge against the hedgehog for having spines on its back seems unaccountable. For the urchin is a very pleasing little animal, exceedingly harmless in a wild state, and both useful and diverting when tame. That it makes garden-paths untidy by rooting up the plantain weeds is a complaint brought against it by Gilbert White, but plantains are in themselves untidy on garden paths. Tennyson notes its fondness for the plant in his " Aylmer's Field "—

> " Then the great hall was wholly broken down,
> And the broad woodland parcelled into farms ;
> And where the two contrived their daughter's good
> Lies the hawk's cast, the mole has made his run,
> The hedgehog underneath the plantain bores,
> The rabbit fondles his own harmless face,
> The slow-worm creeps, and the thin weasel there
> Follows the mouse, and all is open field."

Instead of ridiculing it and reproaching it, why did not the poets take it (as antiquity did) as the symbol of prudence, mother-wit, and self-reliance? Can modesty, honour, virtue, do more than the hedgehog does when attacked—roll itself up, and present to the assailant a front equally defended at every point? What a delightful lesson of patient hopefulness it teaches the Christian! It submits to misfortune without a murmur, waiting till malice shall have spent itself and its troubles cease. What problems too it symbolises, this spherical impossibility! How gingerly you have to handle them. Can you make head or tail out of them? Yet, like most problems, if you will leave them alone long enough, they will solve themselves. It is·surely, too, a type of innocence, being so harmless itself, yet so fully armed. It might stand, too, for law, which runs along on four feet, looking a simple thing enough, but which, the moment any one begins to meddle with it, resolves itself into a hopeless ball of difficulties.

One of the legends of the hedgehog tells us how a viper had come into its hole, and being very much inconvenienced by the hedgehog's prickles, begged it to go away. "Let him go," replied the master of the house, "who cannot stay." The hedgehog's treatment of the mythic wolf is equally delightful.

In folk-lore the urchin possesses occult properties which make it more or less eerie in reputation, but do not prevent it being eaten or kept in houses for clearing them of cockroaches. In Drayton's " Polyolbion " the rustic, enumerating his worldly possessions, says—

> " Sweeting mine, if thou mine own wilt be,
>   I've many a pretty gaud I keepe in store for thee,
>   A nest of broad-faced owls and goodly urchins too ;
>   And better yet than these, a bulkin two years old,
>   A curled-pate calf it is, and oft could have been sold ;
>   And yet besides all this, I've goodly bear-whelps two."

Its voice is a curious, unnatural-sounding snoring, and

sometimes a squeak—"the hedge-pig's whining" of the witches on the heath. It is supposed also to foretell the changes of weather (as indeed nearly all animals do to the careful observer), and so we meet with lines, "as hedgehogs doe foreshew ensuing storms," "observe what way the hedgehog builds her nest." That it had the power of shooting its quills off at pleasure is a popular tradition of wide prevalence. Thus in "Hiawatha"—

> " From a hollow tree the hedgehog
>   With his sleepy eyes looked at him,
>   Shot his shining quills like arrows ;
>   Saying, with a drowsy murmur,
>   Through the tangle of his whiskers,
>   Take my quills, O Hiawatha ! "

Though Drayton speaks of "conies" being "banisht quite from every fertile place," they have since then become a tolerably "common object of the country." Few poets, therefore, describing a rural scene, omit this pretty and familiar incident of

> " Bobbing rabbits,
>   Their white tails glancing."

> " The upright rabbit, where he sits and mocks you,
>   Ere he deigns to hide."

> " The little noises flung,
>   Out of clefts where rabbits play."

Clare is especially full of "coy" and "scouting"[1] and "quirking" rabbits ; his poems are a regular warren.

> " I love to peep out on a summer's morn,
>   Just as the scouting rabbit seeks her shed,
>   And the coy hare squats nestling in the corn,
>   Frit at the bowed ear tott'ring o'er her head."

Somerville and his contemporaries call them "dodging"

[1] An epithet used by Bloomfield and Grahame also.

conies, and, by their suggestions of their feebleness, imply the error of identifying them with the conies of Holy Writ, though the latter are really, in spite of their rabbit size, the connecting links between the enormous hippopotamus and rhinoceros, and not much more nearly related to Bunny than they are to "Welsh rabbits."

It is unfortunate for the rabbit, poor "Wabasso," in one way, that it should be such excellent eating, for if they shared the hedgehog's immunity from the pie-dish, their pleasant republics might never know the recurring massacre. I confess that much as I delight in watching warren-life, and, indebted as I am to the grotesqueness of rabbits at play or at work for many a hearty laugh, I remember them very tenderly in a pie—a cold pie.

I never feel guilty when I shoot rabbits. There is an idea somewhere about me that they multiply under destruction. They are like peppermint plants. If you go and root out the bed in the corner of the garden, the plant breaks out all over the path. It is like fighting with original sin, as Dudley Warner says. So I pepper away in a warren with a light heart. After all, if you smash up a comet it splinters into stars.

Rabbits, they say, taught men sapping and mining,—in " Rasselas," at any rate, the Prince and his companion take the hint of tunnelling a way of escape out of the Happy Valley from these small rodents—and their burrows are certainly sometimes models of ingenious complication, strongholds though without strength, impregnable though without armament. If the poets had wanted an analogous instance of maternal sacrifice to take the place of the wretched old pelican, they might have remembered the rabbit, which lines her nursery with fur pulled off her own body.

Hares go with rabbits by a process of unconscious cerebration. Laprel and Kayward are sympathetic. Each in turn plays the other's shadow. Rabbits, however, are much more familiar to most of us than hares. In a country walk you pass a second rabbit without remark; but you draw attention to a hare every time you see it, and watch it as long as you can.

But in the poets there are fifty hares for every rabbit,— "as numerous as hares on Athos"—and the reasons for this are obvious. The poets go by preference to antiquity, legends, fictions, for their Nature. They do not go to Nature for it.

Now, the "light-foot" hare possesses as voluminous a folk-lore as almost any animal, and ever since there were men and women in the world to be frightened by superstition, this little creature, itself one of the most timid of things, has inspired human beings with dread.

> " Nor did we meet with nimble feet
> A single fearful lepus,
> That certain sign, as some divine,
> Of fortune bad to keep us."

Sir Thomas Browne says, "There are few above the age of threescore and ten who are not perplexed at a hare crossing their path," and a number of poets allude to the superstition of the ill-luck foreboding, when *inauspicatum dat iter oblatus lepus.*

> " If a poor timorous hare but crosse the way,
> Morus will keep the chamber all the day."—*Quarles.*

"The mythical hare," says delightful Gubernatis, "is undoubtedly the moon," and the wide-spread connection of the animal with that luminary gives the myth something of a popular acceptation. Thus the Chinese represent the moon-figure, Jut-ho, with a hare at her feet, and symbolise Luna by a rabbit pounding in a mortar. In Vedic myth, "the leaping one" is the moon, and the spots on the face of it are hares by the shore of the moon-lake. These hares have a king, and it is Death. Buddhists, again, aver that the hare is in the moon as a reward for its self-sacrifice— meeting Buddha hungry the hare cooked herself for his meal, and the Great Master threw her up there to be an object of the world's homage. The Red Indians also have a hare in their moon.

But its peculiarly sinister reputation has arisen from its own timidity—"the hartlesse hare," the most timorous of animals, suggesting fear and so portending something to be feared. And in this significance the whole world at one time or another has taken divination from "the fearful hare." From north to south, from Lapland to Arabia, from east to west, from the Chinese to the Red Indians, all nations in the past, and many in the present, have seen the hand of fate in the movements of this little creature.

Its appearance of perpetual alarm specially attracts the poets. It sits "all trembling in its form" and "springs astonished." It is the "list'ning" hare (Bloomfield); "in act to spring away" (Thomson); "beneath her bramble screen, quaking as astound" (Heber); "afraid to keep or leave her form" (Prior). "To lie and dare, as in a fourme sitteth a weary hare" (Chaucer), is a poetical proverb, and in Herbert's poem, Humility gives "the fearful hare her ears" to Fortitude. The story of the terrified hares being checked in their purpose of suicide by seeing how they had frightened a linnet is versified by Beattie—

> " Is there on earth a wretch, they said,
>   Whom our approach can strike with dread ? "

From this notion of perpetual apprehension, due in part to the nervous restlessness of the hare's ears, arose the fancy that the hare slept with one eye open—the *somnus leporinus.* Thus Keats speaks of the hare's "half-sleeping fit," and another poet has the admirable phrase "hare-eyed unrest."

This sleepless vigilance, however, gives the hare an important place in mythology, where it often figures as the sentinel.

Being thus of ill-omen, the hare's flesh was condemned. Thus Burton advises against it, quoting profusely in support of his advice. "'Tis melancholy meat," says Lady Answerall.

Yet, in spite of their being nominally in such disfavour, we find the Romans maintaining extensive "leporaria," not for coursing but for the table, the shoulder being considered the tit-bit, while the phrase "to live on hares' flesh" became a synonym for "the lap of luxury" or "the fat of the land."

Its flesh being thus reputed, the animal itself becomes "melancholy," and "as melancholy as a hare" is a poetical simile. "The sad hare," says Davenant.

Clare notes its dulness in winter as a striking contrast to its summer gaiety of manners—

> " The woods how gloomy in a winter's morn,
>   The crows and ravens even cease to croak ;
>   The little birds sit chittering on the thorn,
>   The pies scarce chatter when they leave the oak,
>   Startled from slumber by the woodman's stroke.
>
>   The quirking rabbit scarcely leaves her hole,
>   But rolls in torpid slumbers all the day;
>   The fox is loth to 'gin a long patrol,
>   So scouts the woods content with meaner prey ;
>   The hare so frisking, timid once, and gay,
>   Now scarce is scared though in the traveller's way,
>   Though waffling curs and shepherd dogs pursue."

Finally, as melancholy conduces to madness, the hares—especially March hares—are popularly considered a trifle insane.

Yet it is far from being of a triste or solemn kind ; for who has ever watched a hare, when it thought itself in safety, and not been amused by its absurd light-heartedness. Instead of behaving like the witches' familiar, which folk-lore

has made it, it is the veriest elf of frolic.   Faber talks of the
"almost silent gambols of the hares in the tall grass"—
Burns has them on a happy summer's day "hirplin down
the furze," and again "jinking hares in amorous whids"—
and Wordsworth sees her "running races in her mirth."
Cowper has pet ones—

> " I kept him for his humour's sake,
>   For he would oft beguile
> My heart of thoughts that made it ache
>   And force me to a smile "—

that are "still wild Jack-hares," and—

> " A turkey carpet was his lawn,
>   Whereon he loved to bound,
> To skip and gambol like a fawn,
>   And swing his rump around."

Nor is the "panting timorous" hare always "fearful."
Like all wild things in England, where dogs, and guns, and
traps cover the land with such a labyrinth of danger, they
suspect man and all his works.   But a very little will suffice
to gain the confidence of hares, and make them "lose
much of the vigilant instinctive dread," as Cowper, being
himself inoffensive, found—"the timorous hare scarce shuns
me."   Sometimes, indeed, they require only too little encouragement for boldness, and having been invited into the
paddock with cabbage-leaves and parsley, invite themselves
later on into the kitchen garden.   In winter too, when—

> " The foodless wilds
> Pour forth their brown inhabitants, the hare,
> Though timorous of heart and hard beset
> By death in various forms, dark snares and dogs,
> And more unpitying men, the garden seeks,
> Urged on by fearless want."—*Thomson.*

In " Reynard the Fox," the hare, Kayward, though a
simpleton, is certainly not a coward.

But the great majority accept only the sinister, dismal, and unhappy aspects of the hare. It goes "limping" in Grahame, Keats, Thomson, Burns, and others, as if limping were a feature of a woe-begone, mendicant sort of existence, and not its natural gait, when at ease in its mind and quite happy. "The hare limped trembling," "the fearful hare limped awkward," "the limping hare stops, and looks back, and stops and looks on man, his deadliest foe." As a matter of fact, of course, the hare's "limp" is merely its loitering pace, and expressive of poor Watts' only too infrequent tranquillity.

Associated with the hare and rabbit, but in a very disagreeable manner for those animals, are the "thin" weasels, and their relatives the ferrets—

> " In Shetland's grassy holms, the mining tribe
> Skulking, is there well pleased to dwell obscure,
> Regardless they of what loud bustling men
> Concert in clamorous camp or palace high ;
> But what avails their unambitious care,
> If the fierce ferret spies the vaulted cell
> And rushes headlong in to seize his prey ?
> At once the subterraneous state alarmed,
> Shrieks out all over—whither shall they fly ?
> Caught in their inmost chambers, where they slept
> Vainly secure.   The assassin fiery-eyed
> Winding up all their mazes, through and through
> Spreads desolation o'er the feeble race."—*Leyden.*

Not only in the land of Shakspeare's "weasel-Scot," but in England, the ferret may still be found wild; but Scotland alone can now boast of the larger marten.

The "sucke-egg[1] weasele" (Quarles), "night-wandering weasel" (Shakespeare), "wicked" weasel, finds barely a dozen references in all the range of poetry, though to the

[1] "I can suck melancholy out of a song, as a weasel sucks eggs."—*As You Like It.*

prosaic mind this elegant little monster is full of significances.   At any rate it is quite as pretty as the panther—such a favourite for its beauty with the poets—

> " Fayre was this yonge wif, and therewithal
>   As any weasel hire body gent and smal,"—

and quite as fierce as the tiger, while its voracity, agility, and various natural endowments, make it one of the most dreadful little creatures in Nature.   A thousand times better to be a deer in a tiger's jungle than a rabbit in the same copse as a weasel.

> " My lord and I are kindred spirits,
>   Like in our ways as two young ferrets,
>   Both fashioned as that supple race is,
>   To twist into all sorts of places,
>   Creatures lengthy, lean, and hungering,
>   Fond of blood and burrow-mongering."—*Moore.*

Yet the weasel has a benign significance in ancient Hindu myth, as also in Red Indian legends, for one reason, perhaps, that it is erroneously supposed to be the dire foe of snakes and scorpions.   Its leanness of person is due to the fact that, when the beasts were invited to help themselves from Manobozho's fat-pool, the supercilious weasel came last and got none.   Pope has a weasel that grows fat in a corn-loft.   But the poet may mean upon a diet of mice and not corn.

A great many poets, it may be, never saw a wild squirrel, so they refer only to those in cages, and draw the moral of foolish ambition from the sight.   For myself, I think it very pathetic, the hopeless scrambling of the squirrel on its wheel; and such lines as these exasperate me—

> " Contented like the playful squirrel
>   To wanton up and down my cage."

Besides, what privilege have the poets to take it for granted that this creature of liberty, this "merry forester," is deluded by the clattering revolution of its prison into supposing that it is "skimming up the silent beech," or "dancing oak-trees round and round?" It is, I think, a little high-handed to teach a squirrel to spin its wire treadmill, and then to pretend that "the foolish creature thinks he climbs," that it has mistaken your wretched whirligig for its old "mazy forest-house," the tops of the wind-blown pines, or the fragrant bowers of "nut-grown" hazels. I resent the similes of Prior, Mallet, and others, who see in the poor captives illustrations of human weakness and the vanities of foolish ambition. Nor, Mr. Moore, "does the name of the little animal rhyme with 'girl.'"

Of course many poets have really seen it wild, and they delight in it—the "bright-eyed," "busy," "gay," and "wanton creature," "flippant, pert, and full of play."

> " The squirrel, with aspiring mind,
> Disdains to be to earth confined,
>   But mounts aloft in air ;
> The pine-tree's giddiest height he climbs,
> Or scales the beech-tree's loftiest limbs,
>   And builds his castle there.
>
> As Nature's wildest tenants free,
> A merry forester is he,
>   In oak o'ershadowed dells ;
> In glen remote, or woodland lawn,
> Where the doe hides her infant fawn,
>   Among the hills he dwells."

They stop to watch it crack its nuts and drop the shells, hear it "rattling in its hoard of acorns," peep into "the brown hermit's" larder, its winter-store of acorn, pine-cone, and filbert, and note "its prettiness of feigned alarm, and anger insignificantly fierce."

" And he could tell how the shy squirrel fared,
  Who often stood its busy toils to see ;
  How against winter she was well prepared
  With many a store in hollow root or tree,
  As if being told what winter's wants would be ;
  Its nuts and acorns he would often find,
  And hips and haws too, heaped plenteously
  In snug warm corner that broke off the wind,
With leafy nest made nigh, that warm green mosses lined."

"Wingless squirrel," says Montgomery; so Cowper, "swift as bird;" and Charlotte Smith, at greater length—

" Though plumeless, he can dart away,
  Swift as the woodpecker or the jay,
    His sportive mates to woo ;
  His summer's food is berries wild,
  And last year's acorn cups are filled
    For him with sparking dew.

Soft is his shining auburn coat,
As ermine white his downy throat,
  Intelligent his mien ;
With feathery tail and ears alert,
And little paws as hands expert,
  And eyes so black and keen.

Soaring above the earth-born herd
Of beasts, he emulates the bird,
  Yet feels no want of wing ;
Exactly poised, he dares to launch
In air, and bounds from branch to branch,
  With swift elastic spring."

Naturally enough, the poets admire the forethought of the squirrel in furnishing its larder against the winter—

" Within some old fantastic tree,
  Where time has worn a cavity,
    His winter food is stored ;

> The cone beset with many a scale,
> The chestnut in its coat of mail,
> Or nuts complete his hoard."

Or, in Clare—

> " The squirrel bobbing from the eye
> Is busy now about his hoard ;
> And in old nest of crow or pye,
> His winter-store is oft explored."

But this engaging prevision has a charm within a charm. For the squirrel goes to sleep during the winter, and its diligence in collecting food for a time when it does not need it might therefore seem somewhat misdirected. But the squirrel knows that there are often breaks of fine weather in the middle of winter, and it is really for these occasional picnics that the brown hermit provisions himself—

> " When drawn from refuge in some lonely elm,
> That age or injury has hollowed deep,
> Where on his bed of wool and matted leaves
> He has outslept the winter, ventures forth
> To frisk awhile, and bask in the warm sun."

So that as a matter of fact the squirrel does not lay up food against bad weather, but against fine. Moreover, it very often happens that the little creature forgets where it has concealed its hoards; and every one who lives in the country knows how common it is in tumble-down walls or about old trees to find stocks of nuts and acorns that have been laid up but never consumed. The instinct to lay by against heavy snowfalls has been inherited, no doubt, from progenitors who lived in the years of harder winters, and though the necessity for its exercise now hardly exists, the squirrel is still as industrious as ever, and, therefore, twice as industrious as it need be.

Its merry heart is certainly one of the squirrel's many

claims to favour, and its nimble industry, so often noted by the poets, suggests one of the most curious legends of which this delightful little animal is the subject. On the top of the dreadful ash-tree Ygdrasil sits the Death-Eagle, and down among its roots lies coiled Fate, the dragon Nidhöge, and the squirrel is for ever running up and down from one to the other, trying to make them quarrel.

Red men have many superstitions about their squirrels, one species of which closely resembles our own ruddy favourite. As every one knows, it was Hiawatha's benefactor and honoured companion in that perilous voyage on the black pitch-water—

> " On the bows with tail erected
> Sate the squirrel Ajidauno ;
> In his fur the breeze of morning
> Played as in the prairie grasses."

They cough to this day because once they were men, and Manobozho, the mischief-maker, gave them meat which turned to ashes in their mouths, and then, for coughing out his victuals, he turned them all into squirrels. They are one of the Indians' most familiar forms of enchantment, and in many of their tales the hero is turned by beneficent fairies into this animal's form in order to enable him to accomplish his labours. Thus " the wearer of the Ball " becomes a squirrel when he has to chase the flying hut which is built in the top of a pine-tree that keeps on growing up higher the higher the hero climbs.

Moles have in some countries a diabolical, in others only a mysterious reputation. Now and again it has a medicinal aspect, as among the Russians, who say that if you kill a mole by squeezing it in your hand, you can touch for the king's evil, while in England, not so very long ago, a mole was a sure cure for ague—if eaten crisp. But these are exceptional views to take of the " little gentleman in the velvet

coat," and to be accepted with as much reserve as the moles
of Holy Writ, which, owing to errors of translation, should
sometimes be read "Swan !" The intelligent, however,
will do well to regard the mole as a curious little beast,
created apparently for the purpose of providing the earth
with an invaluable system of sub-soil drainage, and, sub-
ordinately, as a moral discipline for landscape gardeners—
and (in Hurdis) for shepherds—

> " Scarce disappears the deluge, when the mole,
> Close prisoner long in subterranean cell
> Frost-bound, again the miner plays, and heaves,
> With treble industry, the mellow mound
> Along the swarded vale. The shepherd's eye
> With unforgiving enmity surveys
> The long concatenated sweep of hills,
> Whose soft and crumbling soil abridges more
> The scanty pittance of his hungry fold."

Cowper, with a wail of sympathy that is almost characteristic of him, finds in the little harmless beast a sinister
analogy—

> " We mount again, and feel at every step
> One foot half sunk in hillocks green and soft,
> Raised by the mole, the miner of the soil.
> He, not unlike the great ones of mankind,
> Disfigures earth, and plotting in the dark,
> Toils much to earn a monumental pile
> That may record the mischief he has done."

Nor is it without interest as being the chief possessor of all
the world below the surface.

> " What need of all this marble crust
> To impack the wanton mole of dust,
> That thinks by breadth the world t' unite
> Though the first builders failed in height."—*Marvell.*

In some places the rat usurps its patrimony, but the

"handed" mole has plenty of room to spare, and though the worms drive their narrow tunnels in subterranean labyrinth, the mole does not complain, for it eats the worms.

With the poets "the mole that scoops with curious toil his subterranean bed" (Montgomery); that "the crumbled earth in hillocks raises" (Gay); "unwearied still roots up many a crumbling hill" (Clare); is a "dark grubbing" and "blinking" creature. Cowper typifies Error as a mole, and Dryden has "like a mole busy and blind, works all his folly up and casts it outward to the world's open air." Eliza Cook is good enough to say that "there's a mission, *no doubt*, for the mole in the dust," and Spenser speaks of the "moldwarp" as a slothful sensualist. Mackay calls all sorts and conditions of men—grasping tyrants, angry bigots, selfish rulers, palace knaves, canting hypocrites, greedy authors, smug philosophers, Malthusians—everybody in fact who tries "to keep the nations down" by plotting against liberty of mind or freedom of conscience, "moles"—

> " Grub, little moles, grub underground,
>   There's sunshine in the sky."

Keats uses the image finely in the following passage from "Isabella"—

> " Who hath not loitered in a green churchyard,
>   And let his spirit, like a demon mole,
>   Work through the clayey soil and gravel hard,
>   To see skull, coffined bones, and funeral stole ;
>   Pitying each form that hungry Death had marred,
>   And filling it once more with human soul."

On the other hand, the poets applaud its acute sense of hearing, and deplore its feeble eyesight—

> " What modes of sight betwixt the wide extreme !
>   The mole's dim curtain, and the lynx's beam."—*Pope.*

The chief point about the natural mole—Tennyson's "four-handed mole"—is its industry in digging ; and the poets, observing the superficial evidences of its diligence, address the "moudiewort" as "patient," draw numerous reflections from its "delving," "earth-piercing," and "mining," which, by the way, the fairies are supposed to have taught them. Thus Pope advises man to imitate the mole in deep-ploughing.

Mice are not suitable subjects for poetry. There is very little of the hieroglyph, few subtle significances, in the pantry-invading, cat-eaten mouse. It is difficult to dignify it. Mouse-character is very one-sided : there are no enormities about it, no picturesque ferocity, or blood-curdling wolfishness ; nor does it conceal itself sufficiently to be worth calling "obscene." Besides, it is so absurdly small. Once in a way it was well enough to make "the crumb ravisher," "cheese-rind nibbler," "bacon-licker," and their comrades-in-arms, heroic ; but the joke does not bear repetition. It is sad that cats should think so well of them as food, and that mouse-traps should be so efficacious, but what is to be done? They insist on being where they should not go, and affront man himself by tampering with his victuals.

Such is the poetical acceptation of the mouse. As "Tom's food" they are benignly congratulated upon their utility, and, though expected to rejoice when cats decease, are sternly reminded that pussy alive was a wholesome corrective to mouse excesses. Thus Clare—

> " Ah mice, rejoice ! ye've lost your foe,
>   Who watched your scheming robb'ries so
>   That, while she lived, twa'nt yours to know
>   A crumb of bread :
>   'Tis yours to triumph, mine's the woe,
>   Now pussy's dead ;
>   While pussy lived ye'd empty maws,
>   No sooner peeped ye out your nose,

> But ye were instant in her claws,
>   With squeakings dread ;
> Ye're now set free from tyrant's laws,
>   Poor pussy's dead."

They may eat crumbs if they can, but if the cat comes, it will serve them right if they get eaten themselves ; as in Herrick—

> " So the brisk mouse may feast herself with crumbs,
>   Till the green-eyed kitling comes,
>   Then to her cabin, blest she can escape
>   The sudden danger of a rape."

So also when the mouse is caught in a trap, the poets hold it inevitable justice that it should die. Thus Somerville speaks of "the rigorous decree of fate" that condemns cheese-hunting mice to execution, and Clare of the "rigid fate" that awaits the tiny pilferer.

But outside the poets, the mouse has considerable dignity. It is "the ravisher" of Vedic legends, and in the solar myth the mice are the shadows which creep out from under the hills, and which the cat-moon and her kitten the twilight hunt. It was turned into a tiger as a reward for assisting a Brahmin, and might have been a tiger still, had it not in its new shape proceeded to eat the Brahmin, and for this been promptly turned back into a mouse again. Nor can an animal be called merely a pantry-thief that sometimes eats kings and archbishops, to say nothing of the sons of Polish dukes.[1] Is the mouse, portentous to Rome, to be perpetually cowering before "green-eyed kitlings?" If poets have no respect for mice, have they none for St. Gertrude, their patron? Take again their position in fairy tales. The mice are always beneficent. Their feud with the sparrows is doubtless deplorable, but did it arise

---

[1] According to legend King Popelus was eaten by mice, also Duke Conrad's son (of Poland), also Otho, Archbishop of Mentz.

from the fault of the mice? Were not they and the sparrows firm friends till the former behaved so meanly in that
matter of the odd poppy seed, eating the whole of it themselves instead of fairly dividing it with the mice? Nor
should it be remembered as discreditable to the mouse
that it is not on good terms with the cat, for the cat behaved very shabbily towards its little partner about that pot
of fat which they had stored away in the church, for joint
winter consumption ; for, not content with faithlessly eating
all the fat by herself, Grimalkin also ate the mouse for
reproaching her. The majority of fables are to the credit
of the mouse : its gratitude is conspicuous, its services to
princes in trouble momentous ; and did it not, at the risk
of its own life, release a lion? Lions are great mouse-
eaters.

But the mouse, apart from man's household and yet more
sacred person, that is to say, the field-mouse—for poets consider corn-stealing in the country merely an amiable weakness as compared with the iniquity of crumb-stealing in the
town—receives more sympathetic treatment. They rejoice
over "the pilfering mouse entrapped and caged" in a
kitchen, and moralise loftily—

> " When the watchful hungry mouse
>   At midnight prowling round the house,
>   Winds in a corner toasted cheese,
>   Glad the luxurious prey to seize,
>   With whiskers curled, and round black eyes,
>   He meditates his luscious prize,
>   Till caught, trepanned, laments too late
>   The rigorous decrees of fate."—*Somerville.*

For the " city mouse, well coated, sleek, and gay, a mouse
of high degree " (Cowley), is looked upon as an animal that
arrives at great personal comfort, and lives luxuriously, by
dishonest practices. But the " fieldish " mouse has somehow acquired a character for industrious honesty and

thrifty struggling against poverty. Thus Wyatt, in his delightful poem " On the Mean and Sure Estate"—

> " The fieldish mouse,
> That for because her livelihood was but thin,
> Would needs go see her townish sister's house,
> She thought herself endured to grievous pain,
> The stormy blasts her cave so sore did souse ;
> That when the furrows swimmed with the rain,
> She must be cold and wet, in sorry plight,
> And worse than that, bare meat there did remain.
> To comfort her, when she her house had dight,
> Sometime a barley corn, sometime a bean,
> For which she laboured hard both day and night
> In harvest time, while she might go and glean.
> And when her store was stroyed with the flood,
> Then welladay ! for she undone was clean."

Thus Clare delights in the pretty little animal with its nest swinging from a wheat-stalk—

> "The little chumbling mouse
> Gnarls the dead weed for her house.
>
> .   .   .   .   .
>
> The fields are cleared, the labouring mice
> To sheltering hedge or wood patrole,
> When hips and haws for food suffice
> That chumbled lie about their hole."

Hurdis sits out to watch

> "The wanton mouse,
> And see him gambol round the primrose head,
> Till the still owl comes smoothly sailing forth,
> And with a shrill ' to-whit' breaks off his dance
> And sends him scouring home."

Indeed, the owl, "whose meteor eyes shoot horror through the dark," often gets well rated for "numbing the tiny revellers with dread." Its habit of "prowling along the fields" is thrown in its beak, and it is reproached for subterfuge, when

> "In a barn
> He sees a mouse creeping in the corn,
> Sits still and shuts his round blue eyes,
> As if he slept, until he spies
> The little beast within his reach,
> Then starts and seizes on the wretch."—*Butler.*

Burns laments over the

> " Wee sleekit, cow'rin', tim'rous beastie,"

and its little home in the stubble ruined by the plough,—

> " That wee bit heap o' leaves an' stibble
> Has cost thee mony a weary nibble."

Two full-grown "harvest-mice" weigh exactly one half-penny, and it was no doubt the marrow of this diminutive species that Titania used to have on her toast. It is not, however, out of place here to remind poets that the "delightful" field-mouse, as they think it, and as it undoubtedly is to all lovers of Nature, is "the corn-destroyer" of Holy Writ, and that they are "the mice that marred the land" of Philistia, the scourge of an angry Jehovah. Nor —to descend to lesser catastrophes—are the field-mice that ate up the Bishop of Bingen altogether trivial creatures. In England and Europe generally, the "pilfering" field-mice that "with far-fetched ear its hole supplies" (Clare), sometimes commit very serious depredations in the barns and rick-yards into which it has been carried at harvest time. Those that have been left behind in the fields become partially torpid, and take refuge in little grass-lined burrows ; but their more fortunate friends in the barns keep awake in winter "as if on purpose to show their gratitude for their liberal provender."

References are made to many of the mice of story— Wyatt's fieldish mouse ; the town mouse and its country cousin ; the golden mice of the covenantal ark ; those that fought the frogs ; the mouse (in Crabbe)

> " That trespassed and the treasure stole,
> Found his lean body fitted to the hole ;
> Till, having fatted, he was forced to stay,
> And, fasting, starve his stolen bulk away,"

and those of the Mouse Tower on the Rhine, while the morals and wise saws derived from the same animal are unexpectedly numerous.

> " I hold a mouse's wit not worth a leke,
> That hath but one hole for to stenten to." —*Chaucer.*

> " 'Tis a bold mouse that nestles in a cat's ear,
> I gave the mouse a hole and she is become my heir."—*Herbert.*

> " Dronke as a mous."— *Chaucer.*

> " The mouse
> Finds no pleasure in a poor man's house.—*Quarles.*

> " State vermin, gnawing into labour's bread."—*E. Cook.*

> " Show him a mouse's tail and he will guess,
> With metaphysic swiftness, at the mouse." –*Keats.*

Women, it is proverbial, dread mice.   Says Crabbe—

> " She who will tremble if her eye explore
> The smallest monstrous mouse that creeps on floor."

But they do not, as a rule, altogether dislike them, or Suckling might regret his pretty simile, who writes—

> " Her feet beneath her petticoat
> Like little mice crept in and out,
> As if they feared the light."

---

[1] Pope has it weakly—

> " The mouse that always trusts to one poor hole,
> Can never be a mouse of any soul."

So Herbert—

> " The mouse that hath but one hole is quickly taken."

In Jean Ingelow there is a pleasant reference to the
"water-mouse" among the reeds—

> " His bright eyes glancing black as beads,
>   So happy with a bunch of seeds,"

and several poets refer kindly to the "drowsy," "wondering,"
"sleepy" dormouse. In Red Indian fairy tales the dormouse, the " blind woman," is a thing of some consequence.
Once upon a time, a dwarf, annoyed by the sun, persuaded
his sister to make a net out of her hair, and going out to
the edge of the prairie next morning, he caught the sun
just as it was rising, and pinned it down inside the net to the
ground. Prodigious was the consternation in Nature when
the sun did not rise, and long and serious the pow-wow of
the beasts. But at last the venerable dormouse (at that
time the largest of all animals and the Ulysses among them)
guessed what was the matter, and going to the edge of the
prairie released the luminary. But in doing so it was
shrivelled up to its present size.

As regards its forethought for the winter, the dormouse
is even more interesting than the squirrel. For not only
does it, like the squirrel, lay up its little hampers for
occasional picnics in the snatches of fine weather, but it
takes care, before turning into its cosy little moss-ball for
the winter, to fatten itself up to an extraordinary obesity.
So fat, indeed, does it become, that without any food at
all laid by, it could sleep out a whole winter comfortably.
But the delightful little Sybarite is not going to run any
risks, so, like the juryman in *Punch*, it first of al eats
itself into invincible fatness, and fills its pockets besides
with condensed foods.

It was this capacity for fattening that endeared the
dormice to Roman epicures. Their "gliralia" or "dormouse parks" were most extensive and costly erections,
planted with oaks and nut-trees for the sustenance of these

small deer, who, as required for the table, were caught and put into jars provided with every sort of mouse luxury.

Rat is a frequent epithet of reproach. Sycophants deserting a declining patron "as rats do a falling house," are vermin. So are beggars "as poor as church rats" (Marvell), and so are thieves. "There be land-rats and water-rats, land-thieves and water-thieves," and so are the Jesuits in Oldham.

> " Prophet, curse me the babbling lip,
>   And curse me the British vermin, the rat ;
>   I know not whether he came in the Hanover ship
>   But I know that he lies and listens mute
>   In an ancient mansion's crannies and holes.
>   Arsenic, arsenic, sure would do it,
>   Except that now we poison our babes, poor souls !
>   It is all used up for that."

Its two great historical iniquities, eating Mrs. Throckmorton's bullfinch—

> " For aided both by ear and scent,
>   Right to his mark the monster went.
>   Ah, muse ! forbear to speak.
>   Minute the horrors that ensued ;
>   His teeth were strong, his cage was wood,
>   He left poor Bully's beak " (*Cowper*)—

And Bishop Hatto—

> " In at the windows, and in at the door,
>   And through the walls by thousands they pour,
>   And down from the ceiling and up from the floor,
>   From the right and the left, from behind and before,
>   From within and without, from above and below,
>   And all at once to the bishop they go.
>   They have whetted their teeth against the stones,
>   And now they pick the bishop's bones.

> They gnawed the flesh from every limb,
> For they were sent to do judgment on him " (*Southey*)—

are each the subject of a poem. Nor is the death of the bishop at all beyond rat capabilities ; for it is beyond doubt that men have been killed and eaten by rats in the sewers, both of London and Paris, while Professor Bell, on the authority of Robert Stephenson, relates the following instance of the extreme ferocity of the rat when driven to hunger.[1] "In a coal-pit," he says, "in which many horses were employed, the rats (which fed upon the fodder provided for the horses) had accumulated in great multitudes. It was customary in holiday times to bring to the surface the horses and the fodder, and to close the pit for the time. On one occasion, when the holiday had extended to ten days or a fortnight, during which the rats had been deprived of food, on reopening the pit, the first man who descended was attacked by the starving multitude, and speedily killed and devoured!" Of their audacity Butler gives delightful illustration—rats getting into his worthy's breeches-pockets to eat his rations—

> " For, as we said, he always chose
> To carry little in his hose.
> That often tempted rats and mice
> The ammunition to surprise ;
> And when he put a hand but in
> The one or t'other magazine,
> They stoutly on defence on't stood,
> And from the wounded foe drew blood.
> And till th' were stormed and beaten out,
> Ne'er left the fortified redoubt "—

while Shenstone records in verse the all-too-frequent vanity of the rat-trap.

[1] Cassell's " Natural History," edited by Professor P. Martin Duncan, F.R.S., F.G.S.

> " But more of trap and bait, sir,
> Why should I sing of either?
> Since the rat who knew the sleight,
> Came in the dead of night,
> And dragged 'em away together.
>
> Then answer this, ye sages!
> Nor deem I mean to wrong ye,
> Had the rat, which thus did seize on
> The trap, less claim to reason
> Than many a skull among ye?"

Tennyson makes "the little rat" a terrific agent in catastrophe—

> " Ah, little rat, that borest in the dyke
> Thy hole by night, to let the boundless deep
> Down upon far-off cities while they dance
> Or dream.

Among British "wild animals" may also be enumerated the polecat, pine-marten, and wild-cat, and each is referred to by our poets.

VIII.

BEASTS OF CHASE.

" THE chase, the sport of kings, image of war without its
guilt," is Somerville's definition; and he tells us that "devo-
tion, pure and strong necessity, first began the chase of
beasts." Thus pious in conception, and innocent in process, "sport" should have no need of apology.

But let us hear the other side, and by preference—as
more nearly corresponding to Somerville in extremity of
prejudice—Thomson :

> "In the gleaming morn
> The beasts of prey retire, that all night long,
> Urged by necessity had ranged the dark,
> As if their conscious ravages shunned the light,
> Ashamed. Not so the steady tyrant man,
> Who, with the thoughtless insolence of power
> Inflamed beyond the most infuriate wrath
> Of the worst monster that e'er roamed the waste,
> For sport alone pursues the cruel chase
> Amid the beamings of the gentle day.
> Upbraid, ye ravening tribes, our wanton rage,
> For hunger kindles you, and lawless want ;
> But lavish fed, in Nature's bounty rolled,
> To joy at anguish, and delight in blood,
> Is what your horrid bosoms never knew."

Nor is Cowper less pronounced in his aversion to the
hard exercise of hunting.

Between these two superlatives stand ranged every conceivable degree of comparison, and it is very difficult indeed to decide whether the poetic instinct is hostile to sport, as sport, or is favourable. A few writers devote whole poems to the glorification of the chase in general and certain forms of hunting in particular. On the other hand, a score and more of poets condemn it root and branch.

Even on special points the diversity of opinion is noteworthy; for, while some go into raptures over the death of the stag, others mingle their tears with those of "the sobbing victim;" one party exults over the fox-hunt, styling the field "bold heroes;" the other calls them "cravens," and says the whole thing is a crying shame. Gay magnifies coursing the hare as a delirious delight; Somerville calls down the vengeance of Heaven upon "the vile crew" who go after Puss with greyhounds.

They are not even agreed on facts. The quarrel commences at the very beginning. For instance, Somerville says—

> "When Nimrod bold,
> A mighty hunter! first made war on beasts;"

while Pope has—

> "Proud Nimrod first the bloody chase began;
> A mighty hunter, and his prey was man."

And they carry on their differences up to their own days. Thus one poet eulogises the modern lady in the hunting-field, as if she were a Florence Nightingale; another cries, Fie on her! and tells the hussy to get home. So that it is not easy to arrive at the just middle of poetical opinion upon the subject of sport.

But a very unmistakable point upon which our poets are agreed, and, in my opinion, are every one of them open to unfavourable criticism, is their deficiency of sympathy. Of "sentiment" they have a constant abundance. I regret its excess in Wordsworth, for instance, and resent it in Cowper; Thomson provokes me almost to apoplexy; and as for Eliza Cook, I weep such tears over her as, I am informed, I wept in childhood over that unfortunate ram which Abraham chanced to sacrifice in the place of his son. There is much pathos in the fate of the ram which had come as a looker-on, and had to take the leading part straight off without even a rehearsal. There is much pathos, too, about Eliza Cook's poetry.

By "sympathy" I mean literally what the word implies; that is, fellow-feeling; and nowhere in poetry do I find this beautiful quality so wanting—as compared with prose—as in the poets' treatment of the chase. When they hold with the hare they séem to have no appreciation of the courage and endurance of the riders, horses, or pack; when they hunt with the hounds they are as pitiless as the dogs them-selves, rush frenzied into the death-worry, and roll in the spilt blood. This loss of balance puzzles me. If a "poet" was of necessity a genius I could understand it. But their madness has not always this justification of alliance.

Shelley may say anything he likes—he does, as a rule—but I do not object to his spotted tigers or his kingfishers that feed on raspberries. He may make his tigers feed on kingfishers, or his kingfishers on tigers—it would not matter. Nor is there anything that might not be forgiven to a Milton, a Crashawe, or a Keats. I would follow a man all round the parish with my bowie-knife who objected (seriously) to Spenser's statements that boars feed upon camels or that bats are birds.

For though these great poets are often wrong in facts— and what decently-thinking man does not hate them? the *accomplished* fact is a simple brute—they are never deficient in sympathy. Yet they never "gush." Without calling man a monster they can admire and feel with the creatures which for his pleasure or his profit he puts to death. But the majority seem unable to do this; they have not the strength for impartiality; they keep themselves perpendicular with sprawling buttresses of prejudice.

To illustrate this. The wild boar is a noble beast; he is the counterpart of the noblest men of an earlier age; a Charles Martel, Charles the Bold, Charles XII.—a grand creature, who treats the odds against him as children treat chronology, as something that he neither understands nor cares to. He takes victory by the ears and drags her along with him into battle. But in poetry none of the courage, this perfection of heroism, is carried to the boar's credit; it all goes to that of the hunters or the boar-hounds. The latter beset it, and do it to death with weapons, nets, and stress of numbers. They are "heroic," but the boar is only "savage."

The stag, again. He is stately and fleet of foot. But if this is true of the quarry, what shall we say, the poets ask, of the men and the stag-hounds that hunt it down? The hare and the otter are wonderfully cunning, but what fools they are compared to the craft of human kind! The fox, too, what do its wiles avail when outraged man is on its racks, thirsting to avenge the duckling and the chicken?

In the poem on "The Chase" Somerville ranges over half the animal kingdom; but, as far as British poets are concerned, the beasts of sport are virtually only five—the wild boar, deer, fox, hare, and otter. The wild-cat, as is proved by old manorial charters, was once included in the list, but it is not a poet's beast.

Incidentally, of course, every quadruped that finds notice in verse is referred to in its relation to man—that of the hunted to the hunter—but, as objects of the chase, the animals finally resolve themselves into the mystic five. The chief of these is the boar.

Homer, describing the outrush of the brothers Ajax, employs it as a simile—

> " Forth from their portals rushed th' intrepid pair,
> Opposed their breasts and stood themselves the war.
> So two wild boars spring furious from their den,
> Roused with the cries of dogs and voice of men.
> On every side the crackling trees they tear,
> And root the shrubs, and lay the forest bare ;
> They gnash their tusks, with fire their eyeballs roll,
> Till some wide wound lets out their mighty soul."

Ovid, in his description of the beast, has the following lines—

> "Sanguine et igne micant oculi, riget horrida cervix,
> Et setæ, densis similes hastilibus horrent,
> Stantque velut vallum, velut alta hastilia setæ.
> Fervida cum rauco latos stridore per armos
> Spuma fluit."

In these two passages are contained the sum total of the English poets' wild boar : Homer's simile and Ovid's description have sufficed.

This animal, by the way, affords us a standard by which to measure our own manhood with that of the "heroic," chivalrous, and historical days. "The destruction of a wild boar," we read, "ranked in the middle ages among the deeds of chivalry, and won for a warrior almost as much renown as the slaying of an enemy in open lists." Think of this, you jolly hog-hunters of India! Regret, when you next ride to pig, with a single spear in your hand, that you did not live in the past, when, if you had gone after the same beast in armour, javelined, and sworded, you might have been a hero. Look at your trophies of tushes and lament. Each pair of those in the days of the Earl Guy might have made you a national hero for life and perhaps even a Saint of Christendom thereafter !

In Windsor Forest the redoubtable Earl "did all to— kill" a "grisly bore," and he lives for ever a mirror of heroism.

> "As also how hee slue
> That cruell boare, whose tusks turned up whole fields of graine
> (And wrooting, raised hills upon the levell plaine,
> Dig'd caverns in the earth, so darke and wondrous deepe
> As that into whose mouth the desperate Roman leepe);
> And, cutting off his head, a trophy thence to beare."—*Drayton.*

Are the Gordons ever likely to forget their illustrious clansman who slew "the boar of Huntley?" or the Boswells how their ancestor avenged the death of Farquhar II., King o' Scots?—

> "When beyond he lyeth languishing,
> Deadly engored of a great wild bore."

In Chetwode once abode a boar, and the terror of it was so great that the country people could not pass that way to Rookwood; and even travellers of quality "passed by on the other side." Then Sir Ryalas, Lord of Chetwode, thinking it great shame that he should be thus isolated from society by an "urchin-snouted boar," goes forth to slay it, as if the beast were a Guillaume le Sanglier with a mighty fanfaronade of castle trumpets.

> "Then the wild boar, being so stout and so strong—
> 　Wind well thy horn, good hunter;
> Thrashed down the trees as he ramped him along,
> 　To Sir Ryalas, the jovial hunter.
>
> Then they fought four hours in a long summer day—
> 　Wind well thy horn, good hunter;
> Till the wild boar fain would have got him away
> 　From Sir Ryalas, the jovial hunter.
>
> Then Sir Ryalas he drew his broadsword with might—
> 　Wind well thy horn, good hunter;
> And he fairly cut the boar's head off quite,
> 　For he was a jovial hunter."[1]

---

[1] "Within a mile of Chetwode Manor-House there existed a large mound, surrounded by a ditch, and bearing the name of 'the Boar's Pond.' It had long been overgrown with gorse and brushwood, when, about the year 1810, the tenant to whose farm it belonged, wishing to

Another illustration of the prodigious importance attached
to such a feat is afforded by the legend of Boarstall, the
seat of the Aubreys. "It is situated within the limits of
the ancient forest of Bernwood, which was very extensive
and thickly wooded. This forest, in the neighbourhood
of Brill, where Edward the Confessor had a palace, was
infested with a ferocious wild boar, which had not only
become a terror to the rustics, but a great annoyance
to the royal hunting expeditions. At length one Nigel,
a huntsman, dug a pit in a certain spot which he had
observed the boar to frequent, and, placing a sow in the pit,
covered it with brushwood. The boar came after the sow,
and, falling into the pit, was easily killed by Nigel, who
carried its head on his sword to the king, who was then
residing at Brill." For this the king knighted him "and
amply rewarded him!"

All this goes to prove the manly courage of the men
who killed boars; yet the boar's courage is all bloodthirsty
ferocity. Adonis will not stay with his celestial charmer;
his thoughts are all given to the boar-hunt he has on hand—

> "But for she saw him bent to cruell play,
> To hunt the salvage beast in forest wyde.
> Dreadfull of danger that mote him betyde,
> She oft and oft advized to refraine
> From chase of greater beastes, whose brutish pryde
> Mote breede him scath unwares."

So, too, the lovely Thyamis wedded to a "loose, unruly
swain,"

---

bring it into cultivation, began to fill up the ditch by levelling the
mound. Having lowered the latter about four feet he came on the
skeleton of an enormous boar lying flat on its side and at full length.
Probably this was the very spot where it had been killed, the earth
around having been heaped over it so as to form the ditch and mound.
The space formerly thus occupied can still be traced. It extends about
thirty feet in length and eighteen in width, and the field containing it
is yet called 'the Boar's Head Field.' "—*Book of Days.*

> "Who had more joy to range the forest wyde,
>   And chase the salvage boar with busie payne,
>   Than serve his lady's love ; "

goes out loveless into the wilderness.

Boar-hunting had therefore—at least so it would appear—momentous consequences in the days of chivalry; now-a-days it is a mere pastime with Englishmen; they call it "sticking pigs." None of them expects knighthood for the performance, nor does the pig-sticker expect his wife to go forth mad during his absence. Of course it may be said that boars are not what they were "in the good old days," and there the poets have the best of it—for their boars are perfect hurricanes. But I protest against their handling of them. The valour of the gallant brute was worth a passing compliment.

> " Hero-like, who on their crest still wore
>   A lion, panther, leopard, or a boar."

Now the three first animals mentioned in Lovelace's lines are, according to the traditions of the College of Arms, one and the same beast. Virtually, therefore, the boar is the only animal except the lion that was considered worthy by ancient chivalry to be worn as a badge.

> " Tusky boars [1]
> Razed out of all thy woods, as trophies hung,
> Grin high-emblazoned on thy children's shields."

So Planché, in his " Pursuivant of Arms," notes how in Glover's Roll (temp. Henry III.) only three beasts were then borne upon English coats-of-arms, and that one of them was the boar. It shared with the lion and the leopard the honourable distinction of emblazonment upon shields. Mrs. Bury Palliser also, in her most fascinating work on

----

[1] Leyden's " Albania."

" Historic Devices," bears ample testimony to the heraldic dignity of the beast.

The device of a boar was used by Richard III. before he was a king, and when Duke of Gloucester he had a pursuivant named Blanc Sanglier. His cognisance was a rose supported on the dexter side by a bull, a badge of the house of Clare, and on the sinister by a boar, which boar he had found among the badges of the house of York. " The latter he selected for his own personal device, and it was that by which he was generally designated, as we know by the doggrel which is said to have caused its composer to be shortened by the head and four quarters "—

> " The Ratte, the Cat, and Lovell our dogge,
> Rule all England under the Hogge,"

meaning by the hog, " the dreadful wild boar " which was the king's crest. But Collingbourne was one of the most seditious of the disaffected, and held correspondence with Richard and deserved his fate.

> " When I meant the king by name of hog,
> I only alluded to his badge the boar."

Queen Margaret calls Richard a " rooting hog," and Hastings says—

> " To fly the boar before the boar pursues
> Were to incense the boar to follow us,
> And make pursuit when he did mean no chase.
> Go, bid thy master rise and come to me,
> And we will both together to the tower,
> Where, he shall see, the boar will use us kindly."

Again, Hastings to Stanley—

> " Come on, come on, where is your boarspear man ?
> Fear you the boar and go so unprovided ?"

Nor was the bristled boar wanting at the battle of Bosworth ; for, gorgeously attired in splendid armour, and rendered still more conspicuous by the royal diadem which surmounted his helmet, Richard rode upon a milk-white charger superbly caparisoned and attended by his body-guards, displaying the banner of England and innumerable pennons glittering with the silver boar. After his death, Richard's body was placed across his war steed "like a hogue calf," the head and arms hanging on one side of the horse and the legs on the other side, and was thus disposed behind his pursuivant-at-arms, Blanc Sanglier, he wearing the silver boar upon his coat, and carried back to Leicester in trophy of the morning's victory.

The poetical boar is a very fine presentment of the noble brute in Nature. It is "the mighty boar," "bristled," "tusked," and foaming. "Fierce as forest boar" is a con-stantly recurring simile in verse, and its "headlong rush" through the brake a familiar figure. But Spenser makes the quaint error of supposing that boars eat camels—

> " He shortly met the tiger and the boar,
> Which with the simple camel ragèd sore
> In bitter words, seeking to take occasion
> Upon his fleshy corpse to make invasion."

And so err all those poets who make it carnivorous. "Throw me to the wild boar" to be devoured is as absurd in Heber as "the boars that roar through the woods" of Ossian.

Perhaps the good bishop had in his mind that episode in the Seven Champions of Christendom, where St. James of Spain goes a-hunting with Neburazadan, the King of Jerusalem, and by the slaying of a great man-eating boar wins the Hebrew's daughter. He found it, we are told, lying in its mossy den, gnawing the mangled joints of some passenger whom it had murdered as he travelled through the forest. It was of wonderful length and size, and so terrible to behold, that at first sight it almost daunted the courage of the Spanish knight; for its monstrous head seemed ugly and deformed, its eyes sparkled like a fiery furnace, its tusks, more sharp than spikes of steel, and from its nostrils fumed such a violent breath, that it seemed like a tempestuous whirlwind; his bristles were harder than seven times solid brass, and his tail more loathsome than a wreath of snakes. A gruesome beast, indeed !—and standing in no need of the wings which Ælian gives to the Flying Hog of Clazomenæ to make it worthy the steel of a knight of Christendom.

But Pope need not have described the wild boar " in silence creeping " upon a sleeping youth, and goring him "with unrelenting tooth." It is far too "generous," in the poets' sense, to attack a sleeping adversary. Why, too, should Scott go out of his way to call it "the felon boar ? " The abuse is not more just than that poet's frequent plagiarisms are creditable.

"No man who has not been an eyewitness of the desperate courage of the wild hog would believe in his utter recklessness of life, or in the fierceness that will make him run up the hunter's spear, which has passed through his vitals, until he buries his tusk in the body of the horse or his rider." "No animal exceeds him in ferocity; he will boldly charge the largest elephant who may have disturbed him without further provocation." "There is hardly a more dangerous brute to cope with. He will fight to the last, and then die game."

These are quotations from the foremost of Indian sportsmen and naturalists—Elliot, Shakespeare, Kinloch, Jerdon, and others of equally established reputation.

They are of the fighting caste—Gadites—men of war from their youth up. If they meet each other there is a duel at once ; any other beast, and a fight immediately commences. They have absolutely no idea of giving way, or yielding the

path.   It is no boxing-gloves with them, always the cestus.
They strike the shield always with the bare lance-point.
Their challenge is "to the death."   So the poets always
have them in conflict.

> " As wilde bores gan they togeder smite,
>   That frothen white as fome for anger wood."

> " As when two bores with rankling malice met,
>   Their gory sides fresh-bleeding fiercely fret,
>   Till breathless both themselves aside retire,
>   Where foaming wrath their cruel tusks they whet,
>   And trample the earth the whiles they may respire,
>   Then back to fight again."

Chaucer and Spenser are especially fond of the wild boar
simile, and employ it with great effect for their furious
knights.   "Hurtling   round,   advantage   for   to   take,"
"chafering and foaming," and "grinte with his teeth so
was he wroth."   Later poets take their cues of course from
the elder.   Thomson has "the brindled boar grins fell
destruction;" Gray, "the tusky boar on surrounding foes
advanced."   Darwin gives a sketch from Nature—

> " Contending boars, with tusk enamelled, strike
>   And guard with shoulder shield the blow oblique,
>   While female bands attend in mute surprise,
>   And view the victor with admiring eyes."

But the wild hog, if I am not mistaken, is monogamous.
Gay, too, has a sketch of combatant boars which reads—from
the introduction of "Westphalia" and the "mire"—as a
mock-heroic.

> " So when two boars in wild Ytene bred,
>   Or on Westphalia's fat'ning chestnuts fed,
>   Gnash their sharp tusks, and, roused with equal fire,
>   Dispute the reign of some luxurious mire ;
>   In the black flood they wallow o'er and o'er,
>   Till their armed jaws distil with foam and gore."

Byron has an admirable line, "the lion and his tusky *rebels*," for though the two animals are not found together —except so infrequently that the error is not justified—the "rebel" is one of the wild boar's most notable characters. The tiger is his natural Raja, but he revolts at the first menace of oppression. The jungle path is his as much as the tiger's, he says, and if they meet, the pig as often as not joins issue as to the right of way. " The native Shikarries affirm that the wild boar will quench his thirst at the river between two tigers, and I (Shakespeare) believe this to be strictly the truth. The tiger and the boar have been heard fighting in the jungle at night, and both have been found dead alongside of one another in the morning." "Though the wild hog often becomes the tiger's prey, it sometimes falls a victim to the successful resistance of its intended victim. I (Elliot) once found a full-grown tiger nearly killed by the rip of a boar's tusk, and two similar instances were related to me by a gentleman who had witnessed them, one of a tiger, the other of a panther."

Once upon a time the boar was lord of British woodlands, and, as Thomson says—

> " The sad barbarian, roving, mixed
> With beasts of prey, or for his acorn meal
> Fought the fierce tusky boar."

As a beast of chase it was extant in England up to the Stuarts' time.

According to Bell, "about the year 940 the laws of Hoel Dha direct that it shall be lawful for the chief of his hunts-men to chase the boar of the woods from the 5th of the Ides of November (9th) until the Calends of December (1st)." In the next century, Bell states that "the numbers had perhaps begun to diminish, since a forest law of William I., established in 1087, ordained that any who were found guilty of killing the stag, the roebuck, or the wild boar, should have the eyes put out, and sometimes the penalty appears to have been a painful death. It appears," continues Bell, "that Charles I. turned out some wild swine in the New Forest for the purpose of restoring the breed to that royal hunting-ground, but they were all of them destroyed during the civil war. A similar attempt was made in Bere Wood in Dorsetshire, but one of the boars having injured a valuable horse belonging to the wealthy Nimrod who exhibited this specimen of sporting epicurism, he caused them to be destroyed."

The wild boar probably became extinct in Britain before the reign of Charles I.; while in Ireland it was abundant as late as the seventeenth century.

Spenser's touches and descriptions are from the life, no doubt. He must have seen Leicester, Essex, Sidney, Raleigh, and others go out hunting, perhaps went with them, and on his estate (some 3000 acres, with a rental of £17) in Ireland must have been familiar enough with the wild boar as a tenant.

Somerville, therefore, wrote too late to speak of the animal —"churning his foam, and on his back erect his pointed bristles rising"—except from hearsay, and "young Redmond" of Rokeby, that "gallant boy in hunter's green" who

> " Loved to wake the felon boar
> In his dark lair on Greta's shore,"

lived barely in time to save Sir Walter from an anachronism. The genius of Shakespeare presents the fierce beast to the life, " with frothy mouth bepainted all with red, like milk and blood being mingled both together." The " blunt " boar he calls it, " the foul, grim, urchin-snouted boar, whose downward eyes still looketh for a grave." But Venus' description is matchless. It has all the majesty of Job's poem on Leviathan.

> " His tushes, never sheathed, he whetteth still,
> Like to a mortal butcher, bent to kill.
> On his bow-back he hath a battle set
> Of bristly pikes, that ever threat his foes ;
> His eyes, like glow-worms, shine when he doth fret ;
> His snout digs sepulchres where'er he goes ;
> Being moved, he strikes whate'er is in his way,
> And whom he strikes his cruel tushes slay.
> His brawny sides, with hairy bristles armed,
> Are better proof than thy spear's point can enter ;
> His short thick neck cannot be easily harmed ;
> Being ireful, on the lion he will venture ;
> The thorny brambles and embracing bushes,
> As fearful of him, part, through whom he rushes."

Keats, too, well imagines the scene " when snouted wild boars rooting the tender corn " anger the huntsmen ; for it is a shrewd beast at furrowing up a field.   " The rage of a wild boar is able to spoil more than one wood," says Herbert.

But Somerville, in his sketch of the " Arabian " chasing the animal, is somewhat " out of the hunt : "

> " The grisly boar is singled from his herd
> As large as that in Erimanthean woods
> A match for Hercules.   Round him they fly
> In circles wide, and each in passing sends
> His feathered death into his brawny sides ;
> But perilous the attempt, for if the steed
> Haply too near approach, or the loose earth
> His footing fail, the watchful angry beast
> Th' advantage spies, and, at one sidelong glance,
> Rips up his groin.
>   Wounded, he rears aloft,
> And, plunging, from his back the rider hurls
> Precipitant : then, bleeding, spurns the ground,
> And drags his reeking entrails o'er the plain.
> Meanwhile the surly monster hurls along,
> But with unequal speed, for still they wound,
> Swift wheeling in the spacious ring.   A wood
> Of darts upon his back he bears : adown
> Pours many a gaping font ; and now, at last,
> Staggering he falls, in blood and foam expires."

The Greeks and Romans, when they hunted him—
"Adonis' bane"—took extraordinary precautions for their
personal safety. They went in large parties, keeping
together, and were attended by the largest and fiercest
hounds—Locrian, Spartan, or Cretan. Nets were carried
with them to throw over the brute, and the javelins used
were of a specially murderous description.

In metaphor the boar is singularly rare. Burns has a
"wild Scandinavian boar" that issued forth "to wanton in
carnage and wallow in gore," but, changing the beast in the
next line into the plural, "brave Caledonia in vain they
assailed, as Largs well can witness and Loncartie tell." In
Gray's "Bard" we find the English king "the bristled boar
that in infant gore wallows beneath the thorny shade;" and
Dryden has a semi-domesticated hog as the type of the
Baptist—

> " The bristled baptist boar, impure as he,
> But whitened with the form of sanctity,
> With fat pollutions filled the sacred place,
> And mountains levelled in his furious race ;
> So first rebellion founded was in grace.
> But since the mighty ravage which he made
> In German forests had his guilt betrayed,
> With broken tusks, and with a borrowed name,
> He shunned the vengeance and concealed the shame."

Yet in folk-lore and myth it is a constantly recurring and a
very formidable figure.

It is sacred to Scandinavian Thor, and drags the car
of Freyya, its bristles golden, its head refulgent. Vishnu
appears as the tusked one, the irresistible piercer ; and the
thunderbolts, the fathers of the winds, are red boars,
horned, bristled, and fierce.

Once upon a time the Trinity of the Hindoos disputed
for supremacy. Brahma, seated on his lotus, could see
nothing else in the universe, and so said to himself, "I am

the beginning of all." But he descended the stalk and came upon Vishnu asleep. "Who are you?" he asked. "I am the beginning of all things," was the reply. Then Brahma raised his arm to strike. But on a sudden Shiva stood before them. "What are you quarrelling about? Am not I, Shiva, the first-born? Which of you can see either the crown of my head or the soles of my feet?" Brahma stood aghast; but Vishnu without a word plunged down, and, ripping up the universe, pierced below the infernal regions, and lo! the feet of Shiva. So the two others did obeisance to him, the sharp-tusked one.

It was one of the labours of Hercules to kill a boar. Meleager's hunt—

> " A great boar, that no man could withstand,
> And many a woe he wrought upon the land "—

gathered all the heroes of Greece together, and for the trophy of the brute's hide cities went to war. Indras, in that he slew the boar that guarded the Demons' treasure, proudly wore its tusks. Mars protected it as the warrior among the beasts : it was once the badge of Rome.

Even the Christians' boar's head, "crested with bays and rosemary," is said to have honorific origin, as a symbol of gloomy winter slain at the solstice. "Aper significat Diabolum," quoth Du Cange.

He is always obtrusive, assailing. Gods and heroes are perpetually after him. There is no guardian of a treasure like him, except perhaps the griffin. It is no use trying to pipe *him* to bed. He will see the whole of Argus asleep and still be awake. He would have rooted Medea out of the garden in no time and tusked Mercury if he had not been too nimble with those heels of his. You never meet with him, in myth, in an amiable mood. He is either red, the colour of fury, or black, the hue of mischief, malignity, and diabolism. He hurtles about bristling and demoniacal.

With the poets the deer is a universal favourite. "The dew-clawed stag" (Keats), "a stag of ten, bearing his branches sturdily" (Scott), always makes a stanza go statelily. Even Ossian's tiresome "dun sons of the bounding hind, the dark-brown deer of Cromla," relieve the dreary monotony of the Phairson's native heath. Every poet likes to talk about them—

> "The wild and frightful herds
> That, hearing no noise but that of chattering birds,
> Feed fairly on the lawns : both sorts of seasoned deer,
> Here walk the stately Red, the freckled Fallow there
> The Bucks and lusty Stags amongst the Rascals strewed,
> As sometime gallant spirits among the multitude."

And they all agree in paying tribute to its courage—"When at bay a desperate foe."

They exult in its escape. Thus even Somerville—

> "Heaven taught, the roebuck swift
> Loiters at ease before the driving pack,
> And mocks their vain pursuit. Nor far he flies,
> But checks his ardour, till the streaming scent
> That freshens on the blade provokes their rage.
> Urged to their speed, his weak, deluded foes
> Soon flag fatigued ; strained to excess, each nerve,
> Each slackened sinew fails : they pant, they foam.
> Then o'er the lawn he bounds, o'er the high hills
> Stretches secure, and leaves the scattered crowd
> To puzzle in the distant vale below."

So, too, Scott seems glad when the "antlered monarch of the glen" baulks those dogs "of black St. Hubert's breed," and, dashing down "into the Trosach's wildest nook," is soon "lost to hound and hunter's ken," and from its place of refuge

> "Hears the baffled dogs in vain
> Rave through the hollow pass amain,
> Chiding the rocks that yelled again."

When it dies the poets weep with it. If it is a fawn no
Lesbia sheds such tears over her sparrow. Read, for instance,
Marvell's dainty poem. But it is a pity that he, so true,
as a rule, to Nature, should err (with many other poets) in
making fawns " white."

> " I have a garden of my own,
> And all the spring-time of the year
> It only lovèd to be there.
> Among the bed of lillies I
> Have sought it oft where it should lye,
> But could not, till itself should rise,
> Find it, although before mine eyes ;
> For in the flaxen lillies' shade
> It like a bunch of lillies laid.
> Upon the roses it would feed
> Until its lips e'en seemed to bleed,
> And then to me 'twould boldly trip
> And print those roses on my lip."

But the wanton troopers riding by shot the fawn, and it
died—

> " Ungentle men ! they cannot thrive
> Who killed thee. Thou ne'er didst alive
> Them any harm : alas ! nor could
> Thy death yet do them any good.
> .   .   .   .
> And nothing may we use in vain ;
> Even beasts must be with justice slain;
> Else men are made their deodands."

Nor, when full-grown and antlered, does sympathy cease.
Thus in Phineas Fletcher's poem—

> " Look as a stagge pierced with a fatal blow,
> As by a wood he walks securely feeding—
> In coverts thick conceals his deadly blow,
> And feeling death swim in his endless bleeding,
> His heavy head his fainting strength exceeding—
> Bids woods adieu, so sinks into his grave ;
> Green brakes and primrose sweet his seemly herse embrave.

In the actual chase itself the poets' sympathies are never

far behind the deer.   Drayton is a poet who is seldom read,
but as he lived in the days when stags were running wild in
England he is well worth the hearing—quite apart from the
rare robustness of his verse—

> " The best of chase, the tall and lusty Red,
>   The stag for goodly shape and statelinesse of head,
>   Is fitt'st to hunt at force."

Such is the beast he starts with.   He shows us the
huntsman in "the thicke," tracking it by its slot or by his
wood-craft, and then on a sudden the stag, startled by the
" bellowing hounds," rushes out—

> " He through the brakes doth drive,
>   As though up by the roots the bushes he would rive."

The hounds fall to, the horns are blown, and the quarry's
afoot—

> " The lusty stag his high palmed head upbears,
>   His body showing state, with unbent knees upright,
>   Expressing (from all beasts) his courage in his flight."

But the pack come up to him, and then he exerts his
utmost speed.   The baying of the hounds dies away, and
the stag, to baffle further pursuit, "doth beat the brooks
and ponds," and "makes among the herds and flocks of
shag-woolled sheep."   But wherever he goes he finds himself shunned or opposed.   In the fields the ploughman
goes after him with his goad, "while his team he letteth
stand."   In the pasture the shepherd chases him, "and to
his dog doth halow."   And all this time the hounds come
creeping up again, while the stag has wearied itself in futile
stratagem.   "Through toyle bereaved of strength, his long
and sinewy legs are fayling him at length."   A village comes
in his way; and he flies for safety to the abodes of men ;
but the people turn out and drive him forth.   There are the
hounds, full in sight ; so there is nothing for it but to stand
at bay.   "Some bank or quick set finds, to which his haunch

opposed, he turns upon his foes," and as the "churlish-throated" hounds attack him "dealeth deadly blows with his sharp-pointed head." Then the huntsmen come up, and one of them kills the stag. And so

> " Opprest by force,
> He who the mourner is to his own dying corse
> Upon the ruthless earth his precious tear lets fall."

Thomson's sententious caricature of this passage in his "Autumn" is well worth noting, but as the poet only knew of fallow deer he makes the stag "spotted" in the face and "chequered" in the sides. But in all matters of fact his animal is simply Somerville's. It starts off with all its faith in its own speed, "bursts through the thickets," and goes away. But—

> " Slow of sure, adhesive to the track,
> Hot-steaming up behind him come again
> The inhuman rout."

And then "oft to full-descending flood he turns," and "oft seeks the herd." But his "once so vivid nerves" begin to fail, and "he stands at bay," "putting his last weak refuge in despair "—

> " The big round tears run down his dappled face;
> He groans in anguish while the growling pack,
> Blood-happy, hang at his fair jutting cheek
> And mark his beauteous checkered sides with gore."

In metaphor also the deer symbol is often used as of a creature that may lay claim to superior intelligence and special protection. Thus in Quarles—

> " Great God of hearts, the world's sole sov'raign Ranger,
> Preserve Thy deer, and let my soul be blest
> In Thy safe forrest when I seek for rest :
> Then let the hell-hounds roar, I fear no ill,
> Rouse me they may, but have no power to kill."

The hare is certainly one of the best hunted of animals, and Swift puts its perpetual pursuit delightfully into rhyme—

> " A hare had long escaped pursuing hounds,
> By often shifting into distant grounds,
> Till finding artifices vain,
> To save his life he leaped into the main ;
> But there, alas, he could no safety find,
> A pack of dogfish had him in the wind.
> He scours away ; and, to avoid the foe,
> Descends for shelter to the shades below.
> There Cerberus lay watching in his den,
> He had not seen a hare the Lord knows when.
> Out bounced the mastiff with the triple head,
> Away the hare with triple swiftness fled,
> Hunted from earth and sea and hell, he flies
> (Fear lent him wings) for safety to the skies :
> Sirius, the fiercest of the heavenly pack,
> Failed but an inch to seize him by the back ! "

Over this universal huntedness of the hare, the poets maintain a very even quarrel. Some applaud the sport, others condemn it. While Gay goes into raptures over coursing, Somerville calls it a "mean, murderous" pastime, and gravely invokes the retributive hand of Heaven upon the " vile crew " who follow it—

> " Nor the tim'rous hare
> O'ermatched destroy, but leave that vile offence
> To the mean murd'rous coursing crew, intent
> On blood and spoil.   O blast their hopes, just Heaven !
> And all their painful drudgeries repay
> With disappointment and severe remorse."

Not that Somerville was not really more cruel than Gay (who was merely thoughtless), but he thought coursing hares was wasting them.   He insisted on their being hunted with beagles.   Drayton has a straightforward description of coursing without effusion of sentiment which Dryden seems to borrow (for the occurrence can hardly be called a familiar one)—

> " So have I seen some fearful hare maintain,
> A course, till tired before the dog she lay,
> Who stretched behind her pants upon the plain,
> Past power to kill, as she to get away."

On the other side are ranged all the rural poets : Hurdis, Clare, Grahame, Bloomfield, Burns, and the rest; and Cowper, Thomson, and Wordsworth weigh in their sympathies with the gentler majority—

> " Poor is the triumph o'er the timid hare,
> O'er a weak, harmless, flying creature "—

and delight with Grahame in her escape either by her fleetness of foot, when—

> " She scorns
> Thy utmost speed, and from the thistly lea
> Espies secure thy puzzled fruitless search ;."

or by her cunning, when—

> " With step reversed
> She forms the doubling maze, then ere the morn
> Peeps through the clouds, leaps to her close recess ;"

or by some accident, as when, according to Grahame,—

> (" As erst befell in Clyde's fair dale)
> She gain some floating rick ; there close she squats,
> Now in the middle current shot along
> In swift career, now near the eddying side,
> Whirling amazed.
>   . . . Onward meanwhile she sails,
> Till through the broadened vale, the stream expands
> In gentle curve and gliding past the bank
> Restores her, fearful, to the fields again."

Nor are coursing, hunting, and poaching the whole of the hare's grievances, for, as Clare laments, there still remains the gun.

> " Poor pussy through the stubble flies,
>   In vain, o'erpowering foes to shun,
>   The lurking spaniel points the prize,
>   And pussy's harmless race is run."

Sometimes, however, the wound is not mortal, and several poets refer with horror to the poor hare's maimed existence. Notable among the humane protests against an unintentional cruelty is Burns—

> " Go live, poor wanderer of the wood and field,
>   The bitter little that of life remains ;
>   No more the thickening brakes and verdant plains
> To thee shall home, or food, or pastime yield.
> Seek, mangled wretch, some place of wonted rest,
>   No more of rest, but now thy dying bed !
>   The sheltering rushes whistling o'er thy head,
> The cold earth with thy bloody bosom prest.
> Oft as by winding Frith, I musing wait
>   The sober eve, or hail the cheerful dawn,
>   I'll miss thee sporting o'er the dewy lawn,
> And curse the ruffian's aim, and mourn thy hapless fate."

It is looked upon as the most melancholy, limping, trembling creature imaginable—intended, apparently, by Nature for the exercise of beagles, and given an extraordinary degree of craft in order to amuse greyhounds. Some poets strangely pity it and, considering it already sufficiently afflicted by natural timidity and general helplessness, think hunting it is a shame. Their argument is a singular one. "See how frightened the poor thing looks, don't frighten it," and "See how fast the unhappy wretch runs away, don't run after it." "Poor is the triumph o'er the timid hare," "o'er a weak, harmless, flying creature"—such is the view taken of the sport by the minority, their expressions of regret being often marked by true pathos, as thus, in the " Deserted Village "—

> " And, as an hare whom hounds and horns pursue,
>   Pants to the place from whence at first she flew,
>   I still had hopes, my long vexations past,
>   Here to return, and die at home at last."

And what can be finer than the distracted Paphian's description of the hunted hare ?

> " His grief may be comparèd well
>   To one sore-sick, that hears the passing bell.
>   Then shalt thou see the dew-bedabbled wretch
>   Turn and return, indenting with the way ;
>   Each envious briar his weary legs doth scratch,
>   Each shadow makes him stop, each murmur stay :
>   For misery is trodden on by many,
>   And being low, never relieved by any."

The rest, strangely enough for poets perhaps, seem to accept the fitness of the hare to be hunted as a matter of course, its suitableness for "the chase" a provision of Nature. "If thou needs *will* hunt," says Venus, "be ruled by me, uncouple at the timorous, flying hare."

Pope, Gay, Rowe, Mallet, Drayton, and Somerville are instances in point. Thus the author of " Polyolbion "—

> " The man whose vacant mind prepares him for the sport
>   The Finder sendeth forth to seek out nimble Wat
>   Which crosseth in the field each furlong, every flat,
>   Till he this pretty beast upon the Forme hath found.
>   Then, viewing for the course which is the fairest ground,
>   The greyhounds forth are brought, for coursing then in case,
>   And choicely in the slip, one leading forth a brace,
>   The finder puts her up and gives her courser's law ;
>   Then whilst the eager dogs upon the start do draw
>   She riseth from her seat, as though on earth she flew,
>   Forced by some yelping curre to give the greyhounds view,
>   Which are at length let slip, when leaping out they goe,
>   As in respect of them the swiftest wind were slow,
>   When each man runs his horse, with fixèd eyes, and notes
>   Which dog first turnes the hare, which first the other coats,
>   Till oft for want of breath to fall to ground they make her,
>   The greyhounds both so spent that they want breath to take her."

Gay was not much of a sportsman, as he himself confesses, for, finding himself committed to the subject of rural sports, he feels that he cannot do less than, at any rate, refer, in passing, to hunting as one of them ; but he pulls himself up with pleasing frankness and a "what on earth do I know about it" sort of apology—

> " The theme demands a more experienced lay.
>   Ye mighty hunters ! spare this weak essay."

Fishing was his weakness, with a fly by preference ; but still he breaks out into an artless linnet-chirrup about "the chase, a pleasing task."   He confines his remarks to hare-hunting, and thus abruptly finishes Wat off—

> "New strategems and doubling wiles she tries—
>   Now circling turns, and now at large she flies—
>   Till, spent at last, she pants and heaves for breath,
>   Then lays her down and waits devouring death !"

Somerville is, however, *par excellence* "the poet of the chase," and the second book of his poem, which is mainly concerned with hare-hunting, cannot be passed over without becoming notice.

Commencing with some general remarks about "that instinct which, unerring, guides the brutal race, which mimics reason's lore, and oft transcends," he passes on to the special instinct "that directs the jealous hare to choose her soft abode" and "oft quit her seat, lest some curious eye should mark her haunt."   He then describes the changes which she makes, according to the season, "as fancy prompts her or as food invites," and counsels the huntsman to make a note of them, as otherwise his labours will be wasted in looking for hares in places they are not likely to be, and "his impatient hounds, with disappoint-ment vexed, each springing lark, babbling pursue, far scat-tered o'er the fields."

So supposing it to be autumn, and the crops all gathered off the ground, he starts out with his harriers—

> "The gay pack
> In the rough, bristly stubbles range unblamed :
> No widow's tears o'erflow, no secret curse
> Swells in the farmer's breast, which his pale lips,
> Trembling, conceal, by his fierce landlord awed :
> But courteous now he levels every fence,
> Joins in the common cry, and halloos loud,
> Charmed with the rattling thunder of the field."

The pack is thrown off; after a while the old hound, with his "authentic voice, avows the recent trail," and away they go. But a double gives them a check, and then they steady down, working the fallow in a business-like way, and all of a sudden the huntsman himself comes upon puss in her form, and away she bolts. The hounds are laid on, and "as winds let loose, from the dark caverns of the blustering god, they burst away."

> "Now, my brave youths !
> Stripped for the chase, give all your souls to joy ;"

for the hare "o'er plains remote now stretches far away." The country side is up at the sound of the "clanging horns ;" the schoolboy, dreading no more the "afflictive birch," runs out of school to see the hunt go by; the travellers on the roads climb up to the highest spots ; the shepherd and ploughman leave their work ; the peasants "desert the unpeopled village."

> "And wild crowds
> Spread o'er the plains, by the sweet frenzy seized."

The hare doubles again, gets behind the pack, and "seems to pursue the foe she flies."

> "Let cavillers deny
> That brutes have reason : Sure 'tis something more.
> 'Tis heaven directs, and stratagems inspires,
> Beyond the short extent of human thought."

But the hounds find her out, and the pack sees her sitting on an eminence, "listening with one ear erect," and wondering what to do next, "pondering and doubtful what new course to take." At length she decides to trust to her heels again, and is off— .

"Once more, ye jovial train, your courage try."

She has gone uphill, which takes it out of the hounds, and down the steep other side, which takes it out of the riders; but "smoking along the vale," the hunt has the hare full in view. A flock of sheep baulks the hounds for a while, but they take up the "streaming scent" again, and "the rustling stubbles bend beneath the driving storm" of harriers—

> "Now the poor chase
> Begins to flag, to her last shifts reduced.
> From brake to brake she flies, and visits all
> Her well-known haunts, where once she ranged secure,
> With love and plenty blessed. See! there she goes;
> She reels along, and by her gait betrays
> Her inward weakness. See how black she looks.
> The sweat that clogs the obstructed pores scarce leaves
> A languid scent.
>   And now in open view
> See, see! she flies; each eager hound exerts
> His utmost speed, and stretches ev'ry nerve.
> How quick she turns, their gaping jaws eludes,
> And yet a moment lives, till round enclosed
> By all the greedy pack, with infant screams
> She yields her breath, and there, reluctant, dies."

After this, of course, there is nothing to come but exultation and, for the hounds, a taste of blood—

> "The huntsman now a deep incision makes,
> Shakes out with hands impure, and dashes down,
> Her reeking entrails and yet quivering heart.
> These claim the pack, the bloody perquisite
> Of all their toils. Stretched on the ground she lies
> A mangled corse; in her dim-glaring eyes
> Cold death exults and stiffens every limb."

After all this, the poet—the *poet*, remember—says this—

> " Thus the poor hare,
> *A puny, dastard animal*, diverts the youthful train."

The fox—what an endless theme the mere name suggests ! The stanchest pen might well despair of running down a creature of such interminable breath, such immeasurable craft.

A proverb says that all the cloth of Ghent, if it were turned into parchment, would not hold the stories of vulpine perfidy and sagacity, and though several scholars have devoted themselves to the "epic exploit" of this little animal, it seems to be far from exhausted. Yet its character is by no means altogether despicable. Bacon and Machiavelli say that for success a little of the fox is indispensable. Pope has a line to the effect that "the lion's skin is lengthened by the fox's tail"—a repetition of Lysander's apothegm, "When the lion's skin does not suffice, add on that of the fox."

Fortunately the poets' fox has but one aspect—the dispeopler of the poultry-yard. It eats chickens, therefore it should be vindictively hunted to death.

In the East the fox is not a familiar beast. It lives a secluded life, and seldom haunts the abodes of men. The jackal, therefore, is the original of those Oriental myths which European fabulists have adapted, and wherein the Western fox takes the place of its foreign congener. The two animals have very much in common in habits and character, though the fox is the superior in physical endurance, speed, and, perhaps, courage. I qualify my opinion on the last point, because it may be that the appearance of inferior pluck in the jackal may be really only due to an extra measure of that astute discretion which has made this animal the foremost figure in myth and folk-lore.

If we accept the myth translations of Gubernatis we see in the fox-jackal the ruddy interval between daylight and darkness that shades off bye-and-bye into twilight-grey with black night-points. It is the crepuscular phenomenon of the heavens taking an animal form. But just as there are two "auroras," the morning and the evening, so the fox-jackal has in every twenty-four hours two chances at the sun-cock, both of which it punctually fails to score, missing the solar fowl with an invariable accuracy that ought by this time to have had a depressing effect upon Reynard.

In fables the character of the fox is also dual. It is generally the deceiver, but also on occasions the dupe. Many animals on occasion fall a victim to it—in the single romance of Reincke Fuchs it outwits and infamously ruins the king-lion and pretty nearly all his courtier quadrupeds— but every now and again the same animals flout it, make fun of it, play tricks on it. Even cocks and kids have a joke occasionally at its expense, which is very true to nature, for we often see the professional sharper, the habitual traitor, exposed and put to shame by simple honesty or innocent mother wit. Betty with her mop routs the fencing-master. But, above all, the fox is always beaten when he tries to pass off his dishonesties upon other foxes; the rogues know each other too well to try to guess where the pea is. So when the fox falls by accident into a dyer's vat, and comes out a fine blue all over, he goes back to his kindred and tells them that he is a peacock of the sky. But they recognise his voice, and worry him till they pull all his blue fur off, and he dies. Stories of the same purport are abundant and familiar to all.

Yet there are plenty of occasions in which the fox behaves very honourably to its friends, and appears in the light of a benefactor, notably, in those tales where Reynard plays the part of Puss-in-boots, such as Cosmo the Quickly Enriched, and others. Moreover, the cock is sometimes found on the most friendly relations with the fox, who helps it against their common enemy, the wolf.

It is almost needless to say that many poets condemn fox-hunting, "which rural gentlemen call sport divine," and perhaps superfluous to add that their reasons hardly justify their condemnation. To them the sportsman appears something rather less than human—

> " To the field he flies,
> Leaps every fence but one, then falls and dies
> Like a slain deer ; the tumbril brings him home,
> Unmissed but by his dogs and by his groom.".

Especially does this class of poet detest to see women in the field—

> " Far be the spirit of the chase from them !
> Uncomely courage, unbeseeming skill,
> To spring the fence, to rein the prancing steed."

They hope "such horrid joy" will never "stain the bosom of the British fair."

Nor when they come to discriminate between one kind of sport and another is their argument such as to increase respect for their opinion. When Venus implores her darling not to hunt fierce beasts, but, if he *must* hunt, to go after the "timid hare," there is womanly reason enough in what she says. But when Thomson begs "ye Britons" not to hunt the poor "dappled" stag with the "chequered" sides, nor the "flying hare," but, if they *must* hunt, to ride after the fox, "the nightly robber of the fold," and, "pitiless, pour their sportive fury" upon it, the fustian of his sentiment is neither masculine nor feminine.

This idea, that Englishmen hunt the fox because it eats ducks, is quite a common one with the poets, and justifies, to their minds, the chase of it. So that it seems incredible that they could ever have seen a fox-hunter, still less have heard him speak with admiration, pride, even affection, of the staunch, plucky, little beast that had given him a fast run, and saved its brush after all.   At any rate, the idea that the animal is hunted because it kills chickens, and, therefore, richly deserves the worst that can happen to it, is utterly foreign to the character of "sport."   The fact that foxes are *preserved* in order to be hunted should have corrected the theories of modern poets.

With the otter it fares exactly the same.   Because the beast catches fish which men wish to catch it is said to merit the death which overtakes it when the hounds pursue and tear it to pieces.   They all seem to hate it, call it "felon," "robber," and " prowler," and Somerville descants at length in a very spirited but most deliberately cruel poem . on the pleasures of murdering an otter.

IX.

THE POETS' FLOCKS.

> " Let me hear
> The morning uproar of the fleecy flock,
> What time, vociferous, their tardy march
> With baying curs impatient their rude load
> To the green pastures urge.   Loud inquires
> The bleating mother for her sundered lamb,
> As loud complaining for his mother lost.
> With quick infallible perception, she,
> Amid the mingled outcry, hears distinct
> His slender shrill entreaty, he remote,
> With nicety that shames our grosser sense,
> Her voice acknowledges, and through the crowd
> Winds his insulted way."

I THINK this stanza is exquisite, and, as a sketch straight from Nature, perfect.   But the poets are, as a rule, exceptionally happy in their treatment of sheep.   Most of them are born shepherds.   They seem to have an instinctive sympathy with the woolly folk..

> " To him the whistling ploughman's artless tune,
>   The bleating flocks, the oxen's hollow crune,
>   Give more delight than the Italian song."

With what a nice accuracy they watch them ; how exactly faithful they are to the real life of the flocks.

At morning the sheep-fold pours out its fleecy tenants "o'er the glade, and, first progressive in a stream, they seek the middle field, but scattered by degrees, each to his choice, soon whiten all the land" (Cowper).   They are the "restless," "ever-wandering" sheep—

> " Russet lawn and fallows grey
>   Where the nibbling flocks do stray."

So the morning passes and the heat increases.   "With numerous bleat," they seek the trees "spreading a shady boon," and "creep close by the grove, to hide from the rigours of day."   Here they lie ruminating ; smoothing the knotted thorns by rubbing against them ; and then spread again over the land till evening, and "in the soft sunshine of departing day" the "cheerful lambs skip in the fields and lead the wanton race."   The twilight falls, and

> " Every mother ruminates apart
> Recumbent in the dusk, and every son
> Sportful no longer, and his bleating hushed,
> Reclines expectant of the dewy night
> Fast by his chewing dam."

Or the shepherd convenes the flock, and they troop to the fold "with hurried bell and dust-provoking feet."

Not that their days are altogether uneventful.   Cowper's "Needless Alarm" is an excellent case in point, when they discuss the propriety of suicide in consequence of the overwhelming horrors of the approaching fox-hunt, thinking all the fiends are let loose upon themselves.   The description of the mutton-headed folk is delightful—

> " Awhile they mused.   Surveying every face,
> Thou hadst supposed them of superior race ;
> Their periwigs of wool and fears combined,
> Stamped on each countenance such marks of mind,
> That sage they seemed as lawyers o'er a doubt,
> Which, puzzling long, at last they puzzle out."

Sometimes, again, dogs worry the flock.   Somerville prescribes the proper punishment for any hound caught in such an act—

> " If at the crowding flock
> He bay presumptuous, or with eager haste
> Pursue them scattered o'er the verdant plain,
> In the foul fact attached, to the strong ram
> Tie fast the rash offender.   See ! at first
> His horned companion, fearful and amazed,
> Shall drag him trembling o'er the rugged ground.
> Then, with his load fatigued, shall turn his head,
> And with his curled hard front incessant peal
> The panting wretch, till, breathless and astunned,
> Stretched on the turf he lie.   Then spare not thou
> The twining whip, but ply his bleeding sides,
> Lash after lash, and with thy threat'ning voice
> Harsh echoing from the hills, inculcate loud
> His vile offence."

Even if there is no malicious intent, the presence of a strange dog is enough to bring excitement into their day. " Look," says Hood,

> " How a panicked flock will stare,
> And huddle close and start and wheel about,
> Watching the roaming mongrel here and there ;"

and Grahame, how " the startled lambs with bickering haste, fly to their mother's side and gaze around."

Sportsmen are out and the guns alarm them, as so many poets note. The passing train, the whirring covey, the shouting plough-boy, are each of them episodes of puzzling interest to the woolly ones. Yet they have their amusements also. Panic is not their only dissipation. They are " sportive "—especially as lambs.

> " I am so old, so old I can write a letter,
> My birthday lessons are done ;
> The lambs play always, they know no better,
> They are only one times one."

The lost lamb affords a theme for countless excellent passages. Who has not, in the course of a country walk, come, as Clare does, upon the small wanderer on the wrong side of the hedge, looking in vain for the hole it got through, "having no sense to find the same again," and "calling for help" as it trots up and down in nervous bewilderment, the mother meanwhile pacing backwards and forwards on the other side, and replying with a grave, troubled voice to the pitiful lamentations of her little one? Indeed, getting lost or thinking that it is lost, and straightway abandoning itself to an excessive pity for itself, is almost the normal condition of the lamb.

> " Soon lost and soon inquiring for its dam,
> Who bleats and mumbles at his slender call."

As the "playful," "dancing" lamb, it is one of the insignia of the poets' Spring, its voice a "vernal note" like the linnet's, its presence contemporary with, and a co-efficient of, the budding flowers and sprouting leaves and birds' nests with their eggs. Spring personified comes with "whinny braes all garlanded with gold" (Grahame), and with lambkins sporting round her, "full of May." Its association with the linnet is often very prettily worked in, as where Crabbe has "browsing by the linnet's bed," and Grahame, the lamb chasing his twin round and round "the linnet's bush." In Phineas Fletcher's eclogue one of the features of the vernal season is the lamb; " they forget their food to mind their sweeter play," and so too in Bloomfield's "Spring" this charming adjunct of the young year finds, with characteristic affection for Nature, conspicuous description. The passage commencing—

> " A few begin a short but vigorous race,
> And indolence astonished soon flies the place.
> Thus challenged forth, see thither, one by one,
> From every side assembling playmates run,"

makes a delightful vignette.

But of all the metaphors and similes drawn from this inexhaustible source, I would give the palm to Lovelace's—

> "Lost hearts, like lambs drove from their fields by fears, .
> May back return by chance, but not by tears."

Then comes Summer, when the flies are abroad, and the shearers a-field—"what time the new-shorn flock stand here and there, with huddled head, impatient of the fly." No one who knows the midsummer pastures can have missed noticing how the restless sheep, worried by insects, can hardly venture to stand still to eat a mouthful, but nibble and walk at the same time, and pitied the poor wretches for their uncomfortable feeding; or how, in despair, they congregate, and, hiding their faces under each other, try to baulk the indefatigable "bot." How carefully they keep their noses down in the grass, even though too fidgety to eat, and then suddenly, when one gives the alarm, how the whole company decamps from one side of the field to the other. Not that the shepherd can do much for them; as a rule, he merely leans on the gate, and extends a passive sympathy; so that Quarles' "Emblem," taken from this pastoral incident, would seem somewhat wide of the fact—

> "Look how the sheep, whose rambling steps do stray
>   From the safe keeping of the shepherd's eye,
> Eftsoon becomes the unprotected prey
>   Of the winged squadron of beleaguering fly."

The shearing of the sheep, once an acknowledged rural festival, gives poetry many a charming passage—as "the gambols and wild freaks at shearing-time," when, after the creatures, soused one by one into the pool, had been hurdled up, and the shearer got him ready for his work, the "queen" of the day, with her chosen "shepherd-king," came, with bravery of summer flowers, and bright clothes and rustic music, upon the scene, and, the short day's work over, headed the long evening's revels—

> "The chief, in gracious dignity enthroned,
>   Shines o'er the rest, the pastoral queen, and lays

> Her smiles, sweet-beaming, on her shepherd-king,
> While the glad circle round them yield their souls
> To festive mirth and wit that knows no gall."

Thomson's description of the scene, "while, ever and anon, to his shorn peers a ram goes bleating" (Keats), is excellent—

> "In one diffusive band
> They drive the troubled flocks, by many a dog
> Compelled, to where the mazy, running brook
> Forms a deep pool: this bank, abrupt and high,
> And that fair-spreading in a pebbled shore,
> Urged to the giddy brink, much is the toil,
> The clamour much of men and boys and dogs,
> Ere the soft, fearful people to the flood
> Commit their woolly sides. And oft the swain,
> On some impatient seizing, hurls them in :
> Emboldened then, nor hesitating more,
> Fast, fast, they plunge amid the flashing wave,
> And, panting, labour to the farthest shore.
> Repeated this, till deep the well-washed fleéce
> Has drunk the flood, and from his lively haunt
> The trout is banished by the sordid stream;
> Heavy and dripping, to the breezy brow
> Slow move the harmless race ; where, as they spread
> Their swelling treasures to the sunny ray,
> Inly disturbed, and wondering what this wild
> Outrageous tumult means, their loud complaints
> The country fill ; and, tost from rock to rock,
> Incessant bleatings run around the hills.
> At last, of snowy white, the gathered flocks
> Are in the wattled pen innumerous pressed,
> Head above head : and, ranged in lusty rows,
> The shepherds sit, and whet the sounding shears."

Then stormy Autumn comes with its "huddling" flocks, and

> "The sheep before the pinching heaven
> To sheltered dale and down are driven
> Where yet some faded herbage pines,
> And yet a watery sunbeam shines.

> In weak despondency they eye
> The withered sward and wintry sky.
> The shepherd shifts his mantle's fold,
> And wraps him closer from the cold ;
> His dogs no merry circles wheel,
> But, shivering, follow at his heel ;
> A cowering glance they often cast,
> As deeper moans the gathering blast."—*Scott.*

And so to Winter, with "the dun-discoloured flocks, untended spread, cropping the wholesome root"—or, as Grahame more prosaically puts it, "on the turnip-field, in portions due, staked off, the bleating flock their juicy meal, nibbling partake"—or it may be with the same poor woolly folk piteously neglected, like Milton's "hungry sheep that look up and are not fed, but, swollen with wind and the rank mist they draw, rot inwardly," or, as in Thomson—

> "The bleating kind
> Eye the bleak heavens, and next the glistening earth,
> With looks of dumb despair, then sad dispersed
> Dig for the withered herb, through heaps of snow."

Fond as poets are of their sheep, they hardly justify their excessive affection for them by the character which they give the "woolly people." Their habit of following their leader, "whether led to the downs or from the wave-worn rock reluctant hurled" (Armstrong), brings down upon their heads frequent contempt. Slaves are as obedient "as sheep," and stupid men are "like sheep that follow." As flocks they are always "silly," "the tame, implicit team" (Armstrong), as individuals they are meekly feeble. Says Swift—

> "Therefore the sheep, those foolish cattle,
> Not fit for courage or for battle,
> And being tolerable meat,
> They're good for nothing but to eat."

"Specious and sage, the sovereign of the flock," the

ram, "the flocke's father," finds but scanty reference ; the truth being that this generous and bold-fronted beast mars the symmetry of the poetical sheep-idea. His independent bearing, his courage in misfortune, spoil the woolly-silky-gentle picture. In the olden verse the rams that "fight for the rule of the rich-fleeced flock," and "meet so fierce with hornèd fronts," receive a robust and becoming sympathy, which is in accordance with the splendid traditions of the beast—

> "As when two rams, stir'd with ambitious pride,
> Fight for the rule of the rich-fleeced flocke,
> Their horned fronts so fierce on either side
> Doe meete, that, with the terror of the shocke
> Astonied, both stand sencelesse as a blocke,
> Forgetfull of the hanging victory :
> So stood these twaine, unmoved as a rocke,
> Both staring fiercely, and holding idëly
> The broken reliques of their former cruelty."

The ewe, the "mumbling" ewe, has but little individuality. They call her "Goody Sheep," and, in Mother Hubbard's delightful tale, the fox and wolf flout her when she comes to complain to the ape—then ruler of the four-footed—of the loss of her young. She is only the mother of the lamb. Eagles stooping from their watch-towers and "gathering large tribute from every vale,"—wolves rushing from the bushes upon the gamboling lambkins,—the butcher levying his toll upon the flock, all relegate her to obscurity. Take away her lamb and she vanishes into nonentity. Give her another, and she reappears.

> "She provident
> Her milky treasures for his life reserves,
> Butting intruders with a frown away.
> At length he finds her, and with bended knees,
> Emblem of innocence and filial grace
> His plenteous meal receives, and bleats no more."

In Nature the mother and her young one are ever a delight-

ful and loveable sight; and the charm is often beautifully
translated into verse. Thus in Blomfield—

> "The teeming ewes, that still their burdens bear :
> Beneath whose sides to-morrow's dawn may see
> The milk-white strangers bow the trembling knee.
> And at their birth the pow'rful instinct's seen
> That fills with champions all the daisied green,
> For ewes that stood aloof with fearful eye,
> With stamping foot now men and dogs defy,
> And obstinately faithful to their young
> Guard their first steps to join the bleating throng."

Hurdis has the following curious passage about the
pastoral artifice of dressing up a lamb in the skin of another,
and thus palming it off upon some bereaved mother— .

> "Often let me mark
> The sullen ewe's authoritative stamp
> Where'er the sheep-dog passes. Let me smile
> At her deluded sense, what time her lamb
> By the bleak season slain, his wilted coat
> Yields to the flayer, and the ravished twin
> Of some fond mother, in the coarse disguise
> Appears loose-coated, and usurps the dug.
> Dull fool, how ill perceives thy stupid eye
> The palpable imposture !"

The lamb, when not "prancing" and "gambolling," is
"witless" and "unconscious." Above all, it is innocent.
"Is not this a lamentable thing, that the skin of an innocent
lamb should be made parchment? that parchment being
scribbled o'er should undo a man?"

That the wolf should eat the lamb is therefore one of that
beast's most infamous points. It is intolerable to the poets,
and they are never weary of denouncing the base assassina-
tion. They admit the provocation the lamb gives by losing
itself, by bleating loudly, by opening doors which its mother
had particularly cautioned it to keep shut; but their indignation against the murderer is none the less unmeasured

and persistent. Their lambs are innocent and white and gentle; so the wolves that eat them are atrociously guilty and unspeakably swarthy and grim. But this is after all only the survival of the world's original pastoral myth.

Judged from any but a poet's standpoint, sheep might almost be accounted the happiest and most fortunate of animals. Death, after all, is the universal lot; the grim policeman calls with his summons upon each in turn. Not that sheep ever seem to contemplate anything farther ahead than their own noses. They are not troubled with visions of cold mutton—

> " The lamb thy riot dooms to bleed to-day,
> Had he thy reason, would he skip and play?
> Pleased to the last he crops the flow'ry food
> And licks the hand just raised to shed his blood." [1]—*Pope.*

But, with the poets, their mildly-idiotic vacuity of face, their senseless imitation of each other's actions, their shambling evasion of anything like vigorous independence for attack or self-defence, are interpreted into innocence, docility, and meekness. Their timidity is called gentleness. Thus invested with many good qualities—those which specially engage the poetic fancy—we find them constantly besung

[1] What an admirable passage is Tennyson's—

> " And in the flocks
> The lamb rejoiceth in the year,
> And raceth freely with his fere,
> And answers to his mother's calls
> From the flowered furrow. In a time
> Of which he wots not, run short pains
> Thro' his warm heart, and then, from whence
> He knows not, on his light there falls
> A shadow; and his native slope,
> Where he was wont to leap and climb,
> Floats from his sick and filmed eyes,
> And something in the darkness draws
> His forehead earthward, and he dies."

as a virtuous people whose lives are sadly oppressed. Their perpetual nervousness, one of the most absurd phenomena of animal life, is excused on the ground that the events that cause the alarm are arbitrary and brutal. Some tyrant or another, a dog that barks, or man with a gun, rudely disturbs the happy calm of the gentle sheep. So all persecuted sects, communities, or persons are called "flocks" and "sheep," although, says Herbert, "to a short-shorn sheep God gives wind by measure."

So it becomes the symbol of home-life, and its peace. In the pet-lamb, Burns' lamented "hoggie," this idea, as in Mary Howitt's very charming poem, reaches its extreme expression, but the flocks in general convey the same significance in a hundred different ways. Their mere presence suffices to tranquillise the scene, and, like some other sounds in Nature, their voices emphasise the rural silence.

> " For sheep-bells chiming from a wold,
>   Or bleat of lamb within its fold,
>   Or cooing of love-legends old
>   To dove-wives makes not quiet less ;
>   Ecstatic chirp of wingèd things,
>   Or bubbling of the water spring,
>   Are sounds that more than silence bring
>   Itself and its delightsomeness."—*Jean Ingelow.*

Wordsworth hears, in the bleat of the lamb on the hill, "the plaintive spirit of the solitude." Thomson is very fond of "the bleating mountains,"[1] the "distant bleatings of the hills," as an emblem of repose. The absence of sheep from the landscape (as in Grahame) reminds the wanderer in other lands of the happy tranquillity of "home." He longs, with Faber, to hear

> " The bleating tribes,
> The nomads of the moorland, which send down
> A plaintive greeting from the windy heights."

---

[1] So too we have with the herds "lowing vales."

Thomson's shepherd therefore "dwells with Peace," and "the porch of his mossy cottage" is in Wordsworth rendered more touchingly home-like by the corner-stones on either side being

> "With dull red stains discoloured, and stuck o'er
> With tufts and hairs of wool,
> As if the sheep that fed upon the common, thither came
> Familiarly, and found a couching place
> Even at the threshold."

It follows therefore that any accidental association of sheep with stirring scenes or sounds of the chase or battle —as lambs "in friskful glee" that sport round "the mossy mound, the rampart once of iron war "—should give the poets a point of strong contrast. So (in Pitt) " the bleating flocks that along the bastion pass, and from the awful ruins, crop the grass," illustrates the peaceful meeting of generals to sign a truce upon their recent battlefield. The utterness of change is shown in Byron by sheep feeding on the lost site of Ilion's outworks—"where I sought for Ilion's walls, the quiet sheep feeds, and the tortoise crawls," and so too in Leyden—

> " Green waves the harvest, and the peasant boy
> Stalls his rough herds, within the towers of Troy ;
> Prowls the sly fox, the jackal rears her brood,
> Where once the towers of mighty Ilion stood."

Though thus idealised as a genus, the various species are all practically rendered. A poet's acquaintance with Nature is not, as a rule, so extensive that he can afford to waste a variety of sheep. The "small black-legged sheep" that, " fleshless, lank, and lean," devour "the meagre herbage" of the Cumbrian hills ; the "goat-horned" animals " of fleece hairy and coarse, of long and nimble shank," that " browse their thinly-scattered meal o'er the bleak wilds " of the Cambrian ; the Cotswold, " hills of milder air, that gently rise, o'er dewy dales, a fairer species boast, of shorter limb and frontlet more ornate, such the Silurian ; " the Southdown, "the larger sorts of head defenceless," " whose fleece is deep and clammy, close and plain ; " the other,

> " Whose tawny fleece in ringlets curls,
> With horns Ammonian circulating twice
> Around each open ear—like those fair scrolls
> That grace the columns of th' Ionic dome,"

and many another, is specifically described, while the elaborate minuteness of Dyer's history of the Fleece, from the ingredients that compose the soil, that grows the grass, that feeds the sheep, that gives the wool, that makes dyers rich, and ought to make England mistress of the world, is probably too well known to need any detailed reference here to that amazing abuse of poetical instinct, and unique infelicity of choice of subject.   But the " poem," for such Akenside declares it to be, contains some delightful references to foreign sheep and shepherds, which are worth a passing notice.   Having put the Indus in Cashmere, he calls the goats of the country sheep, and then, rambling off across Cathay, refers enraptured to the shepherd by " China's long canals," and so, coming round to the west, sees Mississippi " lengthen-on " her sheep-walks, and finally arrives in South America, where he speaks of the llama or the alpaca of Peru as

> " That sheep
> Of fertile Arica, like camels formed,
> Which bear huge burdens to the sea-beat shore
> And shine with fleeces soft as feathery down."

But the whole poem is too pathetic in its vain struggle with the hopeless to be made fun of.   There are lines and occasional passages of tolerable merit, but of the work, as a whole, Johnson's verdict on it will generally commend itself to the majority.

The value of our wool productions is, however, a frequently recurring point in verse; and though the old pastoral days are called (by Phillips), "the unluxurious times of yore, when flocks and herds were no inglorious store," the possession of flocks is usually spoken of as an important factor in individual, local, and national wealth. Says King, "the fleecy produce of the Cotswold field shall equal what Peruvian mountains yield." The beauty of the wool itself comes often also under admiration, its whiteness and its softness exceeding indeed sometimes the poets' stock of simile and comparison. More than one even goes so far as to blame us for dyeing it, and to draw a moral of voluptuous luxury therefrom. So Hammond, for instance—

> " Unwise who first the charm of Nature lost
>   With Tyrian purple soiled the snowy fleece."

As the sheep are, so are the shepherds; creatures of a "witless" innocence, a feeble simplicity. Thus Parnell's—

> " Gaping, tender, apt to weep,
>   Their nature's altered by their sheep."

Or, again, in Spenser—

> " And meek he was, as meek might be,
>   Simple as simple sheep,
> Humble and like in each degree
>   The flock which he did keep."

Indeed, " the cheerful tendance of the flocks " would hardly seem, from the poets' description of those who tend them, to conduce to much dignity of thought or intellectual occupation. They see them grazing, as Crabbe says, " with what a pure and simple joy ! "

> " Perhaps their loves, or else their sheep,
>   Was all that did their silly thoughts so busy keep."

And when they meet they have but a slender stock of intelligence to exchange, as in Herrick—

> " But say, what news
>   Stirs in our sheep-walk ?
>   None. Save that my ewes,
>   Wethers, and lambs, and wanton kids are well,
>   Smooth, fair, and fat."

Yet Faber would seem to be envious of such company—

> " That in mute company with the creatures,
>   And gazing in their patient features,
>   I might receive some sweet sense
>   Of our original innocence."

There are, however, two varieties of the shepherd. The first is the strictly poetical shepherd, " with his artless reed." This is Mallet's " rural king amid his subject flocks," who (Dyer) flutes to " charm his sheep" and (Otway) " pipeth to his feeding sheep." Jean Ingelow has, in " Gladys' Island,"

> " A grassy down,
> Where sheep and lambs were feeding, with a boy
> To tend them. 'Twas the boy who wears that herb
> Called heartsease in his bosom, and he sang
> So sweetly to his flock, that she stole on
> Nearer to listen."

The other is the ordinary rustic, who lies about on the grass, and, when he is awake, gazes at his sheep and the landscape generally, and who has a dog to do all his work for him. A pleasing sub-variety, however, is " the blooming maid," who sometimes drives her flocks afield. Their queen is surely Lovelace's Chloris—that

> " Chloris, the gentlest shepherdess
>   That ever lambs or lawns did bless."

Country folk take omen and augury from so many beasts, birds, and plants, that it would be strange if sheep were exempt from prophetic functions, and not invested with prognostic powers.

> " When Blouzelind expir'd, the wether's bell
> Before the drooping flock toll'd forth her knell,
> The solemn death-watch click'd the hour she dy'd,
> And shrilling crickets in the chimney cry'd.
> The boding raven on her cottage sate,
> And with hoarse croak warn'd us of her fate ;
> The lambkin, which her wonted tendance bred,
> Dropp'd on the plains that fatal instant dead.
> Swarm'd on a rotten stick the bees I spied,
> Which erst I saw when Goody Dobson died."— *Gay.*

Certain noises are said to sicken the ewes ; shrew-mice in the grass, newts in the water, are supposed to " blast " them. The poets take due cognisance of these superstitions ; and the fauns and fairies who avert such disasters are becomingly admired. Of old-world fancies, Keats has beautifully preserved the following—

> " And it had gloomy shades, sequestered deep,
> Where no man went ; and if from shepherd's keep
> A lamb strayed far adown those inmost glens,
> Never again saw he the happy pens
> Whither his brethren, bleating with content,
> Over the hills at every nightfall went.
> Among the shepherds 'twas believed ever,
> That not one fleecy lamb which thus did sever
> From the white flock, but passed unworried
> By any wolf, or pard with prying head,
> Until it came to some unfooted plains
> Where fed the herds of Pan : ay, great his gains
> Who thus one lamb did lose."

This beautiful legend of Pan—" Hearkener to the loud-clapping shears "—and the fauns guarding the shepherd and his sheep — the cloud-flocks of the divinities — of Oceanus—the golden fleece of Colchos—

> " There was a shepe, as it was tolde,
> The whiche his flees bare all of golde,
> And so the goddess had it sette,
> That it ne might awaie be fette " (*Gower*)—

the strange shepherding of Orpheus, "when lambs would scorn their food to hear his lay, and savage beasts stand by as tame as they" (Cowley), and many another fancy of a pastoral antiquity, finds a place in our poets' verse; while the similes, analogies, morals, and metaphors from the sheep of Scripture, the classics, or folk-lore individuality are innumerable. The Lamb of the Messiah—

> "Tell me, was he a Shepherd or a Lamb?
>   Shepherd and Lamb at once. He took each name.
>   Since then our God a Shepherd's name doth wear,
>   The name of lamb who will not wish to bear?
>   And who will not be shepherd, since God deigns
>   To be a Lamb for suffering of sin's pains."—*Crashaw.*

Of Pentecost, of sacrifice, "the useful beast on Isaac's pile consumed" (Cowley), the flocks of David and of the shepherds of Bethlehem, afford again and again an image or a thought—

> "A deceitful concubine, who shore me
>   Like a tame wether, all my precious fleece,"

Una with her milk-white lamb, Joan of Arc with her crook, Don Quixote's army of Pentapolin.

Being thus prepossessed in favour of sheep, it is almost a natural sequence that the poets should be prejudiced against the goat, which is the moral antithesis of their favourite animal. Allan Ramsay's fable admirably illustrates this difference of sentiment. A ram "of upright, hardy spirit, really a hornèd head of merit," who all summer and autumn through had led his family to abundant pastures, takes them, as winter comes on, "to crop contented frozen fare, with honesty, on hills blown bare." Then he meets a goat who by his rascally trespassing upon fields and gardens had earned the hatred of all his neighbours, and who, anxious if possible to secure a friend, offers to give the ram some of his coat, which is close and intact, while the ram's, being torn by brambles, leaves his body half naked to the biting mountain-wind. But the sturdy old ram refuses.

" No," said he, " though my coat's torn,
  Yet ken, thou worthless, that I scorn
  To be obliged at any price
  To sic as you, whose friendship's vice :
  I'd have less favour frae the best,
  Clad in a hatefu' hairy vest
  Bestowed by thee, than as I noo
  Stand but ill-drest in native woo'.
  Boons frae the generous make ane smile ;
  Fro' miscreants, make receivers vile."

X.

"THE BEARD-BLOWN GOAT."

GOATS possess the great advantage over sheep of having beards. This should be especially in their favour with the poets, for the beard makes the animal romantic—it becomes, in Tennyson, the "beard-blown goat"—and gives it that air of the rude and shaggy which Dr. Syntax assures us is the soul and essence of the picturesque.

Bearded is always a favourite epithet with the poets, when they wish to convey an idea of rugged strength or venerable wisdom. Thor, with all his presence, could hardly spare that red torrent from his chin ; Peru's dignity and strength lies in his thunder-black beard. Remember Schaibar. He was a dwarf, and a dreadful ogre at that. But he trailed thirty feet of beard. When the wind blew he looked forth as from a mist of flame. Regiments of guards fell flat before him as he walked. Kings upon their thrones shivered in their golden sandals at the sight of the much-bearded brother of the Peri Banou. How better describe the grim earl than to call him " Hakon Grizzle-beard ? " The portrait is authentic at once. From the beard we straightway deduce the complete man. Barbarossa stands out from the page forthwith.

Conversely, disrespect attaches to the shabby beard : as Don Quixote, admonishing Sancho on the manner of his life when he should come to be governor of an island or an earldom, says, "What thou art will be seen a bow-shot off if thy beard be not as it should be."

The anomalous beard makes the whole man eccentric, grotesque, and absurd. What reverence would attach to the appearance of the Nestors of the Moon-folk, whose beards, as we know, grew just above their knees? or to those elders of the wise sea-folk with their faces smothered in green tangles?

Again, to be altogether beardless has passed into an expression of scornful contempt. It was David's hairless chin that exasperated Goliath. It is true that some races affect to despise the beard—thus the Red Indians, who say that a European's face resembles a dog's with a squirrel in its mouth—but they are those who cannot grow a really handsome and venerable length of beard, and illustrate, therefore, very aptly the fable of the fox that had lost its tail. As a rule, all nations of antiquity prided themselves on this adornment. No oath carried with it the same dignity of earnestness as "by my beard"—even when a Welshman pronounced it with a "p;" no affront such humiliation as that which was offered to the beard. The gods themselves pledged their honour "by their beards." The reddened beard of Ahenobarbus, black till then, was the great Twin Brethren's gage of victory.

When men succumb to the vril-staff of women in the struggle for existence they are to become Ana and beardless.

"So his prophesying thus to the Assyrians moved them to paint Apollo with a large, long beard beseeming an old settled person of a most sedate, staid, and grave demeanour: not young and beardless as he was pourtrayed most usually among the Grecians." In fairy tales, again, what beards the magician, the ogres, and the giants have! When they are blue or scarlet (as in the Red Shoes story), or green, like those of the pine-forest Kobolds, they are a trifle whimsical, no doubt, but never ridiculous.

Thus the goat starts, as it were, with a beard "to the good "—

> " Hung high in air the hoary goat reclined,
> His streaming beard the sport of every wind."

What a delightful confusion of mental pictures the couplet innocently conjures up—Rogers' Swiss mountaineers—Keat's discrowned Titans—the Last Minstrel. Put any other word in the place of "goat" and see the effect. " Hung high in air the hoary *god* reclined," &c. Lo! Saturn overlooking the conflict that shook the Elder Divinities out of the heavens. Try "prince" instead of "goat," and we have doomed Saul lying stretched upon the mountain side, his eyes, ominous of to-morrow's woe, scanning the hosts of Philistia as they darken the spurs of Gilboa. Change it for "chief," or "sage," or "bard," and the effect of the couplet remains the same.

It is the beard that does it. Dignity is inseparable from it—when it is long enough to "stream," and the owner is in repose. "The old romantic goat, his white beard low-waving." Here Coleridge has the vignette complete.

Not that the goat's beard, as such, is in itself a reverend symbol. On the contrary, if it is transplanted from the animal's chin to any other. it carries with it those scarcely-admirable significances which the folk-lore of all nations has attached to the he-goat. "Mad and careless, hot and vain," is the poets' summing-up of the male animal, and Spenser tells us how—

> " The blossoms of lust to bud do begin,
> And spring forth rankly under his chin."

Satyrs and all sorts of misbehaving persons, even Apollyon himself, cohircinate therein, and in the " Beasts' Confession " of Swift we read how—

> " The goat advanced with decent pace,
> And first excused his youthful face ;

> Forgiveness begged that he appeared
> ('Twas Nature's fault) without a beard.
> 'Tis true, he was not much inclined
> To fondness of the female kind,
> For he had made a holy vow
> Of chastity, as monks do now."

Moreover, there is a popular superstition that no he-goat ever remains in sight for twenty-four consecutive hours. For just as every Grimalkin has to be a cat for eight of her lives and a witch for one, so, they darkly hint, the goat has to go once a day to the Devil to have his beard combed.

In the practical household the appendage had its use as a cider-strainer. Thus the Poet of the Apple advises—

> " With timely care
> To shave the goat's shaggy beard, lest thou too late
> In vain should'st seek a strainer to dispart,
> The husky terrene dregs from purer must."

When the Bachelor disguises himself to deceive the Don, he ties on to his face a beard which the innkeeper's wife angrily despoils him of, it being her strainer.

But the poets have very skilfully utilised both aspects. As the beard promiscuous or general it claims for the animal a uniform picturesqueness ; as the beard particular—caprine —it gives the poet an easy simile.

Next to their beards, the sure-footedness of this daring mountaineer that—

> " Mid the cliffs with steady footstep climbs,"

attracts poetical regard, and certainly not without cause. For the amazing confidence of this animal is certainly among the chief marvels of Nature. Caution in moving and deliberateness in setting down the foot on a new spot are characteristics of nearly all wild things, whether furred or feathered. Even cats look carefully before they leap. Birds flutter before settling on an untried perch. But goats appear to have no fear whatever, and never fail in their trust of themselves. They make no pauses between their bounds, but spring from point to point, from sliding shingle to hard rock, sharp peak to sloping boulder, without apparently the least calculation—and sometimes they break their legs. So the poets call them "the careless goats "— Spenser has them "dancing on the craggy cliffs at will," and Montgomery speaks of them "vaulting through the air, as if a thought conveyed them to and fro." They delight to "hang" them upon "dizzy heights," or make them, as Wordsworth does, frolic "by the side of dashing waterfalls."

> " The vine-mantled brows
> The prudent goats unveil, regardless they
> Of hourly peril, tho' the rifted domes
> Tremble to ev'ry wind."

There is, indeed, a fine independence of character about the goat which separates it by many parasangs from the sheep. The latter lives placidly by faith, and seems assured of redemption ; the former is possessed by the restless genius of unbelief. You cannot keep goats on the level road, even though you take the greatest possible pains to show them the farmyard and the fold at the end of it. They detest the commonplace. Rather than plod safely home by the regular way, they prefer to travel adventurously by paths of their own. By choice, they take the ups and downs of life ; and when they do not find them ready made for them, they make them for themselves. If there is a heap of stones by the roadside. they get up on to it—their spirits at once rise at finding themselves on an eminence : and till the herdsman comes up they snatch a precious half-minute in playing "Tom Tiddler's Ground." If there is a ditch it is just the same. As many goats as possible get down into it and pretend it was in their way. They get among the sheep, and deliberately disorder the woolly procession

They jump over the sheep's backs to show their indifference to orthodoxy.

It is very seldom indeed, therefore, that the versatile, generous-minded goat is found in Nature mixed up with the dull but eminently respectable sheep. They are bored by . them. When the herdsman calls his charges together, the sheep come along the valley in a compact body, taking the beaten track. But the goats drop in promiscuously, singly, or in twos or threes ; and most of them from above.

" At feeding time the goats will be browsing in long lines on the mountain sides, while the sheep are grazing in the plain. At midday, when the flocks are gathered round the wells to await the rolling away of the stone that guards the water, the goats assemble on one side and the sheep on the other. And at night, when they are all gathered into one fold by one shepherd, they are still separated from each other."

I confess this exclusiveness commends itself to me, and I cannot find it in me to reproach goats for avoiding the company of sheep. I can imagine no company less exhilarating or improving. Sheep are very woolly.

This independence of character is finely shown in the goat's demeanour. He bears himself in a stately way. Read Proverbs—

"There be three things which go well, yea, four are comely in going.

"A lion which is strongest among beasts, and turneth not away from any.

"A greyhound ; *an he-goat also ;* and a king, against whom there is no rising up."

Indras, therefore, does not derogate from his dignity in assuming the form of the "warrior he-goat," nor Thor select unbecoming steeds for his thunder-car when he yokes the Butting Ones.

Boldness is in the blood of it—an inheritance from its great-horned ancestry of the Asiatic ranges. These are the paseng and the ibex, among the bravest of animals and symbols of proud and fearless freedom. The markhor, too, is a grand type of the mountaineer, with its gravity of bearing, induced as it were by a life of constant peril, and an implacable courage.

As distinct from sheep—the ordinary fleecy flocks of the dawn—goats are the shaggy clouds that hang on the hillside, as in Phillips' lines—

> " On the cliffy height
> Of Penmenmaur and that cloud-piercing hill
> Plinlimmon, from afar the traveller views
> Astonished, how the goats their shrubby browse,
> Gnaw, pendent "—

or are blown about the peaks, as in Montgomery—

> " Goats that swing
> Like spiders on the crags."

They are the darker *nimbus* clouds as contrasted with the lamb's-wool *cirrus* of meteorologists. A suspicion of the sinister lurks about them. They have latent potentialities for mischief. They huddle together at twilight in the wolfish gloaming, and threaten with their horns the monster of Night, whether wolf or witch, that fills the herdsman's hours of darkness with terror—substantial, four-footed terrors, some of them : superstitious, aerial, the others. They patrol the midnight sky lest the enemy with the myriad eyes, the sleepless one, should do them harm. When day breaks, and Aurora opens her folds to drive her charges afield, they separate each after its kind, just as in the pastoral landscape—

> " Goats upon the frowning steep,
>   Fearless with their kidlings browse,
> Here a flock of snowy sheep,
>   There a herd of motley cows."

For the cloud-myth, a fancy of primitive man, is altogether

pastoral; and goats—more common than sheep in the countries where that myth originated—have always their appropriate prominence.

Goatherds differ from shepherds only as their charges differ, being more picturesque and in a manner more vagabond. They are described in prose, in Don Quixote and Gil Blas, for instance, as of a more active, aggressive, and enterprising kind than the Gentle Shepherd. Byron's little goatherd "in his white capote, leaning his boyish form along the rock," affords a pleasing vignette from the rocks, and many speak of him as delighting, like the guardian of the sheep, in music.

> " Meantime on earlier pipe a lowly lay,
>   As my kids browse obscure in shades, I play."

Following goats naturally called for a greater robustness of limb and character, and so, though we occasionally find in the poets an " Acantha roaming in thymy valleys, tending her milk-white goats and gathering honey," the goatherdess is a very rare phenomenon. It may be feminine enough to follow the "silly sheep" among their level pastures; but trying to keep order among goats, or clambering after them to lend assistance to adventurous kids in distress, is scarcely becoming to the sex.

Of the antiquity of their domestication we have some evidence from the first sacrifice, from which we learn that they were kept in herds by the second generation of mankind; and we may, therefore, without any unreasonable license of assumption, suppose that the First Man, "the old gardener," was a goatherd also. By what devices our great Progenitor circumvented the original goat we are not told. But they were not, probably, very different from those by which Robinson Crusoe caught his. For that Adam, cast upon the desert island of the earth outside of Paradise, had a dog for a companion, the traditions of antiquity suffice to assure us, and, given a dog, everything becomes possible for man in the most natural way. Moreover, Lilith, who is called the first wife of Adam, came, it is said, from a pastoral folk ; and it may be that she brought with her into the solitary wigwam that stood among the thistles hard by the gates of Eden, the secret of weaving the primitive pushm.

> " With glossy hair of shaggy goat,
>   Are light tiaras woven that wreath the head,
>   And airy float behind."

There, too, was first made goats'-milk cheese, the original Gruyère, such as the son of Jesse carried down to the camp in the valley of Elah, for a present to the captain of the thousand in which his brothers served. There, too, the wandering jackal first sniffed the odour of the Kibáb, the roasted kid-flesh, such as Rebecca made haste to get ready for old Isaac's deceiving, preparing it like Esau's venison, " the savoury meat which his father loved."

How is it, by the way, that this excellent meat is not more common in England? The empty hills of Wales would surely support innumerable herds of goats, and the flesh of the kid is infinitely better eating, both in flavour and texture, than half the " lamb " which is sold in butchers' shops.

That this animal was selected to bear away upon its head the sins of the people, has somehow brought it obliquely into disrepute, and the " scape-goat " has become a symbol of reproach. Yet it should not be forgotten that when the lots were cast, there were only two chances, and that the goat which was not Azazel, " the departing one," was drawn "*for Jehovah.*" So that it rested only on the hazard of the Levite's choice which of the two remained in the Hebrew camp, consecrated for sacrifice to the Lord, and which was sent forth.

> " The scape-goat on his head
>   The people's trespass bore,
> And to the desert led,
>   Was to be seen no more :
> In him our Surety seemed to say,
> ' Behold, I bear your sins away.' "

Nor also should it be overlooked that the goat which was drawn "for Jehovah" was at once led to the altar and slain for the "Great Atonement." So that the one which was set at liberty was not less honourable than the other which was dedicated to death. Nor can it be said to have been less fortunate.

The legend of the scape-goat is a very widespread one, and belongs indeed to those "primitive fancies" with which each nation seems to have started as a stock in common. In sacrifice, also, it has always been conspicuous. But this is a melancholy distinction which in one way or another has befallen every animal man could manage to catch for the purpose, but which should never be supposed to derogate from the victim's respectability, or else humanity itself becomes contemptible on the altar, and the life of man be held a worthless offering.

In parts of Egypt the he-goat was sacrificed ; in others it was worshipped. Thus, the Memphians held public mourning, whenever one of the "horn-lifting" animals went over to the majority.

As the wet-nurse of the King of Olympus—

> " Above the rest in grace Adraste stood,
>   Who rocked the golden cradle of the God,
>   On his ambrosial lips the goat distilled
>   Her milky store, and fed th' immortal child "—

the she-goat arrives at considerable consequence, and its horns, presented by grateful Jove to Amalthea, the sister of the honey-nymph, flourishes immortal as the cornucopia, the horn of plenty, and glitters among the stars. Indeed, the astral honours of the goat are rather exceptional. The Milky Way, "the bridge of souls," is the she-goat—the same whose milk "nurse Amalthea skimmed for the boy Jupiter," and when called "St. James' Way," is still of caprine significance, though perhaps of a kind somewhat deplorable for the animal concerned, inasmuch as on that Saint's day it was the custom in Germany to throw a goat out of the window. The Pleiades, again, are called in many parts of Europe the Seven She-goats, and no one who has read of the notable ride of Don Quixote and his Squire on the wooden horse Clavileno, can forget how Sancho—wishing to have something to say as to what he saw when blindfolded—declares to the Duchess that he found himself at one point of the journey so near the sky that it was not a span above him.

"And it so fell out that we passed close by the place where the seven she-goats are kept; and, truly, having been a goatherd in my youth, I no sooner saw them but I longed to play with them awhile; and had I not done so, I verily think I should have died; so what does I but, without saying a word, softly slide down from Clavileno, and play with the sweet little creatures, which are like so many violets, for almost three-quarters of an hour."

On being further questioned, he goes on to say that two of them were green, two carnation, two blue, and one motley-coloured. The Duke protests that he had never himself seen such goats. "No," replies Sancho; "but your highness will allow that there must be some difference between celestial goats and those of the lower world."

The she-goat in Aquarius has two kids, and Hindoo astrology knows them as the Rain-bringers. In this aspect they descended to the Romans, and Ovid, Horace, and Virgil have each of them due reference to the "signum pluviale capellæ." Her character is always beneficent and motherly, whether we find her in classical fancy as Galathea, "the milky one," or in contemporary folk-lore as the self-sacrificing she-goat that gives up her life for her less intelligent companions.   "Billy" may be overbearing, hot-tempered, and unprincipled; but "Nanny" is meek and mild and benign.   Though "the goat of El-Akhfash" has passed into Arab proverb as a fool, the adult animal in fable is invariably discreet.   The "wanton kidling" is a trifle imbecile. Wolves and other villainous personages are the cause of "kiddie's" succumbing to the most obvious frauds, as in the Shepherd's Calendar—and thereafter punctually in all poets.

> " All save a bell, which he left behinde
>   In the basket for the kidde to finde ;
>   Which, when the kidde stouped downe to catch,
>   He popt him in, and his basket did latch ;
>   Ne stayed he once the dore to make fast,
>   But ranne away with him in all hast."

That goats carry with them an ungracious aroma—are, in fact, the Bassas of the flock—is a circumstance most reproachfully urged against them ; yet, though, as Sir Thomas Browne would say, " I concede many questionable points, and dispute not the verity of sundry opinions which are of affinity thereto," I know not how to admit that their odour is a diabolical one.   For Chaucer is not the only poet who thus unsavourily associates goats and devils—

> " And evermore wherever that they gon,
>   Men may hem kennen by smell of brimston,
>   For all the world they stinken as a gote."

Now, Sancho Panza, who, having been a goatherd in his youth, was an authority on the subject, speaks endearingly (as we have seen) of certain goats as "little violets," while in another place he refers specifically to the demoniacal odour as something very different.   "Truly, sir," quoth Sancho, " I have already touched them, and this same devil, who is so very busy about us, is as plump as a partridge, and has another property very different from what your devils are wont to have, who all smell of brimstone."

It is a curious point, too, that in England, as well as in other countries, the goat is considered a healthy animal, and its fragrance especially is supposed to be beneficial to cattle, horses, and sheep. For this obsolete reason a single goat is still often kept in our farmyards.

This may have arisen out of the world-wide superstition, that these creatures are wise in simples and the medicine of the fields. Indeed, it is said that man got his first ideas of vegetable efficacies from the leechcraft of this animal and its knowledge of the uses of wild balsam.

" Fresh dittany beloved of goats " is a poet's allusion to the wondrous virtues of the herb which the deer also are said to have recourse to when wounded.

It had other drugs, too, " for its secure." Thus—

> " Here grows melampode everywhere,
> And terebinth good for goats,
> The one my madding kids to smear,
> The next to heal their throats."

Mrs. Bury Palliser, in her delightful work, tells us how the Count of Soriano, who fell by the hand of Francis I. at Pavia, bore the device of the wild goat, " which when pierced by the arrow-shaped leaves of the palm-tree, seeks, to heal its wounds, for the herb dittany, which grows under the shade of the same tree," with the motto " Hinc vulnus, salus et umbra." Of the herb dittany Pliny says, " The goats first showed us the virtue of the herb dictamnus or dittany, to draw out arrows forth of their bodies. Perceiving themselves shot with a shaft, they have recourse presently to that herb, and with eating thereof it is driven out again." So in Virgil we find

Venus, in order to cure her son, speeding to Crete to fetch
the plant

> " Well known to wounded goats, a sure relief
> To draw the pointed steel, and ease the grief."

It is true that "the goddess-mother brews the extracted
liquor with ambrosial dews, and odorous panacea," but the
healing of Æneas' hurt is none the less due to the herb.

In Folkard's " Plant-lore "[1] I find many items about the
weed.   Thus, that Plutarch says that the women of Crete,
seeing how the goats, by eating dittany, cause the arrows to
fall from their wounds, learnt to make use of the plant to
aid them in childbirth.   Gerard recounts that the plant is
most useful in drawing forth splinters of wood, bones, &c.,
and in the healing of wounds, "especially those made with
invenomed weapons, arrowes shot out of guns, and such
like."   The juice, he says, is so powerful, that by its mere
smell it "drives away venomous beasts, and doth astonish
them."   When mixed with wine, the juice was also considered a remedy for the bites of serpents.   According to
Apuleius, however, the plant possessed the property of
killing serpents.   The dittany of Crete, it should be noted,
is not to be confounded with the dittany, dittander, or
pepper-wort of the English herbals.   This plant, the
lepidium latifolium, from its being used by thrifty house-
wives to season dishes with, obtained the name of poor
man's pepper.

From this knowledge of natural medicines, the goat then
became itself medicinal.   Its blood had singular potencies.
False emeralds shivered to pieces under a drop of it.
Smear the palms of a sleeping man with it, and he will tell
you all his secrets.

"To artists who wish to engrave glass handsomely, now
will I disclose to you a method exactly as I myself have

---

[1] " Plant-lore Legends and Lyrics."   Sampson Low & Co.

proved it. I collected fat earthworms turned up by the plough : and at the same time took vinegar and the hot blood out of a big he-goat, which I had skilfully fed upon strengthening herbs for a short time, when kept tied up in-doors. With the hot blood I then rinsed the worms, and the vinegar, and so anointed the whole of the bright glass bowl ; which being done I essayed to engrave upon the glass with the hard stone known by the name of pyrites." Those who " desire to attack with the steel the noble gems which the princes of Rome loved far above gold," had also to use goats' blood, and so, too, had those who wished to engrave on crystals. But whether Heraclius meant what he said, or whether he was only "showing the way the trick was done," after the manner of Maskelyne and Cook—whose delightful explanations of their mysteries only serve to make them more mysterious than before—nobody will ever know. But as far as the professors of the glyptic art have gone yet, the blood of goats appears to be about as inefficient for softening gems as it is for calling up witches. For this also was one of its deplorable potencies.

But the witches had their revenge upon the animal that could thus disturb their rest. For on their " Sabbaths " they murdered goats, black ones—and ate them, raw.

XI.

THE POETS' HERDS.

In the earliest poetry of the world, the prose myth, the "epic exploit" of cattle is so conspicuous a theme that, if I might take poetical license, I should speak of "hornèd legend" and of "lowing verse."

That amazing puzzle, "the Solar myth," is largely bovine, and the primitive mythology being naturally zoological, found its constant illustration and most frequent subject in the bulls, cows, and calves without which man, in the first days of universal discomfort, would have been himself little better than a beast of the field. The phenomena of Nature represented to the bucolic generation a herd of cattle, and nothing more. Everything suggested itself to them as a mode of beef.

Men started with a cow as the original datum of consciousness, and round it, as the one and only positive fact they possessed, their lives and thoughts were grouped. Let their imagination wander as far as it might, it never got outside the cattle-run, and fancy could not stray beyond ear-shot of the lowing kine. As they fed their bodies upon the produce of their herds, so they pastured their minds upon beef and milk. The skies became meadows, and the firmament a cattle-yard. Thunder lowed, and the hurricane bellowed. The lightning was horned, and the storm, rattling overhead, went on hoofs. Black and white, red, dun, and dappled, the clouds went grazing or ramping across the fields of heaven. The lowering, gloomy rain-nimbus tossed its head and pawed the air; in the lighter drift they saw the sporting calves. The end of the world was a slaughter-yard, and Nature closed the volume in a catastrophic Smithfield.

This is no exaggeration of the prominence of the cattle in myth. The bull and the cow represent in turn nearly everything that man then distinguished in the elements of the earth or their functions, everything that he saw in the skies above the earth, and everything that he guessed at in the depths below it. Never were there such kine before.

They wandered about in such a maze of avatars that it seemed impossible they could ever turn up as mere cows again, and no Protean divinity—whether in classical myth or modern fairy tale—had such a phantasmagoric repertory. They impersonated everything, and everything at once. The cow was a cloud in the sky, which was itself a cow. The king in his fortress was a cow, and the forest about the fortress was a cow, and so was the cave within the forest about the fortress, and so was the giant inside the cave within the forest about the fortress in which the cow-king lived. Cow was stuffed within cow, like the bird within bird which we find in the Yorkshire pie; and every incident of Nature—human, zoological, or elementary—revolved round the bovine idea just as things do round the malt "that lay in the house that Jack built." The cow, again, is the thunder and the lightning too, both rain and sunshine, sun, moon, and stars. Then it gets mixed up with auroras and twilights, till, in the confusion of metamorphoses, we find the cow-morning pursuing the cow-night—each being attended by its appropriate twilight calf—and we find them also running away from each other by the light of the cow-stars that are shining out of the cow-sky.

And the bull is alongside all the time, and every now and then there is a calf to complicate the situation. It is a dreadful myth altogether, ranging from language to language with exasperating indifference, and from people to people as if there were no fences in the ethnical and religious pastures in which it roves. It drags in, too, by countless arms, like some octopus of theory, every symbol of the folk-tale and fairy lore.

Cinderella's slipper is proved to be a bull's tail. The bean-stalk which Jack climbs is a cow's tail. The wonderful lamp and the persecuted maiden, the girl that was seven years old whom the thunder carried off, the three dwarf brothers, and the magic flute,—are all of them modifications, we are told, of the bovine idea, and the cock comes in, and the hare and the crow, and the grateful pike, and the quail and the fox, and the red apples, and the kidney bean, and grief that inspires song, and the shrimps that saved the fairy.

Who, too, cannot at once see the connection between the saviour bull and Turn-little-Pea, and Ivan who went out on his crook-backed horse to look for the casket under the oak at the bottom of the sea? and the witch that was burned in the form of a cat, and the cock that came out of the mountain, the Bird of Light that performed such wonders against the serpent and tortoise, and Medea and Orpheus, and the Strong Bear of the Finns? Was not the bull sold to a tree, and did not the tree burst and out of it come gold which turned into bees? And does not all this make it as clear as cow-daylight that stock-raising was the only religion of the earth once upon a time, and justify a firmament filled with stars of beef that illuminate the Milky Way?

Wander as you will in these antique myths, and Nature all round and above you, sunlit or moonlit or eclipsed, is still all cattle. Go where you choose, they still bellow and low, and paw and toss their heads, the luminous calf and the azure cow, the black bull with the golden horns, demoniacal cattle and celestial, malignant and benign.

Time passed, and then came the days of sacrificial honour
and of temple worship.

> " The pontiff knife
> Gleams in the sun, the milk-white heifer lows,
> The pipes go shrilly, the libation flows."

In the melancholy honour of the sacrifice cattle have
been always conspicuous, and in nearly all countries.
Among the Hebrews they were selected for the purposes
of the altar "without blemish," and were conscientiously
consumed to ashes. Among the Spartans the leanest
specimens were specially chosen, and the gods put off with
only the entrails, the attendants of the shrine eating the
meat. Even the Athenians made believe that the deities
preferred the smoke of the sacrifice to the flesh. It was a
convenient credulity, for while Olympus sniffed, the popu-
lace feasted. Hecatombs were therefore vastly popular in
Greece. The pagans of Africa at the present day piously
economise in their burnt-offerings much in the same way,
for though they sacrifice a beast in honour of Aunt Sally—
as one feels irreverently inclined to call their idols—they
eat it themselves. But they are very careful to give the
medicine-man some of the teeth, to put inside his rattle.
None the less, consecration was an honour, and the horned
folk have in their day suffered from a surfeit of it. The poets
prefer to see the heifer at the altar—

> " Who are these coming to the sacrifice ?
> To what green altar, O mysterious priest,
> Lead'st thou that heifer lowing at the skies,
> And all her silken flanks with garlands drest ?"

Yet as a rule it was a bull or bullock—in Egypt always.
Yet Cowley has—

> " With less complaint the Zoan temples sound,
> When the adoréd heifer's drowned,
> And no true marked successor to be found."

S

The allusion is of course to the Egyptian practice of leading out the sacred bull at a stated period and drowning it, the people going into mourning until a successor with the proper marks upon it was found by the priests. It was essential that the animal should be black, with a white spot on the forehead, and a white crescent on the right flank; the image of an eagle on the spine, a knot under the tongue that resembled the scarabæus beetle, and the hairs of the tail double. In Roman sacrifice the white oxen of Umbria that pastured by the Clitumnus were for their size and beauty specially preferred; otherwise the poets' preference for this colour has no countenance from the past. The fact of the devoted animals being gaily garlanded and ornamented, and their consequent appearance of a superior stateliness as they approached the place of doom, has given the poets many occasions for apt simile.

> "Like as the sacred oxe that carelesse stands
> With gilden hornes and flow'ry girlonds crown'd,
> Proud of his dying honor and deare bandes,
> Whiles th' altars fume with frankincense around,
> All suddeinly with mortall stroke astound,
> Doth groveling fall, and with his streaming gore
> Distaines the pillours and the holy grownd,
> And the faire flowres that decked him afore."

Those honours, such as they were, of gilded horns and rose-wreathed neck, of fillet and votive garland, are things of the past—

> "Nor is Osiris seen
> In Memphian grove or green,
> Trampling the unshowered grass with lowings loud."

At any rate, they only survive in the form of Christmas beef. We no longer strew the victim's head with roasted barley and salt; we pin a blue rosette on instead. When the

Smithfield butcher draws the head upwards,[1] it might be whimsically inferred that we still sacrifice to the Olympic deities. In the scrutiny of the sanitary inspector we may recall the careful divination by entrails of the old haruspex, while the poets' descriptions of the ancient holocaust apply to our own Yule-tide immolations.

Indeed, who can say, visiting any great Cattle-show, that the old worship of the horned things is extinct? If the cult is dead, what means this thronging of people to see these fat cattle? Pilgrims come from every part of the kingdom, and among those who officiate in the rites are the highest in the land.

> " The sacred herd march proud and softly by,
> Too fat and gay to think their deaths so nigh.
> Hard fate of beasts, more innocent than we,
> Prey to our luxury and our piety ! "

Suppose a Herodotus on his travels had chanced to pass through London and seen the Show, and inquired of the intelligent native what it meant, would he not have put it down in his note-book that we had a great saint named Christmas, who was commonly depicted as an aged man of jolly countenance, and crowned with evergreens and berries ; that the priests of the temples, of which the chief is called Smithfield, annually sacrificed large numbers of fatted kine or sheep and pigs in his honour, and that the people exhibited the utmost reverence for this festival, never failing, even to the poorest, to do their best to celebrate it with merrymaking? This festival, he might have added, "comes but once a year," and it is commonly alleged by those who sing at night for alms in the streets, and have often to wait a long time before they get them, that this is the reason why they are so punctual in their observance of it.

---

[1] If downwards the Greeks meant that the sacrifice was to heroes or the gods of the lower world ; if upwards, to Olympus.

Nor would any one be surprised at such a conjecture, for whether we look at the solemn crowds that gravely survey the devoted animals and then go away complacent as if a religious duty had been paid, or watch the experts reverently punching a bullock's ribs or handling a fat sheep, it is very difficult not to imagine that one is assisting at a pious rite.   Gazing at these prodigies of beef and mutton, women are serious and men stern.   There is less cheerfulness than, for instance, at any Oriental shrine, where pilgrims from the country meet to offer their dues and chatter, and there is all the difference between the crowd inside and outside, as if the Agricultural Hall were some kind of sacred edifice.   As a matter of fact, indeed, there is something solemn about the uniform nobility of size, something that represses mirth in the monotonous flatness of these prize animals' backs. You could lay out tea upon the back of that Hereford there, or play a game of cards upon that Southdown.   It looks as if a roller had been passed over them all.   On the other hand, there is a tendency to lofty exultation, chastened yet inspiriting, in the contemplation of all this meat to so little bone.   It mollifies the spectator; when he thinks of so much tenderness he melts unconsciously himself.   He would not, if he could help it, harm even the most trifling butcher.   But it does not conduce to much hilarity.   A baron of prize beef is not a thing to jest about.   So the visitors are mostly of a solemn kind.

If the oxen that once, in pre-historic times, wandered about the Thames valley where Islington now stands, could return to the scenes of their lives, and see the Agricultural Hall, with its contents, they would probably be astonished.   It is permissible, at least, to suppose they would be.

For, though the Pleistocene cattle may naturally have been of a kind that required much astonishing, seeing that they were familiar with the mammoth and the woolly rhinoceros and other marvels of Nature, it is still within the possibilities that the alterations which have taken place since their day in Islington and the neighbourhood would be calculated to surprise. When they were in the flesh the site of London was an agreeable forest, interspersed with patches of marsh-land, affording the finest of grazing for everybody. Occasionally, perhaps, a man painted blue would come creeping along and whiz a pebble at them out of a sling, and then scramble up the nearest tree as fast as he could, or a carnivorous beast—lion, bear, or wolf,—would come up from the jungles about King's Cross, and make a meal off one of them.

But if they came back now they would find but poor pasturage in Islington. There is no great luxuriance of meadow-grass in Pentonville, nor would oxen find much of the old bush herbage left in St. John Street Road. On the other hand, there would be no chance of azure aborigines coming up from the Smithfield marshes to annoy them with pebbles out of slings, or of lions and bears lying in wait to eat them as they passed along to the Agricultural Hall. So that, "taking one thing with another," it is not easy to say whether the antiquated old cattle whom we find in the Essex fossil-beds would prefer the present state of things or the old.

Imagine, for instance, an ancient auroch, accustomed all his life to fight for everything he wanted, seeing the modern shorthorn in its stall. In his day, he would say, cattle were cattle. They had horns with which they could drill a hole through a rhinoceros; long and sinewy legs that carried them nimbly up the hills when tigers ran after them; tough and shaggy hides, loose-fitting, that stood them in good stead in many a tussle for the lordship of the herd or the possession of a juicy pasture. In his day it was the hardest head and the stoutest heart that gained for their possessors all the luxuries of life; dexterity in defence and ferocity in attack that won for them the reward of unmolested enjoyments;

and when they were too old to live they died. He only
knew of one kind of food, and that was grass; and as far
as he could remember, never saw but one human being in
all his life, and if that one had not been so remarkably
agile in getting up a tree that happened to be near, he
would have tossed him on his horns sky high.

With the animals of to-day it is vastly different. They
are perpetually being fed upon new kinds of food, none of
which bear the slightest resemblance to grass, and instead
of having to go out and look for it for themselves—and
fight for it, probably, before they could eat it—they find
their meals being constantly replenished and put under
their very noses. The result is that the hide grows fine,
the bones become small, and the fattening beasts get bulkier
every day, and shorter-winded. A pretty figure the prize
beef would look trying to run up Box Hill, with a pack of
wolves after it !

Yet the comfort of such arrangements—a thickly-littered
stall and a pail of appetising " patent food " always at hand,
and nothing to worry him—would certainly suggest itself to
the old-world visitor. For, after all, this was the utmost
ambition of his own life in the Pleistocene days—plenty of
food, comfortable quarters, and absence of enemies. For
a moment, perhaps, he would regret that he had been born
in such early times ; but on a sudden, probably, he would
remember that, though the lives of these stalled cattle were
made very pleasant for them, they did not last long, and so
in the end he would come to the conclusion that liberty,
with length of years, was better than domestication and
sudden death.

Yet a very little further on he will find some of his
posterity that have the true old feral ring about them, and
all the shaggy romance of mountain and forest, as fleet and
fierce as any primeval beast that had to fight with lions or
escape from them.

They are the Highland cattle, with their long-haired ruddy coats, their bison heads, bold wild eyes peering out through the overhanging locks, and horns with a menacing up-lift and terribly keen at the points.

> " Mightiest of all beasts of chase
>   That roam in woody Caledon,
> Crashing the forest in his race
>   The mountain bull comes thundering on.
>
> Fierce, on the hunter's quivered hand
>   He rolls his eyes of swarthy glow,
> Spurns, with black hoof and horn, the sand,
>   And tosses high his mane of snow."

Some are coal-black, the veritable beasts of Ossian, and at once suggestive of those old myths in which they figure as storm clouds and malignant agencies.

Nor are the Welsh cattle on the other side of the Hall much behind them in wild picturesqueness, while that fine black fellow, for ever restlessly tramping and turning his horns this way and that in the vain hope of finding something near enough to prod, is a beast that the gladiators must have found some trouble with when the Romans imported British bulls for the spectacles of the amphitheatre. It looks as if it could go up hill as fast as down, and is fierce enough to perplex even a Texan cow-boy. But the breeder, when he selects his stock, thinks of Smithfield and not of the prairies, and lays his plans for the approval of the Christmas judges and not of wild herds of bison.

Yet the spectacle of a prize bullock set down in the middle of a prairie, and submitted to the criticism of a herd of American bison, or taken down to the source of the Congo and left alone with some old buffaloes, would be a very interesting one. What a puzzle such a phenomenon of beef would be to them. How they would walk round it, and snort and wonder.

> " Stood all astound, like a sort of steeres,
>   'Mongst whom some beast of strange and forraine race
>   Unwares is chaunc't, far straying from his peers."

Then familiarity with the object would probably lead to personalities, and when it came to fighting the prize-winner of Smithfield would have but a hard time of it. So it is better that he should remain where he is appreciated, and where his points are understood.

The beef again, when sporting in the meadow, is not the master of its own fate.

> " The pampered wanton steer of the sharp axe,
>   Regardless that o'er his devoted head
>   Hangs menacing, crops his delicious bane,
>   Nor knows the juice is life."

It may think it is, and behave as if it thought so. But other hands shape its destiny, rough-hew it as it may, and the widely divergent results are such as to justify any conscientious person in hesitation before he decides to commit the heedless bullock to the unhonoured publicity of the suburban meat-stall, or to reserve it for the blue-riband dignities of Smithfield in December. What does the horned yearling know of Christmas or its possibilities of obsequious sacrifice? It is of Christmas but not in it. Pantomimes do not compete for its patronage; the shops expect no purchases of him. In all the acres of fir forest robbed for Christmas trees not one is lit up for his amusement. No one sends him hampers of game or barrels of oysters. He knows nothing of plum-puddings, snapdragon, or crackers. How is he to do so? Is he not himself part of the festivity, a passive actor in the bright scenes of social enjoyment? Who can have time to think of the animal that gives us the beef we eat, even though his life was given with it? Yet if we do think of him why not remember that he has had a life of jollity himself in order that he might add to the pleasures of the season; that but for our great annual holiday he would have died long ago, unwept, unhonoured, and unsung? If it had not been for the Christian institution of the 25th he would have been a common bullock. As it is, he has had a twelvemonth's grace of life, and luxurious life too. Fed upon the best of everything, and tended as if he were an emperor's favourite, he has dreamed away his days in obese contentment, and now that the end has overtaken him he goes to his fate surrounded with every accessory of importance.

The influence, therefore, of human society upon the bullock is all for its advantage. If it had not been for Christmas he would have been common beef long ago. But as it is he is prize beef, and those who bred him, sold him, and ate him, are all the better for the time and money spent upon his education.

In Greece and Rome it was a matter of popular belief that animals devoted to sacrifice walked to the altar with something of a nobler gait than when at liberty in the grass. They were conscious of an exceptional dignity in the occasion, and paced to death with a becoming stateliness.

"The fatter the ox," says the Pilgrim, "the more gamesomely he goes to the slaughter." The significance of the fancy is of course obvious. The ancients wished to think that the animal world was in alliance with them in the honours that were conferred upon their divinities, and in harmony with themselves. The thought of unwilling death jars upon the dignified composure of the sacrificial rite.

Whether or not bullocks look upon Yule-tide as an occasion for high spirits, is of course a point involved in some doubt. But I do not think we need feel any hesitation in congratulating ourselves upon having given these amiable animals the opportunity of doing so if they liked. We bring a great moral purpose into their lives and add a dignity to decease. If they do their duty in death, they live in ease and peace. Fate spins them a more generous length of days, and when the fatal day comes it is really an altar that awaits them.

For what is Christmas in its festal aspect but a feast in honour of the genius of good living, and what are the store of choice viands that we prepare for it but sacrifices? So the pig, the bullock, and the sheep find, just as in the old pagan days, the fillets of sacrificial flowers, the garlands, and the ornaments ready. There is ceremony over the act of offering, and reverent appreciation of the remains.

The Pontifex Maximus of the market himself prepares the prize beef, and the ordinary ministers of the place attend the rite in deferential attention. With what scientific nicety the joints are got ready; with what conciseness of skill and brave affectations of gesture the operator does his work. He might be a surgeon with an emperor for his subject. And then with what parade of circumspection each portion is removed, with what fine quibblings as to trifles of position each is placed aside. Dexterous hands have already carved the lucid turnip and the glowing carrot into floral effigies, and the blue satin bows have fringes of silver tinsel, and the skewer is gilt. Under the master's own eye the decorations are affixed. In private there are many rehearsals, till at length taste is satisfied, and then the lordly fragments are brought out for public view. Now all this circumstance of demise, this consequential pomp of posthumous adornment, ought surely to have an elevating influence upon the bullock and his friends.

They are the descendants of "the wild herds that own no master's stall," of the reem—the animal that had such wide horns that Noah (so the Talmudists say) could not get it into the ark, and had to tow it behind—and of the urus, which Julius Cæsar says was only a trifle smaller than the elephant. And to-day they are the brothers of the American bison, "the majestic brute that roams in herds which shake the earth," and of the gigantic gour of the Indian swamps. It is not true (though the natives believe it is) that the latter snuffs up chunks of stone with its nostrils, and then discharges them with the force of a catapult at those who attack it, but it is beyond doubt that the gour shows no hesitation whatever in charging anything that stands in front of it.

In the East the whole family of "horned beasts" is treated with superstitious reverence, for all the animals which are the "vahans" or "vehicles" of the gods are sacred, and amongst these are the bull and buffalo—but above all the cow. For Brahma is said to have created the Brahmin and the cow at the same birth; the former to offer sacrifice, the latter to yield the "ghee" for anointing the offering. The eating of ghee (or "clarified butter") in sufficient quantities destroys all sin—so the Hindoos say—while the consumption of the five products of the cow cleanses from all pollution. One of these is used all over India for spreading over the floors and walls on scrubbing days, and, strange to say, it has the effect of cleansing them perfectly, and giving the rooms the fragrance of the Tonquin bean. "How," asks Sir George Birdwood, "would Dr. Richardson explain this?" The Hindoo explains it easily by a miracle. Yet the enormous importance of the cow in Hindooism is only of comparatively recent date, for, as the Brahmins themselves confess, the blessed animal is only coeval with themselves, and until recently India has known so little of its ancient self that Hindoos have come to believe that it was ordained at the creation that man should not eat beef. The impulse to literary research given by British encouragement of education has, however, resulted in showing that the original. ante-Brahminical gods of the Hindoos used to eat beefsteaks habitually—it was their favourite diet, in fact—and, what is more, that they got very drunk on soma after their meals.

No animal in all the range of zoolatry has ever arrived at such dignities as the Hindoo cow. The monkey is sufficiently sacred, and it goes hard with the novice who, unconscious of any sacrilege, shoots the village peacocks. In other countries, as in the case of the dog and baboon, bull and ram, crocodile, hawk, and ibis of ancient Egypt, or the eagle and crow, snake, wolf, shark, and pike of the modern clan-animal worship, many birds and beasts, reptiles and fishes, have attracted to themselves the homage of nations. But, putting them all together, whether in fur, feather, or scales, they do not collectively outweigh the stupendous sanctity with which Brahminism has invested the cow. The bull shares in some degree his consort's honours, and in the more exclusively Hindoo towns sacred cattle of both sexes lounge about the streets. No place is forbidden to them, and they are free of every stall. Wherever they choose to feed, there they are at liberty to eat; and wherever they choose to lie down, that place is theirs. The sweetmeat-seller may bribe the sacred bull with a lump of sugar-stuff to pass on to the next stall, or the grain-seller may exchange a chatty of cheaper grain for that into which the fastidious beast has plunged its black muzzle. Yet they are never struck and seldom reproached, except with qualifying phrases of respect, in which the merchant deprecates his four-legged visitor's displeasure, or apologises for his refusal of more viands on the score of his own poverty.

The cow, and not the bull, however, is pre-eminently the object of worship. The latter may be specially sacred as the "vehicle" of this god or a particular symbol of that, but the former pervades the whole religion, and itself adds a sanctity to every deity in the Pantheon. When Brahma, the All-Father, took upon himself the beneficent function of creation, he first made the gods and then the holy men, and the cow and the Brahmin were produced by the same act of creative power. So Brahminism and the cow are inseparable, and the animal, the twin, as it were, of the holy "twice-born," takes rank above many castes of men. To save the life of a cow, to do it a service, to tend it in sickness, to revere it at all times, are almost as advantageous in the hereafter as if the same acts had been done towards a Brahmin. To kill a cow, to wound it, or to insult it, is reckoned, in the full austerity of Brahminism, a more heinous offence than similar wrongs inflicted upon the lower orders of Hindoos.

The camel selected to carry the Sultan's annual gift of the new veil to Mecca is, in memory of El Kaswa which the Prophet rode, treated, while on the road, with all the pomp and care that would be extended to majesty itself, and the competition for the honourable posts of attendance upon the brute is sometimes very keen. So too in Egypt the sacred animals became, once a year, by priestly condescension, the objects of public solicitude and recipients of public services. But among the Hindoos the kine live in the same sanctity perennially, and enjoy a universal tenderness of treatment from year's end to year's end. During all the rest of the twelvemonth, when it is not loitering along the caravan-route to the Holy City, the camel of Islam receives but scant respect from a provoked rider or short-tempered owner. So, too, the furry obliquities of Egyptian adoration relapsed in the majority of cases and for the greater part of the year into their proper places in the animal world. But the glory of the cow of Hindostan, like that of its prototype in Vedic legends, is never in eclipse. It is always at the meridian. So to this day we find it in Hindoo zoolatry as the supreme expression of the kindliness of the powers of Nature to man, an authentic proof of the goodness of the gods. Though all the herds that other peoples worshipped have gone from the earth with the credulities upon which they pastured, the bull of Shiva and the cow of Brahma have still their altars in a thousand temples, and arrogate the central dignity in a religion which has two hundred millions of believers.   To this day Hindoos devoutly believe in Kamadhuk, the "cow of plenty," which yields in heaven, from her exuberant udders, every gift and blessing which the spirit of the dead can demand.

Yet, elsewhere, in the West, cattle are called prosaic animals, and it is a common thing for men to speak superciliously of the bovine atmosphere of bucolic society. From the supposed stupidity of kine the dulness of all such as have their being among them is arbitrarily inferred. The companionship of the bulky, slow-moving, cud-chewing things is presumed to have a corresponding effect upon the temperaments of those who are much with them. To call a man a bullock is to suggest that he is clumsy-footed and thick-headed, with an inert mind in a heavy body.

Even the poets are of this way of thinking.   They have the same name for the animals and the men that tend them; they are all "herds" together, and which is the more "simple," the quadruped or the biped, it were hard to decide.   But it is quite certain that the poetical "herd" is as nearly an idiot as man could be without positively gibbering, and his "patient charges," if absence of character be significant of defective intelligence, are not much above him.

> " The bound of all his vanity, to deck
>   With one bright bell a fav'rite heifer's neck."

Yet the poets make excellent use of their cattle, and the complete calendar of the year might be easily constructed out of the moods of the kine in verse.

Spring is quiet with "placid beeves" "unworried in the meads," "the calm pleasures of the pasturing herds," and "the tranquil tinkle of the heifer's bell."

"Straight to the meadow then he whistling goes,
  With well-known halloo calls his lazy cows,
  Down the rich pasture heedlessly they graze,
  Or hear the summons with an idle gaze ;
  For well they know the cow-yard yields no more
  Its tempting fragrance, nor its wint'ry store.
  Reluctance marks their steps, sedate and slow,
  The right of conquest all the law they know.
  Subordinate they one by one succeed,
  And one among them always takes the lead,
  Is ever foremost, wheresoe'er they stray,
  Allowed precedence, undisputed sway.
  With jealous pride her station is maintained,
  For many a broil that post of honour gained."

Then comes Summer with its flies and "restless herds"
with tails perpetually on the swing. They rush from their
tormentors into the pools.

"What time the cow stands knee-deep in the pool,
  Lashing her sides for anguish,
  Scaring off with sudden head reversed the insect swarm,
  That basks and preys upon her sunny hide,
  Or when she flies with tufted tail erect,
  The breeze-fly's keen invasion to the shade,
  Scampering madly."

This breeze-fly is specially popular with the poets as
a summer detail. Spenser draws an illustration of the
"World's Vanity" therefrom—

"In summer's day, when Phœbus fairly shone,
  I saw a Bull as white as driven snowe,
  With gilden hornes embowed like the moone,
  In a fresh flowring meadow lying lowe ;
  Up to his eares the verdant grasse did growe,
  And the gay flowres did offer to be eaten ;
  But he with fatnes so did overflowe,
  That he all wallowed in the weedes downe beaten,
  Ne car'd with them his daintie lips to sweeten :
  Till that a Brize, a scorned little creature,

> Through his faire hide his angrie sting did threaten,
> And vext so sore, that all his goodly feature
> And all his plenteous pasture nought him pleased :
> So by the small the great is oft diseased."

Next Autumn with its cattle "conscious of storms," "and huddling side by side, in closest ambush seek to hide," Winter with its "miry herds" or "kine in stalls."

Winter is, indeed, a season of horrors for the poets' herds. In the morning—

> " Driven from their stalls to take the air,
> How stupidly they stare ! and feel how strange !
> They open wide their smoking mouths to low,
> But scarcely can their feeble sound be heard ;
> Then turn and lick themselves, and step by step
> Move, dull and heavy, to their stalls again."—*J. Baillie.*

This is bad enough, but it is much worse sometimes. They go afield, but there " in icy garments mourn, and wildly murmur for the spring's return " (Crabbe).   They then return " from the untasted fields," and " wail their wonted fodder, not, like hungering man, fretful if unsupplied, but silent, meek " (Cowper), while " drooping the labourer-ox, stands covered o'er with snow, and then demands the fruit of all his toil " (Thomson).   After this the end cannot be far—

> " The grazing ox lows to the gelid skies,
> Walks o'er the marble meads with with'ring eyes ;
> Walks o'er the solid lakes, snuffs up the wind, and dies."

The seasons, again, could be divided off almost into months—so punctually are the changes in cattle-life noted ; while the different periods of the day have each of them their herds characteristic of the hour and in keeping with the weather.

The cool air of the dewy morning, the still heat of noon, the languor of the afternoon, the quiet of evening—are all marked off by their special cattle features ; and rainy weather and fine, hot and cold, present us with just as different aspects of the herds as the seasons. In the morning

> " The cattle are grazing,
>   Their heads never raising,
>   There are forty feeding like one " (*Wordsworth*) ;

and there is

> " A balm,
> Of palpable and breathing calm,
> By song of birds confessed,
> And gentle kine that graze and move,
> Spotting the misty pastures o'er."—*Faber*.

The sun rises higher over "green valleys musical with lowing kine"—the "lowing vales," as several poets audaciously called them [1]—and with "the heifer's wandering bell." And then noon. If it be summer—

> "A various group the herds and flocks compose—
> Rural confusion ! On the grassy bank
> Some ruminating lie ; while others stand
> Half in the flood, and, often bending, sip
> The circling surface. In the middle droops
> The strong laborious ox, of honest front,
> Which incomposed he shakes ; and from his sides
> The troublous insects lashes with his tail,
> Returning still. Amid his subjects safe,
> Slumbers the monarch swain ; his careless arm
> Thrown round his head, on downy moss sustained ;
> Here laid his scrip, with wholesome viands filled ;
> There, listening every noise, his watchful dog."

If winter, there is Cowper's picture—

> "The very kine that gambol at high noon,
> The total herd receiving first from one
> That leads the dance, a summons to be gay,

---

[1] Tennyson says the ox fills "the horned valleys" with his lowing. Is this an analogous instance of the transfer of epithet ?

T

> Though wild their strange vagaries, and uncouth
> Their efforts, yet resolved with one consent
> To give such act and utterance as they may
> To ecstacy too big to be suppressed."

The herds "screened from the sun and from molesting bite of vexing flies, peaceful enjoy the cool and fragrant meal," and so on to evening, when "the horned cattle will forget to feed, and come home lowing from the grassy mead." We hear them "rub the pasture's creaking gate," and see them, in the yard, "their rustling feast enjoy, and snatch sweet mouthfuls from the passing boy." If the weather be stormy, we see them in the morning "on the scowling heavens cast a despairing eye," at noon "gaze upon the gloom, and, seemly, dread the threatened storm to come," "with broadened nostril to the sky upturned, the conscious heifer sniffs the stormy gale."

In poetry, therefore, the cow is regularly recurrent as a feature of the passing day or changing year; indeed, if we except the birds as a class, no other image is such a favourite with the bards as the herd. Whether they speak of them collectively as "soft beavies," and "patient kine," or, individually, as the "lordly stiff-necked bull," "the tyrant of the field,"—the "milky mother,"—"the strong laborious ox with honest front," or "the slow team of steers with down-sunk forehead and depending tongue,"—"the lowing heifer, loveliest of the herd,"—the "stubborn" bullock, or "the sportive calves with lifted tails," we find them extending to the horned things all that sympathetic admiration which is characteristic of the poets when speaking of animals that are of direct use to man.

The bull is a really noble animal when you are not on the same side of the hedge. As Hurdis says—

> "'Tis pleasure to approach,
> the strong fence shielded, view secure
> Nature, in the savage bull.

> Soon as he marks me, he, the tyrant fierce,
> To earth descends his head ; hard breathe his lungs
> Upon the dusty sod ; a sulky leer
> Gives double horror to the frowning curls
> That wrap his forehead, and ere long is heard
> From the deep cavern of his lordly throat
> The growl insufferable."

But when you and it are both on the same side of the palings, the spectacle of the bull—

> "To the hollowed earth
> Whence the sand flies, muttering bloody deeds,
> And groaning deep,"

is not nearly so inspiriting. For the beast has a reckless way about it that defies the calculations of the amateur—

> "At random faces,
> And whom he hits nought knows, and
> Whom he hurts nought cares."

The professional torreador has the creature at his mercy, and I can conceive nothing better calculated to impress upon the mind a befitting sense of the superiority of human reason over brute force and cunning, than the Portuguese bull-ring. The vile cruelty of Madrid is not permitted in Lisbon, and in the latter city therefore is to be seen the perfection of courage and skill—

> "The bull's hoarse rage in dreadful sport to mock,
> And meet with single sword his bellowing shock."

Byron has given an admirable description of the Spanish scene.

The contests for "the lordship of the lowing herds" afford the poets some fine touches—how they "fill the fields with troublous bellowing," and "in impetuous battle mix." The baited bull was a specially favourite image with Spenser, perhaps a favourite sport. His sympathy is always with the bull, as in the following—

> " Like a wylde bull, that, being at a bay,
> Is bayted of a mastiffe, and a hound,
> And a curre-dog, that doe him sharp assay
> On every side, and beat about him round ;
> But most that curre, barking with bitter sownd,
> And creeping still behinde, doth him incomber,
> That, in his chauffe, he digs the trampled ground,
> And threats his horns, and bellows like the thonder :
> So did that squire his foes disperse and drive asonder."

The bullock is, in the poets, very properly the type of headstrong, unmanageable youth, without the mature dignity of the bull, but a sufficient measure of dangerous potentiality.

Oxen are "sluggish," "stubborn," "dull," "toiling," "moyling," "tired," "patient," " willing," "slowpaced," "faint."

> "The slow team
> Of steers, reluctant pressing on the yoke,
> With down-sunk forehead and depending tongue,
> With winding shoulders and slow-pacing foot,
> Pants."

Hurdis wrote this from the life, or he could never have used the word " winding " for that laboured circular working of the fore-legs. Yet what noble upstanding brutes the oxen of the East are, and how admirably they look trotting along an Indian road to the rhythmic tinkling of their bells, with the crimson-canopied carriage behind them.

One great poet called the cow " the milky mother," a phrase that does not sound so well in English as in Latin, but five or six adopt it from him. She is a ponderous, lethargic, slow-footed personage, but benevolent and tranquil. Those who live in the country may not be of the same opinion, for many milky mothers are very awkward to meet—

> "Straight down she ran like an enragèd cow
> That is berobbed of her youngling dear "—

and after all, in the matter of being tossed, it does not matter much whether you are pitchforked by a "tyrant of the herd" or a "milky mother." Sancho swore they were clothworkers from Segovia : thè Don said they were magicians. Whichever they were, the squire's bones ached for ever so many days, and his self-respect was tossed out of him for the rest of his life.

The heifer is always, in the poets, a thing of beauty, "gentle," "balmy-breathing," "sleeker than night-swollen mushrooms " (Keats). Yet they like to see it, in the traditional tigress fashion, looking on while rivals combat to the death for her possession—

> "A lowing heifer, loveliest of the herd,
> Stood feeding by, while two fierce bulls prepared
> Their armèd heads for fight, by fate of war to prove
> The victor worthy of the fair one's love."

Nor outside the natural animal do the poets neglect their kine. Scattered up and down are references to bull-baiting—

> "When through the town, with slow and solemn air,
> Led by the nostril, walks the muzzled bear ;
> Behind him moves, majestically dull,
> The pride of Hockley Hole, the surly bull "—

and bull-fights—the sympathy of the poet being always with the baited beast—to the kine that Egypt worshipped, the bovine metamorphoses of Jupiter and of Io, the beast of the Bethlehem stable—

> "When He incradled was,
> In simple cratch, wrapt in a wad of hay,
> Betweene the toylful oxe and humble asse."

the punishment of Nebuchadnezzar—

> "That great proud King of Babylon,
> That would compel all nations to adore,
> And him as only God to call upon,
> Till, through celestial doom thrown out of door,
> Into an ox he was transformed of yore "—

Brahma's white bull and Europa's—

> "Now lows the milk-white bull on Afric's strand,
> And crops with dancing head the daisied land ;
> With rosy wreaths Europa's hand adorns
> His fringèd forehead, and his pearly horns ;
> Light on his back the sportive damsel bounds,
> And pleased he moves along the flowery grounds,
> Bears with slow step his beauteous prize aloof,
> Dips in the lucid flood his ivory hoof ;
> Then wets his velvet knees, and wading laves
> His silky sides amid the dimpling waves "—

the bulls of heraldry, notably the "dun" the bulls of Percy—

> "Lord Westmoreland his ancient raised,
> The Dun Bull he raised on high "—

the cows of popular superstition—white, black, and "shelly coated," dappled, and sand-red, and brindled—and many other creatures of story and myth, from Taurus of the zodiac to the cow of Dunsmore Heath, of which the horn, albeit an elephant's tusk is shown to this day, in proof of the great Earl's great achievement.

XII.

SOME POETS' HORSES.

IT is curious that poets should see so little of the natural
animal in the horse. As a beast, a quadruped, they
absolutely ignore it. It is only in its artificial varieties
that they recognise it at all, and even then so seldom as
to surprise the student of their pages. About the horse
particular, individual steeds of fame, a volume might easily
be gathered from our poets. But of the creature in Nature
they say nothing. The beast has become so thoroughly
relative that it has lost all individuality. It is either the
other half of a cavalier, a warrior, a war-chariot, a plough,
a coach, or a cart, or something else, that it cannot be
contemplated apart from its rider, its accoutrements, or the
vehicle it draws. All other animals have characters of their
own. The horse has none. It varies only according to the
kind of man on its back or the kind of thing behind it.
Attach a plough to it, and it becomes at once "heavy" and
"dull;" set a soldier upon it, and it is "fiery" and
"proud." When ladies ride, their horses turn to "milk-
white palfreys;" the hero of a poem, whether knight or
highwayman, bestrides, as a rule, a "courser." There are
also "swift-heeled Arabians," and "barbs," and "jennets;"
but these are not meant for real horses.

There is, of course, nothing surprising in the fact that
poets have but little in sympathy with stable-boys or book-

makers. When they do speak of grooms they rate them as second-class horses, and the " horsey" gentleman as an inferior amateur groom. This is, poetically, as it should be ; but, on the other hand, when we remember that nearly all history has been made on horseback, and that it is to the character of that animal that man is indebted for the moiety of his achievements, it strikes strangely to find the poets so consistently disregarding the strongly-marked individuality of the horse. Its sympathy with human beings—as is the case with the poets' dogs also—has doubtless much to do with the doubling-up of the animal with its master. Whatever nature it may show, it is always in accordance with that of its rider. Its temper always matches its trappings, is strictly in keeping with its harness.

Once upon a time—so the Greeks had the story[1]—Athena and Poseidon contended for the honour of being the best friend of humanity, and, to clinch his claim, the ocean-god created for the use of man the horse. Olympus had to arbitrate between the rival divinities, and eventually decreed in favour of Athena's olive-tree, "for," said Zeus, " I foresee that man will pervert the gift of Poseidon to the purposes of war."

Appeal, however, lies from the judgment of the Thunderer to the ultimate voice of history, and if " in the fulness of time" we could ask the question again, Eternity would certainly reverse the decree of the Olympian bench, for the horse has done far more for man than salad oil.

In myth it is always noble. No monstrous form in the classics has dignity except the Centaur, the Asvinau of the Hindoos. The conjunction of man and horse in one being was not considered degrading.

---

[1] How miserably the poets use this beautiful episode. See, for instance, Congreve (To the Earl of Godolphin), or Parnell (The Horse and the Olive).

To complete the majesty of deities, they rode or drove horses. In primitive legend they go in pairs—the black steed of Night with the grey of the Morning, the red horse of Carnage and the white of Death. In the sunrise and the sunset there glitter the peacock-feathered manes of the coursers of the sky. The spirit of the Whirlwind sweeps along charioted by a swarthy team. Thunder and Lightning, the terrific Dioscuri, ride in the heavens upon their neighing, fire-breathing, stallions. The rain-god Indras comes up drawn by the Rohits, " the brown ones;" the Dawn has harnessed to her car three dappled greys. From the stables of Asgard issue Hrimfaxe and Skimfaxe, the steeds of Day and Night, just as from the stalls of Olympus the Hours lead forth Xanthos "the golden," and Belios "the mottled," and Memnon's mother—"Tithonia conjux"—springs from bed to chariot, and, shaking their dewy manes, Lampas and Phæthon whirl her upwards through the reddening skies to awaken gods and men.

The spirits are all mounted—" Heaven's cherubim, horsed upon the sightless coursers of the air "—"night-roaming ghosts, by saucer-eyeballs known " (Gay)—"the Kelpy on its water-palfrey" (Wordsworth)—the angels of death, whose "coal-black steeds wait for men " (Jean Ingelow)—the fays of Collins on milk-white steeds, and of Shelley on "the coursers of the air," the elfin king of Leyden on his coal-black horse that goes with noiseless hoofs. Ossian's steeds—"bounding sons of the hill," like every other animal in that tiresome imposture—are wreaths of mist. But more substantial, in their way, are the night-steeds of the moon in Campbell, the "pale horses" of famine, war, and plague (Mallet), the white horse, splashed with blood, which Anarchy rides in Shelley, and the "pale horse," which is the steed of death in a score of poets. Coleridge makes fun of it—

" A Pothecary on a white horse,
Rode by on his vocations,
And the Devil thought of his old friend
Death in the Revelations."

But it is reserved for Eliza Cook to speak of " the brave iron-grey," which is *Eternity's Arab!*

The Oriental horse-myths have their exponent in Sir William Jones, whose "green-haired steeds," "with verdant manes," gallop through the skies.   "The seven coursers green" of Love and Bounty, "with many an agate hoofed, and pasterns fringed with pearl," and those others, "the steeds of noon's effulgent king, that shake their green manes, and blaze with rubied eyes," are strictly in sympathy with Hindoo tradition.   Campbell, on the same theme, wanders, as usual, into sunless skies of error.

Of horses more specifically, historically, individual, there is a multitude, of course.   Starting from the commencement, there is the wild Scythian, supposed (by Phineas Fletcher) to drink the blood of the horse he is riding— "yet worse! this fiend makes his own flesh his meat" — and the horses of ancient tradition, such as that "wondrous horse of brass on which the Tartar king did ride;" and so we pass, through the classic steeds of Greece and Rome, the steeds of Cæsar and Alexander, to those of mediæval heroes, Arthur and the Cid; and so along the picketed lines of Rhenish steeds, knightly coursers, and milk-white palfreys of the old-ballad age, to the horse of Mazeppa, and the Tartar steeds of the revolt of Islam.

The horses of St. Mark and of Pharaoh, of which Miriam sang when she went up before the host, with all the women with timbrels and dances—of Darius, which neighed him into the throne of Persia—of Diomed, anthropophagous brutes, "Thracian steeds with human carnage wild"—

" Which fell Geryon nursed, their food
The flesh of man, their drink his blood"

—of Nereus, the sea-horses, a very favourite fancy of the poets—of Dan Phœbus—

> " When he doth tighten up the golden reins
> And paces leisurely down amber plains
> His snorting four "—

the air-bred and wind-begotten steeds of Thrace — the winged steeds of Perseus and Endymion,—and all the " other foales of Pegasus, his kynde." So, step by step, pass to Black Besses of the heath and road, the chargers of our Joan-of-Arcs and other warriors of history, of Queen Elizabeth and other sovereigns, to the Rozinantes, Grizzles, and Dobbins, of Cervantes, Hudibras, and Syntax, to hacks of John Gilpin and the " Parish Doctor," and many a local hero and heroine beside whose jades are the subjects of a passing jest.

I remember having seen somewhere a picture of Adam, in the garb of Eden, riding a bare-backed mustang, a lion gamboling by his side. But in Holy Writ the horse appears in only one aspect—as the war-horse. " He saith among the trumpets, Ha ! ha ! and he smelleth the battle afar off, the thunder of the captains and the shouting." [1]

In Genesis the name does not occur at all. Nor, as a matter of fact, could it do so, seeing that the first " horse " (the first that science knows of) was a little, five-toed, sharp-nosed creature, much too small for a man of even our degenerate stature to ride upon, and otherwise also unsuitable for a steed ; and it is, therefore, very probable that " the first man " never was on horseback.

Yet the use of the animal dates back to a prodigious antiquity. The Assyrian sculptures show us high-bred and carefully-caparisoned chargers, three thousand years and more ago. Nor is it at all likely that they were the first to

---

[1] Job's splendid poem has incited several poets (Quarles, Young, Broome, for instance) to attempt the same theme, which, however, gains no accession of beauty or power from their paraphrases.

train them, for the horse is a native of Central Asia, and the early Aryan is hardly likely to have wasted such a useful beast. At any rate, the perfection to which the extremely ancient Assyrian monuments show us that the breeding had attained some eighteen hundred years before Christ, must certainly have taken a long time in development.

The poets, therefore, do not take more than their usual license when they describe a primitive race catching the wild horse and breaking it into their use. Thus in " Before the Flood "—

> " With flying forelock and dishevelled mane,
>   They caught the wild steed prancing o'er the plain,
>   For war or pastime reined his fiery force ;
>   Fleet as the wind he stretched along the course,
>   Or, loudly neighing at the trumpet's sound,
>   With hoofs of thunder smote the indented ground."

The colt "with heels unclipped and shaggy mane promiss," and "nothing conscious of his future toils," "approving all pastures but his own" (Hurdis), grows up, and for a while longer retains his liberty.

> " Wanton
> He skims the spacious meadows,
> Then stops and snorts, and throwing up his heels,
> Starts to the voluntary race again."

But in due time he becomes a full-grown horse.

> " Then think how short the time, since, joyous, free,
>   He roamed the mead, or, by his mother's side,
>   Attended plough or harrow, scampering gay ;
>   And think how soon his years of youth and strength
>   Will fly, and leave him to that wretched doom
>   Which ever terminates the horse's life.
>   Toil more and more severe, as age, decay,
>   Disease, unnerve his limbs, till sinking faint
>   Upon the road, the brutal stroke resounds."

The phrase "which ever" is not, however, strictly correct in England, whatever, according to Grahame, may be the universal rule in Scotland. For, as Cowper says—

> " The veteran steed excused his task at length,
> In kind compassion of his failing strength,
> And turned into the park or mead to graze,
> Exempt from future service all his days,
> There feels a pleasure perfect in its kind."

This may be accepted as almost the total sum of the natural horse in poetry. That episode in Venus and Adonis, where the conduct of the young boar-hunter's steed suggests to the quick-witted goddess an argument from analogies, has suggested several exaggerated descriptions of the stallion at large, but they are scarcely sketches from the life.

In the chase, Somerville of course excepted, the horse does not occupy the prominent place that might have been expected. Hunting is not a favourite pastime of the poet. He does not ride as Byron says Don Juan did—

> " So that his horse, or charger, hunter, hack,
> Knew that he had a rider on his back."

And they skirt the subject, except so far as sentiment goes, with the utmost delicacy. Some, indeed, contemn "the squire" who takes a pride in his steed.

Somerville, of course, is a unique exception, and his apostrophes of the "brave youths" who go a-hunting are delightful rubbish, as the opening rhapsody goes to show—

> " Hail, happy Britain ! highly favoured isle,
> And Heaven's peculiar care ! to thee 'tis given
> To train the sprightly steed, more fleet than those
> Begot by Winds, or the celestial breed
> That bore the great Pelides thro' the press
> Of heroes armed, and broke their crowded ranks."

But he knew a good horse as well as Hurdis did, and

was a far better sportsman than he was a poet. For tł
utter humiliation of the noble brute read Eliza Cook.

The race-horse finds but few friends among the poel
They see only the cruelty of the sport. The jockeys a
" murderers," and the animals come in with " rivers
sweat and blood flowing from gorèd sides." They admi
the animal " with his nostrils thin, blown abroad by tł
pride within," but they avoid it.

The war-horse finds more frequent and appreciati·
reference, but the poets cannot shake Job off. The fe
lines of the Patriarch's poem stretch farther than all the
laboured eulogies, just as the staff of Moses reached farth
than the linked sceptres of all the Kings of Edom.
neighs and paws and snorts, but it gets no further, after a
than the 25th verse of the 39th chapter of the Book of Jo
" Taboring the ground" is, however, an excellent conce
of Quarles, and shows an unusual judgment in plagiari
ing.

The poet's cart-horse is a most dismal creation. N
long ago cruelty to animals was much more prevalent thа
it is now—thanks to a society that has the eyes of Argu
the funds of Crœsus, and the sympathy of the country-
and from Chaucer to Wordsworth the draught-horse is
miserable brute, habitually ill-treated, and dying from cru
over-work. It is " as lene as is a rake" (Chaucer); " ε
bones and leather" (Butler); " a wretched unlucky corse
(Ramsay); " toil-worn" in Grahame, who seems to ha·
had an exceptionally bad opinion of Scotch treatment
horses. Cowper implores the carter to spare his " po
beasts;" Wordsworth beseeches the waggoner to be min·
ful of his responsibilities. Both these poets, however, pε
a tribute of respect to the draught-horse's willingness, whi
those who know him better—Hurdis, Clare, and Bloo1
field, for instance—admire it, " patient of the slow-pacε
swain's delay;" or as

> " Up against the hill they strain,
> Tugging at the iron chain."

Joanna Baillie has a bitter passage : is there still all the old truth about it ?

> " What forms are these with lean galled sides ?   In vain
> Their laxed and ropy sinews sorely strain
> Heaped loads to draw, with lash and goad urged on.
> They were in other days, but lately gone,
> The useful servants, dearly prized, of those
> Who to their failing age give no repose—
> Of thankless, heartless owners.   Then full oft
> Their arched, graceful necks, so sleek and soft,
> Beneath a master's stroking hand would rear
> Right proudly, as they neighed his voice to hear.
> But now how changed !   And what marred things are these,
> Starved, hooted, scarred, denied or food or ease ;
> Whose humbled looks their bitter thraldrom show,
> Familiar with the kick, the pinch, the blow ?
> Alas ! in this sad fellowship are found
> The playful kitten and the faithful hound."

In metaphors and analogies, similes and morals drawn from an original so exceptionally promising as the horse, the poets show themselves strangely self-denying and even parsimonious.   In a great measure the dog forestalls it. Moreover, when comparisons of courage, speed, or a generous spirit are sought there are the poets' lions and eagles to draw upon.   The horse therefore is made an adjunct in description rather than a moral auxiliary.   It adds a material feature to the scene, but affords no lesson.   The poets, in fact, do not recognise the horse as an animal.   It is an equipment, an adornment, furniture.

Herbert is a very striking exception ; he has a whole quiver full of equine "jacula."   Thus, for example, "a jade eats as much as a good horse ; " "Who lets his wife go to every feast, and his horse drink at every water, shall neither have good wife nor horse ; " "The master's eye

fattens the horse;" "For want of a nail the shoe is l
for want of a shoe the horse is lost : for want of a h
the rider is lost;" "The horse thinks one thing, anc
that saddles him another;" "Speed without pains, a hoi
These must suffice. Cowper uses the metaphor "p
horse constancy," and Churchill, though with defic
skill, utilises the colt as a simile for "loose Digressi
that "spurning connection and her formal yoke, boi
through the forest and wanders far astray." The colt
deed, furnishes an analogy to many things and persons
depreciate it, for the poets too often forget that, after
innocence in the young beast sets it quite apart from
deliberate obliquities of reasoning humanity.

XIII.

SOME POETS' DOGS.

> " Mastiff, greyhound, mongrel grim,
>   Hound or spaniel, brach or lym,
>   Or bobtail-tyke or trundle-tail."

PREMISING, in the poet's humour, that animals are only worthy of regard relatively to man, it follows that no animal is so suitable for poetical treatment as the dog, for the dog has virtually no independent existence. Apart from man it has no identity.

For the wild dog is hardly a dog. It smells like a fox, has eyes that gleam in the twilight like a wolf's, is silent under all canine provocations to bark, and when it does give tongue, its howling is in a voice that is absolutely unlike any other created utterance. In appearance it is a cross between a jackal and a wolf, assuming a furry winter coat in high latitudes, while its manners in captivity resemble neither the one nor the other. In Byron it " howls o'er the fountain brim, with baffled thirst and famine grim," but as he is speaking of the deserted courts of Hassan's palace, the animal intended is probably only the " pariah-dog " of the East, as also in the following—

> " He saw the lean dogs beneath the wall
>   Hold o'er the dead their carnival;

U

Gorging and growling o'er carcass and limb,
They were too busy to bark at him !
From a Tartar's skull they had stripped the flesh,
As ye peel the fig when its fruit is fresh ;
And their white tusks crunched o'er the whiter skull,
As it slipped through their jaws when their edge grew dull,
As they lazily mumbled the bones of the dead,
When they scarce could rise from the spot where they fed ;
So well had they broken a lingering fast
With those who had fall'n for that night's repast.
The scalps were in the wild dog's maw,
The hair was tangled round his jaw ;
But close by the shore, on the edge of the gulf,
There sat a vulture flapping a wolf,
Who had stolen from the hills, but kept away,
Scared by the dogs, from the human prey ;
But he seized on his share of a steed that lay,
Picked by the birds, on the sands of the bay,
And see, worms of the earth, and fowls of the air,
Beasts of the forest, all gathering there;
All regarding man as their prey,
All rejoicing in his decay."

By the way, were pariah-dogs ever a feature of English life ? Or how is it that Spenser, Chaucer, and others talk so often of vagrant curs that beset well-bred dogs; of "a sort of hungry dogs y-met, about a carcass in the common way," and so forth. It is very probable that we once had pariahs, just as every other half-civilised country still has them. This opens up, it seems to me, rather an interesting point for inquiry and research. At any rate, our older poets evidently *saw* them in packs quarrelling over offal on the roads.

When, therefore, the poets speak of dogs they mean the tamed descendants of the creatures which were given to man by a compassionate Providence to be his eyes and ears, and which centuries of experience have proved to be the best servants beyond all comparison that humanity has ever dignified into utility. Under domestication the dog has varied from its original types with such extraordinary ingenuity that it would now be very difficult indeed to resolve the different species of Europe into their primal elements or to refer each to its old wild-brier stock.

I do not say it would be impossible, for I have myself seen so many transition-varieties between the *bonâ fide* "wild dog"—the tiger-hunting pack of the Indian jungles—and the thoroughly civilised animal, that I have no doubt that if travellers put their experiences together, the existence of most of our dogs, with their present special characteristics in full development, could be traced back to the remotest ages. Thus, long before white men went to North America, the Red Indians had possessed the greyhound; the dames of old Mexico centuries ago cherished curly-haired lap-dogs; the villagers of the Himalayas guarded their hill-paths in the Vedic days with ferocious thick-coated shepherd-dogs ; Nineveh borrowed the mastiff from Egypt—and Egypt from " Accadia."

I yield to no one in my honourable and affectionate regard for the dog. But I place it far below man ; for man, I contend, made the dog, and I agree with him who says that " man is the Providence of the dog." The sagacity, fidelity, and disinterested, passionate attachments of the dog are such old facts that the person who would disbelieve in them can hardly be imagined ; and for myself, I am almost afraid to think of the dog's possibilities in intelligence and affection, if its life were only commensurate with our own. Yet granting all this, I always find myself resenting the irrational infatuation of dog enthusiasts, and being thus apprehensive of the excesses of others, am perhaps inclined to weigh out the measure of my own admiration with too exact a hand. For a margin of eulogy is excusable for an animal that without reason learns in its short span of years so nearly to simulate it; that without inherited data evolves from its own perceptions such an admirable morality; that without free agency formulates so fearlessly and faithfully its table of duties to be done and temptations to be resisted; that without any hope of a hereafter, so often seems to be living in expectation of a life to come. But the sum of all this does not reach by many figures the full equation of man.

Yet the dog is a beautiful symbol, and though here and there individuals may exceed into Egyptian idolatry of the animal, it is as a type of courageous, self-forgetful friendship that the poets use it most justly.

Occasionally, too, they confess that the best of dogs may "from the path of duty err."[1]   As Somerville admits—·

> "He may mistake sometimes, 'tis true,
> None are infallible but you ;
> The dog whom nothing can mislead
> Must be a dog of parts indeed ; "

and as Eliza Cook delightfully illustrates in her address to the staghound Bran—

> "You have strength of muscle and length of limb,
> Your jaws are deep and your beard is grim,
> Your fangs are strong and ivory white,
> Your mouth is as black as a cloudy night.
> 'Tis pleasant to hear the wise ones utter
>   The worth of your power and pace ;
> But why did you swallow that pound of butter,
>   Dog of an ancient race?"

So, too, Cowper, rising for once out of his indolent, timid life, to impatience with a little dog that persisted in quarrelling with others, orders it to—"go !"

[1] "E'en the docile pointer knows disgrace,
    Thwarting the gen'ral instincts of his race ;
    E'en so the mastiff or the meaner cur
    At times will from the path of duty err."

> " I care not whether east or north,
>   So I no more may find thee ;
>   The angry Muse thus sings thee forth,
>   And claps the gate behind thee."

To measure the real worth of a dog's attachment, the true value of its friendship, we have only to take any one of the poets' desperate assertions that the dog they deplore was their " only " friend.   Thus Byron—

> " Ye who perchance behold this simple urn
>   Pass on—it honours none you wish to mourn ;
>   To mark a friend's remains these stones arise,
>   I never knew but one—and here he lies."

Now, what is the effect of this stanza on the mind ?   Does it exalt the worth of a dog's fidelity ? or does it not rather fill the reader with an indignant pity for the man who in all this world of men and women says he could find, or keep, no better friend than a dog? Sympathy is of so subtle a crystal that it shivers to pieces at the first drop of cynicism, and so, instead of admiring Byron's dog the more, I feel inclined to admire the dog's master the less.

By his own showing, too, the poet was barely honest to his one friend—

> " Perchance my dog will whine in vain
>   Till fed by stranger hands ;
>   But long ere I come back again,
>   He'd tear me where he stands "—

and there is either gross injustice in this verse or false sentiment in the other.   And each is alike disagreeable and unjust.

Meanwhile, the beauty of the dog's fidelity remains unimpaired, and when the same poet (in his terrific dream of " Darkness ") pays the tribute of his verse to the hound faithful even to death, he commands a universal sympathy—

> " With a piteous and perpetual moan
> And a quick desolate cry, licking the hand
> Which answered not with a caress—he died."

Mary Howitt's lines—

> " My mother is dead, and my father loves
> His dogs far more than me,"

are within the facts, and so too is Tennyson's

> " He will hold thee when his passion shall have spent its moral force
> Something better than his dog, something dearer than his horse."

Nothing, of course, can prevent a Cowper making even a dog's friendship sometimes ridiculous, nor an Eliza Cook arousing one's furious scorn with such a couplet as this—

> " Nor deem me impious if I say
> That next to God I hold my hound."

What a confession of faith—to worship God, and love her dog better than her neighbour ! But where the poet does not fall a victim to want of taste or to cheap cynicism, the expression of affection for a worthy dog is always sure to command a reasonable sympathy with the writer, if only for the reason that the dog is one of man's finest triumphs.

King Lear bemoans it as "the most unkindest cut of all," that the dogs about his palace, "the little dogs and all," should bark at him. How many men have said it in half earnest that they place their hopes no higher than the Red Indian who "in another life expects his dog, his bottle, and his wife," and that they envy Tobit and Arjuna their canine companions in heaven—

> " He asks no angel's wings, no seraph's fire,
> But thinks, admitted to that equal sky,
> His faithful dog shall bear him company."—*Pope.*

It forms a feature, therefore, of all the happiest aspects of life, is an emblem of the security and tranquil domestic simplicity that are accepted as characteristic of the poetical country-side.

The dog at ease is significant of auspicious times and events; the miserable one ominous of disaster present or to come. The lazy dog is a feature of the summer's day, and the active one of winter and spring. It is on the hills with the shepherd, on the road with the carter, in the corner of the field with the ploughman. No door or gate opens without its appropriate dog. Guests, good and bad, are to be distinguished by the kind of dogs that meet them.

And there are few incidents of the animal's life that have not been noted. The meeting of strange dogs, their making acquaintance, their courtships, the birth of puppies, their blindness, and sometimes untimely death by drowning; the playing of the puppies with the children of the house, their being reared as members of the family circle, their entering upon the duties of life, their different careers, and the various incidents of each. And what delightful vignettes they often suggest! Grahame's haymaking dog for instance, or Joanna Baillie's summer-afternoon dog—

> " Silence prevails—
> Nor low, nor bark, nor chirping bird is heard,
> The shady nooks the sheep and kine convene;
> Within the narrow shadow of the cot
> The sleepy dog lies stretched upon his side,
> Nor heeds the footsteps of the passer-by,
> Or at the sound but raises half an eyelid,
> Then gives a feeble growl and sleeps again,
> While puss composed and grave on threshold stone
> Sits winking in the light."

And Jean Ingelow's delightful sketch of the fisherman's puppies—

> " The village dogs and ours, elate and brave,
> Lay looking over, barking at the fish;

> Fast, fast, the silver creatures took the bait,
> And when they heaved and floundered on the rock
> In beauteous misery, a sudden pat
> Some shaggy pup would deal, then back away,
> At distance eye them with sagacious doubt,
> And shrink half-frightened from the slippery things."

At play or at war, snarling over a bone, quarrelling over a piece of meat, crouching under the lash, barking at passing beggars, barking at nothing, asleep, awaking, awake, rolling in the grass or dust, eating, drinking, chasing cats, dreaming of chasing cats, annoyed by flies, wistful, honest, suspicious, confiding, fawning; big dogs beset by little ones, "generous" hounds by curs of low degree; the poor man's dog, the blind man's dog, the poacher's dog, the mad dog; —in each and all these phases we find the dog in poetry. Indeed, there is no mood of temper, no circumstance of life whatever, in which, in one poet or another, the animal does not figure, from the puppy blind to the dog cooked—

> " A kettle slung
> Between two poles upon a stick transverse
> Receives the morsel, flesh obscene of dog
> Or vermin, or at best of cock purloined
> From his accustomed perch."

Yet of all terms of reproach, the whole world over, and from time immemorial, none is comparable in frequency of use or in its provocative potentialities on the individual abused, to the name of our best friend. "Treacherous, false, ungrateful dog!" and so forth, could be multiplied indefinitely from the poets if there were any need to go beyond the streets for evidence to the ignominy of the name. Spenser has ("Fairy Queen," Book vi. c. vi. 33) the phrase " vile *cowheard* dogge," and in the next stanza "cowheard feare." In stanza 26, however, we find "craven cowherd knight" who in "cowardize doth delight." These spellings occur in Johnson's edition, and, though I have not met with it, I make no doubt commentators have elucidated this complexity of etymology.

Even more curious, perhaps, is it that the hound, held in such special honour, should if possible suggest an aggravation of the dog reproach. All over the world, in every language from the far East to the far West, among savages of all countries and from the earliest days to the present time, "dog" is the supreme epithet of scorn. Whenever a European goes among an unfriendly population he is a "dog of an infidel," "a Christian dog;" and the worst that savages can say of him is that he "eats dog's meat," and has "dog's teeth." But for us, who have evolved the hound from the dog, the former stands a point in contempt below even the latter.

In the same spirit the canine element in a composite monster horribly enhances its deformity. How abominable the Scylla form always is—

> " Thereto the body of a dog she had,
> Full of fell ravin and fierce greedinesse."

"Cur" is in poetry a genus which includes many specific varieties—"mongrel of low degree," "bob-tailed tyke," "trundle-tail," "curtail dog," and so forth. It has long been in use as a term of reproach; and in this sense the poets always use it. Thus Wyatt's "curs do fall by kind on him that hath the overthrow," and Herbert's "babbling curs never want sore ears." And King's

> " Cur of shabby race,
> The first by wand'ring beggars fed;
> His sire, advanced, turned spit for bread,
> Himself each trust had still abused,
> To steal what he should guard was used
> From puppy; known where'er he came,
> Both vile and base, and void of shame."

In the same way " puppy " and, with less reason perhaps

"whelp." "A fierce Hibernian whelp" is, in Hurdis, curiously enough, a metaphor for a Scotchman, and "wanton whelp that loves to gnaw," in Davenant for disease. Now, seeing that man has given the young of a dog its name, it is an illustration of human unfairness to arbitrarily attach to the word any disagreeable significance. But whether we call them puppies or whelps the result is much the same to the animal.

Poetical proverbs and metaphors, all harping on the worst points of the dog, are very numerous ; and as curious as any, to my mind, are Watt's well-known lines, "Let dogs delight to bark and bite, *for God hath made them so,*" in which he throws the responsibility for the dog's implacable ferocity upon an inscrutable Providence. "He that lies with the dogs riseth with the fleas" (Herbert); "dog in office, set to bark all beggars from the door" (Hood); "the miserable pack that ever howl against fallen greatness" (Rogers); "two-legged dogs still pawing on the peers" (Pitt); "he can snap as well as whine" (Pope); "in every country dogs bite," and "look not for musk in a dog's kennel" (Herbert); "it is an houndes kynde, to bark upon a man behynde" (Gower). Avarice is a dog-madness (Young); Russians are "the dogs of Moscow," "Jews the curs of Nazareth" (Byron); "Malice is a cursed cur" (Pope). The Furies, like clinging crime, in Shelley, "track all things that weep and bleed and live, as lean dogs pursue through wood and lake some struck and sobbing fawn." Spaniards, in Phineas Fletcher, are "curres whelpt in Spain"—the laws of murder (Mallet); the meanly envious, that "ever howl against fallen greatness" (Rogers). Quarles likens the prayers of an unrepentant man to the howling of a dog, and associates dogs and devils in a curious way—

> " Depart like dogs, with devils take your lot,
> Depart like devils, for I know ye not ;

> Like dogs, like devils goe, goe howle and barke,
> Depart in darknesse, for your deeds were darke."

But not only, of course, does every mood of the canine character find abundant recognition in our poets, but every variety also of the animal; above all, each variety of hound used in sport.

> " Trusty household guardians,' mastiffs fell
>   Nightly to watch the walls,
>   Stout terriers that in high-hilled Sutherland
>   Beat up the wild cat's lodge or badgers rouse ;
>   And russet bloodhounds, wont near Annand's stream
>   To trace the sly thief with avenging foot,
>   Close as an evil conscience, still at hand :
>   Fleet greyhounds that outrun the fearful hare
>   And many a dog beside the faithful scent
>   To snuff his prey, on eager heel to scour
>   The purple heath and snap the flying game." [1]

Supreme of course as a creature of the chase is the fox, and its correlative, the foxhound, is therefore proportionately conspicuous.

> " Of horn and morn and hark and bark,
>   And echo's answering sounds,
> All poets' wit hath ever writ
>   In doggrel verse of hounds."

A reasonable quantity of rubbish was only therefore to be expected. But bearing in mind the excessive sympathy of the poets for the birds of sport and their habitual lamentations over pheasants and partridges, the robust tone in which they approve of the doings of foxhounds, beagles, staghounds, otter-hounds, badger-hounds, spaniels, pointers, and the rest, comes upon the student of poetical psychology as a surprise. It would be too much, of course, to say that the general tendency of poets to dislike wild beasts

[1] Leyden.

influences them in their opinion of the animals which man has taught to kill those quadrupeds; but it really does seem as if the poets' aversion to foxes, wolves, otters, badgers, boars, and their indifference to rabbits and hares, made them rather unfairly partial to their destroyers. In the single case of the deer (for which they have a very sincere admiration), there arose an obvious difficulty, which the poets have audaciously met by exulting with the hounds, and weeping with the deer. They "hang on the haunches" of stags, while tears chase each other "down the innocent noses" of their victims.

Some poets of the chase, however, have very decided opinions as to its morality generally. On the one side are, as examples, Somerville and Gay, on the other Thomson and Cowper. These, being altogether on the side of the victims, hold with the hares. Those, affecting a prodigious indignation against the robbers of hen-roosts and consumers of sprouting wheat, hunt with the hounds. These exhaust their satire and denunciation against the hunters. Those against the hunted. And neither are just.

Yet the just middle of sport is an easy one to hit, and the significances of our national pastime are admirable themes for the moralist and poet. It is not necessary for poetical fidelity to be either cruel with the one or gush with the other. It is not more remarkable that foxes should eat geese than that geese should eat grass, nor more culpable; and for the men whom England has been most proud of, they are rather those who have ridden straight to hounds with Somerville, not those who went nutting with Thomson. We can never have too many fox-hunting youths, but a very few Cowpers are enough. For myself, all sport has a dark side in the death of the victim. I eat the lamb with equanimity, and "the pullet of tender years" without mingling my tears with its sauce. But I regret the death of the fox and the otter. My sympathy is with Nature, and not with the stock-yard. I had rather, if sheep had the speed and pluck of foxes, hunt a sheep than a fox. But the poets' sympathy is with the villatic and the domesticated, not with the independent and the wild.

One poet at any rate—Somerville—was sportsman first and poet afterwards, and his rhymed instructions for the breeding, rearing, and hunting of hounds is an admirable instance of poetical ingenuity applied to an obstinately technical subject. A notice of his poem in some detail will cover all the others on the same subject, and may be accepted, from the unswerving similarity of poetical " hunts," as typical of all ; while by selecting Somerville as the spokesman I give the other poets the advantage of that knowledge of the subject in which they are so conspicuously deficient.

He commences by describing the origin of hunting, and the rude manner of the first hunters—

> " When Nimrod bold,
> That mighty hunter ! first made war on beasts
> And stained the woodland green with purple dye,
> New and unpolished was the huntsman's art ; "

and goes on to state that at first the chase was only a means towards sacrifice, but afterwards a necessity for food, the Creator having added flesh to man's vegetable diet—

> " So just is Heaven
> To give us in proportion to our wants."

Then comes a gap from Cain to William the Conqueror, bridged over by the poet only with a passing allusion to " our painted ancestors being slow to learn." But the Conquest arrives, and

> " Victorious William to more decent rules
> Subdued our Saxon fathers, taught to speak
> The proper dialect, with horn and voice
> To cheer the busy hound, whose well-known cry
> His listening peers approve with joint acclaim.

> From him successive huntsmen learned to join
> In bloody social leagues, the multitudes
> Dispersed, to size, to sort, train various tribes
> To rear, feed, hunt, and discipline the pack.
> Hail, happy Britain ! highly favoured isle,
> And Heaven's peculiar care ! "

He then describes in detail the arrangements for the kennel, insisting upon the necessity for perpetual watchfulness, especially when the hounds are at food or at play.

> " Which too often ends
> In bloody broils and death,
>   . . . for oft in sport
> Begun, combat ensues ; growling they snarl,
> Then on their haunches reared, rampant they seize
> Each others' throats ; with teeth and claws in gore
> Besmeared, they wound, they tear, till on the ground
> Panting, half-dead, the conquered champion lies,
> Then sudden all the base ignoble crowd
> Loud clam'ring seize the helpless, worried wretch,
> And thirsting for his blood, drag diff'rent ways
> His mangled carcass o'er the ensanguined plain.
> O breasts of pity void ! t'oppress the weak,
> To point your vengeance at the friendless head,
> And with one mutual cry insult the fall'n ;
> Emblem too just of man's degenerate race."

Directions are then given for the choice of hounds for the different kinds of chase, pointing out the necessity for selecting animals of medium size, and containing the following description of the poet's " perfect " foxhound—

> " See there, with count'nance blithe,
> And with a courtly grin, the fawning hound
> Salutes thee cow'ring, his wide-op'ning nose
> Upward he curls, and his large sloe-black eyes
> Melt in soft blandishments and humble joy.
> His glossy skin, or yellow pied, or blue,
> In lights or shades by Nature's pencil drawn,
> Reflects the various tints ; his ears and legs,

Flecked here and there, in gay enamelled pride
Rival the speckled pard ; his rush-grown tail
O'er his broad back bends in an ample arch :
On shoulders clean, upright and firm he stands :
His round cat-foot, straight hams, and wide-spread thighs,
And his low-dropping chest, confess his speed,
His strength, his wind, or on the steepy hill
Or far extended plain ; in ev'ry part
So well proportioned that the nicer skill
Of Phidias himself can't blame thy choice ;
Of such compose the pack.

                          But here a mean
Observe, nor the large hound prefer.
  .   .   .   .
For hounds of middle size, active and strong,
Will better answer all thy various ends
And crown thy pleasing labours with success."

For " the amphibious otter " or " stately stag " he advises

        " The deep-flewed hound,
Strong, heavy, slow, but sure ;
Whose ears down-hanging from his thick round head
Shall sweep the morning dew, whose clanging voice
Awake the mountain echo in her cell
And shake the forests."

And then comes a page or two on the "lime-hound"—

      "The bold Talbot kind
Of these the prime, as white as Alpine snows,
And great their use of old "

on the Borders to track human culprits, cattle-lifters, and horse-thieves.

A whole book then follows on the virtues of the beagle and the merits of hare-hunting, but reverting, as antithesis to " so mean a prey," to the sketch of a wild beast hunt in the days of the Great Mogul. Book III. finds us back in England in the days of King Edgar and wolves, and from the wolf the transition is easy to the fox.

> "Oh! how glorious 'tis
> To right th' oppressed, and bring the felon vile
> To just disgrace!"

And then follows a eulogy of fox-hunting—

> "Heav'ns! what melodious strains, how beat our hearts,
> Big with tumultuous joy!   The loaded gales
> ·Breathe harmony; and as the tempest drives
> From wood to wood, thro' every dark recess
> The forest thunders, and the mountains shake.
> The chorus swells.
>
> .   .   .   .
>
> See how they range
> Dispersed, how busily this way and that
> They cross, examining with curious nose
> Each likely haunt.   Hark! on the drag I hear
> Their doubtful notes, preluding to a cry
> More nobly full, and swelled with ev'ry mouth.
>
> .   .   .   .
>
> The gay pack
> In the rough bristly stubbles range unblamed.
> No widow's tears o'erflow, no secret curse
> Swells in the farmer's breast, which his pale lips
> Trembling conceal, by his fierce landlord awed;
> But courteous now he levels every fence,
> Joins in the common cry, and halloos loud,
> Charmed with the rattling thunder of the field."

The book then proceeds to give instructions for catching foxes in traps, and thence digresses to pitfalls for lions and elephants, with some hints how to hunt leopards with looking-glasses, returning again to England with an account of the royal staghounds out in Windsor Forest, remarkable, apart from the ecstatic narrative of the actual hunt, for an address to the ladies in the field—

> "How melts my beating heart! as I behold
> Each lovely nymph, our island's boast and pride,
> Their garments loosely waving in the wind,
> And all the flush of beauty in their cheeks!

While at their sides their pensive lovers wait,
Direct their dubious course, now chilled with fear
Solicitous, and now with love inflamed.
O grant, indulgent Heaven, no rising storm
May darken with black wings this glorious scene.
Should some malignant pow'r thus damp our joys
Vain were the gloomy cave, such as of old
Betrayed to lawless love the Tyrian queen—
For Britain's virtuous nymphs are chaste as fair ; "

and an equally preposterous address to the King, who
orders the hounds off the stag when it has been run
into—

" O mercy, heavenly born ! sweet attribute ! "

Book IV. reverts to details of the kennel, the care necessary in selecting "the parents of the pack "—

" The vain babbler shun,
Ever loquacious, ever in the wrong ;
His foolish offspring shall offend thy ears
With false alarms and loud impertinence.
Nor less the shifting cur avoid, that breaks
Illusive from the pack : to the next hedge
Devious he strays, there ev'ry muse he tries ;
If haply then he cross the steaming scent,
Away he flies vain-glorious, and exults
As of the pack supreme, and in his speed
And strength unrivalled.   Lo ! cast far behind,
His vexed associates pant and lab'ring strain
To climb the steep ascent.   Soon as they reach
Th' insulting boaster, his false courage fails,
Behind he lags, doomed to the fatal noose,
His master's hate, and scorn of all the field.
What can from such be hoped but a base brood
Of coward curs, a frantic, vagrant race ? "

Counsel is then given for curing sheep-worrying by strap-
ping the offender to a ram to be butted into repentance,

and a long dissertation on hydrophobia, elaborately horrible, leads the poem to its conclusion.　But

> " One labour yet remains, celestial maid !
> Another element demands my song ; "

and a spirited description of an otter-hunt closes "The Chase."

For fairness sake, and to strike the balance equally between the enthusiasts in praise and denunciation, Thomson's "Autumn," where (plagiarising as he goes) he condemns the "falsely-cheerful, barbarous game of death," should be read, especially the delightful account of the tipsy fox-hunters up at the Hall—

> " The table floating round
> And pavement faithless to the fuddled foot ;
> Thus as they swim in mutual swill, the talk,
> Vociferous at once from twenty tongues,
> Reels fast from theme to theme ; from horses, hounds,
> To church or mistress, politics or ghost,
> In endless mazes, intricate, perplexed.
> .　　.　　.　　.　　.　　.　　.
> Their feeble tongues
> Unable to take up the cumbrous word
> Lie quite dissolved.　Before the maudlin eyes
> Seen dim and blue, the double tapers dance,
> Then sliding soft—they drop."

This is a counterblast of course to Somerville's "short repast and temperate," to which the grateful farmer invites the avengers of his hen-roosts.　Nor less pointed is Thomson's reproof to ladies in the hunting ground, that commences—

> " Let not such horrid joy
> E'er stain the bosom of the British fair ;
> Far be the spirit of the chase from them ! "

Taken together, the poems are excellent illustrations of

poetical extremes, and of the poetical weakness of false sympathies.

Metaphors and similes from the chase are very numerous, and the "deep-mouthed," "cannon-mouthed" (Davenant), "chiming," "yelling," "baying" hounds are as industrious and as apt in poetical pursuit and apothegm as in the field. Wordsworth's line—"Keen as a fine-nosed hound, by soul-engrossing instinct driven along"—is one of the many fine metaphors which the subject affords.

Remembering the lamentations of the poets over the "wheeling coveys" pursued by "leaden showers," it is remarkable that the "full-eared" pointer and "wise-eyed" setter should be so warmly eulogised. When the wolf eats a sheep, all the sympathy is with the sheep, and when the leopard kills a deer the poets bewail the dead. Yet when the dogs of men hunt and murder a little animal which they are not going to eat, they applaud the dogs. And so, extending this incongruous partiality for human weaknesses a step further, they congratulate the pointer, setter, spaniel, and retriever, upon their success in assisting man to kill. Even Cowper, usually so fierce in his satire and denunciation of sport of all kinds, epitaphises a pointer without a word of disparagement : indeed, after the manner of epitaphs generally, with many compliments on his successful complicity in bloodshed—

> " Here lies one who never drew
> Blood himself, yet many slew ;
> Gave the gun its aim, and figure
> Made in field, yet ne'er pulled trigger.
> Armed men have gladly made
> Him their guide, and him obeyed ;
> At his signified desire,
> Would advance, present, and fire.
> Stout he was and large of limb,
> Scores have fled at sight of him,

> And to all this fame he rose
> Only by following his nose.
> Neptune was he called ; not he
> Who controls the boisterous sea,
> But of happier command,
> Neptune of the furrowed land ;
> And, your wonder vain to shorten,
> Pointer to Sir John Throckmorton."

That Gay should applaud " the obsequious ranger " is not to be wondered at.

The staghound—its very name is knightly—is an adjunct of all baronial scenes, of royal sport, of chivalrous society. It is the companion of chiefs and their daughters, a feature of earls' firesides. How Scott delighted in it, its power and grace. His verse is full of staghounds, though sometimes, as in the " Lady of the Lake," he employs bloodhounds of black St. Hubert's breed in pursuit of the antlered quarry. But what an unmitigated bore they are in Ossian, those "grey-bounding dogs," "long-bounding sons of the chase," that are for ever pursuing the everlasting "dun sons of the bounding roe !" In a score of our poets, conspicuously the older and more robust, the staghound occupies a place of considerable dignity, and not without reason, for it is a noble animal.

Greyhounds are " gentle " and " graceful "—" a grey-hound's gentle grace " is becoming both in a ship ("the vessel from the land, like a greyhound from the slips, darted forth ") and an elegant woman—so that they are popular with the poets. "A gentleman's greyhound and a salt-box, seek them at the fire." But it is as the pursuer of the hare that it receives most frequent notice ; and, singularly enough, in spite of the poets' usual sympathy with the hare apart from greyhounds, coursing is only here and there considered cruel. Gay, for instance, forgets all his kindness . for the hare as soon as the greyhound is after it—

> " Let thy fleet greyhound urge his flying foe,
>   With what delight the rapid course I view !
>   How does my eye the circling race pursue !
>   He snaps deceitful air with empty jaws,
>   The subtle hare darts swift between his paws.
>   She flies, he stretches ; now with nimble bound
>   Eager he presses on, but overshoots his ground ;
>   She turns, he winds, and soon regains the way,
>   Then tears with gory mouth the screaming prey."

Nor less emphatic than Gay's "delight" at such a scene is Somerville's denunciation of it. Not, be it remembered, from any sympathy with the hare, but because he preferred killing it with harriers—

> " Nor the tim'rous hare
> O'ermatched destroy, but leave that vile offence
> To the mean, murdering, coursing crew, intent
> On blood and spoil. Oh blast their hopes, just Heaven !"

The spaniel, as a pet—"household spaniel," "parlour spaniel," "fond spaniel"—is a touch of description which the poets use with excellent effect as completing the domestic scene or rounding off strong family emotions. As the water-spaniel it is utilised as the disturbing element of water-fowl existence, the acid in the mixture that effervesces the general tranquillity of life among water-lilies.

As the ordinary spaniel of bird-shooting, and "skilful to betray" when it is usually " the snuffing spaniel "—its habit of making a point often makes another for the poets. Thus Thomson—

> " In his mid career the spaniel struck
>   Stiff by the tainted gale, with open nose
>   Outstretched and finely sensible, draws full,
>   Fearful and cautious, on the latent prey."

While Grahame, Hurdis, Pope, and others find the simile of the spaniel that—

> " Scent struck,
> With lifted paw, stands stiffened."

Gay has the cocker, " the roving spy," at the copse side.

> " Cool breathes the morning air, and winter's hand
>   Spreads wide her hoary mantle o'er the land ;
>   Now to the copse thy lesser spaniel take,
>   Teach him to range the ditch and force the brake ;
>   Not closest coverts can protect the game.
>   Hark ! the dog opens, take thy certain aim ;
>   The woodcock flutters ; now he wav'ring flies !
>   The wood resounds : he wheels, he drops, he dies."

In character the spaniel appears to be more feminine than other dogs (though Cowley uses it as a simile for death) and proverb has extended the resemblance into a humility that women of spirit will hardly concede,[1] and that is hardly creditable to the spaniel—" like a thorough true-bred spaniel licks, the hand which cuffs him and the foot which kicks " (Churchill). Nor indeed do the poets carry it altogether to the credit of the spaniel that it should be so eager to forgive—" the beaten spaniel's fondness not so strange " as a woman's love that is abused, and that, in spite of abuse, strengthens. " No sycophant *although* of spaniel race," says Cowper of his fop. Its extreme docility, again, affords many a contemptuous simile ; as in Pope,

> " So well-bred spaniels civilly delight
>   In mumbling of the game they dare not bite."

The sea, "spaniel-like with parasitic kiss," laps on the shore.

The " baying beagle " is a general favourite, in spite of the hare being its victim, and a score of poets are to be found in the meet when puss is the game. To

---

[1] " A woman, a spaniel, a walnut-tree,
    The more you beat them the better they be."

> " See the deep-mouthed beagles catch
>   The tainted mazes, and on eager sport
>   Intent, with emulous impatience try
>   Each doubtful trace,"

is one of Armstrong's counsels for " Preserving Health," and Allan Ramsay asks—

> " What sweeter music wad ye hear
>   Than hounds and beagles crying?
>   The started hare runs hard wi' fear
>   Upon her speed relying."

Now and again the poets draw a sad moral from the chase, as Pope, after admiring the beagles on the track, interpolates in brackets—

> " Beasts, urged by us, their fellow-beasts pursue,
>   And learn of man each other to undo."

There are " wolf-dogs " in Leyden, Byron, and Wordsworth ; and the boar-hound—not a favourite with the poets—being the " dastard curres " of Spenser, the defeated assailants in Venus and Adonis—is a frequent species—

> " Here kennelled in a brake she finds a hound,
>   And asks the weary caitiff for his master,
>   And there another licking of his wound
>   'Gainst venomed sores the only sovereign plaster ;
>   And here she meets another sadly scowling
>   To whom she speaks, and he replies with howling.
>   When he hath ceased his ill-resounding noise,
>   Another flap-mouthed mourner, black and grim,
>   Against the welkin volleys out his voice.
>   Another and another answer him,
>   Clapping their proud tails to the ground below,
>   Shaking their scratched ears, bleeding as they go."

Bloodhounds, " sure-nosed as fasting tigers " (Davenant)

are, not unnaturally perhaps, even less popular with the poets. They never forget the abuse of this animal's terrific instinct—Moore's " precious scent "—of which man has at different periods of history been guilty, and the crime is poetically transferred from the human criminal to his innocent instrument. They are gloomily apostrophised as " bandogs." The flying slave,

> " 'Midst the shrieks of murder on the wind,
> Heard the mute bloodhound's death-step close behind,"

and the poets have never ceased to hear it ever since. It is " the sagacious bloodhound " in many poets, but the sagacity is that of the sleuth-hound, " skilled too well in all the murd'ring qualities of hell " (Pomfret). It is " staunch " also, but only in its fearful steadfastness to " the bloody trail." Shelley adds a horror to imprisonment in " the prison bloodhounds huge and grim " that were permitted to become familiar with the convicts whom they might have to track, and they are used as similes for the relentless whirlwind in Faber, and for famine and pestilence in Shelley. Says Byron, " Kings ! 'tis a great name for bloodhounds," and Shelley, " the bloodhound of Religion's hungry zeal."

As the " limehound," " creatures whose cold secrecy was meant, by Nature, for a surprise," this animal was at one time in demand on the Cheviot marches for tracking human delinquents—

> " Soon the sagacious brute, his curling tail
> Flourished in the air, low bending plies around
> His busy nose, the steaming vapour snuffs
> Inquisitive, nor leaves one turf untry'd,
> Till, conscious of the recent stains, his heart
> Beats quick ; his snuffing nose, his active tail,
> Attest his joy ; then with deep op'ning mouth
> That makes the welkin tremble, he proclaims

> Th' audacious felon : foot by foot he marks
> His winding way, while all the list'ning crowd
> Applaud his reas'nings.
> > O'er the wat'ry flood,
> Dry sandy heaths and stony barren hills
> O'er beaten paths with men and beasts detained,
> Unerring he pursues, till at the cot
> Arrived, and seizing by his guilty throat
> The caitiff vile, redeems the captive prey :
> So exquisitely delicate his sense."

Davenant pays them the compliment of saying "Wise, temperate limehounds that proclaim no scent, nor harb'ring will their mouths in boasting spend," and Spenser and others of the older poets refer to the sleuth-hound with respect. Barry Cornwall's poem on the animal is an enthusiastic panegyric of "the resolute fond bloodhound."

The mastiff, strangely enough, arrives at little honour in the poets' company. "Sagacious of his prey," "with eye of fire," says Falconer, and as the opponent of "the salvage bull" it arrives at many compliments. In Chaucer they are a noble figure—

> "About his car there wenten white alauns,
> Twenty and more, as great as any steer,
> To hunten at the leon and the deer,
> And followed him with muzzle fast y'bound."

But it is "an ill-conditioned carl," "gaunt," and "gruff," has to be taught manners by being kicked in the mouth by donkeys in Wordsworth, and, "growling at the gate," is possessed with a horrible longing to eat beggars in Pope. The sea when rough is, in Hurdis, a furious mastiff—

> "Lo ! as we speak,
> The wolfish monster kindles into rage.
> Enormous mastiff, how he gnaws his chain
> And struggles to be free, fast bound by fate
> And never to be let loose on man.

> Aloud he bellows, with uplifted paw
> Dances upreared, menaces the foot
> Of earth with trembling diffidence protruded.
> Lo ! the saliva of his deafening tongue
> Her pebbled instep stains : his rugged coat
> Is whitened o'er with foam."

On the whole, it seems to me, a poet's sentiments towards animals generally are very much like those of an average girl. Both prefer little animals, with smooth skins, and, for choice, white.

In this analogy perhaps is to be found the prevalent fastidiousness with regard to mastiffs. Ladies as a rule do not like them, nor do poets. When they baited bulls they always received a measure of admiration, and in the stouter verse of our older poets "the fell mastiffe" was a frequent simile for furious ferocity.

> " When an eager mastiffe once doth prove
> The taste of blood of some engored beast,
> No words may rate, nor rigour him remove
> From greedy hold of that his bloudy feast."

> " With that all mad and furious he grew
> Like a fell mastiffe."

An especial favourite is of course the "officious" sheep-dog, "faithful to teach thy stragglers to return" (Dyer). But just as it is impossible to think of dogs apart from man, so it is very difficult to think of the shepherd-dog apart from sheep. For the pet "colley," so rapidly being degenerated by town fashion into a cowardly sycophant, is not the typical shepherd-dog. It is becoming a variety by itself, "the colley," and seen in the street recalls no rural sound or sight. Far different is the unkempt muddy dog that may be sometimes seen driving a flock of sheep through the busiest thoroughfares of London. For as a rule the shepherd's dog is a mongrel—"shaggy and lean and shrewd, with pointed ears and tail cropped short, half lurcher and half cur;" but in Scotland, "there still of genuine breed, the colley, barking shrill-toned "—

> " Indeed, thy Ball is a bold bigge cur
> And could make a jolly hole in their fur "—

we meet with the beautiful beast, now so popular as a pet in England, that Burns had before him in his glorious sketch of the " Twa Dogs "—

> " The tither was a ploughman's collie,
> A rhyming, ranting, roving billie,
> Wha for his friend and comrade had him,
> And in his freaks had Luath ca'd him,
> After some dog in Highland sang,
> Was made lang syne—Lord knows how lang,
> He was a gash an' faithfu' tyke,
> As ever lap a sheugh or dyke.
> His honest, sonsie, baws'nt face,
> Aye gat him friends in ilka place ;
> His breast was white, his towzie back
> Weel clad wi' coat o' glossy black ;
> His gawcie tail, wi' upward curl,
> Hung o'er his hurdies wi' a swirL"

They are part of "the household" of the shepherd— "two brave dogs tried in many a storm made all their household "—and the reaper's children lie on the summer's afternoon "curled up with the sheep-dogs asleep." For to him they are veritably his eyes and his ears, and his legs besides.

> " Waving his hat, the shepherd from the vale
> Directs his winding dog the cliffs to scale
> That, barking busy, 'mid the glittering rocks
> Hunts, where he points, the intercepted flocks."

In the house their honesty and discipline raise them

almost to the level of human companions.   The gilly's wife
says, in Wordsworth—

> " This honest sheep-dog's countenance I read,
>   With him can talk, nor blush to waste a word
>   On creatures less intelligent and shrewd."

Now and again, in order to point the extraordinary
depravity of the wolf, the moral tone of the colley is so
lowered that it connives with Sir Isegrim to destroy its
master's flocks; and in Mother Hubbard's Tale will be
found the deplorable narrative of the demoralised dog that
demoralised its master, the " disguised dog that loved
blood to spill, and drew the wicked shepherd to his will,
so 'twixt them both they not a lambkin left."   Nor does
Southey hesitate to picture the dog reverting to lupine
habits : " The shepherd's dog preyed on the scattered flock,
for there was now no hand to feed him."

The bulldog, "with black mouth," the turnspit, that
affords the poets the same moral and similes as the caged
squirrel—

> " That climbs the wheel, but all in vain,
>   His own weight brings him down again,
>   And still he's in the self-same place
>   Where at the setting out he was."

The St. Bernard's dog, "the dog of the Alps," "of grave
demeanour, all meekness, gentleness, though large of limb "
finds honourable mention, in spite of Eliza Cook's assurance that

> " It is not ambition that leads him to danger,
>   He toils not for trophy, he seeks not for fame,
>   He faces all peril and succours the stranger,
>   But asks not the wide world to blazon his name,"—

in the verse of Thomson, Rogers, and others.   The New-
foundland, " the brave diver," in several, notably Burns—

> " The first I'll name, they ca'd him Cæsar,
>   Was keepit for his honour's pleasure :
>   His hair, his size, his mouth, his lugs,
>   Showed he was nane o' Scotland's dogs,
>   But whalpit some place far abroad,
>   Where sailors gang to fish for cod.
>   His lockit, lettered, braw brass collar,
>   Showed him the gentleman and scholar.
>   But though he was o' high degree,
>   The fient a pride, nae pride had he ;
>   But wad hae spent an hour caressin'
>   E'en wi' a tinkler-gipsy's messin :
>   At kirk or market, mill or smiddie,
>   Nae tauted tyke, though e'er sae duddie,
>   But he wad stan't as glad to see him,
>   And stroaned on stanes an' hillocks wi' him."

The "wiry terrier rough and grim," used "to hunt the tod;" the "fierce otter-hounds," are all duly immortalised.

> " Would you preserve a num'rous finny race ?
>   Let your fierce dogs the rav'nous otter chase ;
>   Th' amphibious monster ranges all the shores,
>   Darts thro' the waves, and ev'ry haunt explores,
>   Or let the gin his roving steps betray,
>   And save from hostile jaws the scaly prey."

Poets, by the way, are unanimous in their dislike of otters, which I attribute to the same reason as so many other antipathies—a false sentiment. The " hairy," " fierce " otter devours the " silver," " innocent " fishes ; therefore the otter should be detested and, if possible, murdered.

No village is complete without its "honest watch-dog," whose "deep-mouthed welcome" sweetens return. Joanna Baillie and Clare compliment it excellently. Thomson, too, has a delightful scrap—

> " In a corner of the buzzing shade,
>   The house-dog with the vacant greyhound lies,
>   Out-stretched and sleepy. In his slumbers one
>   Attacks the nightly thief, and one exults

> O'er hill and dale ; till, wakened by the wasp,
> They starting snap."

The poor man's dog, that shares the proverbial crust with its master; the blind man's dog, which alone of all their kind other dogs respect ; the dancing dog—all these, and others, find their poets. How too can I omit Goldsmith's mad dog.

> " And in that town a dog was found,
>   As many dogs there be,
> Both mongrel, puppy, whelp and hound
>   And curs of low degree.
> This dog and man at first were friends ;
>   But when a pique began,
> The dog, to gain his private ends,
>   Went mad, and bit the man."

Of the individual animals known to fame the list that our poets immortalise is very long.

Lufra, Cavall, " King Arthur's hound of deepest-mouth," Luath, Beth-gelert, Berezillo (who drew the full allowance of a soldier in the Spanish army), Bran, Herod, Tray, Fop, Beau, Blanch, Sweetheart, " St. Hubert's breed ; " His Highness' dog at Kew—the hounds of Actæon " that knew him naught,"

> " Those mistaken hounds of yore,
> That for the stag their master tore "—

and of Adonis and Diana, " this goddess on an hart full high sate, withsmall hounds all about her feet " (Chaucer) ; Geryon and Cerberus ; Malaia's dog ; the dogs of Lazarus, of Tobit, as in Quarles—

> " What luck has Tobit's dog ! what grace ! what glory !
> Thus to be kennelled in eternal story !
> Until th' Apocrypha and Scripture sever
> The mem'ry of Tobit's dog shall live for ever "—

and of Jezreel, an interminable series.

In addition to all these more familiar species and individuals, the poets have many others not so well known to sport or science. Gower has a "wood-hound" that is of a benign character. Rogers, Shelley, and others have a "dog of carnage," and others a "carrion-hound." A "hell-hound" also is to be found occasionally in their kennels—

> " Behold where Melecan, a dog in fierceness,
> The savage dog of hell,
> Darts growling to his prey ;
> He flies and he returns
> All covered and all drenched with human gore."

Superstitions about dogs are very numerous—"females with tormenting spells, consult their dogs as oracles " (Montgomery)—and none more widely spread than that which supposes dogs to be able to see visitors from another world—

> " His noble hound sprang from his lair,
> The midnight rouse to greet,
> Then, like a timid trembling hare,
> Crouched at his master's feet.
> Between his legs his drooping tail,
> Like dog of vulgar race,
> He hid, and with strange piteous wail
> Looked in his master's face " (*Joanna Baillie*)—

and that their howling, which is therefore ominous, "making men deem some mischief is at hand," is caused by these supernatural visions. " Ossian's grey dogs are always howling at home ; they see his passing ghost." So in Kirke White, "filled with fear, the howling dogs bespoke unholy spirits near ; " and "disturbed by dreams, with wild affright, the deep-mouthed mastiff bays the troubled night ; " in Joanna Baillie's " Ghost of Faden," and in " The Elder Tree," where

> " Cowering hounds the board beneath
>   Are howling with piteous moan ;
> While lords and dames sit still as death,
>   And words are uttered none ; "

frequently in Scott, as—

> " Sudden the hounds erect their ears,
>   And sudden cease their moaning howl ;
> Close pressed to Moy, they mark their fears
>   By shivering limbs and stifled growl ; "

and regularly in every poet who, wanting a rhyme to owl—
and wolves failing—or a sound of dread to complete a
scene of general eeriness,

> " Hears upon the mountain forest's brow
>   The death-dog howling loud and long."

SOME POETS' CATS.

"A familiar beast to man, and signifies love."
—*M. W. of W.*

JUST as the dog is the poetical register of the out-of-door
life of man, the index of the pleasures and occupations of
the open air, the "power," so to speak, of the human
quantity, so the cat, in its differing moods and aspects, ex-
presses the various phases of domestic life, and stands for
the symbol of the alternations of existence within doors.

The Chinese, so I have read, take their time from cats'
eyes. So the history of the family inside the house might
be hieroglyphically written in a series of cats.

On the garden-wall, soliloquising at the top of its voice,
it means the household abed ; on the doorstep, with a too-
much-whisky-overnight expression of face, it denotes the
hour when the milkman and the sweep, like larks, "lead on
the merry hours and rouse the day ;" before the kitchen
fire, blinking at the kettle, it signifies breakfast ; rubbing
itself, all on the slant, against the cook's petticoats, we know
that it is the hour of noon—of scraps from the early
dinner ; asleep on the hearth all the afternoon, it wakes up
with a start when the jack cracks under the twirling joint
for the later meal ; the children's tea-hour finds it in the
nursery ; as evening closes in it sits before the fire musing—
"Shall I go to the club ? or what shall I do with myself

to-night ?"—and then comes darkness, and the cat is in the garden or on the pantiles, sitting in moonstruck reverie or sharing a most melancholy dialogue—

> "Or making gallantry in gutter-tiles,
> And sporting in delightful faggot-piles ;
> Or bolting out of bushes in the dark
> (As ladies use at midnight in the park),
> Or seeking in tall garrets and alcove
> For assignations with affairs of love."—*Butler*.

Dejected or elated, morose or amiable, distant or familiar, acrimonious or conciliatory, alarmed or tranquil, dreadfully awake or fast asleep—in a score of other tempers and states of mind—puss reflects a corresponding variation in the domestic barometer. It is the indicator of the fluctuations of family emotions, and apparently without spontaneity in its moods, without independence in its actions. Its existence would seem to be wholly relative and magnetised. It lives within the influence of perpetual attractions. The joint roasting at the fire draws it to the hearth with just the same mechanical regularity as the voice of the cats'-meat-man does to the garden-gate. These are natural forces which it seems powerless to resist.

Now how is it that this little creature—the incarnation of evasive vagrancy, one of the most hopeless of Bohemians, as restless as the tides, and as fickle as the breeze, the ancient symbol of the goddess of Liberty, whose amiabilities are nearly all self-indulgence, and gratitudes self-interest—has come to be regarded as the type of domesticity and symbol of the hearth, where "the little Lares keep their vigils round ?"

> "Thou sayst also, I walke out like a cat ;
> For who so wolde senge the cattes skin,
> Than wol the cat wel dwellen in hire inn :
> And if the cattes skin be sleke and gay,
> She wol nat dwellen in hous half a day,
> But forth she wol,"

to "show her fur and be caterwauled," as Pope has it in his translation of the " Wif of Bathe's Prologue.

The kitten's position in the household is easier to understand.   It is one of the most beautiful and amusing of pets. The man who could watch kittens' "gambolling excessive," as Hurdis calls it, and not laugh, must have had a death-rattle as his only plaything when a baby.   Richelieu and Colbert delighted in cats' company.   Wriothesley's pet found him out in prison, and was his solace.   Mahomet, rather than disturb his cat, which was asleep on it, cut off the skirt of his robe.   Pope Gregory made his cat a cardinal. How Gautier l.ked them.   Do you remember Zizi (which means "too beautiful for anything ") that had a nose like a truffle and adored books ? or that other which had a resemblance to a tiger, which he found, he says, "very pleasing ; " the cat that saw the parrot and said, "This is decidedly —yes it is—a green chicken ! "

Not only is their unconscious absurdity immense, but they have a deliberate appreciation of humour.   They know exactly when they are being played with and when teased—Montaigne "playing with his cat, complains she thought him but an ass."

> " Ye who can smile—to wisdom no disgrace
> At the arch meaning of a kitten's face,"

must remember many a time and oft when the small thing, with its elegant overtures to a frolic, has tempted you into joining it in a fit of nonsense.   And how it acted all the time, the fluffy little impostor !   What an enthusiasm it obviously feigned for the trailing worsted, what desperate struggles it made believe to have with a tassel, how it pranced and cavorted, standing ridiculously on two legs and skipping sideways!   With what matchless art did it not pretend to get itself into inextricable difficulties with a chair leg, in order to show off a hundred pretty devices of paddling with its paws, and then in an instant how it was up and off, with its tail all crooked, its ears anyhow, and an absurd affectation of being scared! Or, when two are together and one is lazy, with what adroitness will the other beguile its companion into a romp, gradually coaxing it on till it is in an equal frenzy of light-heartedness with itself.

> " What intenseness of desire
> In her upward eye of fire !
> With a tiger-leap half-way
> Now she meets the coming prey,
> Lets it go as fast, and then
> Has it in her power again :
> Now she works with three or four
> Like an Indian conjurer ;
> Quick as he in feats of art,
> Far beyond in joy of heart.
> Were her antics played in the eye
> Of a thousand standers-by,
> Clapping hands with shout and stare,
> What would little tabby care
> For the plaudits of the crowd?
> Over happy to be proud."

No wonder children love them so. Their faces are as sweetly innocent as their own. Is it possible that these winning little fluffinesses could ever descend to the surreptitious consumption of the family canary? or that such guileless faces could ever be stained with the purloined bloater? Their delightful little cosy bodies seem made for a baby's cuddling. Their natures are curiously alike. A kitten will seldom take offence at what a little child does to it—and the outrageous liberties taken with pussy are sometimes dreadful to contemplate. I have seen a small boy go through a meal with a kitten held in bagpipe fashion under his arm ; and the poor animal stayed there with a half-squeezed look on its face that was infinitely pathetic, but made no complaint. Its confidence in the child carried it through the ordeal.

It knew he would not do it if it was not all right.   And so
it was; for by-and-by the boy got the kitten and a saucer
of milk together, and, though there was a good deal
of unnecessary bobbing of its nose into the milk, the
kitten took it all as meant in kindness, and, when it had
had its face dried on a pinafore, was ready for another
romp.

But they can scratch when they are put out, as Joanna
Baillie's fat Tommy found—

> "He did her hinder parts assail,
> And pinched and pulled the kitten's tail.
> On this her sudden anger rose,
> She turned and straightway scratched his nose."

But it is of course the good-humoured and playful kitten
that chiefly attracts the poets.   Many such are to be found
gamboling in verse: Wordsworth's yellow one, playing with
the falling leaves—

> "Over-wealthy in the treasure
> Of her own exceeding pleasure;"

Gray's tortoiseshell tabby, "the pensive Selina," that got
drowned trying to catch gold-fish—

> "Malignant Fate sate by and smiled,
> The slipp'ry verge her feet beguiled—
> She tumbled headlong in.
> Eight times emerging from the flood,
> She mewed to every wat'ry god
> Some speedy aid to send.
> No dolphin came, no Nereid stirred,
> Nor cruel Tom nor Susan heard—
> A fav'rite has no friend !
> From hence, ye beauties undeceived,
> Know one false step is ne'er retrieved,
> And be with caution bold.
> Not all that tempts your wand'ring eyes
> And heedless hearts is lawful prize—
> Nor all that glitters gold;"

the kittens of Cowper that found the snake in the garden,
and Hurdis, "cuffing the suspended cork," of Blomfield and
Gay, and a score of others who delight in "the instinct joy
of kittens," and "the kitling ever happy."   By-and-by, and
all too soon, they grow into cats.

> "And so, poor kit ! must thou endure,
>   When thou becomest a cat demure,
>   Full many a cuff and angry word,
>   Chased roughly from the tempting board.
>   But yet, for that thou hast, I ween,
>   So oft our favoured playmate been,
>   Soft be the change which thou shalt prove !
>   When time hath spoiled thee of our love,
>   Still be thou deemed by housewife fat,
>   A comely, careful, mousing cat ;
>   Whose dish is, for the public good,
>   Replenished oft with savoury food.
>   Nor, when thy span of life is past,
>   Be thou to pond or dung-hill cast ;
>   But, gently borne on gardener's spade,
>   Beneath the decent sod be laid ;
>   And children show, with glistening eyes,
>   The place where poor old pussy lies."

In connection with the adage that the cat has nine lives
—found very useful, by the way, in verse—a very delightful
instance of what Bain would call eccentric ratiocination
occurs in Barry Cornwall.   The line is this—

> "One bite of a mad cat—*no more than would kill a tailor.*"

The relation here of a nine-lived cat (each cat being really,
therefore, only a ninth of one) to a tailor who, they say, is
only the ninth of a man, is, it seems to me, most humor-
ously involved.

For myself, I discredit the theory of sartorial fractions,
and hold with the poet (Taylor) who says—

> "Some foolish knave, I think, it first began
>   The slander that three tailors make one man."

I always feel inclined to retort upon it with the other adage that "'tis the tailor makes the man;" so in "King Lear"—

"A tailor makes a man?   Ay, a tailor, sir;"

and hesitate to contribute my acquiescence in the circuitous arithmetic of the playwright who makes a character, on meeting eighteen tailors, cry out to them all, "Come on, I'll fight you both."   The inadequate championship of Teufelsdrock does not satisfy me.   He goes not far enough.

I remember well enough what Petruchio says to his tailor—

"O monstrous arrogance !   Thou liest,
Thou thread, thou thimble,
Thou yard, three-quarters, half
Yard, quarter, nail,
Thou flea, thou nit, thou winter-cricket, thou,
Away, thou rag, thou quantity, thou remnant !"

and do not forget Montaigne's evidence.   "I have," he says, "an honest lad to my taylor, who I never knew guilty of one truth—no, not when it had been to his advantage not to lye."

But I remember also how Master Feeble, "the forcible Feeble," proved himself the best man of all Falstaff's recruits; with what discretion Robin Starveling played the part of Thisbe's mother before the Duke; and carry it to their credit the public spirit of those stitchers of Tooley Street.

"Give the gods a thankful sacrifice.   When it pleaseth their deities to take the wife of a man from him, it shows to man the tailors of the earth."

I have no wish to rehabilitate Urquiza of Paita, nor apologise for the tailor who pricked the elephant's trunk with his needle and got squirted with a puddle by Behemoth for doing so—except to say that I think the elephant was an ill-mannered beast to go thrusting several feet of trunk into a tailor's shop. Nor do I ask to have that nursery rhyme abolished which makes the tailors go forth to attack a snail, but retire defeated on seeing her horns.

Yet, when I think of all the valiant tailors of story, I hesitate to believe that four-and-twenty of the trade should have been panic-stricken at the spectacle of an enraged snail. What shall we say of that Snip of Basle who kissed the dragon-princess? It is true that, the worst accomplished, he turned and fled, leaving his victory incomplete. Not so much, perhaps, as a Hercules or a Sir Gawain would have done; yet how many heroes had failed before the tailor succeeded! Then, again, there was that other who passed the night with a bear, and won the princess; that other who slew seven at a blow, and lived himself to be a king; that brave journeyman whom De Quincey has made immortal for his courage. In many other ways they have been distinguished, these knights of the needle, from the father of Thumbling to that tailor of Yarrow who beat Mr. Tickler hollow at backgammon. Who was it charitably mended the bean, and who that sewed up the ship that was smashed on the rocks? Oriental story is full of tailors of consequence. Remember that one who befriended Prince Amgiad when he fell among the fire-worshippers, and him that took in the poor hunchback who choked with a fish-bone. Was not Aladdin himself the son of Mustapha the tailor?—and a right good father he was, dying at last out of sheer grief at Aladdin's scapegrace ways. In the great Mosque at Mecca there is a Tailors' Gate.

But there is no need to accumulate such testimonies to the worth of the cross-legged craft—and not more use. For it has got into our system—into the British Constitution, in fact—that it takes nine tailors to make one man, and the equation will never probably be abandoned. So after this digression let me return to Barry Cornwall and his mad cat and its nine lives.

> " Cats there lay, divers had been flayed and roasted,
>   And after mouldy grown were toasted ;
>   Then, selling not, a dish was ta'en to mince them,
>   But still it seemed, the rankness did convince 'em,
>   For here they were thrown in with the melted pewter,
>   Yet drowned they not ; they had five lives in future."

In every town there is a constant proportion of vagabond cats that have no homes ; and what house is there that has not at one time or another mysteriously lost its cat ?   Now, is there no connection between these two phenomena ?   For myself, I cannot help thinking that the "lost" cats are merely animals that, "to serve some private ends," have deliberately, gone elsewhere.   The gipsy instinct has overtaken them, and they have decamped in quest of adventure, and on the chance of "bettering" themselves.   Some of them, perhaps, go away to die—for is it not a curious fact that so few of these pets ever die at home ?   But the majority simply disappear.   The children are told pussy has " run away."   By-and-by another cat comes ; that is to say, it installs itself.   No one probably invited it, but, as it was mewing very much, the hall door or the kitchen door was opened, and it was allowed to come in, on approbation. But the small stranger made itself at home at once, rubbed against the cook's petticoats—cats have an extraordinary instinct for cooks—and sat down in the very middle of the hearth opposite the fire, and there it remained.

As there was no other cat in the house, it was taken on. Now, it must have come from somewhere, as certainly as its predecessor went somewhere ; so that perhaps there is a perpetual exchanging of cats going on.   Everybody gets everybody else's in turn.

This mysterious but periodical disappearance of the household pets finds, however, an explanation in the popular tradition that every cat has to spend one life out of its nine as a witch. The time comes when Death beckons to Grimalkin, and, whatever she is doing, she has to obey. But, unless it be for the ninth, and fatal time, there are no corporal remains to show for the decease, no dead cat lying in the garden, or on the outhouse roof, or wherever it may have been that the dread summons reached her. On each of the eight occasions the cat that had been simply vanished from the earth, and in the same instant reappeared in a new avatar. Tabby yesterday, she is black to-day. But the supreme moment arrives at last. The ninth messenger is at the door. The cat, conscious of coming change, sits before the fire, looking into the heart of the blaze, and lost in thought. A voice she dare not refuse to hear calls her away from the comfortable hearth, and she goes, pensively, out into the dark night. The wind blows shrill, the clouds are driving fast. She would like to go back to the fire and the cook. But something she may not resist draws her onward, farther into the garden, deeper into the gloom. The bushes round her hide the lights of the house. In the distance she hears the caterwauling of familiar voices. And while she sits, shivering, wondering, waiting, lo! it all happens, and Grimalkin suddenly finds herself whisked off up into the sky. A long cloak streams backwards from her shoulders. A broomstick is between her legs. She is a witch.

Several poets refer to her as a thing of " venomed spite and cruel scratch," " from a witch transformed." So in Southey's " Witch "—

> " What makes her sit there moping by herself,
> With no soul near her but that great black cat,
> And do but look at her !"

and in Herrick's " Hag "—

> " In a dirty hair trace
> She leads on a brace

> Of black boar-cats to attend her,
> Who scratch at the moon
> And threaten at noon
> Of night from heaven to rend her."

"Old Grimalkin's glaring eyes," so often a terror to "wee sleekit cowerin'" mice, are thus at times uncanny for human beings. Envy, "spitting spite," is symbolised as a cat.

Not that the familiar of the "wise woman" seems to take any very active part in her unkind performances. Her function appears to be that of a tacit accomplice—one who looks on at the wickednesses of the Black Art without actually putting her hand to any particular villainy. She is the sleeping partner of the confederacy. Sometimes, indeed—as in the story where the witch's cat is grateful to the good girl who has given it some ham to eat—the dabbler in occult science is even beneficent.

In Sicily—where the animal is sacred to St. Martha —the cats that walk on the pantiles in the month of February are supposed to be witches, and as such considered worthy of death. Somewhat analogous is our own "March cat," which combines with the eccentricity of the "March hare" a suspicion of necromantic leanings and diabolic conspiracy.

Relativity, thy name is Cat. It is not easy to imagine Grimalkin in a vacuum, isolated, alone in space. As easy to think of matter without giving it form as to conceive puss without either a hearth, a mouse, or a dog.

> "Not such thy spirit when insulted, puss,
> Scampers the garden path, and climbs alert
> The high espalier, there to dwell and swear,
> Or, in close corner pent, upheaves her coat,
> And blust'ring cuffs thee with vindictive claw."

"Dire foe of mouse," "Grimalkin to domestic vermin sworn an everlasting foe." Such are the usual "connotations," if I may use the word, of the cat in verse. She is the "mouse-eater," and because the poets, who dislike mice, applaud her taste, becomes the "harmless *necessary* cat."

It is a curious fact, however, that classic legend makes this animal the protector of the innocent: that in Hindoo mythology she is sometimes the ally of little birds, and that in monkish tradition St. Gertrude, a funereal saint, who is the patroness of mice, is also the protector of cats. Moreover, puss, in occasional myths, is the crony of the dog, and figures as the protector of poultry from the fox, of lambs from wolves.

On the other hand, "the vermin-hunter" is a much more frequent character. "By the austerity which it practises on the banks of the Ganges it inspires confidence in the birds, who gather round it to pay reverence to its sanctity. The mice imitate their example, and place themselves under the cat's tutorship. The cat of course eats them, and by inducing them to go with it only two or three at a time, grows mysteriously fat for a fakir." This assumption of sanctimoniousness is not an uncommon characteristic of the cat of fable. "Il fait le saint, il fait la chatte!" The oldest of all myths shows us the cat-moon eating up the grey mice of twilight. That Diana, a lunar divinity, should have taken the feline form is therefore strictly in accordance with the original Aryan fancy; and so, too, we find Freyya, the Scandinavian Selene, drawn sometimes by a team of cats.

But it pleases me immensely to remark how this little animal of contradictions and perplexities puzzle mythologists. They mix it up with the lynx and the ichneumon and the mole. These are thieving, hunting, secret animals, and so are distorted into the myth-phrases of night, and the nocturnal forest, and so forth. In the Sanskrit, so we are assured, the same epithet is indiscriminately applied to cat and thief. It is in fact the beast "of three letters." So also, in Vedic metaphor, the cat is "the cleanser," the one that washes its face, and also "the hunter;" as the white cat, the moon, it protects innocent animals; as a black cat, the dark night, it persecutes them. "It is easy," says Gubernatis, "to pass from the Latin *mustela* to the Sanskrit mûshikâutakrit." But then Gubernatis can stretch farther with a foot-rule than any other man, and to go from a stoat to a cat because the names happen in Sanskrit and Latin to begin with the same letter of the alphabet (which is all they really do) is to him the most natural transition in the world. Yet if there is one Grimalkin more puzzling than another it is surely "the cat in the bag of proverbs."

Our mousers, however, seem to have declined deplorably from their old standards of diligence and dexterity. In other respects the type has been immeasurably improved. The size of some of these animals gives promise that before long we shall have cats to rival that Brobdingnagian creature that purred like a dozen stocking-weavers at work and thought Gulliver too small an insect to run after, and carrying such a fleece as shall make the shearing of cats an operation of commercial value. In beauty we have Grimalkins that would have driven Egypt mad with envy; while for downright wild-beastishness what can we have fiercer-looking than the Russian lynx-like breed?

As a rule, people look upon cats as being without variety. They know that these animals catch mice, have evil designs upon cream-jugs and canaries, scratch Baby, and hold melancholy concerts in the back garden. But beyond these points, common to all the species, the great majority of people have no standards of distinction. It is true that the creatures vary in colour, but somehow, as a rule, we lump them all together into the common or garden cat, and regard them as being of a monotonous sort. Yet there is just as much variety in a Cat-show as among the pippins in a Chiswick "Apple Congress," or the chrysanthemums at the Temple.

Some, for instance, are pure wild animals in miniature.
One is an undeniable lynx, only half-size, and another a
mimic ocelot ; a third imitates the puma, and a fourth is
an excellent imitation of a raccoon.   In colour of course the
range is very large, from pure whites and blacks to smudged
tortoiseshells.   Some wear the pelts of rabbit and hare,
others the soft blue greys of the lemurs or the silvery fur
of the Arctic foxes.   They are blotched, and barred, and
brindled, "ring-straked, speckled, and spotted," their pat-
terned skins producing in combination or by accident of position the most singular results of expression.   Indeed, nothing
is more surprising than the immense diversity of character
which the faces illustrate.   Placid dignity and street-boy
impudence are caged side by side, and a very little trouble
would give an artist the whole series of human types.   The
cat with a black blotch in the middle of a white countenance is obviously a burglar among his kind, and what deeds
of midnight violence would be too dreadful for some of
those smudged-faced Toms to commit.   They seem to
have deliberately disguised themselves, as if they were
Thugs out on a murderous errand, and peer at you, as from
behind a mask, from a confusion of red and tan and black
fur like the demon cat of the Japanese.   One would almost
hesitate to leave such a cat alone in a room with one's
purse.

Yet, all the same, in spite of their Merovingian length
of disorderly fur, or their furious aspect, in spite too of
their surpassing elegance of colour and form, a suspicion
widely prevails that the town-cat is abandoning its taste for
mice.

Daily familiarities with milkmen, the certainty of regular
and ample meals, have dulled its appetite for the chase.
Though it may not have forgotten that the mouse is tooth-
some, it remembers more than it used to do that the mouse
is nimble, and very troublesome to catch.   An ordinary cat

will studiously devote a whole day to the circumvention of the lodger's canary rather than spend an hour upon the landlady's rats. A single bullfinch in the drawing-room is worth a wilderness of mice in the pantry.

> " Let take a cat, foster her with milk,
> And tender flesh, and make her couch of silk,
> And let her see a mouse go by the wall,
> Anon she scorneth milk and flesh and all,
> And every dainty that is in that house,
> Such appetite hath she to eat the mouse.
> Lo here hath kind her domination,
> And appetite o'ercomes discretion."

This may be an allusion to that fable in Æsop where the youth " falls in love " with a cat, and in a moment of caprice calls upon Venus to change the pretty animal into a pretty woman. The goddess does so. But the happy couple have hardly met before a mouse happens to run by and the bride rushes away in feline pursuit—"and appetite o'er-comes discretion."

However diligent and habitual mousing may have been a characteristic of cats in Chaucer's time, it may even be true still. But yet there is abundant proof for the accusation that mouse-catching has become for the town-cat a mere pastime, or at best an avocation, a parergon. Just as the town-sparrow now only eats insects by way of dessert, as it were, and never goes among trees except for an occasional picnic, so the cat amuses itself, of a wet afternoon, over the mouse-hole in the cupboard—and as often as not goes to sleep at her post.

If there be any other just cause of complaint against this pretty little favourite, it is surely its habit of vociferous dialogue during our hours of sleep. " Foul night-waking cats," "clamorous o'er their joys," " who amant misere " (Shelley). How heartily the poets hated it.

> " I would rather hear cat-courtship
> Under my bedroom window "

is the worst that Southey can say of odious sounds.   Nor
is it easy to imagine any disturbance of slumber more exasperating than the melancholy love-makings of cats when
they foregather immoderately on the garden wall and pro-
long their woeful canticles into the hours of dawn—the
dismal soliloquy uttered

> " From the depths of a divine despair "

that by-and-by becomes a gruesome dialogue, in which the
two voices rise in unison, from the expression of a profound
longing, cavernous and sepulchral, up and up and up
through the scale of sharpening grief to the utmost peaks of
anguish, and then in a frenzied climax the two hearts break
as one in a piercing discord of mutual appeal.

Is all over?   Are the two cats lying dead?   Did their
great hearts burst their little bodies in that last unspeakable
moment of tender despair?   Not a bit of it.   Listen.   They
are beginning again, exactly where they began before, at
the " *De profundis*," and they will climb up the keys in
precisely the same abominable *crescendo* of misery, and when
they can no longer restrain the pent-up torrent of their tor-
tured affections they will mingle their voices in one wild
shattering yell of pity for themselves.

Yet though the householder empties the phials of his
wrath—and, if of a choleric soul, also all the movable
trifles about the bedroom that may seem to an exasperated
imagination suitable for throwing—upon the wretches for
their nocturnal ululations, there comes with daylight a
milder frame of mind.   The tranquil spectacle of pussy
snugly curled up in front of the fire routs all suspicions as
to its having had any share in the outrageous frolics that
broke the slumbers of the household, and causes the dis-
turbances of over-night to be placed to the discredit of the

cat "next door." The truth is, we are all too fond of our cats to continue long in wrath with them.

Yet in fable and fairy tale they are not treated with the tenderness and consideration one would expect for such a universal favourite, and the poets accept this tendency of folk-lore to laugh at and depreciate Grimalkin. All the cat-poems banter the animal, or place it in a ridiculous light. Besides those already noted, there is Allan Ramsay's fable of the cats and the cheese, of which the monkey ate two-thirds in trying to make an exactly equal division, and kept the other third for his trouble. In the fable of the cat and the fox that reproach the wolf for killing a lamb, and immediately go off and kill a chicken themselves, as also in the stories where the cat is fooled by the mice, made to take the hot nuts off the bars by the ape, and beguiled into the oven by the sparrows, the motive seems always to turn the laugh against puss.

In Cowper's poem of the "Retired Cat," an excellent illustration is given of the creature's complacent self-assurance that everything in a household is specially arranged with relation to its own comforts. She finds the garden draughty, and, searching the house for a convenient couch, "some place of more serene repose," discovers an open drawer half-filled with linen of "the softest kind, such as merchants introduce, from India for the ladies' use," and curls herself up for sleep "lulled by her own humdrum song." By-and-by Susan, "housewifely inclined," comes in and shuts the drawer, "all unconscious whom it held,"— pussy taking it for granted that this is done for her greater tranquillity.

> "Was ever cat attended thus?
> The open drawer was left, I see,
> Merely to prove a nest for me ;
> For soon as I was well composed,
> Then came the maid, and it was closed.

> How smooth these kerchiefs, and how sweet !
> Oh what a delicate retreat !
> I will resign myself to rest
> Till Sol, declining in the west,
> Shall call to supper, when, no doubt,
> Susan will come and let me out."

But Susan does not, and the cat nearly starves to death.

> " So, beware of too sublime a sense
> Of your own worth and consequence ;
> The man who dreams himself so great,
> And his importance of such weight,
> That all around and all that's done
> Must move and act for him alone,
> Will learn in school of tribulation
> The folly of his expectation."

Even the fact of their having been worshipped in Egypt brings them little credit; it only makes Egyptian worship discreditable—

> " Cats and dogs, and each obscener beast,
> To which Egyptian dotards once did bow."

Or again—

> " Lang syne in Egypt beasts were gods,
> Sae mony that the men turned beasts,
> Vermin and brutes, boot house or hold,
> Had offerings, temples, and their priests."

And then the poet goes on to say how one day the people of the Nile sacrificed a rat to the great glory of the cat, and next day a cat to the great glory of the rat.

Not that their worship is by any means extinct. You have only to go to a Cat-show to be assured of the survival of the whimsical homage of Memphis, Bubastis, and Thebes. The old-world dignities of priestly service, temple ceremonial, and posthumous embalming have of course broken in the lapse of time, but their place has been turban filled by a homage which is certainly more intelligent and scarcely less sincere. The days are long gone by when, to bury a cat, processions of white-robed Egyptians, crowned with convolvulus, acacia, and chrysanthemum, trailed their effigies of water-beast and reptile, and images of dog-headed or hawk-headed gods, with the clashing of cymbals and the singing of the choirs of Isis, down through long aisles of reverent folk, from the Memphian temple-gates to the catacombs under the rocks.

It is to this day a fetish animal. Indeed, in Siam, a curious variation of the cult obtains. For there, in the land of the White Elephant, there is a royal breed of cats, and, so it is said, it is death for any one to take one beyond the precincts of the palace. The colour of these illustrious Grimalkins is very striking, being something between buff and tan, with ears, nose, and other "points" jet-black. Indeed, with a little trimming here and there, they might easily pass for tolerable pug-dogs. But we need hardly go so far as Bangkok for vestiges of the old worship, for it is obvious to the most casual observer at a Cat-show, from the epithets applied by visitors to the animals under exhibition and the exclamations of pious rapture, that there are plenty of persons of both sexes, who, if they do not actually set puss up on an altar and sacrifice to it with music and incense and temple rites, as was done in the palmy days of the Pharaohs, are sufficiently in love with the species to be enthusiastic in admiration. To hear a fierce old Russian cat described as "adorable," and a snowy Persian apostrophised as "divine," bridges over the interval between the Crystal Palace and the cat temples of Bubastis, and narrows the chasm somewhat between Pharaoh-Necho and the cats'-meat man.

And the modern taxidermist, as well as he can, has taken up the duties of the priests, and where the creatures of the Egyptians' adoration used to be spiced, they are now stuffed.

Instead of lying swathed in cloths and steeped in aromatic gums within a syenite sarcophagus, Puss stands in the back parlour, and fixes with her glassy eye the new tenant of the hearth-rug, and, from the cold neutrality of wires and wadding, gazes upon the domestic circle of which once *pars magna fuit.*

THE END.

PRINTED BY BALLANTYNE, HANSON AND CO.
EDINBURGH AND LONDON.

CHATTO & WINDUS'S
LIST OF BOOKS.

✳ ✳ ✳ ✳ ✳ ✳ ✳ ✳ ✳ ✳ ✳ ✳ ✳

About.—The Fellah: An Egyptian Novel. By EDMOND ABOUT. Translated by Sir RANDAL ROBERTS. Post 8vo, illustrated boards, 2s. ; cloth limp, 2s. 6d.

Adams (W. Davenport), Works by:

A Dictionary of the Drama. Being a comprehensive Guide to the Plays, Playwrights, Players, and Playhouses of the United Kingdom and America, from the Earliest to the Present Times. Crown 8vo, half-bound, 12s. 6d. [*Preparing.*

Latter-Day Lyrics. Edited by W. DAVENPORT ADAMS. Post 8vo, cloth limp, 2s. 6d.

Quips and Quiddities. Selected by W. DAVENPORT ADAMS. Post 8vo, cloth limp, 2s. 6d.

Advertising, A History of, from the Earliest Times. Illustrated by Anecdotes, Curious Specimens, and Notices of Successful Advertisers. By HENRY SAMPSON. Crown 8vo, with Coloured Frontispiece and Illustrations, cloth gilt, 7s. 6d.

Agony Column (The) of "The Times," from 1800 to 1870. Edited, with an Introduction, by ALICE CLAY. Post 8vo, cloth limp, 2s. 6d.

Aide (Hamilton), Works by:

Carr of Carrlyon. Post 8vo, illustrated boards, 2s.

Confidences. Post 8vo, illustrated boards, 2s.

Alexander (Mrs.).—Maid, Wife, or Widow? A Romance. By Mrs. ALEXANDER. Post 8vo, illustrated boards, 2s. ; cr. 8vo, cloth extra, 3s. 6d.

Allen (Grant), Works by:

Crown 8vo, cloth extra, 6s. each,
The Evolutionist at Large. Second Edition, revised.
Vignettes from Nature.
Colin Clout's Calendar.
Nightmares: A Collection of Stories.
Strange Stories. With a Frontispiece by GEORGE DU MAURIER. Crown 8vo, cloth extra, 6s.

Architectural Styles, A Handbook of. Translated from the German of A. ROSENGARTEN, by W. COLLETT-SANDARS. Crown 8vo, cloth extra, with 639 Illustrations, 7s. 6d.

Art (The) of Amusing: A Collection of Graceful Arts, Games, Tricks, Puzzles, and Charades. By FRANK BELLEW. With 300 Illustrations. Cr. 8vo, cloth extra, 4s. 6d.

Artemus Ward:

Artemus Ward's Works: The Works of CHARLES FARRER BROWNE, better known as ARTEMUS WARD. With Portrait and Facsimile. Crown 8vo, cloth extra, 7s. 6d.

Artemus Ward's Lecture on the Mormons. With 32 Illustrations. Edited, with Preface, by EDWARD P. HINGSTON. Crown 8vo, 6d.

The Genial Showman: Life and Adventures of Artemus Ward. By EDWARD P. HINGSTON. With a Frontispiece. Cr. 8vo, cl. extra, 3s. 6d.

Ashton (John), Works by:

A History of the Chap-Books of the Eighteenth Century. With nearly 400 Illusts., engraved in facsimile of the originals. Cr. 8vo, cl. ex., 7s. 6d.

Social Life in the Reign of Queen Anne. From Original Sources. With nearly 100 Illusts. Cr. 8vo, cl. ex., 7s. 6d.

Humour, Wit, and Satire of the Seventeenth Century. With nearly 100 Illusts. Cr. 8vo, cl. extra, 7s. 6d.

English Caricature and Satire on Napoleon the First. 120 Illusts. from Originals. Two Vols., demy 8vo, 28s.

Bacteria.—A Synopsis of the Bacteria and Yeast Fungi and Allied Species. By W. B. GROVE, B.A. With 87 Illusts. Crown 8vo, cl. extra, 3s. 6d.

Balzac's " Comedie Humaine " and its Author. With Translations by H. H. WALKER. Post 8vo, cl. limp, 2s. 6d.

Bankers, A Handbook of Lon- don; together with Lists of Bankers from 1677. By F. G. HILTON PRICE. Crown 8vo, cloth extra, 7s. 6d.

Bardsley (Rev. C.W.), Works by:

English Surnames: Their Sources and Significations. Third Ed., revised. Cr. 8vo, cl. extra, 7s. 6d.

Curiosities of Puritan Nomenclature. Crown 8vo, cloth extra, 7s. 6d.

Bartholomew Fair, Memoirs of. By HENRY MORLEY. With 100 Illusts. Crown 8vo, cloth extra, 7s. 6d.

Basil, Novels by:

A Drawn Game. Three Vols., cr. 8vo.

The Wearing of the Green. Three Vols., crown 8vo.

Beaconsfield, Lord: A Biography. By T. P. O'CONNOR, M.P. Sixth Edit., New Preface. Cr. 8vo, cl. ex. 7s. 6d.

Beauchamp. — Grantley Grange: A Novel. By SHELSLEY BEAUCHAMP. Post 8vo, illust. bds., 2s.

Beautiful Pictures by British Artists: A Gathering of Favourites from our Picture Galleries. In Two Series. All engraved on Steel in the highest style of Art. Edited, with Notices of the Artists, by SYDNEY ARMYTAGE, M.A. Imperial 4to, cloth extra, gilt and gilt edges, 21s. per Vol.

Bechstein. — As Pretty as Seven, and other German Stories. Collected by LUDWIG BECHSTEIN. With Additional Tales by the Brothers GRIMM, and 100 Illusts. by RICHTER. Small 4to, green and gold, 6s. 6d.; gilt edges, 7s. 6d.

Beerbohm. — Wanderings in Patagonia; or, Life among the Ostrich Hunters. By JULIUS BEERBOHM. With Illusts. Crown 8vo, cloth extra, 3s. 6d.

Belgravia for 1885. One Shilling Monthly, Illustrated by P. MACNAB. — A Strange Voyage, by W. CLARK RUSSELL, is begun in the JANUARY Number, and will be continued throughout the year. This Number contains also the Opening Chapters of a New Story by CECIL POWER, Author of " Philistia," entitled Babylon.

*** Now ready, the Volume for JULY to OCTOBER, 1884, cloth extra, gilt edges, 7s. 6d.; Cases for binding Vols., 2s. each.*

Belgravia Annual. With Stories by F. W. ROBINSON, J. ARBUTHNOT WILSON, JUSTIN H. McCARTHY, B. MONTGOMERIE RANKING, and others. Demy 8vo, with Illusts., 1s.

Bennett (W.C.,LL.D.), Works by:

A Ballad History of England. Post 8vo, cloth limp, 2s.

Songs for Sailors. Post 8vo, cloth limp, 2s.

Besant (Walter) and James Rice, Novels by. Post 8vo, illust. boards, 2s. each; cloth limp, 2s. 6d. each; or cr. 8vo, cl. extra, 3s. 6d. each.

Ready-Money Mortiboy.

With Harp and Crown.

This Son of Vulcan.

My Little Girl.

The Case of Mr. Lucraft.

The Golden Butterfly.

By Celia's Arbour.

The Monks of Thelema.

'Twas in Trafalgar's Bay.

The Seamy Side.

The Ten Years' Tenant.

The Chaplain of the Fleet.

Besant (Walter), Novels by:

All Sorts and Conditions of Men: An Impossible Story. With Illustrations by FRED. BARNARD. Crown 8vo, cloth extra, 3s. 6d.; post 8vo, illust. boards, 2s.; cloth limp, 2s. 6d.

The Captains' Room, &c. With Frontispiece by E. J. WHEELER. Crown 8vo, cloth extra, 3s. 6d.; post 8vo, illust. bds., 2s.; cl. limp, 2s. 6d.

All in a Garden Fair. With 6 Illusts. by H. FURNISS. New and Cheaper Edition. Cr. 8vo, cl. extra, 3s. 6d.

Dorothy Forster. New and Cheaper Edition. With Illustrations by CHAS. GREEN. Cr. 8vo, cloth extra, 3s. 6d.

Uncle Jack, and other Stories. Crown 8vo, cloth extra, 6s. *[In the press.*

The Art of Fiction. Demy 8vo, 1s.

Betham-Edwards (M.), Novels by. Crown 8vo, cloth extra, 3s. 6d. each.; post 8vo, illust. bds., 2s. each.
Felicia. | Kitty.

Bewick (Thos.) and his Pupils. By Austin Dobson. With 95 Illustrations. Square 8vo, cloth extra, 10s. 6d.

Birthday Books:—
The Starry Heavens: A Poetical Birthday Book. Square 8vo, handsomely bound in cloth, 2s. 6d.

Birthday Flowers: Their Language and Legends. By W. J. Gordon. Beautifully Illustrated in Colours by Viola Boughton. In illuminated cover, crown 4to, 6s.

The Lowell Birthday Book. With Illusts., small 8vo, cloth extra, 4s. 6d.

Blackburn's (Henry) Art Handbooks. Demy 8vo, Illustrated, uniform in size for binding.
Academy Notes, separate years, from 1875 to 1883, each 1s.
Academy Notes, 1884. With 152 Illustrations. 1s.
Academy Notes, 1875-79. Complete in One Vol.,with nearly 600 Illusts. in Facsimile. Demy 8vo, cloth limp, 6s.
Academy Notes, 1880-84. Complete in One Volume, with about 700 Facsimile Illustrations. Cloth limp, 6s.
Grosvenor Notes, 1877. 6d.
Grosvenor Notes, separate years, from 1878 to 1883, each 1s.
Grosvenor Notes, 1884. With 78 Illustrations. 1s.
Grosvenor Notes, 1877-82. With upwards of 300 Illustrations. Demy 8vo, cloth limp, 6s.
Pictures at South Kensington. With 70 Illustrations. 1s.
The English Pictures at the National Gallery. 114 Illustrations. 1s.
The Old Masters at the National Gallery. 128 Illustrations. 1s. 6d.
A Complete Illustrated Catalogue to the National Gallery. With Notes by H. Blackburn, and 242 Illusts. Demy 8vo, cloth limp, 3s.

Illustrated Catalogue of the Luxembourg Gallery. Containing about 250 Reproductions after the Original Drawings of the Artists. Edited by F. G. Dumas. Demy 8vo, 3s. 6d.

The Paris Salon, 1884. With over 300 Illusts. Edited by F. G. Dumas. Demy 8vo, 3s.

Art Handbooks, *continued—*
The Art Annual, 1883-4. Edited by F. G. Dumas. With 300 full-page Illustrations. Demy 8vo, 5s.

Boccaccio's Decameron ; or, Ten Days' Entertainment. Translated into English, with an Introduction by Thomas Wright, F.S.A. With Portrait, and Stothard's beautiful Copperplates. Cr. 8vo, cloth extra, gilt, 7s. 6d.

Blake (William): Etchings from his Works. By W. B. Scott. With descriptive Text. Folio, half-bound boards, India Proofs, 21s.

Bowers'(G.) Hunting Sketches:
Canters in Crampshire. Oblong 4to, half-bound boards, 21s.
Leaves from a Hunting Journal. Coloured in facsimile of the originals. Oblong 4to, half-bound, 21s.

Boyle (Frederick), Works by :
Camp Notes: Stories of Sport and Adventure in Asia, Africa, and America. Crown 8vo, cloth extra, 3s. 6d.; post 8vo, illustrated bds., 2s.
Savage Life' Crown 8vo, cloth extra 3s. 6d.; post 8vo, illustrated bds., 2s.
Chronicles of No-Man's Land. Crown 8vo, cloth extra, 6s.

Brand's Observations on Popular Antiquities, chiefly Illustrating the Origin of our Vulgar Customs, Ceremonies, and Superstitions. With the Additions of Sir Henry Ellis. Crown 8vo, cloth extra, gilt, with numerous Illustrations, 7s. 6d.

Bret Harte, Works by :
Bret Harte's Collected Works. Arranged and Revised by the Author. Complete in Five Vols., crown 8vo, cloth extra, 6s. each.
Vol. I. Complete Poetical and Dramatic Works. With Steel Portrait, and Introduction by Author.
Vol. II. Earlier Papers—Luck of Roaring Camp, and other Sketches—Bohemian Papers — Spanish and American Legends.
Vol. III. Tales of the Argonauts—Eastern Sketches.
Vol. IV. Gabriel Conroy.
Vol. V. Stories — Condensed Novels, &c.
The Select Works of Bret Harte, in Prose and Poetry. With Introductory Essay by J. M. Bellew, Portrait of the Author, and 50 Illustrations. Crown 8vo, cloth extra, 7s. 6d.
Gabriel Conroy: A Novel. Post 8vo, illustrated boards, 2s.

Bret Harte's Works, *continued—*

An Heiress of Red Dog, and other Stories. Post 8vo, illustrated boards, 2s.; cloth limp, 2s. 6d.

The Twins of Table Mountain. Fcap. 8vo, picture cover, 1s.; crown 8vo, cloth extra, 3s. 6d.

Luck of Roaring Camp, and other Sketches. Post 8vo, illust. bds., 2s.

Jeff Briggs's Love Story. Fcap. 8vo, picture cover, 1s.; cloth extra, 2s. 6d.

Flip. Post 8vo, illustrated boards, 2s.; cloth limp, 2s. 6d.

Californian Stories (including The Twins of Table Mountain, Jeff Briggs's Love Story, &c.) Post 8vo, illustrated boards, 2s.

Brewer (Rev. Dr.), Works by :

The Reader's Handbook of Allusions, References, Plots, and Stories. Fourth Edition, revised throughout, with a New Appendix, containing a Complete English Bibliography. Cr. 8vo, 1,400 pp., cloth extra, 7s. 6d.

Authors and their Works, with the Dates: Being the Appendices to "The Reader's Handbook," separately printed. Cr. 8vo, cloth limp, 2s.

A Dictionary of Miracles: Imitative, Realistic, and Dogmatic. Crown 8vo, cloth extra, 7s. 6d.; half-bound, 9s.

Brewster (Sir David), Works by:

More Worlds than One: The Creed of the Philosopher and the Hope of the Christian. With Plates. Post 8vo, cloth extra, 4s. 6d.

The Martyrs of Science: Lives of Galileo, Tycho Brahe, and Kepler. With Portraits. Post 8vo, cloth extra, 4s. 6d.

Letters on Natural Magic. A New Edition, with numerous Illustrations, and Chapters on the Being and Faculties of Man, and Additional Phenomena of Natural Magic, by J. A. Smith. Post 8vo, cloth extra, 4s. 6d.

Brillat-Savarin.—Gastronomy as a Fine Art. By Brillat-Savarin. Translated by R. E. Anderson, M.A. Post 8vo, cloth limp, 2s. 6d.

Burnett (Mrs.), Novels by :

Surly Tim, and other Stories. Post 8vo, illustrated boards, 2s.

Kathleen Mavourneen. Fcap. 8vo, picture cover, 1s.

Lindsay's Luck. Fcap. 8vo, picture cover, 1s.

Pretty Polly Pemberton. Fcap. 8vo, picture cover, 1s.

Buchanan's (Robert) Works :

Ballads of Life, Love, and Humour. With a Frontispiece by Arthur Hughes. Crown 8vo, cloth extra, 6s.

Selected Poems of Robert Buchanan. With Frontispiece by T. Dalziel. Crown 8vo, cloth extra, 6s.

Undertones. Cr. 8vo, cloth extra, 6s.

London Poems. Cr. 8vo, cl. extra, 6s.

The Book of Orm. Crown 8vo, cloth extra, 6s.

White Rose and Red: A Love Story. Crown 8vo, cloth extra, 6s.

Idylls and Legends of Inverburn. Crown 8vo, cloth extra, 6s.

St. Abe and his Seven Wives : A Tale of Salt Lake City. With a Frontispiece by A. B. Houghton. Crown 8vo, cloth extra, 5s.

Robert Buchanan's Complete Poetical Works. With Steel-plate Portrait. Crown 8vo, cloth extra, 7s. 6d.

The Hebrid Isles: Wanderings in the Land of Lorne and the Outer Hebrides. With Frontispiece by W. Small. Crown 8vo, cloth extra, 6s.

A Poet's Sketch-Book: Selections from the Prose Writings of Robert Buchanan. Crown 8vo, cl. extra, 6s.

The Shadow of the Sword: A Romance. Crown 8vo, cloth extra, 3s. 6d.; post 8vo, illust. boards, 2s.

A Child of Nature: A Romance. With a Frontispiece. Crown 8vo, cloth extra, 3s. 6d.; post 8vo, illust. bds., 2s.

God and the Man: A Romance. With Illustrations by Fred. Barnard. Crown 8vo, cloth extra, 3s. 6d.; post 8vo, illustrated boards, 2s.

The Martyrdom of Madeline: A Romance. With Frontispiece by A. W. Cooper. Cr. 8vo, cloth extra, 3s. 6d.; post 8vo, illustrated boards, 2s.

Love Me for Ever. With a Frontispiece by P. Macnab. Crown 8vo, cloth extra, 3s. 6d.; post 8vo, illustrated boards, 2s.

Annan Water: A Romance. Crown 8vo, cloth extra, 3s. 6d.

The New Abelard: A Romance. Crown 8vo, cloth extra, 3s. 6d.

Foxglove Manor: A Novel. Three Vols., crown 8vo.

Matt: A Romance. Crown 8vo, cloth extra, 3s. 6d.   [*Shortly*.

Burton (Robert):

The Anatomy of Melancholy. A New Edition, complete, corrected and enriched by Translations of the Classical Extracts. Demy 8vo, cloth extra, 7s. 6d.

Melancholy Anatomised: Being an Abridgment, for popular use, of Burton's Anatomy of Melancholy. Post 8vo, cloth limp, 2s. 6d.

Burton (Captain), Works by:

To the Gold Coast for Gold: A Personal Narrative. By RICHARD F. BURTON and VERNEY LOVETT CAMERON. With Maps and Frontispiece. Two Vols., crown 8vo, cloth extra, 21s.

The Book of the Sword: Being a History of the Sword and its Use in all Countries, from the Earliest Times. By RICHARD F. BURTON. With over 400 Illustrations. Square 8vo, cloth extra, 32s.

Bunyan's Pilgrim's Progress.
Edited by Rev. T. SCOTT. With 17 Steel Plates by STOTHARD, engraved by GOODALL, and numerous Woodcuts. Crown 8vo, cloth extra, gilt, 7s. 6d.

Byron (Lord):

Byron's Letters and Journals. With Notices of his Life. By THOMAS MOORE. A Reprint of the Original Edition, newly revised, with Twelve full-page Plates. Crown 8vo, cloth extra, gilt, 7s. 6d.

Byron's Don Juan. Complete in One Vol., post 8vo, cloth limp, 2s.

Cameron (Commander) and Captain Burton.—To the Gold Coast for Gold: A Personal Narrative. By RICHARD F. BURTON and VERNEY LOVETT CAMERON. With Frontispiece and Maps. Two Vols., crown 8vo, cloth extra, 21s.

Cameron (Mrs. H. Lovett), Novels by:

Crown 8vo, cloth extra, 3s. 6d. each; post 8vo, illustrated boards, 2s. each.

Juliet's Guardian.
Deceivers Ever.

Campbell.—White and Black:
Travels in the United States. By Sir GEORGE CAMPBELL, M.P. Demy 8vo, cloth extra, 14s.

Carlyle (Thomas):

Thomas Carlyle: Letters and Recollections. By MONCURE D. CONWAY, M.A. Crown 8vo, cloth extra, with Illustrations, 6s.

On the Choice of Books. By THOMAS CARLYLE. With a Life of the Author by R. H. SHEPHERD. New and Revised Edition, post 8vo, cloth extra, Illustrated, 1s. 6d.

The Correspondence of Thomas Carlyle and Ralph Waldo Emerson, 1834 to 1872. Edited by CHARLES ELIOT NORTON. With Portraits. Two Vols., crown 8vo, cloth extra, 24s.

Chapman's (George) Works:
Vol. I. contains the Plays complete, including the doubtful ones. Vol. II., the Poems and Minor Translations, with an Introductory Essay by ALGERNON CHARLES SWINBURNE. Vol. III., the Translations of the Iliad and Odyssey. Three Vols., crown 8vo, cloth extra, 18s.; or separately, 6s. each.

Chatto & Jackson.—A Treatise on Wood Engraving, Historical and Practical. By WM. ANDREW CHATTO and JOHN JACKSON. With an Additional Chapter by HENRY G. BOHN; and 450 fine Illustrations. A Reprint of the last Revised Edition. Large 4to, half-bound, 28s.

Chaucer:

Chaucer for Children: A Golden Key. By Mrs. H. R. HAWEIS. With Eight Coloured Pictures and numerous Woodcuts by the Author. New Ed., small 4to, cloth extra, 6s.

Chaucer for Schools. By Mrs. H. R. HAWEIS. Demy 8vo, cloth limp, 2s. 6d.

Clodd. — Myths and Dreams.
By EDWARD CLODD, F.R.A.S., Author of "The Childhood of Religions," &c. Crown 8vo, cloth extra, 5s. [*Shortly.*

City (The) of Dream: A Poem.
Fcap. 8vo, cloth extra, 6s. [*In the press.*

Cobban.—The Cure of Souls:
A Story. By J. MACLAREN COBBAN. Post 8vo, illustrated boards, 2s.

Collins (C. Allston).—The Bar Sinister: A Story. By C. ALLSTON COLLINS. Post 8vo, illustrated bds., 2s.

Collins (Mortimer & Frances), Novels by:

Sweet and Twenty. Post 8vo, illustrated boards, 2s.

Frances. Post 8vo, illust. bds., 2s.

Blacksmith and Scholar. Post 8vo, illustrated boards, 2s.; crown 8vo, cloth extra, 3s. 6d.

The Village Comedy. Post 8vo, illust. boards, 2s.; cr. 8vo, cloth extra, 3s. 6d.

You Play Me False. Post 8vo, illust. boards, 2s.; cr. 8vo, cloth extra, 3s. 6d.

Collins (Mortimer), Novels by:

Sweet Anne Page. Post 8vo, illustrated boards, 2s.; crown 8vo, cloth extra, 3s. 6d.

Transmigration. Post 8vo, illust. bds., 2s.; crown 8vo, cloth extra, 3s. 6d.

From Midnight to Midnight. Post 8vo, illustrated boards, 2s.; crown 8vo, cloth extra, 3s. 6d.

A Fight with Fortune. Post 8vo, Illustrated boards, 2s.

Collins (Wilkie), Novels by.
Each post 8vo, illustrated boards, 2s; cloth limp, 2s. 6d.; or crown 8vo, cloth extra, Illustrated, 3s. 6d.

Antonina. Illust. by A. CONCANEN.

Basil. Illustrated by Sir JOHN GILBERT and J. MAHONEY.

Hide and Seek. Illustrated by Sir JOHN GILBERT and J. MAHONEY.

The Dead Secret. Illustrated by Sir JOHN GILBERT and A. CONCANEN.

Queen of Hearts. Illustrated by Sir JOHN GILBERT and A. CONCANEN.

My Miscellanies. With Illustrations by A. CONCANEN, and a Steel-plate Portrait of WILKIE COLLINS.

The Woman in White. With Illustrations by Sir JOHN GILBERT and F. A. FRASER.

The Moonstone. With Illustrations by G. DU MAURIER and F. A. FRASER.

Man and Wife. Illust. by W. SMALL.

Poor Miss Finch. Illustrated by G. DU MAURIER and EDWARD HUGHES.

Miss or Mrs.? With Illustrations by S. L. FILDES and HENRY WOODS.

The New Magdalen. Illustrated by G. DU MAURIER and C. S. RANDS.

The Frozen Deep. Illustrated by G. DU MAURIER and J. MAHONEY.

The Law and the Lady. Illustrated by S. L. FILDES and SYDNEY HALL.

The Two Destinies.

The Haunted Hotel. Illustrated by ARTHUR HOPKINS.

The Fallen Leaves.

Jezebel's Daughter.

The Black Robe.

Heart and Science: A Story of the Present Time. Crown 8vo, cloth extra, 3s. 6d.

"I Say No." Three Vols., crown 8vo, 31s 6d.

Colman's Humorous Works:
"Broad Grins," "My Nightgown and Slippers," and other Humorous Works, Prose and Poetical, of GEORGE COLMAN. With Life by G. B. BUCKSTONE, and Frontispiece by HOGARTH. Crown 8vo, cloth extra, gilt, 7s. 6d.

Convalescent Cookery: A Family Handbook. By CATHERINE RYAN. Crown 8vo, 1s.; cloth, 1s. 6d.

Conway (Moncure D.), Works by:
Demonology and Devil-Lore. Two Vols., royal 8vo, with 65 Illusts., 28s.

CONWAY'S (M. D.) WORKS, *continued*—

A Necklace of Stories. Illustrated by W. J. HENNESSY. Square 8vo, cloth extra, 6s.

The Wandering Jew. Crown 8vo, cloth extra, 6s.

Thomas Carlyle: Letters and Recollections. With Illustrations. Crown 8vo, cloth extra, 6s.

Cook (Dutton), Works by:
Hours with the Players. With a Steel Plate Frontispiece. New and Cheaper Edit., cr. 8vo, cloth extra, 6s.

Nights at the Play: A View of the English Stage. New and Cheaper Edition. Crown 8vo, cloth extra, 6s.

Leo: A Novel. Post 8vo, illustrated boards, 2s.

Paul Foster's Daughter. Post 8vo, illustrated boards, 2s.; crown 8vo, cloth extra, 3s. 6d.

Cooper.—Heart Salvage, by Sea and Land. Stories by Mrs. COOPER (KATHARINE SAUNDERS). Three Vols., crown 8vo.

Copyright. — A Handbook of English and Foreign Copyright in Literary and Dramatic Works. By SIDNEY JERROLD, of the Middle Temple, Esq., Barrister-at-Law. Post 8vo, cloth limp, 2s. 6d.

Cornwall.—Popular Romances of the West of England; or, The Drolls, Traditions, and Superstitions of Old Cornwall. Collected and Edited by ROBERT HUNT, F.R.S. New and Revised Edition, with Additions, and Two Steel-plate Illustrations by GEORGE CRUIKSHANK. Crown 8vo, cloth extra, 7s. 6d.

Creasy.—Memoirs of Eminent Etonians: with Notices of the Early History of Eton College. By Sir EDWARD CREASY, Author of "The Fifteen Decisive Battles of the World." Crown 8vo, cloth extra, gilt, with 13 Portraits, 7s. 6d.

Cruikshank (George):
The Comic Almanack. Complete in TWO SERIES: The FIRST from 1835 to 1843; the SECOND from 1844 to 1853. A Gathering of the BEST HUMOUR of THACKERAY, HOOD, MAYHEW, ALBERT SMITH, A'BECKETT, ROBERT BROUGH, &c. With 2,000 Woodcuts and Steel Engravings by CRUIKSHANK, HINE, LANDELLS, &c. Crown 8vo, cloth gilt, two very thick volumes, 7s. 6d. each.

CRUIKSHANK (G.), *continued*—

The Life of George Cruikshank. By BLANCHARD JERROLD, Author of "The Life of Napoleon III.," &c. With 84 Illustrations. New and Cheaper Edition, enlarged, with Additional Plates, and a very carefully compiled Bibliography. Crown 8vo, cloth extra, 7s. 6d.

Robinson Crusoe. A beautiful reproduction of Major's Edition, with 37 Woodcuts and Two Steel Plates by GEORGE CRUIKSHANK, choicely printed. Crown 8vo, cloth extra, 7s. 6d. A few Large-Paper copies, printed on hand-made paper, with India proofs of the Illustrations, 36s.

Cussans.—Handbook of Heraldry; with Instructions for Tracing Pedigrees and Deciphering Ancient MSS., &c. By JOHN E. CUSSANS. Entirely New and Revised Edition, illustrated with over 400 Woodcuts and Coloured Plates. Crown 8vo, cloth extra, 7s. 6d.

Cyples.—Hearts of Gold: A Novel. By WILLIAM CYPLES. Crown 8vo, cloth extra, 3s. 6d.

Daniel. — Merrie England in the Olden Time. By GEORGE DANIEL. With Illustrations by ROBT. CRUIKSHANK. Crown 8vo, cloth extra, 3s. 6d.

Daudet.—Port Salvation; or, The Evangelist. By ALPHONSE DAUDET. Translated by C. HARRY MELTZER. With Portrait of the Author. Crown 8vo, cloth extra, 3s. 6d.

Davenant. — What shall my Son be? Hints for Parents on the Choice of a Profession or Trade for their Sons. By FRANCIS DAVENANT, M.A. Post 8vo, cloth limp, 2s. 6d.

Davies (Dr. N. E.), Works by:

One Thousand Medical Maxims. Crown 8vo, 1s.; cloth, 1s. 6d.

Nursery Hints: A Mother's Guide. Crown 8vo, 1s.; cloth, 1s. 6d.

Aids to Long Life. Crown 8vo, 2s.; cloth limp, 2s. 6d.

Davies' (Sir John) Complete Poetical Works, including Psalms I. to L. in Verse, and other hitherto Unpublished MSS., for the first time Collected and Edited, with Memorial-Introduction and Notes, by the Rev. A. B. GROSART, D.D. Two Vols., crown 8vo, cloth boards, 12s.

De Maistre.—A Journey Round My Room. By XAVIER DE MAISTRE. Translated by HENRY ATTWELL. Post 8vo, cloth limp, 2s. 6d.

De Mille.—A Castle in Spain. A Novel. By JAMES DE MILLE. With a Frontispiece. Crown 8vo, cloth extra, 3s. 6d.

Derwent (Leith), Novels by:

Our Lady of Tears. Cr. 8vo, cloth extra, 3s. 6d.; post 8vo, illust. bds., 2s.

Circe's Lovers. Crown 8vo, cloth extra, 3s. 6d.

Dickens (Charles), Novels by:

Post 8vo, illustrated boards, 2s. each.

Sketches by Boz. | Nicholas Nickleby.
Pickwick Papers. | Oliver Twist.

The Speeches of Charles Dickens. (*Mayfair Library*.) Post 8vo, cloth limp, 2s. 6d.

The Speeches of Charles Dickens, 1841-1870. With a New Bibliography, revised and enlarged. Edited and Prefaced by RICHARD HERNE SHEPHERD. Crown 8vo, cloth extra, 6s.

About England with Dickens. By ALFRED RIMMER. With 57 Illustrations by C. A. VANDERHOOF, ALFRED RIMMER, and others. Sq. 8vo, cloth extra, 10s. 6d.

Dictionaries:

A Dictionary of Miracles: Imitative, Realistic, and Dogmatic. By the Rev. E. C. BREWER, LL.D. Crown 8vo, cloth extra, 7s. 6d.; hf.-bound, 9s.

The Reader's Handbook of Allusions, References, Plots, and Stories. By the Rev. E. C. BREWER, LL.D. Fourth Edition, revised throughout, with a New Appendix, containing a Complete English Bibliography. Crown 8vo, 1,400 pages, cloth extra, 7s. 6d.

Authors and their Works, with the Dates. Being the Appendices to "The Reader's Handbook," separately printed. By the Rev. E. C. BREWER, LL.D. Crown 8vo, cloth limp, 2s.

Familiar Allusions: A Handbook of Miscellaneous Information; including the Names of Celebrated Statues, Paintings, Palaces, Country Seats, Ruins, Churches, Ships, Streets, Clubs, Natural Curiosities, and the like. By WM. A. WHEELER and CHARLES G. WHEELER. Demy 8vo, cloth extra, 7s. 6d.

DICTIONARIES, *continued—*
Short Sayings of Great Men. With Historical and Explanatory Notes. By SAMUEL A. BENT, M.A. Demy 8vo, cloth extra, 7s. 6d.
A Dictionary of the Drama: Being a comprehensive Guide to the Plays, Playwrights, Players, and Playhouses of the United Kingdom and America, from the Earliest to the Present Times. By W. DAVENPORT ADAMS. A thick volume, crown 8vo, half-bound, 12s. 6d. [*In preparation.*
The Slang Dictionary: Etymological, Historical, and Anecdotal. Crown 8vo, cloth extra, 6s. 6d.
Women of the Day: A Biographical Dictionary. By FRANCES HAYS. Cr. 8vo, cloth extra, 6s.
Words, Facts, and Phrases: A Dictionary of Curious, Quaint, and Out-of-the-Way Matters. By ELIEZER EDWARDS. New and Cheaper Issue. Cr. 8vo, cl. ex., 7s. 6d. ; bf.-bd., 9s.

Diderot.—The Paradox of Acting. Translated, with Annotations, from Diderot's "Le Paradoxe sur le Comédien," by WALTER HERRIES POLLOCK. With a Preface by HENRY IRVING. Cr. 8vo, in parchment, 4s. 6d.

Dobson (W. T.), Works by :
Literary Frivolities, Fancies, Follies, and Frolics. Post 8vo, cl. lp., 2s. 6d.
Poetical Ingenuities and Eccentricities. Post 8vo, cloth limp, 2s. 6d.

Doran. — Memories of our Great Towns ; with Anecdotic Gleanings concerning their Worthies and their Oddities. By Dr. JOHN DORAN, F.S.A. With 38 Illustrations. New and Cheaper Ed., cr. 8vo, cl. ex., 7s. 6d.

Drama, A Dictionary of the. Being a comprehensive Guide to the Plays, Playwrights, Players, and Playhouses of the United Kingdom and America, from the Earliest to the Present Times. By W. DAVENPORT ADAMS. (Uniform with BREWER'S "Reader's Handbook.") Crown 8vo, half-bound, 12s. 6d. [*In preparation.*

Dramatists, The Old. Cr. 8vo, cl. ex., Vignette Portraits, 6s. per Vol.
Ben Jonson's Works. With Notes Critical and Explanatory, and a Biographical Memoir by WM. GIFFORD. Edit. by Col. CUNNINGHAM. 3 Vols.
Chapman's Works. Complete in Three Vols. Vol. I. contains the Plays complete, including doubtful ones ; Vol. II., Poems and Minor Translations, with Introductory Essay by A. C. SWINBURNE ; Vol. III., Translations of the Iliad and Odyssey.

DRAMATISTS, THE OLD, *continued—*
Marlowe's Works. Including his Translations. Edited, with Notes and Introduction, by Col. CUNNINGHAM. One Vol.
Massinger's Plays. From the Text of WILLIAM GIFFORD. Edited by Col. CUNNINGHAM. One Vol.

Dyer. — The Folk - Lore of Plants. By T. F. THISELTON DYER, M.A., &c. Crown 8vo, cloth extra, 7s. 6d. [*In preparation.*

Early English Poets. Edited, with Introductions and Annotations, by Rev. A. B. GROSART, D.D. Crown 8vo, cloth boards, 6s. per Volume.
Fletcher's (Giles, B.D.) Complete Poems. One Vol.
Davies' (Sir John) Complete Poetical Works. Two Vols.
Herrick's (Robert) Complete Collected Poems. Three Vols.
Sidney's (Sir Philip) Complete Poetical Works. Three Vols.

Herbert (Lord) of Cherbury's Poems. Edited, with Introduction, by J. CHURTON COLLINS. Crown 8vo, parchment, 8s.

Edwardes (Mrs. A.), Novels by :
A Point of Honour. Post 8vo, illustrated boards, 2s.
Archie Lovell. Post 8vo, illust. bds., 2s. ; crown 8vo, cloth extra, 3s. 6d.

Eggleston.—Roxy: A Novel. By EDWARD EGGLESTON. Post 8vo, illust. boards, 2s. ; cr. 8vo, cloth extra, 3s. 6d.

Emanuel.—On Diamonds and Precious Stones: their History, Value, and Properties ; with Simple Tests for ascertaining their Reality. By HARRY EMANUEL, F.R.G.S. With numerous Illustrations, tinted and plain. Crown 8vo, cloth extra, gilt, 6s.

Englishman's House, The : A Practical Guide to all interested in Selecting or Building a House, with full Estimates of Cost, Quantities, &c. By C. J. RICHARDSON. Third Edition. Nearly 600 Illusts. Cr. 8vo, cl. ex., 7s. 6d.

Ewald (Alex. Charles, F.S.A.), Works by :
Stories from the State Papers. With an Autotype Facsimile. Crown 8vo, cloth extra, 6s.
The Life and Times of Prince Charles Stuart, Count of Albany, commonly called the Young Pretender. From the State Papers and other Sources. New and Cheaper Edition, with a Portrait, crown 8vo, cloth extra, 7s. 6d.

Eyes, The.—How to Use our Eyes, and How to Preserve Them. By JOHN BROWNING, F.R.A.S., &c. With 52 Illustrations. 1s.; cloth, 1s. 6d.

Fairholt.—Tobacco: Its History and Associations; with an Account of the Plant and its Manufacture, and its Modes of Use in all Ages and Countries. By F. W. FAIRHOLT, F.S.A. With Coloured Frontispiece and upwards of 100 Illustrations by the Author. Cr. 8vo. cl. ex., 6s.

Familiar Allusions: A Handbook of Miscellaneous Information; including the Names of Celebrated Statues, Paintings, Palaces, Country Seats, Ruins, Churches, Ships, Streets, Clubs, Natural Curiosities, and the like. By WILLIAM A. WHEELER, Author of " Noted Names of Fiction ; " and CHARLES G. WHEELER. Demy 8vo. cloth extra, 7s. 6d.

Faraday (Michael), Works by :
The Chemical History of a Candle : Lectures delivered before a Juvenile Audience at the Royal Institution. Edited by WILLIAM CROOKES, F.C.S. Post 8vo, cloth extra, with numerous Illustrations, 4s. 6d.
On the Various Forces of Nature, and their Relations to each other : Lectures delivered before a Juvenile Audience at the Royal Institution. Edited by WILLIAM CROOKES, F.C.S. Post 8vo, cloth extra, with numerous Illustrations, 4s. 6d.

Farrer. — Military Manners and Customs. By J. A. FARRER, Author of "Primitive Manners and Customs," &c. Crown 8vo, cloth extra, 6s. [*In preparation.*

Fin-Bec. — The Cupboard Papers : Observations on the Art of Living and Dining. By FIN-BEC. Post 8vo, cloth limp, 2s. 6d.

Fitzgerald (Percy), Works by :
The Recreations of a Literary Man ; or, Does Writing Pay ? With Recollections of some Literary Men, and a View of a Literary Man's Working Life. Cr. 8vo, cloth extra, 6s.
The World Behind the Scenes. Crown 8vo, cloth extra, 3s. 6d.
Little Essays: Passages from the Letters of CHARLES LAMB. Post 8vo, cloth limp, 2s. 6d.

Post 8vo, Illustrated boards, 2s. each.
Bella Donna. | Never Forgotten.
The Second Mrs. Tillotson.
Polly.
Seventy-five Brooke Street.
The Lady of Brantome.

Fletcher's (Giles, B.D.) Complete Poems : Christ's Victorie in Heaven, Christ's Victorie on Earth, Christ's Triumph over Death, and Minor Poems. With Memorial-Introduction and Notes by the Rev. A. B. GROSART, D.D. Cr. 8vo, cloth bds., 6s.

Fonblanque.—Filthy Lucre : A Novel. By ALBANY DE FONBLANQUE. Post 8vo, illustrated boards, 2s.

Francillon (R. E.), Novels by :
Crown 8vo, cloth extra, 3s. 6d. each ; post 8vo, illust. boards, 2s. each.
Olympia. | Queen Cophetua
One by One.

Esther's Glove. Fcap. 8vo, picture cover. 1s.
A Real Queen. Cr. 8vo, cl. extra. 3s. 6d.

French Literature, History of. By HENRY VAN LAUN. Complete in 3 Vols., demy 8vo, cl. bds., 7s. 6d. each.

Frere.—Pandurang Hari ; or, Memoirs of a Hindoo. With a Preface by Sir H. BARTLE FRERE, G.C.S.I., &c. Crown 8vo, cloth extra, 3s. 6d. ; post 8vo, illustrated boards, 2s.

Friswell.—One of Two: A Novel. By HAIN FRISWELL. Post 8vo, illustrated boards, 2s.

Frost (Thomas), Works by :
Crown 8vo, cloth extra, 3s. 6d. each.
Circus Life and Circus Celebrities.
The Lives of the Conjurers.
The Old Showmen and the Old London Fairs.

Fry.—Royal Guide to the London Charities, 1884-5. By HERBERT FRY. Showing their Name, Date of Foundation, Objects, Income, Officials, &c. Published Annually. Crown 8vo, cloth, 1s. 6d.

Gardening Books:
A Year's Work in Garden and Greenhouse : Practical Advice to Amateur Gardeners as to the Management of the Flower, Fruit, and Frame Garden. By GEORGE GLENNY. Post 8vo, 1s. : cloth, 1s. 6d.
Our Kitchen Garden : The Plants we Grow, and How we Cook Them. By TOM JERROLD. Post 8vo, cloth limp, 2s. 6d.
Household Horticulture: A Gossip about Flowers. By TOM and JANE JERROLD. Illust. Post 8vo, cl. lp. 3s. 6d.
The Garden that Paid the Rent. By TOM JERROLD. Fcap. 8vo, illustrated cover. 1s. ; cloth limp, 1s. 6d.
My Garden Wild, and What I Grew there. By F. G. HEATH. Crown 8vo, cloth extra, 5s. · gilt edges, 6s.

Garrett.—The Capel Girls: A
Novel. By EDWARD GARRETT. Post
8vo, illust. bds., 2s.; cr. 8vo, cl. ex., 3s. 6d.

Gentleman's Magazine (The)
for 1885. One Shilling Monthly. A
New Serial Story, entitled "The
Unforeseen," by ALICE O'HANLON,
begins in the JANUARY Number.
"Science Notes," by W. MATTIEU
WILLIAMS, F.R.A.S., and "Table
Talk," by SYLVANUS URBAN, are also
continued monthly.
*** *Now ready, the Volume for* JULY *to*
DECEMBER, 1884, *cloth extra, price* 8s. 6d.;
Cases for binding, 2s. *each.*

German Popular Stories. Collected by the Brothers GRIMM, and
Translated by EDGAR TAYLOR. Edited,
with an Introduction, by JOHN RUSKIN.
With 22 Illustrations on Steel by
GEORGE CRUIKSHANK. Square 8vo,
cloth extra, 6s. 6d.; gilt edges, 7s. 6d.

Gibbon (Charles), Novels by:
Crown 8vo, cloth extra, 3s. 6d. each;
post 8vo, illustrated boards, 2s. each.

Robin Gray.	Queen of the
For Lack of Gold.	Meadow.
What will the	In Pastures Green
World Say?	Braes of Yarrow.
In Honour Bound.	The Flower of the
In Love and War.	Forest. [lem.
For the King.	A Heart's Prob-

Post 8vo, illustrated boards, 2s.
The Dead Heart.

Crown 8vo, cloth extra, 3s. 6d. each.
The Golden Shaft.
Of High Degree.
Fancy Free.
Loving a Dream.

By Mead and Stream. Three Vols.,
crown 8vo.
Found Out. Three Vols., crown
8vo.   [*Shortly.*

Gilbert (William), Novels by:
Post 8vo, illustrated boards, 2s. each.
Dr. Austin's Guests.
The Wizard of the Mountain.
James Duke, Costermonger.

Gilbert (W. S.), Original Plays
by: In Two Series, each complete in
itself, price 2s. 6d. each.
The FIRST SERIES contains — The
Wicked World—Pygmalion and Ga-
latea — Charity — The Princess — The
Palace of Truth—Trial by Jury.
The SECOND SERIES contains—Bro-
ken Hearts—Engaged—Sweethearts—
Gretchen—Dan'l Druce—Tom Cobb—
H.M.S. Pinafore—The Sorcerer—The
Pirates of Penzance.

Glenny.—A Year's Work In
Garden and Greenhouse: Practical
Advice to Amateur Gardeners as to
the Management of the Flower, Fruit,
and Frame Garden. By GEORGE
GLENNY. Post 8vo, 1s.; cloth, 1s. 6d.

Godwin.—Lives of the Necro-
mancers. By WILLIAM GODWIN.
Post 8vo, cloth limp, 2s.

Golden Library, The:
Square 16mo (Tauchnitz size), cloth
limp, 2s. per volume.
Bayard Taylor's Diversions of the
Echo Club.
Bennett's (Dr. W. C.) Ballad History
of England.
Bennett's (Dr.) Songs for Sailors.
Byron's Don Juan.
Godwin's (William) Lives of the
Necromancers.
Holmes's Autocrat of the Break-
fast Table. With an Introduction
by G. A. SALA.
Holmes's Professor at the Break-
fast Table.
Hood's Whims and Oddities. Com-
plete. All the original Illustrations.
Irving's (Washington) Tales of a
Traveller.
Irving's (Washington) Tales of the
Alhambra.
Jesse's (Edward) Scenes and Oc-
cupations of a Country Life.
Lamb's Essays of Elia. Both Series
Complete in One Vol.
Leigh Hunt's Essays: A Tale for a
Chimney Corner, and other Pieces.
With Portrait, and Introduction by
EDMUND OLLIER.
Mallory's (Sir Thomas) Mort
d'Arthur: The Stories of King
Arthur and of the Knights of the
Round Table. Edited by B. MONT-
GOMERIE RANKING.
Pascal's Provincial Letters. A New
Translation, with Historical Intro-
duction and Notes, by T. M'CRIE, D.D.
Pope's Poetical Works. Complete.
Rochefoucauld's Maxims and Moral
Reflections. With Notes, and In-
troductory Essay by SAINTE-BEUVE.
St. Pierre's Paul and Virginia, and
The Indian Cottage. Edited, with
Life, by the Rev. E. CLARKE.
Shelley's Early Poems, and Queen
Mab. With Essay by LEIGH HUNT.
Shelley's Later Poems: Laon and
Cytinna, &c.
Shelley's Posthumous Poems, the
Shelley Papers, &c.

GOLDEN LIBRARY, THE, *continued*—
Shelley's Prose Works, including A Refutation of Deism, Zastrozzi, St. Irvyne, &c.
White's Natural History of Selborne. Edited, with Additions, by THOMAS BROWN, F.L.S.

Golden Treasury of Thought, The: An ENCYCLOPÆDIA OF QUOTATIONS from Writers of all Times and Countries. Selected and Edited by THEODORE TAYLOR. Crown 8vo, cloth gilt and gilt edges, 7s. 6d.

Gordon Cumming (C. F.), Works by:
In the Hebrides. With Autotype Facsimile and numerous full-page Illustrations. Demy 8vo, cloth extra, 8s. 6d.
In the Himalayas and on the Indian Plains. With numerous Illustrations. Demy 8vo, cloth extra, 8s. 6d.

Graham. — The Professor's Wife: A Story. By LEONARD GRAHAM. Fcap. 8vo, picture cover, 1s.; cloth extra, 2s. 6d.

Greeks and Romans, The Life of the, Described from Antique Monuments. By ERNST GUHL and W. KONER. Translated from the Third German Edition, and Edited by Dr. F. HUEFFER. With 545 Illustrations. New and Cheaper Edition, demy 8vo, cloth extra, 7s. 6d.

Greenwood (James), Works by:
The Wilds of London. Crown 8vo, cloth extra, 3s. 6d.
Low-Life Deeps: An Account of the Strange Fish to be Found There. Crown 8vo, cloth extra, 3s. 6d.
Dick Temple: A Novel. Post 8vo, illustrated boards, 2s.

Guyot.—The Earth and Man; or, Physical Geography in its relation to the History of Mankind. By ARNOLD GUYOT. With Additions by Professors AGASSIZ, PIERCE, and GRAY; 12 Maps and Engravings on Steel, some Coloured, and copious Index. Crown 8vo, cloth extra, gilt, 4s. 6d.

Hair (The): Its Treatment in Health, Weakness, and Disease. Translated from the German of Dr. J. PINCUS. Crown 8vo, 1s.; cloth, 1s. 6d.

Hake (Dr. Thomas Gordon), Poems by:
Maiden Ecstasy. Small 4to, cloth extra, 8s.

HAKE'S (Dr. T. G.) POEMS, *continued*—
New Symbols. Cr. 8vo, cloth extra, 6s.
Legends of the Morrow. Crown 8vo, cloth extra, 6s.
The Serpent Play. Crown 8vo, cloth extra, 6s.

Hall.—Sketches of Irish Character. By Mrs. S. C. HALL. With numerous Illustrations on Steel and Wood by MACLISE, GILBERT, HARVEY, and G. CRUIKSHANK. Medium 8vo, cloth extra, gilt, 7s. 6d.

Hall Caine.—The Shadow of a Crime: A Novel. By HALL CAINE. 3 vols., crown 8vo. [*Immediately*.

Halliday.—Every-day Papers. By ANDREW HALLIDAY. Post 8vo, illustrated boards, 2s.

Handwriting, The Philosophy of. With over 100 Facsimiles and Explanatory Text. By DON FELIX DE SALAMANCA. Post 8vo, cl. limp, 2s. 6d.

Hanky-Panky: A Collection of Very Easy Tricks, Very Difficult Tricks, White Magic, Sleight of Hand, &c. Edited by W. H. CREMER. With 200 Illusts. Crown 8vo, cloth extra, 4s. 6d.

Hardy (Lady Duffus). — Paul Wynter's Sacrifice: A Story. By Lady DUFFUS HARDY. Post 8vo, illust. boards, 2s.

Hardy (Thomas).—Under the Greenwood Tree. By THOMAS HARDY, Author of "Far from the Madding Crowd." Crown 8vo, cloth extra, 3s. 6d.; post 8vo, illustrated bds., 2s.

Haweis (Mrs. H. R.), Works by:
The Art of Dress. With numerous Illustrations. Small 8vo, illustrated cover, 1s.; cloth limp, 1s. 6d.
The Art of Beauty. New and Cheaper Edition. Crown 8vo, cloth extra, with Coloured Frontispiece and Illustrations, 6s.
The Art of Decoration. Square 8vo, handsomely bound and profusely Illustrated, 10s. 6d.
Chaucer for Children: A Golden Key. With Eight Coloured Pictures and numerous Woodcuts. New Edition, small 4to, cloth extra, 6s.
Chaucer for Schools. Demy 8vo, cloth limp, 2s. 6d.

Haweis (Rev. H. R.).—American Humorists. Including WASHINGTON IRVING, OLIVER WENDELL HOLMES, JAMES RUSSELL LOWELL, ARTEMUS WARD, MARK TWAIN, and BRET HARTE. By the Rev. H. R. HAWEIS, M.A. Crown 8vo, cloth extra, 6s.

Hawthorne (Julian), Novels by.
Crown 8vo, cloth extra, 3s. 6d. each;
post 8vo, illustrated boards, 2s. each.

Garth.
Ellice Quentin.
Sebastian Strome.
Dust.
Prince Seroni's Wife.

Mrs. Gainsborough's Diamonds.
Fcap. 8vo, illustrated cover, 1s.;
cloth extra, 2s. 6d.

Crown 8vo, cloth extra, 3s. 6d. each.
Fortune's Fool.
Beatrix Randolph. With Illustrations
by A. FREDERICKS.
Miss Cadogna.   [*Shortly.*

IMPORTANT NEW BIOGRAPHY.

Hawthorne (Nathaniel) and
his Wife. By JULIAN HAWTHORNE.
With 6 Steel-plate Portraits. Two
Vols., crown 8vo, cloth extra, 24s.

[Twenty-five copies of an *Edition de
Luxe*, printed on the best hand-made
paper, large 8vo size, and with India
proofs of the Illustrations, are reserved
for sale in England, price 48s. per set.
Immediate application should be made
by anyone desiring a copy of this
special and very limited Edition.]

Hays.—Women of the Day: A
Biographical Dictionary of Notable
Contemporaries. By FRANCES HAYS.
Crown 8vo, cloth extra, 5s.

Heath (F. G.). — My Garden
Wild, and What I Grew There. By
FRANCIS GEORGE HEATH, Author of
"The Fern World," &c. Crown 8vo,
cl. ex., 5s.; cl. gilt, gilt edges, 6s.

Helps (Sir Arthur), Works by:
Animals and their Masters. Post
8vo, cloth limp, 2s. 6d.
Social Pressure. Post 8vo, cloth limp,
2s. 6d.
Ivan de Biron: A Novel. Crown 8vo,
cloth extra, 3s. 6d.; post 8vo, illustrated boards, 2s.

Heptalogia (The); or, The
Seven against Sense. A Cap with
Seven Bells. Cr. 8vo, cloth extra, 6s.

Herbert.—The Poems of Lord
Herbert of Cherbury. Edited, with
Introduction, by J. CHURTON COLLINS.
Crown 8vo, bound in parchment, 8s.

Herrick's (Robert) Hesperides,
Noble Numbers, and Complete Collected Poems. With Memorial-Introduction and Notes by the Rev. A. B.
GROSART, D.D., Steel Portrait, Index
of First Lines, and Glossarial Index,
&c. Three Vols., crown 8vo, cloth, 18s.

Hesse-Wartegg (Chevalier
Ernst von), Works by:
Tunis: The Land and the People.
With 22 Illustrations. Crown 8vo,
cloth extra, 3s. 6d.
The New South-West: Travelling
Sketches from Kansas, New Mexico,
Arizona, and Northern Mexico.
With 100 fine Illustrations and Three
Maps. Demy 8vo, cloth extra,
14s.   [*In preparation.*

Hindley (Charles), Works by:
Crown 8vo, cloth extra, 3s. 6d. each.
Tavern Anecdotes and Sayings: In-
cluding the Origin of Signs, and
Reminiscences connected with
Taverns, Coffee Houses, Clubs, &c.
With Illustrations.
The Life and Adventures of a Cheap
Jack. By One of the Fraternity.
Edited by CHARLES HINDLEY.

Hoey.—The Lover's Creed.
By Mrs. CASHEL HOEY. With 12 Illustrations by P. MACNAB. Three Vols.,
crown 8vo.

Holmes (O. Wendell), Works by:
The Autocrat of the Breakfast-
Table. Illustrated by J. GORDON
THOMSON. Post 8vo, cloth limp,
2s. 6d.; another Edition in smaller
type, with an Introduction by G. A.
SALA. Post 8vo, cloth limp, 2s.
The Professor at the Breakfast-
Table; with the Story of Iris. Post
8vo, cloth limp, 2s.

Holmes. — The Science of
Voice Production and Voice Preser-
vation: A Popular Manual for the
Use of Speakers and Singers. By
GORDON HOLMES, M.D. With Illus-
trations. Crown 8vo, 1s.; cloth, 1s. 6d.

Hood (Thomas):
Hood's Choice Works, in Prose and
Verse. Including the Cream of the
Comic Annuals. With Life of the
Author, Portrait, and 200 Illustra-
tions. Crown 8vo, cloth extra, 7s. 6d.
Hood's Whims and Oddities. Com-
plete. With all the original Illus-
trations. Post 8vo, cloth limp, 2s.

Hood (Tom), Works by:
From Nowhere to the North Pole:
A Noah's Arkæological Narrative.
With 25 Illustrations by W. BRUN-
TON and E. C. BARNES. Square
crown 8vo, cloth extra, gilt edges, 6s.
A Golden Heart: A Novel. Post 8vo,
illustrated boards, 2s.

Hook's (Theodore) Choice Humorous Works, including his Ludicrous Adventures, Bons Mots, Puns and Hoaxes. With a New Life of the Author, Portraits, Facsimiles, and Illusts. Cr. 8vo, cl. extra, gilt, 7s. 6d.

Hooper.—The House of Raby: A Novel. By Mrs. GEORGE HOOPER. Post 8vo, illustrated boards, 2s.

Horne.—Orion: An Epic Poem, in Three Books. By RICHARD HENGIST HORNE. With Photographic Portrait from a Medallion by SUMMERS. Tenth Edition, crown 8vo, cloth extra, 7s.

Howell.—Conflicts of Capital and Labour, Historically and Economically considered: Being a History and Review of the Trade Unions of Great Britain, showing their Origin, Progress, Constitution, and Objects, in their Political, Social, Economical, and Industrial Aspects. By GEORGE HOWELL. Cr. 8vo, cloth extra, 7s. 6d.

Hugo. — The Hunchback of Notre Dame. By VICTOR HUGO. Post 8vo, illustrated boards, 2s.

Hunt.—Essays by Leigh Hunt. A Tale for a Chimney Corner, and other Pieces. With Portrait and Introduction by EDMUND OLLIER. Post 8vo, cloth limp, 2s.

Hunt (Mrs. Alfred), Novels by: Crown 8vo, cloth extra, 3s. 6d. each; post 8vo, illustrated boards, 2s. each.

> Thornicroft's Model.
> The Leaden Casket.
> Self-Condemned.

Ingelow.—Fated to be Free: A Novel. By JEAN INGELOW. Crown 8vo, cloth extra, 3s. 6d.; post 8vo, illustrated boards, 2s.

Irish Wit and Humour, Songs of. Collected and Edited by A. PERCEVAL GRAVES. Post 8vo, cl. limp, 2s. 6d.

Irving (Washington), Works by: Post 8vo, cloth limp, 2s. each.
> Tales of a Traveller.
> Tales of the Alhambra.

Janvier.—Practical Keramics for Students. By CATHERINE A. JANVIER. Crown 8vo, cloth extra, 6s.

Jay (Harriett), Novels by. Each crown 8vo, cloth extra, 3s. 6d.; or post 8vo, illustrated boards, 2s.
> The Dark Colleen.
> The Queen of Connaught.

Jefferies (Richard), Works by:
Nature near London. Crown 8vo, cloth extra, 6s.
The Life of the Fields. Crown 8vo, cloth extra, 6s.

Jennings (H. J.), Works by:
Curiosities of Criticism. Post 8vo, cloth limp, 2s. 6d.
Lord Tennyson: A Biographical Sketch. With a Photograph-Portrait. Crown 8vo, cloth extra, 6s.

Jennings (Hargrave). — The Rosicrucians: Their Rites and Mysteries. With Chapters on the Ancient Fire and Serpent Worshippers. By HARGRAVE JENNINGS. With Five full-page Plates and upwards of 300 Illustrations. A New Edition, crown 8vo, cloth extra, 7s. 6d.

Jerrold (Tom), Works by:
The Garden that Paid the Rent. By TOM JERROLD. Fcap. 8vo, illustrated cover, 1s.; cloth limp, 1s. 6d.
Household Horticulture: A Gossip about Flowers. By TOM and JANE JERROLD. Illust. Post 8vo, cl. lp., 2s. 6d.
Our Kitchen Garden: The Plants we Grow, and How we Cook Them. By TOM JERROLD. Post 8vo, cloth limp, 2s. 6d.

Jesse.—Scenes and Occupations of a Country Life. By EDWARD JESSE. Post 8vo, cloth limp, 2s.

Jones (Wm., F.S.A.), Works by:
Finger-Ring Lore: Historical, Legendary, and Anecdotal. With over 200 Illusts. Cr. 8vo, cl. extra, 7s. 6d.
Credulities, Past and Present; including the Sea and Seamen, Miners, Talismans, Word and Letter Divination, Exorcising and Blessing of Animals, Birds, Eggs, Luck, &c. With an Etched Frontispiece. Crown 8vo, cloth extra, 7s. 6d.
Crowns and Coronations: A History of Regalia in all Times and Countries. With One Hundred Illustrations. Cr. 8vo, cloth extra, 7s. 6d.

Jonson's (Ben) Works. With Notes Critical and Explanatory, and a Biographical Memoir by WILLIAM GIFFORD. Edited by Colonel CUNNINGHAM. Three Vols., crown 8vo, cloth extra, 18s.; or separately, 6s. each.

Josephus, The Complete Works of. Translated by WHISTON. Containing both "The Antiquities of the Jews" and "The Wars of the Jews." Two Vols., 8vo, with 52 Illustrations and Maps, cloth extra, gilt, 14s.

Kavanagh.—The Pearl Fountain, and other Fairy Stories. By BRIDGET and JULIA KAVANAGH. With Thirty Illustrations by J. MOYR SMITH. Small 8vo, cloth gilt, 6s.

Kempt.—Pencil and Palette: Chapters on Art and Artists. By ROBERT KEMPT. Post 8vo, cloth limp, 2s. 6d.

Kingsley (Henry), Novels by: Each crown 8vo, cloth extra, 3s. 6d.; or post 8vo, illustrated boards, 2s.

Oakshott Castle. | Number Seventeen

Knight.—The Patient's Vade Mecum: How to get most Benefit from Medical Advice. By WILLIAM KNIGHT, M.R.C.S., and EDWARD KNIGHT, L.R.C.P. Crown 8vo, 1s.; cloth, 1s. 6d.

Lamb (Charles):

Mary and Charles Lamb: Their Poems, Letters, and Remains. With Reminiscences and Notes by W. CAREW HAZLITT. With HANCOCK'S Portrait of the Essayist, Facsimiles of the Title-pages of the rare First Editions of Lamb's and Coleridge's Works, and numerous Illustrations. Crown 8vo, cloth extra, 10s. 6d.

Lamb's Complete Works, in Prose and Verse, reprinted from the Original Editions, with many Pieces hitherto unpublished. Edited, with Notes and Introduction, by R. H. SHEPHERD. With Two Portraits and Facsimile of Page of the "Essay on Roast Pig." Cr. 8vo, cloth extra, 7s. 6d.

The Essays of Ella. Complete Edition. Post 8vo, cloth extra, 2s.

Poetry for Children, and Prince Dorus. By CHARLES LAMB. Carefully reprinted from unique copies. Small 8vo, cloth extra, 5s.

Little Essays: Sketches and Characters. By CHARLES LAMB. Selected from his Letters by PERCY FITZGERALD. Post 8vo, cloth limp, 2s. 6d.

Lane's Arabian Nights, &c.:

The Thousand and One Nights: commonly called, in England, "THE ARABIAN NIGHTS' ENTERTAINMENTS." A New Translation from the Arabic, with copious Notes, by EDWARD WILLIAM LANE. Illustrated by many hundred Engravings on Wood, from Original Designs by WM. HARVEY. A New Edition, from a Copy annotated by the Translator, edited by his Nephew, EDWARD STANLEY POOLE. With a Preface by STANLEY LANE-POOLE. Three Vols., demy 8vo, cloth extra, 7s. 6d. each.

LANE'S ARABIAN NIGHTS, *continued—*
Arabian Society in the Middle Ages: Studies from "The Thousand and One Nights." By EDWARD WILLIAM LANE, Author of "The Modern Egyptians," &c. Edited by STANLEY LANE-POOLE. Cr. 8vo, cloth extra, 6s.

Lares and Penates; or, The Background of Life. By FLORENCE CADDY. Crown 8vo, cloth extra, 6s.

Larwood (Jacob), Works by:

The Story of the London Parks. With Illustrations. Crown 8vo, cloth extra, 3s. 6d.

Clerical Anecdotes. Post 8vo, cloth limp, 2s. 6d.

Forensic Anecdotes Post 8vo, cloth limp, 2s. 6d.

Theatrical Anecdotes. Post 8vo, cloth limp, 2s. 6d.

Leigh (Henry S.), Works by:

Carols of Cockayne. With numerous Illustrations. Post 8vo, cloth limp, 2s. 6d.

Jeux d'Esprit. Collected and Edited by HENRY S. LEIGH. Post 8vo, cloth limp, 2s. 6d.

Life in London; or, The History of Jerry Hawthorn and Corinthian Tom. With the whole of CRUIKSHANK'S Illustrations, in Colours, after the Originals. Crown 8vo, cloth extra, 7s. 6d.

Linton (E. Lynn), Works by: Post 8vo, cloth limp, 2s. 6d. each.
Witch Stories.
The True Story of Joshua Davidson.
Ourselves: Essays on Women.

Crown 8vo, cloth extra, 3s. 6d. each; post 8vo, illustrated boards, 2s. each.
Patricia Kemball.
The Atonement of Leam Dundas.
The World Well Lost.
Under which Lord?
With a Silken Thread.
The Rebel of the Family.
"My Love!"
Ione.

Locks and Keys.—On the Development and Distribution of Primitive Locks and Keys. By Lieut.-Gen. PITT-RIVERS, F.R.S. With numerous Illustrations. Demy 4to, half Roxburghe, 16s.

Longfellow:

Longfellow's Complete Prose Works. Including "Outre Mer," "Hyperion," "Kavanagh," "The Poets and Poetry of Europe," and "Driftwood." With Portrait and Illustrations by VALENTINE BROMLEY. Crown 8vo, cloth extra, 7s. 6d.

Longfellow's Poetical Works. Carefully Reprinted from the Original Editions. With numerous fine Illustrations on Steel and Wood. Crown 8vo, cloth extra, 7s. 6d.

Long Life, Aids to: A Medical, Dietetic, and General Guide in Health and Disease. By N. E. DAVIES, L.R.C.P. Crown 8vo, 2s; cloth limp, 2s. 6d. [*Shortly*.

Lucy.—Gideon Fleyce: A Novel. By HENRY W. LUCY. Crown 8vo, cl. extra, 3s. 6d.; post 8vo, illust. bds., 2s.

Lusiad (The) of Camoens. Translated into English Spenserian Verse by ROBERT FFRENCH DUFF. Demy 8vo, with Fourteen full-page Plates, cloth boards, 18s.

McCarthy (Justin, M.P.), Works by:

A History of Our Own Times, from the Accession of Queen Victoria to the General Election of 1880. Four Vols. demy 8vo, cloth extra, 12s. each.—Also a POPULAR EDITION, in Four Vols. cr. 8vo, cl. extra, 6s. each.

A Short History of Our Own Times. One Vol., crown 8vo, cloth extra, 6s.

History of the Four Georges. Four Vols. demy 8vo, cloth extra, 12s. each. [Vol. I. *now ready*.

Crown 8vo, cloth extra, 3s. 6d. each; post 8vo, illustrated boards, 2s. each.

Dear Lady Disdain.

The Waterdale Neighbours.

My Enemy's Daughter.

A Fair Saxon.

Linley Rochford

Miss Misanthrope.

Donna Quixote.

The Comet of a Season.

Maid of Athens. With 12 Illustrations by F. BARNARD. Crown 8vo, cloth extra, 3s. 6d.

McCarthy (Justin H., M.P.), Works by:

An Outline of the History of Ireland, from the Earliest Times to the Present Day. Cr. 8vo, 1s.; cloth, 1s. 6d.

England under Gladstone. Crown 8vo, cloth extra, 6s.

MacDonald (George, LL.D.), Works by:

The Princess and Curdie. With 11 Illustrations by JAMES ALLEN. Small crown 8vo, cloth extra, 5s.

Gutta-Percha Willie, the Working Genius. With 9 Illustrations by ARTHUR HUGHES. Square 8vo, cloth extra, 3s. 6d.

Paul Faber, Surgeon. With a Frontispiece by J. E. MILLAIS. Crown 8vo, cloth extra, 3s. 6d.; post 8vo, illustrated boards, 2s.

Thomas Wingfold, Curate. With a Frontispiece by C. J. STANILAND. Crown 8vo, cloth extra, 3s. 6d.; post 8vo, illustrated boards, 2s.

Macdonell.—Quaker Cousins: A Novel. By AGNES MACDONELL. Crown 8vo, cloth extra, 3s. 6d.; post 8vo, illustrated boards, 2s.

Macgregor. — Pastimes and Players. Notes on Popular Games. By ROBERT MACGREGOR. Post 8vo, cloth limp, 2s. 6d.

Maclise Portrait-Gallery (The) of Illustrious Literary Characters; with Memoirs—Biographical, Critical, Bibliographical, and Anecdotal—illustrative of the Literature of the former half of the Present Century. By WILLIAM BATES, B.A. With 85 Portraits printed on an India Tint. Crown 8vo, cloth extra, 7s. 6d.

Macquoid (Mrs.), Works by:

In the Ardennes. With 50 fine Illustrations by THOMAS R. MACQUOID. Square 8vo, cloth extra, 10s. 6d.

Pictures and Legends from Normandy and Brittany. With numerous Illustrations by THOMAS R. MACQUOID. Square 8vo, cloth gilt, 10s. 6d.

Through Normandy. With 90 Illustrations by T. R. MACQUOID. Square 8vo, cloth extra, 7s. 6d.

Through Brittany. With numerous Illustrations by T. R. MACQUOID. Square 8vo, cloth extra, 7s. 6d.

About Yorkshire With 67 Illustrations by T. R. MACQUOID, Engraved by SWAIN. Square 8vo, cloth extra, 10s. 6d.

The Evil Eye, and other Stories. Crown 8vo, cloth extra, 3s. 6d.; post 8vo, illustrated boards, 2s.

Lost Rose, and other Stories. Crown 8vo, cloth extra, 3s. 6d.; post 8vo, illustrated boards, 2s.

Mackay.—Interludes and Undertones: or, Music at Twilight. By CHARLES MACKAY, LL.D. Crown 8vo, cloth extra, 6s.

Magic Lantern (The), and its Management: including Full Practical Directions for producing the Limelight, making Oxygen Gas, and preparing Lantern Slides. By T. C. HEPWORTH. With 10 Illustrations. Crown 8vo, 1s. ; cloth, 1s. 6d.

Magician's Own Book (The): Performances with Cups and Balls, Eggs, Hats, Handkerchiefs, &c. All from actual Experience. Edited by W. H. CREMER. With 200 Illustrations. Crown 8vo, cloth extra, 4s. 6d.

Magic No Mystery: Tricks with Cards, Dice, Balls, &c., with fully descriptive Directions; the Art of Secret Writing; Training of Performing Animals, &c. With Coloured Frontispiece and many Illustrations. Crown 8vo, cloth extra, 4s. 6d.

Magna Charta. An exact Facsimile of the Original in the British Museum, printed on fine plate paper, 3 feet by 2 feet, with Arms and Seals emblazoned in Gold and Colours. Price 5s.

Mallock (W. H.), Works by :
The New Republic; or, Culture, Faith and Philosophy in an English Country House. Post 8vo, cloth limp, 2s. 6d. ; Cheap Edition, illustrated boards, 2s.
The New Paul and Virginia; or, Positivism on an Island. Post 8vo, cloth limp, 2s. 6d.
Poems. Small 4to, bound in parchment, 8s.
Is Life worth Living? Crown 8vo, cloth extra, 6s.

Mallory's (Sir Thomas) Mort d'Arthur: The Stories of King Arthur and of the Knights of the Round Table. Edited by B. MONTGOMERIE RANKING. Post 8vo, cloth limp, 2s.

Marlowe's Works. Including his Translations. Edited, with Notes and Introduction, by Col. CUNNINGHAM. Crown 8vo, cloth extra, 6s.

Marryat (Florence), Novels by:
Crown 8vo, cloth extra, 3s. 6d. each ; or, post 8vo, illustrated boards, 2s.
Open ! Sesame !
Written in Fire.

Post 8vo, illustrated boards, 2s. **each.**
A Harvest of Wild Oats.
A Little Stepson.
Fighting the Air.

Masterman.—Half a Dozen Daughters: A Novel. By J. MASTERMAN. Post 8vo, illustrated boards, 2s.

Mark Twain, Works by :
The Choice Works of Mark Twain. Revised and Corrected throughout by the Author. With Life, Portrait, and numerous Illustrations. Crown 8vo, cloth extra, 7s. 6d.
The Adventures of Tom Sawyer. Post 8vo, illustrated boards, 2s.
An Idle Excursion, and other Sketches. Post 8vo, illustrated boards, 2s.
The Prince and the Pauper. With nearly 200 Illustrations. Crown 8vo, cloth extra, 7s. 6d.
The Innocents Abroad; or, The New Pilgrim's Progress: Being some Account of the Steamship " Quaker City's " Pleasure Excursion to Europe and the Holy Land. With 234 Illustrations. Crown 8vo, cloth extra, 7s. 6d. CHEAP EDITION (under the title of " MARK TWAIN'S PLEASURE TRIP "), post 8vo, illust. boards, 2s.
A Tramp Abroad. With 314 Illustrations. Crown 8vo, cloth extra, 7s. 6d.; Post 8vo, illustrated boards, 2s.
The Stolen White Elephant, &c. Crown 8vo, cloth extra, 6s.; post 8vo, illustrated boards, 2s.
Life on the Mississippi. With about 300 Original Illustrations. Crown 8vo, cloth extra, 7s. 6d.
The Adventures of Huckleberry Finn. With 174 Illustrations by E. W. KEMBLE. Crown 8vo, cloth extra, 7s. 6d.

Massinger's Plays. From the Text of WILLIAM GIFFORD. Edited by Col. CUNNINGHAM. Crown 8vo, cloth extra, 6s.

Mayhew.—London Characters and the Humorous Side of London Life. By HENRY MAYHEW. With numerous Illustrations. Crown 8vo, cloth extra, 3s. 6d.

Mayfair Library, The :
Post 8vo, cloth limp, 2s. 6d. per Volume.
A Journey Round My Room. By XAVIER DE MAISTRE. Translated by HENRY ATTWELL.
Latter-Day Lyrics. Edited by W. DAVENPORT ADAMS.
Quips and Quiddities. Selected by W. DAVENPORT ADAMS.
The Agony Column of "The Times," from 1800 to 1870. Edited, with an Introduction, by ALICE CLAY.
Balzac's "Comedie Humaine" and its Author. With Translations by H. H. WALKER.
Melancholy Anatomised: A Popular Abridgment of " Burton's Anatomy of Melancholy."

MAYFAIR LIBRARY, *continued—*

Gastronomy as a Fine Art. By BRILLAT-SAVARIN.

The Speeches of Charles Dickens.

Literary Frivolities, Fancies, Follies, and Frolics. By W. T. DOBSON.

Poetical Ingenuities and Eccentricities. Selected and Edited by W. T. DOBSON.

The Cupboard Papers. By FIN-BEC.

Original Plays by W. S. GILBERT. FIRST SERIES. Containing: The Wicked World — Pygmalion and Galatea— Charity — The Princess— The Palace of Truth—Trial by Jury.

Original Plays by W. S. GILBERT. SECOND SERIES. Containing: Broken Hearts — Engaged — Sweethearts— Gretchen—Dan'l Druce—Tom Cobb —H.M.S. Pinafore — The Sorcerer —The Pirates of Penzance.

Songs of Irish Wit and Humour. Collected and Edited by A. PERCEVAL GRAVES.

Animals and their Masters. By Sir ARTHUR HELPS.

Social Pressure. By Sir A. HELPS.

Curiosities of Criticism. By HENRY J. JENNINGS.

The Autocrat of the Breakfast-Table. By OLIVER WENDELL HOLMES. Illustrated by J. GORDON THOMSON.

Pencil and Palette. By ROBERT KEMPT.

Little Essays: Sketches and Characters. By CHAS. LAMB. Selected from his Letters by PERCY FITZGERALD.

Clerical Anecdotes. By JACOB LARWOOD.

Forensic Anecdotes; or, Humour and Curiosities of the Law and Men of Law. By JACOB LARWOOD.

Theatrical Anecdotes. By JACOB LARWOOD.

Carols of Cockayne. By HENRY S. LEIGH.

Jeux d'Esprit. Edited by HENRY S. LEIGH.

True History of Joshua Davidson. By E. LYNN LINTON.

Witch Stories. By E. LYNN LINTON.

Ourselves: Essays on Women. By E. LYNN LINTON.

Pastimes and Players. By ROBERT MACGREGOR.

The New Paul and Virginia. By W. H. MALLOCK.

The New Republic. By W. H. MALLOCK.

Puck on Pegasus. By H. CHOLMONDELEY-PENNELL.

MAYFAIR LIBRARY, *continued—*

Pegasus Re-Saddled. By H. CHOLMONDELEY-PENNELL. Illustrated by GEORGE DU MAURIER.

Muses of Mayfair. Edited by H. CHOLMONDELEY-PENNELL.

Thoreau: His Life and Aims. By H. A. PAGE.

Puniana. By the Hon. HUGH ROWLEY.

More Puniana. By the Hon. HUGH ROWLEY.

The Philosophy of Handwriting. By DON FELIX DE SALAMANCA.

By Stream and Sea. By WILLIAM SENIOR.

Old Stories Re-told. By WALTER THORNBURY.

Leaves from a Naturalist's Note-Book. By Dr. ANDREW WILSON.

Medicine, Family.—One Thousand Medical Maxims and Surgical Hints, for Infancy, Adult Life, Middle Age, and Old Age. By N. E. DAVIES, L.R.C.P. Lond. Cr. Svo, 1s.; cl., 1s. 6d.

Merry Circle (The): A Book of New Intellectual Games and Amusements. By CLARA BELLEW. With numerous Illustrations. Crown Svo, cloth extra, 4s. 6d.

Mexican Mustang (On a). Through Texas, from the Gulf to the Rio Grande. A New Book of American Humour. By ALEX. E. SWEET and J. ARMOY KNOX, Editors of "Texas Siftings." 265 Illusts. Cr. 8vo, cloth extra, 7s. 6d.

Middlemass (Jean), Novels by: Touch and Go. Crown 8vo, cloth extra, 3s. 6d.; post 8vo, illust. bds., 2s.
Mr. Dorillion. Post 8vo, illust. bds., 2s.

Miller. — Physiology for the Young; or, The House of Life: Human Physiology, with its application to the Preservation of Health. For use in Classes and Popular Reading. With numerous Illustrations. By Mrs. F. FENWICK MILLER. Small 8vo, cloth limp, 2s. 6d.

Milton (J. L), Works by: The Hygiene of the Skin. A Concise Set of Rules for the Management of the Skin; with Directions for Diet, Wines, Soaps, Baths, &c. Small Svo, 1s.; cloth extra, 1s. 6d.

The Bath in Diseases of the Skin. Small Svo, 1s.; cloth extra, 1s. 6d.

The Laws of Life, and their Relation to Diseases of the Skin. Small Svo, 1s.; cloth extra, 1s. 6d

Moncrieff. — The Abdication; or, Time Tries All. An Historical Drama. By W. D. SCOTT-MONCRIEFF. With Seven Etchings by JOHN PETTIE, R.A., W. Q. ORCHARDSON, R.A., J. MACWHIRTER, A.R.A., COLIN HUNTER, R. MACBETH, and TOM GRAHAM. Large 4to, bound in buckram, 21s.

Murray (D. Christie), Novels by. Crown 8vo, cloth extra, 3s. 6d. each; post 8vo, illustrated boards, 2s. each.
A Life's Atonement.
A Model Father.
Joseph's Coat.
Coals of Fire.
By the Gate of the Sea.

Crown 8vo, cloth extra, 3s. 6d. each.
Val Strange: A Story of the Primrose Way.
Hearts.
The Way of the World.
A Bit of Human Nature. [*Shortly.*

North Italian Folk. By Mrs. COMYNS CARR. Illust. by RANDOLPH CALDECOTT. Square 8vo, cloth extra, 7s. 6d.

Number Nip (Stories about), the Spirit of the Giant Mountains. Retold for Children by WALTER GRAHAME. With Illustrations by J. MOYR SMITH. Post 8vo, cloth extra, 5s.

Nursery Hints: A Mother's Guide in Health and Disease. By N. E. DAVIES, L.R.C.P. Crown 8vo, 1s.; cloth, 1s. 6d.

Oliphant. — Whiteladies: A Novel. With Illustrations by ARTHUR HOPKINS and HENRY WOODS. Crown 8vo, cloth extra, 3s. 6d.; post 8vo, illustrated boards, 2s.

O Connor.—Lord Beaconsfield A Biography. By T. P. O'CONNOR, M.P. Sixth Edition, with a New Preface, bringing the work down to the Death of Lord Beaconsfield. Crown 8vo, cloth extra, 7s. 6d.

O'Reilly.—Phœbe's Fortunes: A Novel. With Illustrations by HENRY TUCK. Post 8vo, illustrated boards, 2s.

O'Shaughnessy (Arth.), Works by:
Songs of a Worker. Fcap. 8vo, cloth extra, 7s. 6d.
Music and Moonlight. Fcap. 8vo, cloth extra, 7s. 6d.
Lays of France. Crown 8vo, cloth extra, 10s. 6d.

Ouida, Novels by. Crown 8vo, cloth extra, 5s. each; post 8vo, illustrated boards, 2s. each.

Held in Bondage.	A Dog of Flanders.
Strathmore.	Pascarel.
Chandos.	Signa.
Under Two Flags.	In a Winter City
Cecil Castle-	Ariadne.
maine's Gage.	Friendship.
Idalia.	Moths.
Tricotrin.	Pipistrello.
Puck.	A Village Com-
Folle Farine.	mune.
Two Little Wooden	Bimbi.
Shoes.	In Maremma

Wanda: A Novel. Crown 8vo, cloth extra, 5s.
Frescoes: Dramatic Sketches. Crown 8vo, cloth extra, 5s.
Bimbi: PRESENTATION EDITION. Sq. 8vo, cloth gilt, cinnamon edges, 7s. 6d.
Princess Napraxine. New and Cheaper Edition. Crown 8vo, cloth extra, 5s. [*Shortly.*

Wisdom, Wit, and Pathos. Selected from the Works of OUIDA by F. SYDNEY MORRIS. Small crown 8vo, cloth extra, 5s.

Page (H. A.), Works by:
Thoreau: His Life and Aims: A Study. With a Portrait. Post 8vo, cloth limp, 2s. 6d.
Lights on the Way: Some Tales within a Tale. By the late J. H. ALEXANDER, B.A. Edited by H. A. PAGE. Crown 8vo, cloth extra, 6s.

Pascal's Provincial Letters. A New Translation, with Historical Introduction and Notes, by T. M'CRIE, D.D. Post 8vo, cloth limp, 2s.

Patient's (The) Vade Mecum: How to get most Benefit from Medical Advice. By WILLIAM KNIGHT, M.R.C.S., and EDWARD KNIGHT, L.R.C.P. Crown 8vo, 1s.; cloth, 1s. 6d.

Paul Ferroll:
Post 8vo, illustrated boards, 2s. each.
Paul Ferroll: A Novel.
Why Paul Ferroll Killed his Wife.

Paul.—Gentle and Simple. By MARGARET AGNES PAUL. With a Frontispiece by HELEN PATERSON. Cr. 8vo, cloth extra, 3s. 6d.; post 8vo, illustrated boards, 2s.

Payn (James), Novels by.
Crown 8vo, cloth extra, 3s. 6d. each;
post 8vo, illustrated boards, 2s. each.
Lost Sir Massingberd.
The Best of Husbands.
Walter's Word.
Halves. | Fallen Fortunes.
What He Cost Her.
Less Black than we're Painted.
By Proxy. | High Spirits.
Under One Roof. | Carlyon's Year.
A Confidential Agent.
Some Private Views.
A Grape from a Thorn.
For Cash Only | From Exile.

Post 8vo, illustrated boards, 2s. each.
A Perfect Treasure.
Bentinck's Tutor.
Murphy's Master.
A County Family. | At Her Mercy.
A Woman's Vengeance.
Cecil's Tryst.
The Clyffards of Clyffe.
The Family Scapegrace
The Foster Brothers. | Found Dead.
Gwendoline's Harvest.
Humorous Stories.
Like Father, Like Son.
A Marine Residence.
Married Beneath Him.
Mirk Abbey.
Not Wooed, but Won.
Two Hundred Pounds Reward.

Kit: A Memory. Crown 8vo, cloth
extra, 3s. 6d.

The Canon's Ward. With a Steel-
plate Portrait of the Author. Crown
8vo, cloth extra, 3s. 6d.

In Peril and Privation: A Book for
Boys.   With numerous Illustra-
tions. Crown 8vo, cloth extra, 6s.
[In preparation.

Pennell (H. Cholmondeley),
Works by: Post 8vo, cloth limp,
2s. 6d. each.

Puck on Pegasus. With Illustrations.

The Muses of Mayfair. Vers de
Société, Selected and Edited by H.
C. Pennell.

Pegasus Re-Saddled. With Ten full-
page Illusts. by G. Du Maurier.

Phelps.—Beyond the Gates.
By Elizabeth Stuart Phelps,
Author of "The Gates Ajar." Crown
8vo, cloth extra, 2s. 6d.

Pirkis.—Trooping with Crows:
A Story. By Catherine Pirkis. Fcap.
8vo, picture cover, 1s.

Planche (J. R.), Works by:
The Cyclopædia of Costume; or,
A Dictionary of Dress—Regal, Ec-
clesiastical, Civil, and Military—from
the Earliest Period in England to the
Reign of George the Third. Including Notices of Contemporaneous
Fashions on the Continent, and a
General History of the Costumes of
the Principal Countries of Europe.
Two Vols., demy 4to, half morocco
profusely Illustrated with Coloured
and Plain Plates and Woodcuts,
£7 7s. The Vols. may also be had
separately (each complete in itself)
at £3 13s. 6d. each: Vol. I. The
Dictionary. Vol. II. A General
History of Costume in Europe.
The Pursuivant of Arms; or, Her-
aldry Founded upon Facts. With
Coloured Frontispiece and 200 Illus-
trations. Cr. 8vo, cloth extra, 7s. 6d.
Songs and Poems, from 1819 to 1879.
Edited, with an Introduction, by his
Daughter, Mrs. Mackarness. Crown
8vo, cloth extra, 6s.

Play-time: Sayings and Doings
of Baby-land. By Edward Stanford.
Large 4to, handsomely printed in
Colours, 5s.

Plutarch's Lives of Illustrious
Men. Translated from the Greek,
with Notes Critical and Historical, and
a Life of Plutarch, by John and
William Langhorne. Two Vols.,
8vo, cloth extra, with Portraits, 10s. 6d.

Poe (Edgar Allan):—
The Choice Works, in Prose and
Poetry, of Edgar Allan Poe. With
an Introductory Essay by Charles
Baudelaire, Portrait and Fac-
similes. Crown 8vo, cl. extra, 7s. 6d.
The Mystery of Marie Roget, and
other Stories. Post 8vo, illust. bds. 2s.

Pope's Poetical Works. Complete in One Vol. Post 8vo, cl. limp, 2s.

Power.—Philistia: A Novel. By
Cecil Power. Three Vols., crown
8vo.

Price (E. C.), Novels by:
Valentina: A Sketch. With a Fron-
tispiece by Hal Ludlow. Cr. 8vo,
cl. ex., 3s. 6d.; post 8vo, illust. bds., 2s.
The Foreigners. Cr. 8vo, cl. ex., 3s. 6d.
Mrs. Lancaster's Rival. Crown 8vo,
cloth extra, 3s. 6d.
Gerald. Three Vols., crown 8vo.

Proctor (Richd. A.), Works by:
Flowers of the Sky. With 55 Illusts. Small crown 8vo, cloth extra, 4s. 6d.

Easy Star Lessons. With Star Maps for Every Night in the Year, Drawings of the Constellations, &c. Crown 8vo, cloth extra, 6s.

Familiar Science Studies. Crown 8vo, cloth extra, 7s. 6d.

Rough Ways made Smooth: A Series of Familiar Essays on Scientific Subjects. Cr. 8vo, cloth extra, 6s.

Our Place among Infinities: A Series of Essays contrasting our Little Abode in Space and Time with the Infinities Around us. Crown 8vo, cloth extra, 6s.

The Expanse of Heaven: A Series of Essays on the Wonders of the Firmament. Cr. 8vo, cloth extra, 6s.

Saturn and Its System. New and Revised Edition, with 13 Steel Plates. Demy 8vo, cloth extra, 10s. 6d.

The Great Pyramid: Observatory, Tomb, and Temple. With Illustrations. Crown 8vo, cloth extra, 6s.

Mysteries of Time and Space. With Illusts. Cr. 8vo, cloth extra, 7s. 6d.

The Universe of Suns, and other Science Gleanings. With numerous Illusts. Cr. 8vo, cloth extra, 7s. 6d.

Wages and Wants of Science Workers. Crown 8vo, 1s. 6d.

Pyrotechnist's Treasury (The); or, Complete Art of Making Fireworks. By THOMAS KENTISH. With numerous Illustrations. Cr. 8vo, cl. extra, 4s. 6d.

Rabelais' Works. Faithfully Translated from the French, with variorum Notes, and numerous characteristic Illustrations by GUSTAVE DORÉ. Crown 8vo, cloth extra, 7s. 6d.

Rambosson.—Popular Astronomy. By J. RAMBOSSON, Laureate of the Institute of France. Translated by C. B. PITMAN. Crown 8vo, cloth gilt, with numerous Illustrations, and a beautifully executed Chart of Spectra, 7s. 6d.

Reader's Handbook (The) of Allusions, References, Plots, and Stories. By the Rev. Dr. BREWER. Fourth Edition, revised throughout, with a New Appendix, containing a COMPLETE ENGLISH BIBLIOGRAPHY. Cr. 8vo, 1,400 pages, cloth extra, 7s. 6d.

Richardson. — A Ministry of Health, and other Papers. By BENJAMIN WARD RICHARDSON, M.D., &c. Crown 8vo, cloth extra, 6s.

Reade (Charles, D.C.L.), Novels by. Post 8vo, illust., bds., 2s. each; or cr. 8vo, cl. ex., illust..3s. 6d. each.
Peg Woffington. Illustrated by S. L. FILDES, A.R.A.
Christie Johnstone. Illustrated by WILLIAM SMALL.
It is Never Too Late to Mend. Illustrated by G. J. PINWELL.
The Course of True Love Never did run Smooth. Illustrated by HELEN PATERSON.
The Autobiography of a Thief; Jack of all Trades; and James Lambert. Illustrated by MATT STRETCH.
Love me Little, Love me Long. Illustrated by M. ELLEN EDWARDS.
The Double Marriage. Illust. by Sir JOHN GILBERT, R.A., and C. KEENE.
The Cloister and the Hearth. Illustrated by CHARLES KEENE.
Hard Cash. Illust. by F. W. LAWSON.
Griffith Gaunt. Illustrated by S. L. FILDES, A.R.A., and WM. SMALL.
Foul Play. Illust. by DU MAURIER.
Put Yourself in His Place. Illustrated by ROBERT BARNES.
A Terrible Temptation. Illustrated by EDW. HUGHES and A. W. COOPER.
The Wandering Heir. Illustrated by H. PATERSON, S. L. FILDES, A.R.A., C. GREEN, and H WOODS, A.R.A.
A Simpleton. Illustrated by KATE CRAUFORD.
A Woman-Hater. Illustrated by THOS. COULDERY.
Readiana. With a Steel-plate Portrait of CHARLES READE.

Crown 8vo, cloth extra, 3s. 6d. each.
Singleheart and Doubleface: A Matter-of-fact Romance. Illustrated by P. MACNAB.
Good Stories of Men and other Animals. Illustrated by E. A. ABBEY, PERCY MACQUOID, and JOSEPH NASH.
The Jilt, and other Stories. Illustrated by JOSEPH NASH.

Riddell (Mrs. J. H.), Novels by:
Crown 8vo, cloth extra, 3s. 6d. each; post 8vo, illustrated boards, 2s. each.
Her Mother's Darling.
The Prince of Wales's Garden Party.

Weird Stories. Crown 8vo, cloth extra, 3s. 6d.

Rimmer (Alfred), Works by:
Our Old Country Towns. With over 50 Illusts. Sq. 8vo, cloth gilt, 10s. 6d.
Rambles Round Eton and Harrow. 50 Illusts. Sq. 8vo, cloth gilt, 10s. 6d.
About England with Dickens. With 58 Illusts. by ALFRED RIMMER and C. A. VANDERHOOF. Sq. 8vo, cl. gilt, 10s. 6d.

Robinson (F. W.), Novels by:

Women are Strange. Cr. 8vo, cloth extra, 3s. 6d.; post 8vo, illust. bds., 2s.

The Hands of Justice. Crown 8vo, cloth extra, 3s. 6d.

Robinson (Phil), Works by:

The Poets' Birds. Crown 8vo, cloth extra, 7s. 6d.

The Poets' Beasts. Crown 8vo, cloth extra, 7s. 6d. [*In preparation.*

Robinson Crusoe: A beautiful reproduction of Major's Edition, with 37 Woodcuts and Two Steel Plates by GEORGE CRUIKSHANK, choicely printed. Crown 8vo, cloth extra, 7s. 6d. A few Large-Paper copies, printed on hand-made paper, with India proofs of the Illustrations, price 36s.

Rochefoucauld's Maxims and Moral Reflections. With Notes, and an Introductory Essay by SAINTE-BEUVE. Post 8vo, cloth limp, 2s.

Roll of Battle Abbey, The; or, A List of the Principal Warriors who came over from Normandy with William the Conqueror, and Settled in this Country, A.D. 1066-7. With the principal Arms emblazoned in Gold and Colours. Handsomely printed, 5s.

Rowley (Hon. Hugh), Works by:
Post 8vo, cloth limp, 2s. 6d. each.

Puniana: Riddles and Jokes. With numerous Illustrations.

More Puniana. Profusely Illustrated.

Russell (W. Clark), Works by:

Round the Galley-Fire. Crown 8vo, cloth extra, 6s.

On the Fo'k'sle Head: A Collection of Yarns and Sea Descriptions. Crown 8vo, cloth extra, 6s.

Sala.—Gaslight and Daylight. By GEORGE AUGUSTUS SALA. Post 8vo, illustrated boards, 2s.

Sanson.—Seven Generations of Executioners: Memoirs of the Sanson Family (1688 to 1847). Edited by HENRY SANSON. Cr. 8vo, cl. ex. 3s. 6d.

Saunders (John), Novels by:
Crown 8vo, cloth extra, 3s. 6d. each; post 8vo, illustrated boards, 2s. each.

Bound to the Wheel.
One Against the World.
Guy Waterman.
The Lion in the Path.
The Two Dreamers.

Saunders (Katharine), Novels by:
Crown 8vo, cloth extra, 3s. 6d. each.

Joan Merryweather.
Margaret and Elizabeth.
Gideon's Rock.
The High Mills.

Heart Salvage, by Sea and Land. Three Vols., crown 8vo.

Science Gossip: An Illustrated Medium of Interchange for Students and Lovers of Nature. Edited by J. E. TAYLOR, F.L.S., &c. Devoted to Geology, Botany, Physiology, Chemistry, Zoology, Microscopy, Telescopy, Physiography, &c. Price 4d. Monthly; or 5s. per year, post free. Each Number contains a Coloured Plate and numerous Woodcuts. Vols. I. to XIV. may be had at 7s. 6d. each; and Vols. XV. to XIX. (1883), at 5s. each. Cases for Binding, 1s. 6d. each.

Scott's (Sir Walter) Marmion. An entirely New Edition of this famous and popular Poem, with over 100 new Illustrations by leading Artists. Elegantly and appropriately bound, small 4to, cloth extra, 16s.

[The immediate success of "The Lady of the Lake," published in 1882, has encouraged Messrs. CHATTO and WINDUS to bring out a Companion Edition of this not less popular and famous poem. Produced in the same form, and with the same careful and elaborate style of illustration, regardless of cost, Mr. Anthony's skilful supervision is sufficient guarantee that the work is elegant and tasteful as well as correct.]

"Secret Out" Series, The:
Crown 8vo, cloth extra, profusely Illustrated, 4s. 6d. each.

The Secret Out: One Thousand Tricks with Cards, and other Recreations; with Entertaining Experiments in Drawing-room or "White Magic." By W. H. CREMER. 300 Engravings.

The Pyrotechnist's Treasury; or, Complete Art of Making Fireworks. By THOMAS KENTISH. With numerous Illustrations.

The Art of Amusing: A Collection of Graceful Arts, Games, Tricks, Puzzles, and Charades. By FRANK BELLEW. With 300 Illustrations.

Hanky-Panky: Very Easy Tricks, Very Difficult Tricks, White Magic, Sleight of Hand. Edited by W. H. CREMER. With 200 Illustrations.

"Secret Out" Series, *continued—*

The Merry Circle: A Book of New Intellectual Games and Amusements. By Clara Bellew. With many Illustrations.

Magician's Own Book: Performances with Cups and Balls, Eggs, Hats, Handkerchiefs, &c. All from actual Experience. Edited by W. H. Cremer. 200 Illustrations.

Magic No Mystery: Tricks with Cards, Dice, Balls, &c., with fully descriptive Directions; the Art of Secret Writing; Training of Performing Animals, &c. With Coloured Frontispiece and many Illustrations.

Senior (William), Works by :

Travel and Trout in the Antipodes. Crown 8vo, cloth extra, 6s.

By Stream and Sea. Post 8vo, cloth limp, 2s. 6d.

Seven Sagas (The) of Prehistoric Man. By James H. Stoddart, Author of "The Village Life." Crown 8vo, cloth extra, 6s.

Shakespeare :

The First Folio Shakespeare.—Mr. William Shakespeare's Comedies, Histories, and Tragedies. Published according to the true Originall Copies. London, Printed by Isaac Iaggard and Ed. Blount. 1623.—A Reproduction of the extremely rare original, in reduced facsimile, by a photographic process—ensuring the strictest accuracy in every detail. Small 8vo, half-Roxburghe, 7s. 6d.

The Lansdowne Shakespeare. Beautifully printed in red and black, in small but very clear type. With engraved facsimile of Droeshout's Portrait. Post 8vo, cloth extra, 7s. 6d.

Shakespeare for Children: Tales from Shakespeare. By Charles and Mary Lamb. With numerous Illustrations, coloured and plain, by J. Moyr Smith. Crown 4to, cloth gilt, 6s.

The Handbook of Shakespeare Music. Being an Account of 350 Pieces of Music, set to Words taken from the Plays and Poems of Shakespeare, the compositions ranging from the Elizabethan Age to the Present Time. By Alfred Roffe. 4to, half-Roxburghe, 7s.

A Study of Shakespeare. By Algernon Charles Swinburne. Crown 8vo, cloth extra, 8s.

Shelley's Complete Works, in Four Vols., post 8vo, cloth limp, 8s.; or separately, 2s. each. Vol. I. contains his Early Poems, Queen Mab, &c., with an Introduction by Leigh Hunt; Vol. II., his Later Poems, Laon and Cythna, &c.; Vol. III., Posthumous Poems, the Shelley Papers, &c.; Vol. IV., his Prose Works, including A Refutation of Deism, Zastrozzi, St. Irvyne, &c.

Sheridan :—

Sheridan's Complete Works, with Life and Anecdotes. Including his Dramatic Writings, printed from the Original Editions, his Works in Prose and Poetry, Translations, Speeches, Jokes, Puns, &c. With a Collection of Sheridaniana. Crown 8vo, cloth extra, gilt, with 10 full-page Tinted Illustrations, 7s. 6d.

Sheridan's Comedies: The Rivals, and The School for Scandal. Edited, with an Introduction and Notes to each Play, and a Biographical Sketch of Sheridan, by Brander Matthews. With Decorative Vignettes and 10 full-page Illustrations. Demy 8vo, cl. bds., 12s. 6d.

Short Sayings of Great Men. With Historical and Explanatory Notes by Samuel A. Bent, M.A. Demy 8vo, cloth extra, 7s. 6d.

Sidney's (Sir Philip) Complete Poetical Works, including all those in "Arcadia." With Portrait, Memorial-Introduction, Essay on the Poetry of Sidney, and Notes, by the Rev. A. B. Grosart, D.D. Three Vols., crown 8vo, cloth boards, 18s.

Signboards : Their History. With Anecdotes of Famous Taverns and Remarkable Characters. By Jacob Larwood and John Camden Hotten. Crown 8vo, cloth extra, with 100 Illustrations, 7s. 6d.

Sims (G. R.)—How the Poor Live. With 60 Illustrations by Fred. Barnard. Large 4to, 1s.

Sketchley.—A Match in the Dark. By Arthur Sketchley. Post 8vo, illustrated boards, 2s.

Slang Dictionary, The: Etymological, Historical, and Anecdotal. Crown 8vo, cloth extra, gilt, 6s. 6d.

Smith (J. Moyr), Works by :

The Prince of Argolis: A Story of the Old Greek Fairy Time. By J. Moyr Smith. Small 8vo, cloth extra, with 130 Illustrations, 3s. 6d.

Smith's (J. Moyr) Works, *continued*—
Tales of Old Thule. Collected and Illustrated by J. Moyr Smith. Cr. 8vo, cloth gilt, profusely Illust., 6s.
The Wooing of the Water Witch: A Northern Oddity. By Evan Daldorne. Illustrated by J. Moyr Smith. Small 8vo, cloth extra, 6s.

Spalding.—Elizabethan Demonology: An Essay in Illustration of the Belief in the Existence of Devils, and the Powers possessed by Them. By T. Alfred Spalding, LL.B. Crown 8vo, cloth extra, 5s.

Speight. — The Mysteries of Heron Dyke. By T. W. Speight. With a Frontispiece by M. Ellen Edwards. Crown 8vo, cloth extra, 3s. 6d. ; post 8vo, illustrated boards, 2s.

Spenser for Children. By M. H. Towry. With Illustrations by Walter J. Morgan. Crown 4to, with Coloured Illustrations, cloth gilt, 6s.

Staunton.—Laws and Practice of Chess; Together with an Analysis of the Openings, and a Treatise on End Games. By Howard Staunton. Edited by Robert B. Wormald. New Edition, small cr. 8vo, cloth extra, 5s.

Sterndale.—The Afghan Knife: A Novel. By Robert Armitage Sterndale. Cr. 8vo, cloth extra, 3s. 6d.; post 8vo, illustrated boards, 2s.

Stevenson (R. Louis), Works by:
Travels with a Donkey In the Cevennes. Frontispiece by Walter Crane. Post 8vo, cloth limp, 2s. 6d.
An Inland Voyage. With Front. by W. Crane. Post 8vo, cl. lp., 2s. 6d.
Virginibus Puerisque, and other Papers. Crown 8vo, cloth extra, 6s.
Familiar Studies of Men and Books. Crown 8vo, cloth extra, 6s.
New Arabian Nights. Crown 8vo, cl. extra, 6s.; post 8vo, illust. bds., 2s.
The Silverado Squatters. With Frontispiece. Cr. 8vo, cloth extra, 6s.
Prince Otto: A Romance. Crown 8vo, cloth extra, 6s. [*In preparation.*

St. John.—A Levantine Family. By Bayle St. John. Post 8vo, illustrated boards, 2s.

Stoddard.—Summer Cruising In the South Seas. By Charles Warren Stoddard. Illust. by Wallis Mackay. Crown 8vo, cl. extra, 3s. 6d.

St. Pierre.—Paul and Virginia, and The Indian Cottage. By Bernardin St. Pierre. Edited, with Life, by Rev. E. Clarke. Post 8vo, cl. lp., 2s.

Stories from Foreign Novelists. With Notices of their Lives and Writings. By Helen and Alice Zimmern; and a Frontispiece. Crown 8vo cloth extra, 3s. 6d.

Strutt's Sports and Pastimes of the People of England; including the Rural and Domestic Recreations, May Games, Mummeries, Shows, Processions, Pageants, and Pompous Spectacles, from the Earliest Period to the Present Time. With 140 Illustrations. Edited by William Hone. Crown 8vo, cloth extra, 7s. 6d.

Suburban Homes (The) of London: A Residential Guide to Favourite London Localities, their Society, Celebrities, and Associations. With Notes on their Rental, Rates, and House Accommodation. With Map of Suburban London. Cr. 8vo, cl. ex., 7s. 6d.

Swift's Choice Works, in Prose and Verse. With Memoir, Portrait, and Facsimiles of the Maps in the Original Edition of "Gulliver's Travels." Cr. 8vo, cloth extra, 7s. 6d.

Swinburne (Algernon C.), Works by:
The Queen Mother and Rosamond. Fcap. 8vo, 5s.
Atalanta In Calydon. Crown 8vo, 6s.
Chastelard. A Tragedy. Cr. 8vo, 7s.
Poems and Ballads. First Series. Fcap. 8vo, 9s. Also in crown 8vo, at same price.
Poems and Ballads. Second Series. Fcap. 8vo, 9s. Cr. 8vo, same price.
Notes on Poems and Reviews. 8vo 1s.
William Blake: A Critical Essay. With Facsimile Paintings. Demy 8vo, 16s.
Songs before Sunrise. Cr. 8vo, 10s. 6d.
Bothwell: A Tragedy. Cr. 8vo, 12s. 6d.
George Chapman: An Essay. Crown 8vo, 7s.
Songs of Two Nations. Cr. 8vo, 6s.
Essays and Studies. Crown 8vo, 12s.
Erechtheus: A Tragedy. Cr. 8vo, 6s.
Note of an English Republican on the Muscovite Crusade. 8vo, 1s.
A Note on Charlotte Bronte. Crown 8vo, 6s.
A Study of Shakespeare. Cr. 8vo, 8s.
Songs of the Springtides. Crown 8vo, 6s.
Studies In Song. Crown 8vo, 7s.
Mary Stuart: A Tragedy. Cr. 8vo. 8s.
Tristram of Lyonesse, and other Poems. Crown 8vo, 9s.
A Century of Roundels. Small 4to, cloth extra, 8s.
A Midsummer Holiday, and other Poems. Crown 8vo, cloth extra, 7s.

Symonds.—Wine, Women and Song: Mediæval Latin Students' Songs. Now first translated into English Verse, with an Essay by J. ADDINGTON SYMONDS. Small 8vo, parchment, **6s.**

Syntax's (Dr.) Three Tours: In Search of the Picturesque, in Search of Consolation, and in Search of a Wife. With the whole of ROWLANDSON'S droll page Illustrations in Colours and a Life of the Author by J. C. HOTTEN. Medium 8vo, cloth extra, **7s. 6d.**

Taine's History of English Literature. Translated by HENRY VAN LAUN. Four Vols., small 8vo, cloth boards, **30s.**—POPULAR EDITION, Two Vols., crown 8vo, cloth extra, **15s.**

Taylor (Dr. J. E., F.L.S.), Works by:
The Sagacity and Morality of Plants: A Sketch of the Life and Conduct of the Vegetable Kingdom. With Coloured Frontispiece and 100 Illusts. Crown 8vo, cl. extra, **7s. 6d.**
Our Common British Fossils, and Where to Find Them. With numerous Illustrations. Crown 8vo, cloth extra, **7s. 6d.** [*In the press.*

Taylor's (Bayard) Diversions of the Echo Club: Burlesques of Modern Writers. Post 8vo, cl. limp, **2s.**

Taylor's (Tom) Historical Dramas: "Clancarty," "Jeanne Darc," "'Twixt Axe and Crown," "The Fool's Revenge," "Arkwright's Wife," "Anne Boleyn," "Plot and Passion." One Vol., crown 8vo, cloth extra, **7s. 6d.**
. The Plays may also be had separately, at **1s.** each.

Tennyson (Lord): A Biographical Sketch. By H. J. JENNINGS. With a Photograph-Portrait. Crown 8vo, cloth extra, **6s.**

Thackerayana: Notes and Anecdotes. Illustrated by Hundreds of Sketches by WILLIAM MAKEPEACE THACKERAY, depicting Humorous Incidents in his School-life, and Favourite Characters in the books of his every-day reading. With Coloured Frontispiece. Cr. 8vo, cl. extra, **7s. 6d.**

Thomas (Bertha), Novels by.
Crown 8vo, cloth extra, **3s. 6d.** each; post 8vo, illustrated boards, **2s.** each.
Cressida.
Proud Maisie.
The Violin-Player.

Thomas (M.).—A Fight for Life: A Novel. By W. MOY THOMAS. Post 8vo, illustrated boards, **2s.**

Thomson's Seasons and Castle of Indolence. With a Biographical and Critical Introduction by ALLAN CUNNINGHAM, and over 50 fine Illustrations on Steel and Wood. Crown 8vo, cloth extra, gilt edges, **7s. 6d.**

Thornbury (Walter), Works by
Haunted London. Edited by EDWARD WALFORD, M.A. With Illustrations by F. W. FAIRHOLT, F.S.A. Crown 8vo, cloth extra, **7s. 6d.**
The Life and Correspondence of J. M. W. Turner. Founded upon Letters and Papers furnished by his Friends and fellow Academicians. With numerous Illusts. in Colours, facsimiled from Turner's Original Drawings. Cr. 8vo, cl. extra, **7s. 6d.**
Old Stories Re-told. Post 8vo, cloth limp, **2s. 6d.**
Tales for the Marines. Post 8vo, illustrated boards, **2s.**

Timbs (John), Works by:
The History of Clubs and Club Life in London. With Anecdotes of its Famous Coffee-houses, Hostelries, and Taverns. With numerous Illustrations. Cr. 8vo, cloth extra, **7s. 6d.**
English Eccentrics and Eccentricities: Stories of Wealth and Fashion, Delusions, Impostures, and Fanatic Missions, Strange Sights and Sporting Scenes, Eccentric Artists, Theatrical Folks, Men of Letters, &c. With nearly 50 Illusts. Crown 8vo, cloth extra, **7s. 6d.**

Torrens. — The Marquess Wellesley, Architect of Empire. An Historic Portrait. By W. M. TORRENS, M.P. Demy 8vo, cloth extra, **14s.**

Trollope (Anthony), Novels by:
Crown 8vo, cloth extra, **3s. 6d.** each post 8vo, illustrated boards, **2s.** each.
The Way We Live Now.
The American Senator.
Kept in the Dark.
Frau Frohmann.
Marion Fay.

Crown 8vo, cloth extra, **3s. 6d.** each.
Mr. Scarborough's Family.
The Land-Leaguers.

Trollope (Frances E.), Novels by
Like Ships upon the Sea. Crown 8vo, cloth extra, **3s. 6d.**; post 8vo, illustrated boards, **2s.**
Mabel's Progress. Crown 8vo, cloth extra, **3s. 6d.**
Anne Furness. Cr. 8vo, cl. ex., **3s. 6d.**

Trollope (T. A.).—Diamond Cut Diamond, and other Stories. By T. ADOLPHUS TROLLOPE. Cr. 8vo, cl. ex.. 3s. 6d.; post 8vo, illust. boards, 2s.

Trowbridge.—Farnell's Folly: A Novel. By J. T. TROWBRIDGE. Two Vols., crown 8vo, 12s.

Tytler (Sarah), Novels by:
Crown 8vo, cloth extra, 3s. 6d. each; post 8vo, illustrated boards, 2s. each.
What She Came Through.
The Bride's Pass.

Saint Mungo's City. Crown 8vo, cloth extra, 3s. 6d.
Beauty and the Beast. Three Vols., crown 8vo, 31s. 6d.

Tytler (C. C. Fraser-). — Mistress Judith: A Novel. By C. C. FRASER-TYTLER. Cr.8vo, cl.ex., 3s. 6d.

Van Laun.—History of French Literature. By HENRY VAN LAUN. Complete in Three Vols., demy 8vo, cloth boards, 7s. 6d. each.

Villari. — A Double Bond: A Story. By LINDA VILLARI. Fcap. 8vo, picture cover, 1s.

Walcott.— Church Work and Life in English Minsters; and the English Student's Monasticon. By the Rev. MACKENZIE E. C. WALCOTT, B.D. Two Vols., crown 8vo, cloth extra, with Map and Ground-Plans, 14s.

Walford (Edw., M.A.),Works by:
The County Families of the United Kingdom. Containing Notices of the Descent, Birth, Marriage, Education, &c., of more than 12,000 distinguished Heads of Families, their Heirs Apparent or Presumptive, the Offices they hold or have held, their Town and Country Addresses, Clubs, &c. Twenty-fifth Annual Edition, for 1885, cloth, full gilt, 50s.
The Shilling Peerage (1885). Containing an Alphabetical List of the House of Lords, Dates of Creation, Lists of Scotch and Irish Peers, Addresses, &c. 32mo, cloth, 1s. Published annually.
The Shilling Baronetage (1885). Containing an Alphabetical List of the Baronets of the United Kingdom, short Biographical Notices, Dates of Creation, Addresses, &c. 32mo, cloth, 1s. Published annually.
The Shilling Knightage (1885). Containing an Alphabetical List of the Knights of the United Kingdom, short Biographical Notices, Dates of Creation. Addresses, &c. 32mo, cloth, 1s. Published annually.

Walford's (EDW., M.A.) WORKS, *con.*—
The Shilling House of Commons (1885). Containing a List of all the Members of the British Parliament, their Town and Country Addresses, &c. 32mo, cloth, 1s. Published annually.
The Complete Peerage, Baronetage, Knightage, and House of Commons (1885). In One Volume, royal 32mo, cloth extra, gilt edges, 5s. Published annually.
Haunted London. By WALTER THORNBURY. Edited by EDWARD WALFORD, M.A. With Illustrations by F. W. FAIRHOLT, F.S.A. Crown 8vo, cloth extra, 7s. 6d.

Walton and Cotton's Complete Angler; or, The Contemplative Man's Recreation; being a Discourse of Rivers, Fishponds, Fish and Fishing, written by IZAAK WALTON; and Instructions how to Angle for a Trout or Grayling in a clear Stream, by CHARLES COTTON. With Original Memoirs and Notes by Sir HARRIS NICOLAS, and 61 Copperplate Illustrations. Large crown 8vo, cloth antique, 7s. 6d.

Wanderer's Library, The:
Crown 8vo, cloth extra, 3s. 6d. each.
Wanderings in Patagonia; or, Life among the Ostrich Hunters. By JULIUS BEERBOHM. Illustrated.
Camp Notes: Stories of Sport and Adventure in Asia, Africa, and America. By FREDERICK BOYLE.
Savage Life. By FREDERICK BOYLE.
Merrie England in the Olden Time. By GEORGE DANIEL. With Illustrations by ROBT. CRUIKSHANK.
Circus Life and Circus Celebrities. By THOMAS FROST.
The Lives of the Conjurers. By THOMAS FROST.
The Old Showmen and the Old London Fairs. By THOMAS FROST.
Low-Life Deeps. An Account of the Strange Fish to be found there. By JAMES GREENWOOD.
The Wilds of London. By JAMES GREENWOOD.
Tunis: The Land and the People. By the Chevalier de HESSE-WARTEGG. With 22 Illustrations.
The Life and Adventures of a Cheap Jack. By One of the Fraternity. Edited by CHARLES HINDLEY.
The World Behind the Scenes. By PERCY FITZGERALD.
Tavern Anecdotes and Sayings: Including the Origin of Signs, and Reminiscences connected with Taverns, Coffee Houses, Clubs, &c. By CHARLES HINDLEY. With Illusts.

WANDERER'S LIBRARY, THE, *continued—*

The Genial Showman: Life and Adventures of Artemus Ward. By E. P. HINGSTON. With a Frontispiece.

The Story of the London Parks. By JACOB LARWOOD. With Illusts.

London Characters. By HENRY MAYHEW. Illustrated.

Seven Generations of Executioners: Memoirs of the Sanson Family (1688 to 1847). Edited by HENRY SANSON.

Summer Cruising in the South Seas. By C. WARREN STODDARD. Illustrated by WALLIS MACKAY.

Warner.—A Roundabout Journey. By CHARLES DUDLEY WARNER, Author of "My Summer in a Garden." Crown 8vo, cloth extra, 6s.

Warrants, &c. :—

Warrant to Execute Charles I. An exact Facsimile, with the Fifty-nine Signatures, and corresponding Seals. Carefully printed on paper to imitate the Original, 22 in. by 14 in. Price 2s.

Warrant to Execute Mary Queen of Scots. An exact Facsimile, including the Signature of Queen Elizabeth, and a Facsimile of the Great Seal. Beautifully printed on paper to imitate the Original MS. Price 2s.

Magna Charta. An exact Facsimile of the Original Document in the British Museum, printed on fine plate paper, nearly 3 feet long by 2 feet wide, with the Arms and Seals emblazoned in Gold and Colours. Price 5s.

The Roll of Battle Abbey; or, A List of the Principal Warriors who came over from Normandy with William the Conqueror, and Settled in this Country, A.D. 1066-7. With the principal Arms emblazoned in Gold and Colours. Price 5s.

Weather, How to Foretell the, with the Pocket Spectroscope. By F. W. CORY, M.R.C.S. Eng., F.R.Met. Soc., &c. With 10 Illustrations. Crown 8vo, 1s.; cloth, 1s. 6d.

**Westropp.—Handbook of Pottery and Porcelain; or, History of those Arts from the Earliest Period. By HODDER M. WESTROPP. With numerous Illustrations, and a List of Marks. Crown 8vo, cloth limp, 4s. 6d.

Whistler v. Ruskin: Art and Art Critics. By J. A. MACNEILL WHISTLER. 7th Edition, sq. 8vo, 1s.

White's Natural History of Selborne. Edited, with Additions, by THOMAS BROWN, F.L.S. Post 8vo, cloth limp, 2s.

Williams (W. Mattieu, F.R.A.S.), Works by:

Science Notes. See the GENTLEMAN'S MAGAZINE. 1s. Monthly.

Science in Short Chapters. Crown 8vo, cloth extra, 7s. 6d.

A Simple Treatise on Heat. Crown 8vo, cloth limp, with Illusts., 2s. 6d.

The Chemistry of Cookery. Crown 8vo, cloth extra, 6s.   [*In the press.*

Wilson (Dr. Andrew, F.R.S.E.), Works by:

Chapters on Evolution: A Popular History of the Darwinian and Allied Theories of Development. Second Edition. Crown 8vo, cloth extra, with 259 Illustrations, 7s. 6d.

Leaves from a Naturalist's Notebook. Post 8vo, cloth limp, 2s. 6d.

Leisure-Time Studies, chiefly Biological. Third Edition, with a New Preface. Crown 8vo, cloth extra, with Illustrations, 6s.

Winter (J. S.), Stories by: Crown 8vo, cloth extra, 3s. 6d. each. post 8vo, illustrated boards, 2s. each.

Cavalry Life. | Regimental Legends.

Women of the Day: A Biographical Dictionary of Notable Contemporaries. By FRANCES HAYS. Crown 8vo, cloth extra, 5s.

Wood.—Sabina: A Novel. By Lady WOOD. Post 8vo, illust. bds., 2s.

Words, Facts, and Phrases: A Dictionary of Curious, Quaint, and Out-of-the-Way Matters. By ELIEZER EDWARDS. New and cheaper issue, cr. 8vo, cl. ex., 7s. 6d.; half-bound, 9s.

Wright (Thomas), Works by:

Caricature History of the Georges. (The House of Hanover.) With 400 Pictures, Caricatures, Squibs, Broadsides, Window Pictures, &c. Crown 8vo, cloth extra, 7s. 6d.

History of Caricature and of the Grotesque in Art, Literature, Sculpture, and Painting. Profusely Illustrated by F. W. FAIRHOLT, F.S.A. Large post 8vo, cl. ex., 7s. 6d.

Yates (Edmund), Novels by: Post 8vo, illustrated boards, 2s. each.

Castaway. | The Forlorn Hope. Land at Last.

NOVELS BY THE BEST AUTHORS.

WILKIE COLLINS'S NEW NOVEL.

"I Say No." By WILKIE COLLINS. Three Vols., crown 8vo.

Mrs. CASHEL HOEY'S NEW NOVEL

The Lover's Creed. By Mrs. CASHEL HOEY, Author of "The Blossoming of an Aloe," &c. With 12 Illustrations by P. MACNAB. Three Vols., cr. 8vo.

SARAH TYTLER'S NEW NOVEL.

Beauty and the Beast. By SARAH TYTLER, Author of "The Bride's Pass," "Saint Mungo's City," "Citoyenne Jacqueline," &c. Three Vols., cr. 8vo.

NEW NOVELS BY CHAS. GIBBON.

By Mead and Stream. By CHARLES GIBBON, Author of "Robin Gray," "The Golden Shaft," "Queen of the Meadow," &c. Three Vols., cr 8vo.

Found Out. By CHARLES GIBBON. Three Vols., crown 8vo. [*Shortly.*

NEW NOVEL BY CECIL POWER.

Philistia. By CECIL POWER. Three Vols., crown 8vo.

ROBT. BUCHANAN'S NEW NOVEL.

Foxglove Manor. By ROBT. BUCHANAN, Author of "The Shadow of the Sword," "God and the Man," &c. Three Vols., crown 8vo.

NEW NOVEL BY THE AUTHOR OF "VALENTINA."

Gerald. By ELEANOR C. PRICE. Three Vols., crown 8vo.

BASIL'S NEW NOVEL.

"The Wearing of the Green." By BASIL, Author of "Love the Debt," "A Drawn Game," &c. Three Vols., crown 8vo.

NEW NOVEL BY J. T. TROWBRIDGE.

Farnell's Folly. Two Vols., crown 8vo, 12s.

HALL CAINE'S NEW NOVEL.

The Shadow of a Crime. By HALL CAINE. Three Vols., crown 8vo. [*Immediately*

THE PICCADILLY NOVELS.

Popular Stories by the Best Authors. LIBRARY EDITIONS, many Illustrated, crown 8vo, cloth extra, 3s. 6d. each.

BY MRS. ALEXANDER.

Maid, Wife, or Widow?

BY W. BESANT & JAMES RICE.

Ready-Money Mortiboy.
My Little Girl.
The Case of Mr. Lucraft.
This Son of Vulcan.
With Harp and Crown.
The Golden Butterfly.
By Celia's Arbour.
The Monks of Thelema.
'Twas in Trafalgar's Bay.
The Seamy Side.
The Ten Years' Tenant.
The Chaplain of the Fleet.

BY WALTER BESANT.

All Sorts and Conditions of Men.
The Captains' Room.
All in a Garden Fair.
Dorothy Forster.

BY ROBERT BUCHANAN.

A Child of Nature.
God and the Man.
The Shadow of the Sword.
The Martyrdom of Madeline.
Love Me for Ever.
Annan Water.
The New Abelard.
Matt.

BY MRS. H. LOVETT CAMERON.

Deceivers Ever. | Juliet's Guardian.

BY MORTIMER COLLINS.

Sweet Anne Page.
Transmigration
From Midnight to Midnight.

MORTIMER & FRANCES COLLINS.

Blacksmith and Scholar.
The Village Comedy.
You Play me False.

BY WILKIE COLLINS.

Antonina.
Basil.
Hide and Seek.
The Dead Secret.
Queen of Hearts.
My Miscellanies.
Woman in White.
The Moonstone.
Man and Wife.
Poor Miss Finch.
Miss or Mrs. ?
New Magdalen.
The Frozen Deep.
The Law and the Lady.
The Two Destinies
Haunted Hotel.
The Fallen Leaves
Jezebel's Daughter
The Black Robe.
Heart and Science

BY DUTTON COOK.

Paul Foster's Daughter

BY WILLIAM CYPLES.

Hearts of Gold.

BY ALPHONSE DAUDET.

Port Salvation.

BY JAMES DE MILLE.

A Castle in Spain.

Piccadilly Novels, *continued—*

BY J. LEITH DERWENT.
Our Lady of Tears. | Circe's Lovers.

BY M. BETHAM-EDWARDS.
Felicia. | Kitty.

BY MRS. ANNIE EDWARDES.
Archie Lovell.

BY R. E. FRANCILLON.
Olympia. | One by One.
Queen Cophetua. | A Real Queen.

Prefaced by Sir BARTLE FRERE.
Pandurang Hari.

BY EDWARD GARRETT.
The Capel Girls.

BY CHARLES GIBBON.
Robin Gray.
For Lack of Gold.
In Love and War.
What will the World Say?
For the King.
In Honour Bound.
Queen of the Meadow.
In Pastures Green.
The Flower of the Forest.
A Heart's Problem.
The Braes of Yarrow.
The Golden Shaft.
Of High Degree.
Fancy Free.
Loving a Dream.

BY THOMAS HARDY.
Under the Greenwood Tree.

BY JULIAN HAWTHORNE.
Garth.
Ellice Quentin.
Sebastian Strome.
Prince Saroni's Wife.
Dust. | Fortune's Fool.
Beatrix Randolph.
Miss Cadogna.

BY SIR A. HELPS.
Ivan de Biron.

BY MRS. ALFRED HUNT.
Thornicroft's Model.
The Leaden Casket.
Self-Condemned.

BY JEAN INGELOW.
Fated to be Free.

BY HARRIETT JAY.
The Queen of Connaught
The Dark Colleen.

BY HENRY KINGSLEY.
Number Seventeen.
Oakshott Castle.

Piccadilly Novels, *continued—*

BY E. LYNN LINTON.
Patricia Kemball.
Atonement of Leam Dundas.
The World Well Lost.
Under which Lord?
With a Silken Thread.
The Rebel of the Family
"My Love!" | Ione.

BY HENRY W. LUCY.
Gideon Fleyce.

BY JUSTIN McCARTHY, M.P.
The Waterdale Neighbours.
My Enemy's Daughter.
Linley Rochford. | A Fair Saxon.
Dear Lady Disdain.
Miss Misanthrope.
Donna Quixote.
The Comet of a Season.
Maid of Athens.

BY GEORGE MAC DONALD, LL.D
Paul Faber, Surgeon.
Thomas Wingfold, Curate.

BY MRS. MACDONELL.
Quaker Cousins.

BY KATHARINE S. MACQUOID.
Lost Rose. | The Evil Eye.

BY FLORENCE MARRYAT.
Open! Sesame! | Written in Fire.

BY JEAN MIDDLEMASS.
Touch and Go.

BY D. CHRISTIE MURRAY.
Life's Atonement. | Coals of Fire.
Joseph's Coat. | Val Strange.
A Model Father. | Hearts.
By the Gate of the Sea
The Way of the World.
A Bit of Human Nature.

BY MRS. OLIPHANT
Whiteladies.

BY MARGARET A. PAUL.
Gentle and Simple.

BY JAMES PAYN.
Lost Sir Massingberd. | Carlyon's Year.
Best of Husbands | A Confidential Agent.
Fallen Fortunes. | From Exile.
Halves. | A Grape from a Thorn.
Walter's Word. |
What He Cost Her | For Cash Only.
Less Black than We're Painted. | Some Private Views.
By Proxy. | Kit: A Memory.
High Spirits. | The Canon's Ward.
Under One Roof. |

PICCADILLY NOVELS, *continued*—
BY E. C. PRICE.
Valentina. | The Foreigners.
Mrs. Lancaster's Rival.

BY CHARLES READE, D.C.L.
It Is Never Too Late to Mend.
Hard Cash. | Peg Woffington.
Christie Johnstone.
Griffith Gaunt. | Foul Play.
The Double Marriage.
Love Me Little, Love Me Long.
The Cloister and the Hearth.
The Course of True Love.
The Autobiography of a Thief.
Put Yourself in His Place.
A Terrible Temptation.
The Wandering Heir. | A Simpleton.
A Woman-Hater. | Readiana.

BY MRS. J. H. RIDDELL.
Her Mother's Darling.
Prince of Wales's Garden-Party.
Weird Stories.

BY F. W. ROBINSON.
Women are Strange.
The Hands of Justice.

BY JOHN SAUNDERS.
Bound to the Wheel.
Guy Waterman. | Two Dreamers.
One Against the World.
The Lion in the Path.

BY KATHARINE SAUNDERS.
Joan Merryweather.
Margaret and Elizabeth.
Gideon's Rock. | The High Mills.

PICCADILLY NOVELS, *continued*—
BY T. W. SPEIGHT.
The Mysteries of Heron Dyke.

BY R. A. STERNDALE.
The Afghan Knife.

BY BERTHA THOMAS.
Proud Maisie. | Cressida.
The Violin-Player.

BY ANTHONY TROLLOPE.
The Way we Live Now.
The American Senator
Frau Frohmann. | Marion Fay.
Kept in the Dark.
Mr. Scarborough's Family.
The Land-Leaguers.

BY FRANCES E. TROLLOPE.
Like Ships upon the Sea.
Anne Furness.
Mabel's Progress.

BY T. A. TROLLOPE.
Diamond Cut Diamond

By IVAN TURGENIEFF and Others.
Stories from Foreign Novelists.

BY SARAH TYTLER.
What She Came Through.
The Bride's Pass.
Saint Mungo's City.

BY C. C. FRASER-TYTLER.
Mistress Judith.

BY J. S. WINTER.
Cavalry Life.
Regimental Legends.

CHEAP EDITIONS OF POPULAR NOVELS.
Post 8vo, illustrated boards, 2s. each.

BY EDMOND ABOUT.
The Fellah.

BY HAMILTON AÏDÉ.
Carr of Carrlyon. | Confidences.

BY MRS. ALEXANDER.
Maid, Wife, or Widow?

BY SHELSLEY BEAUCHAMP.
Grantley Grange.

BY W. BESANT & JAMES RICE.
Ready-Money Mortiboy.
With Harp and Crown.
This Son of Vulcan. | My Little Girl.
The Case of Mr. Lucraft.
The Golden Butterfly.
By Celia's Arbour.

BY BESANT AND RICE, *continued*—
The Monks of Thelema.
'Twas in Trafalgar's Bay.
The Seamy Side.
The Ten Years' Tenant.
The Chaplain of the Fleet.

BY WALTER BESANT.
All Sorts and Conditions of
The Captains' Room.

BY FREDERICK BOYLE.
Camp Notes. | Savage Life.

BY BRET HARTE.
An Heiress of Red Dog.
The Luck of Roaring Camp.
Californian Stories.
Gabriel Conroy. | Flip.

CHEAP POPULAR NOVELS, *continued—*
BY ROBERT BUCHANAN.
The Shadow of the Sword.
A Child of Nature.
God and the Man.
The Martyrdom of Madeline.
Love Me for Ever.

BY MRS. BURNETT.
Surly Tim.

BY MRS. LOVETT CAMERON.
Deceivers Ever. | Juliet's Guardian.

BY MACLAREN COBBAN.
The Cure of Souls.

BY C. ALLSTON COLLINS.
The Bar Sinister.

BY WILKIE COLLINS.

Antonina.	Miss or Mrs.?
Basil.	The New Magda-
Hide and Seek.	len.
The Dead Secret.	The Frozen Deep.
Queen of Hearts.	Law and the Lady.
My Miscellanies.	The Two Destinies
Woman in White.	Haunted Hotel.
The Moonstone.	The Fallen Leaves.
Man and Wife.	Jezebel's Daughter
Poor Miss Finch.	The Black Robe.

BY MORTIMER COLLINS.
Sweet Anne Page.
Transmigration.
From Midnight to Midnight.
A Fight with Fortune.

MORTIMER & FRANCES COLLINS.
Sweet and Twenty. | Frances.
Blacksmith and Scholar.
The Village Comedy.
You Play me False.

BY DUTTON COOK.
Leo. | Paul Foster's Daughter.

BY J. LEITH DERWENT.
Our Lady of Tears.

BY CHARLES DICKENS.
Sketches by Boz.
The Pickwick Papers.
Oliver Twist.
Nicholas Nickleby.

BY MRS. ANNIE EDWARDES.
A Point of Honour. | Archie Lovell.

BY M. BETHAM-EDWARDS.
Felicia. | Kitty.

BY EDWARD EGGLESTON.
Roxy.

CHEAP POPULAR NOVELS, *continued—*
BY PERCY FITZGERALD.
Bella Donna. | Never Forgotten.
The Second Mrs. Tillotson.
Polly.
Seventy-five Brooke Street.
The Lady of Brantome.

BY ALBANY DE FONBLANQUE.
Filthy Lucre.

BY R. E. FRANCILLON.
Olympia. | Queen Cophetua.
One by One.

Prefaced by Sir H. BARTLE FRERE.
Pandurang Hari.

BY HAIN FRISWELL.
One of Two.

BY EDWARD GARRETT
The Capel Girls.

BY CHARLES GIBBON.

Robin Gray.	Queen of the Mea-
For Lack of Gold.	dow.
What will the World Say?	In Pastures Green
In Honour Bound.	The Flower of the Forest.
The Dead Heart.	A Heart's Problem
In Love and War.	The Braes of Yar-
For the King.	row.

BY WILLIAM GILBERT.
Dr. Austin's Guests.
The Wizard of the Mountain.
James Duke.

BY JAMES GREENWOOD.
Dick Temple.

BY ANDREW HALLIDAY.
Every-Day Papers.

BY LADY DUFFUS HARDY.
Paul Wynter's Sacrifice.

BY THOMAS HARDY.
Under the Greenwood Tree.

BY JULIAN HAWTHORNE.

Garth.	Sebastian Strome
Ellice Quentin.	Dust.
Prince Saroni's Wife.	

BY SIR ARTHUR HELPS.
Ivan de Biron.

BY TOM HOOD.
A Golden Heart.

BY MRS. GEORGE HOOPER.
The House of Raby.

BY VICTOR HUGO.
The Hunchback of Notre Dame.

Cheap Popular Novels, *continued*—

BY MRS. ALFRED HUNT.
Thornicroft's Model.
The Leaden Casket.
Self-Condemned.

BY JEAN INGELOW.
Fated to be Free.

BY HARRIETT JAY.
The Dark Colleen.
The Queen of Connaught.

BY HENRY KINGSLEY.
Oakshott Castle. | Number Seventeen

BY E. LYNN LINTON.
Patricia Kemball.
The Atonement of Leam Dundas.
The World Well Lost.
Under which Lord?
With a Silken Thread.
The Rebel of the Family.
"My Love!"

BY HENRY W. LUCY.
Gideon Fleyce.

BY JUSTIN McCARTHY, M.P.
Dear Lady Disdain.
The Waterdale Neighbours.
My Enemy's Daughter.
A Fair Saxon.
Linley Rochford.
Miss Misanthrope.
Donna Quixote.
The Comet of a Season.

BY GEORGE MACDONALD.
Paul Faber, Surgeon.
Thomas Wingfold, Curate.

BY MRS. MACDONELL.
Quaker Cousins.

BY KATHARINE S. MACQUOID.
The Evil Eye. | Lost Rose.

BY W. H. MALLOCK.
The New Republic.

BY FLORENCE MARRYAT.
Open! Sesame! | A Little Stepson.
A Harvest of Wild | Fighting the Air.
Oats. | Written in Fire.

BY J. MASTERMAN.
Half-a-dozen Daughters.

BY JEAN MIDDLEMASS.
Touch and Go. | Mr. Dorillion.

Cheap Popular Novels, *continued*—

BY D. CHRISTIE MURRAY.
A Life's Atonement.
A Model Father.
Joseph's Coat.
Coals of Fire.
By the Gate of the Sea.

BY MRS. OLIPHANT.
Whiteladies.

BY MRS. ROBERT O'REILLY.
Phœbe's Fortunes.

BY OUIDA.
Held in Bondage.
Strathmore.
Chandos.
Under Two Flags.
Idalia.
Cecil Castlemaine.
Tricotrin.
Puck.
Folle Farine.
A Dog of Flanders.
Pascarel.
Two Little Wooden Shoes.
Signa.
In a Winter City.
Ariadne.
Friendship.
Moths.
Pipistrello.
A Village Commune.
Bimbi.
In Maremma.

BY MARGARET AGNES PAUL.
Gentle and Simple.

BY JAMES PAYN.
Lost Sir Massingberd.
A Perfect Treasure.
Bentinck's Tutor.
Murphy's Master.
A County Family.
At Her Mercy.
A Woman's Vengeance.
Cecil's Tryst.
Clyffards of Clyffe.
The Family Scapegrace.
Foster Brothers.
Found Dead.
Best of Husbands
Walter's Word.
Halves.
Fallen Fortunes.
What He Cost Her
Humorous Stories
Gwendoline's Harvest.
Like Father, Like Son.
A Marine Residence.
Married Beneath Him.
Mirk Abbey.
Not Wooed, but Won.
£200 Reward.
Less Black than We're Painted.
By Proxy.
Under One Roof.
High Spirits.
Carlyon's Year.
A Confidential Agent.
Some Private Views.
From Exile.
A Grape from a Thorn.
For Cash Only.

BY EDGAR A. POE.
The Mystery of Marie Roget.

CHEAP POPULAR NOVELS, *continued—*

BY E. C. PRICE.

Valentina.

BY CHARLES READE.

It Is Never Too Late to Mend.
Hard Cash.
Peg Woffington.
Christie Johnstone.
Griffith Gaunt.
Put Yourself In His Place.
The Double Marriage.
Love Me Little, Love Me Long.
Foul Play.
The Cloister and the Hearth.
The Course of True Love.
Autobiography of a Thief.
A Terrible Temptation.
The Wandering Heir.
A Simpleton.
A Woman-Hater.
Readiana.

BY MRS. J. H. RIDDELL.

Her Mother's Darling.
Prince of Wales's Garden Party.

BY F. W. ROBINSON.

Women are Strange.

BY BAYLE ST. JOHN.

A Levantine Family.

BY GEORGE AUGUSTUS SALA.

Gaslight and Daylight.

BY JOHN SAUNDERS.

Bound to the Wheel.
One Against the World.
Guy Waterman.
The Lion in the Path.
Two Dreamers.

BY ARTHUR SKETCHLEY.

A Match in the Dark.

BY T. W. SPEIGHT.

The Mysteries of Heron Dyke.

BY R. A. STERNDALE.

The Afghan Knife.

BY R. LOUIS STEVENSON.

New Arabian Nights.

BY BERTHA THOMAS.

Cressida. | Proud Maisie.
The Violin Player.

BY W. MOY THOMAS.

A Fight for Life.

CHEAP POPULAR NOVELS, *continued—*

BY WALTER THORNBURY.

Tales for the Marines.

BY T. ADOLPHUS TROLLOPE.

Diamond Cut Diamond.

BY ANTHONY TROLLOPE.

The Way We Live Now.
The American Senator.
Frau Frohmann.
Marion Fay.
Kept in the Dark.

By FRANCES ELEANOR TROLLOPE

Like Ships upon the Sea.

BY MARK TWAIN.

Tom Sawyer.
An Idle Excursion.
A Pleasure Trip on the Continent of Europe.
A Tramp Abroad.
The Stolen White Elephant.

BY SARAH TYTLER.

What She Came Through.
The Bride's Pass.

BY J. S. WINTER.

Cavalry Life. | Regimental Legends

BY LADY WOOD.

Sabina.

BY EDMUND YATES.

Castaway. | The Forlorn Hope.
Land at Last.

ANONYMOUS.

Paul Ferroll.
Why Paul Ferroll Killed his Wife.

Fcap. 8vo, picture covers, 1s. each.

Jeff Briggs's Love Story. By BRET HARTE.
The Twins of Table Mountain. By BRET HARTE.
Mrs. Gainsborough's Diamonds. By JULIAN HAWTHORNE.
Kathleen Mavourneen. By Author of " That Lass o' Lowrie's,"
Lindsay's Luck. By the Author of " That Lass o' Lowrie's,"
Pretty Polly Pemberton. By the Author of " That Lass o' Lowrie's,"
Trooping with Crows. By Mrs. PIRKIS.
The Professor's Wife. By LEONARD GRAHAM.
A Double Bond. By LINDA VILLARI.
Esther's Glove. By R. E. FRANCILLON.
The Garden that Paid the Rent. By TOM JERROLD.

J. OGDEN AND CO., PRINTERS, 172, ST. JOHN STREET, E.C.